DEAD MAN WALKING

A MYSTERY THRILLER

JOHN CORWIN

OVERWORLD PUBLISHING

DEAD CITY

Amos Carver is out camping when he's forced to kill two men.

To be fair, they shot at him first. But they missed and Carver didn't. It turns out these men were tracking down a drug addict who stole something valuable from them. A briefcase full of money and drugs.

Just before he dies, the drug addict tells Carver that he left the briefcase just over the Golden Gate Bridge in San Francisco. He left it with a woman named Sally.

Carver decides his camping trip is over and ventures into San Francisco. He plays tourist and looks for Sally and the briefcase. But while he's out, his Dodge Ramcharger is broken into. Looted. All his money and guns are taken.

Most importantly, his phone is taken. The encrypted messaging app on it is the only way he can contact Paola. The woman he saved in Morganville. If he doesn't get his phone back, he'll lose contact with her forever.

He soon discovers that retrieving his belongings won't be all that simple. The local kingpin runs all the crime in San Francisco. That kingpin might also be connected to the shadowy organization that ran the Farm in Oregon.

None of that matters to Carver. He'll do whatever it takes to get back that phone. And if anyone gets in his way, they'll find out real fast that it's a bad idea. Because people who get in Carver's way don't live long.

They're just dead men walking.

BOOKS BY JOHN CORWIN

PSYCHOLOGICAL THRILLERS

The Family Business

AMOS CARVER THRILLERS

Dead Before Dawn

Dead List

Dead and Buried

Dead Man Walking

Dead By The Dozen

Dead Run

Dead Weather Days

Dead to Rights

Dead but not Forgotten

CHRONICLES OF CAIN

To Kill a Unicorn

Enter Oblivion

Throne of Lies

At The Forest of Madness

The Dead Never Die

Shadow of Cthulhu

Cabal of Chaos

Monster Squad

Gates of Yog-Sothoth

Shadow Over Tokyo

Into the Multiverse

THE OVERWORLD CHRONICLES

Sweet Blood of Mine

Dark Light of Mine

Fallen Angel of Mine

Dread Nemesis of Mine

Twisted Sister of Mine

Dearest Mother of Mine

Infernal Father of Mine

Sinister Seraphim of Mine

Wicked War of Mine

Dire Destiny of Ours

Aetherial Annihilation

Baleful Betrayal

Ominous Odyssey

Insidious Insurrection

Utopia Undone

Overworld Apocalypse

Apocryphan Rising

Soul Storm

Devil's Due

Overworld Ascension

Assignment Zero (An Elyssa Short Story)

OVERWORLD UNDERGROUND

Soul Seer

Demonicus

Infernal Blade

OVERWORLD ARCANUM

Conrad Edison and the Living Curse

Conrad Edison and the Anchored World

Conrad Edison and the Broken Relic

Conrad Edison and the Infernal Design

Conrad Edison and the First Power

STAND ALONE NOVELS

Mars Rising

No Darker Fate
The Next Thing I Knew
Outsourced
Seventh

CHAPTER 1

A cry for help echoed in the forest.

Carver was hiking off the beaten trail. He paused. Turned around. Tried to gauge where the sound came from. He heard another shout. It was somewhere to the north. Further up the mountain.

He'd noticed smoke coming from that area the previous day. Someone was illegally camping in the forest. Someone who didn't know how to hide their fires. Carver hadn't cared. He wasn't supposed to be out here either.

He'd seen the forest on his way through northern California and had decided to check it out. Signs posted every few yards sternly told people not to leave the trail. Carver ignored them. Cut out across the wilderness.

There was plenty of wildlife here. Some of it harmless. Some of it not so harmless. It was possible the person shouting had come across a bear or a bobcat. Neither one was good for your health. Climbing a tree wasn't going to save you, either.

At least not for long.

That was why Carver was carrying a Glock and a Colt M4. Since he wasn't supposed to be out here, he'd brought suppressors for both weapons. Just in case.

The suppressors would keep any gunfire quiet. Quiet enough, at least, not to alert everyone within two miles. Shooting wildlife in a national forest was a big no-no. Even if you did it to save a life.

Carver walked up the slope. He didn't hear any more shouts. Didn't hear the snarls or roars of a wild animal either. They might be feasting on the camper already. He figured it was best to make sure.

He kept walking. Leaning against the slope. Using a thick stick he'd found for added support. He reached the crest a few minutes later. Climbed over a log. Walked between the trees until he saw the campsite.

It wasn't much. A small, dingy tent. A blackened spot in the ground where the campfire had been. No signs of wild animals. No signs of anything.

Carver slowed his pace. Kept his footsteps quiet. He reached the edge of the small clearing. Heard voices.

"Just how stupid are you?" It was a man speaking. He sounded young. Like his voice hadn't transitioned through puberty just yet. But it wasn't the voice of a boy either.

Another man spoke. A deep voice. Rough from a lifetime of smoking. He'd gone through puberty a long time ago. "He's an addict. What do you expect?"

A third voice joined the conversation. "I didn't see anything. I swear!"

"Bobby, Bobby, Bobby." The first guy sighed. "We saw you. And to top it off, you stole something very valuable."

"I just wanted to see what it was." Bobby's voice shook. It had that underlying edge of desperation. The tone of someone who'd do anything for that next fix.

The second guy spoke. "You tell me and Demetrius what you saw. But most importantly, you tell us what you did with the briefcase. You tell us now, or we're going to torture you until you tell us."

Carver couldn't get an angle on the speakers. They were behind a tree on the other side of the tent. It sounded like it was none of his business anyway. He crouched. Slid the Glock from the holster. Screwed on the suppressor.

He crept closer. Curious to hear what this was all about. It wasn't the smartest thing he'd ever done. Wasn't the dumbest either. The right thing to do was turn around. Walk away. Let events run their course.

But he wasn't all that good at doing the right thing.

The conversation was still going. But the voices were lower. Hard to hear from this position. He kept moving forward. Kept creeping toward the tent. It was maybe twenty feet away. It was about seven feet tall. Probably seven feet squared.

There was a cry of pain and surprise. The first guy shouted, "He cut me!"

Feet pounded. A thin man with a patchy beard raced around the tent. His eyes flared when he saw Carver. Two figures ran around the tent after him. One was short and thin. The other was medium height and round in the midriff.

The taller one leveled a pistol and fired. Carver rolled to the side. The bearded guy, presumably Bobby, screamed and went down like a rag doll.

The two men aimed at Carver. Carver squeezed off two rounds. The taller guy's head snapped back. He dropped. The shorter guy squealed. Gurgled. He dropped his pistol. Grabbed the side of his throat.

Blood bubbled between his fingers. Carver had been aiming for the head. He'd hit the neck by mistake. It would do the trick, but it wasn't ideal. The other guy was dead before he hit the ground. This guy was still squirming. Bleeding out.

Carver watched him until he went still. He was wearing gloves, so he went through their pockets. No wallets. No IDs. Just spare magazines for their Beretta 92s. He didn't bother taking them.

"Help." Bobby was struggling weakly. "Please."

Carver rolled him onto his back. There was an exit wound near the stomach. A nasty one. He was bleeding out fast. Bits and pieces of his intestines were on the ground. He didn't have a chance even if he was already in an emergency room.

"Sorry. You're done for."

Bobby's eyes widened. "No, please."

"Nothing I can do." Carver stood. Went to the tent. Looked inside. There were empty plastic baggies all over the floor. A few empty plastic bottles. One had a little liquid in it. Carver knew from the label that it was fentanyl.

It looked like something from a pharmacy. Probably stolen. It was bad stuff, but there was one thing it was good at.

Pain management.

He took it outside. Knelt next to Bobby. "This is all I can do." He unscrewed the lid.

Bobby gasped with excitement. Opened his mouth. Carver trickled the fentanyl under the man's tongue. It would absorb into the bloodstream fast.

The other man's eyelids went heavy a moment later. He sighed. Shivered. Blood loss was probably numbing the pain just as fast as the fentanyl.

"What was this about?" Carver said.

Bobby's eyes fluttered open. "T-thought I could trade that briefcase for a fix. I always was stupid."

"What briefcase?"

"It was metal. Locked up tight. Couldn't open it. It was too heavy, so I left it in the city." He tried to laugh. Didn't have the energy for it.

"What was in it?"

"Money, I think." He shivered again. "A drug. Flood."

Carver raised an eyebrow. "That's the name of the drug?"

"Yeah. I think that's what they called it."

"Where did you drop the briefcase?"

"Sally has it. Tenderloin..." His words turned to a death rattle. Bobby's eyes glazed over. He stopped breathing.

Carver closed the man's eyes. Bobby had all the markings of an addict. Needle scars on the arms. Thin, wasted musculature. Plenty of tattoos. The most noticeable was the tattoo of a black widow crawling up his throat.

At least, it was supposed to be a black widow. The red hourglass was on the top of the spider's abdomen. It was supposed to be on the bottom. It had probably once been sharp and glossy. The skin was saggy and wrinkled from weight loss.

Carver stood. Looked around. He found his shell casings. Picked them up. Didn't bother looking for the slugs. He took the Beretta from the man who'd shot Bobby. Put it in Bobby's hand.

He considered squeezing off a round with Bobby's hand. But there was probably plenty of gunshot residue on the handle. The original gunshot probably attracted some attention. Firing again was risky. If a ranger was nearby, they'd come running.

There was a lot of vegetation on the ground. Enough to hide most footprints. There wasn't much else Carver could do to taint the scene. He probably didn't need to. Any investigator who saw this scene would come to a quick conclusion.

A drug addict got into trouble with local dealers. Tried to hide in the forest. Ran out of drugs and went back into town for more. The dealers saw him. Followed him out here. Things didn't go as planned.

The addict had a knife. Cut one of the guys. Got his gun. Tried to run. They shot at each other. Everyone died. Maybe they wouldn't bother matching the slugs to the guns.

It was hard to believe the morning's peaceful hike had led him to this. Three more corpses for the worms. These three men had woken up this morning. Made decisions. Those decisions led them to this moment.

They were all dead men walking this morning and they didn't even know it. One day, he'd be in their shoes. He'd be hours away from the grave. Hopefully, he got in a lot more camping before then.

Carver nodded to himself. Turned around. Hiked back into the forest. This might be off the beaten path, but it wasn't far from the main path. There were probably hundreds of people hiking the trails on any given day.

Probably plenty of forest rangers on duty too. They were supposed to keep people from doing what Carver was doing. They were supposed to find illegal campers. Keep them from despoiling nature.

They weren't doing a very good job of it. Bobby's campfire smoke had been highly visible the night before. At least to Carver. Maybe it wasn't as visible to people not trained to notice it.

Regardless, it was time to get out of this neck of the woods. Carver had been working his way south from Oregon. Leaving the roads when he felt like it. Camping. Enjoying life away from the cities.

Now he was just a little over an hour north of San Francisco. Whether he liked it or not, it was the next stop on this western tour. And it was probably worth seeing. Even if only for a day.

He was also curious about the briefcase. The drugs didn't matter, but the money would be nice. If it was a metal briefcase and locked like Bobby said, then Sally probably hadn't gotten into it.

Maybe Carver would combine a little tourist activity with a search and recovery. It might be interesting. Might be worth his time, too. He had access to a healthy bank account through an encrypted app on his burner phone.

But it would be nice to have some extra cash. It was always nice not to worry about money. Especially when it was someone else's money.

It took him the better part of three hours to get back to the public parking lot where he'd parked his Dodge Ramcharger. He'd thought owning a car would be a drag. But it had been liberating. Fun, even.

It especially beat taking the bus. It gave him the freedom to carry all his stuff around and let him wander whenever the mood took him. It was hard to wander when someone else was at the wheel.

He still hadn't bothered changing the registration into his name. It was still registered to the guy he'd bought it from up in Montana. Carver still wasn't sure if he'd ever put it in his name. That would create a paper trail. Carver didn't like paper trails.

Once the current tags expired, he might just have to let go of the Ramcharger. Might have to leave it abandoned in a parking lot. Or maybe he'd give it to someone. Let them register it. The title was signed. All the papers were in order. It was too nice of a car to let it rot.

Carver would keep driving it for the next few months. See more of the west coast. Eventually make his way to another beach. Then he'd find a nice forever home for the Ramcharger.

He'd say his goodbyes and move onto the next chapter in his life. But for now, he'd enjoy every minute of it.

Carver put his gear in the back. He'd accumulated some nice stuff. Mostly camping gear. Survival equipment. Guns and ammo. The essentials.

He needed a new razor. His scruff was turning into a beard. He didn't much care for beards. Beards held onto dirt and food. And he didn't like the feeling of hair on his face.

Carver pulled the burner phone from the backpack. Turned it on. A couple messages popped up in his encrypted messaging app when he turned it on. One was from yesterday. It was from Paola.

Getting a new phone tomorrow. Will text number. I hope you're doing okay, Carver. Miss you.

Carver stared long and hard at the text. He felt something stirring inside him. Something like a longing. A part of him wanted to drop everything. Ask her where she was. Ask if she wanted to see him.

He hadn't seen Paola since she left him on that beach. He'd given her a burner. Told her to switch it out every month for a new one. He'd installed an encrypted messaging app. Showed her how to use the encryption key to install it on different phones.

The app wouldn't accept texts from unregistered numbers. He'd showed her how to add numbers. Taught her how to change phones. Just in case, the cartel that used to own her was still looking for her.

Paola texted him every month. Just to tell him she was okay. To tell him she was getting a new number. Carver sent her his new numbers too. It had become a ritual during all these months. Like he was still with her even if he wasn't.

Carver clamped down on that feeling. He was no good for her. She'd figured that out for herself after living with him for a while. After seeing that he just wasn't the type to settle into any kind of relationship.

But maybe. Just maybe. He could ask her where she was. Visit for a little while. Make sure everything was good. Make sure the Brazilian cartel wasn't hunting her down.

Another feeling stirred deep inside. Fear. The kind of fear that wasn't for himself. It was that helpless kind of fear. The kind he felt when he knew he couldn't do anything to prevent something. To help someone.

He hadn't felt that kind of fear for anyone for a long time. And he didn't like that he felt it for Paola. She was living her life. He was living his. It was in the past. Dead and buried. Gone for good.

Carver cleared his throat. Looked at the other text. It was from Leon. The other person he stayed in touch with.

Carver, these people aren't done with you. Please consider helping me clean house. You'll be doing yourself a favor.

Leon was always a man on a mission. Always out to do what he felt was good and right. It had cost him Breakstone, the private military company. He'd become the de facto CEO after Carver killed off the other partners.

Leon refused to play ball with the feds. Refused to continue doing what the founder had been doing. Refused to turn the company into a private wing of the federal government. So, politicians did what politicians do.

They'd exacted retribution. Shut down the company. Taken everything and left Leon with nothing.

Well, almost nothing. Leon had funneled Breakstone money from overseas accounts into his own secret coffers. He was using that money to hunt down the people behind it. And it was probably going to get him killed.

Carver preferred life on the open road. Camping. Drinking beer. Cooking over an open campfire. And even out here, he hadn't been able to escape the gunfire. Even now, he was about to do something stupid.

He was going to hunt down the briefcase that got three men killed.

CHAPTER 2

The man with the rifle watched the target.

The target was a hundred yards out. Walking left to right. Windspeed was low. The air was cold. He'd already accounted for the variables. All he had to do was pull the trigger. Put down the target.

It would be easy. So easy. But that wasn't how they wanted it. They wanted it up close. Personal. Brutal and messy. It was supposed to send a message. It was supposed to paint a target on someone else's back. Frame them for the violent killing.

The man with the rifle could do clean. He could do messy. He could hit a target from a quarter mile out. He could get up close and personal. He was versatile. A man of many skills. Relentless and ruthless.

But he had a vice. A vice that even he couldn't control despite his best efforts. He liked to watch the prey. Stalk them. See how they spent their remaining hours on Earth. Most people did routine things. Most, if not all.

They woke up. Went to work. Ate lunch. Drove by the grocery store on their way home. Texted their spouse and asked if they needed something. Picked up a few things. Went home. Ate dinner. Entertained themselves with meaningless activities until bedtime. Wash. Rinse. Repeat.

Little did they know they were dead men walking.

This target was different. He moved around a lot. Didn't do many of the same things every day. There wasn't much of a pattern to follow. But there was just enough to make this job doable. And it was almost time to finish it.

The man with the rifle had been watching and plotting for three weeks. His employers knew his methods. Understood them. Didn't question them. They knew the job would be done and it would be done perfectly.

He lowered the rifle. Knelt behind the concrete barrier. Packed the rifle in its case. He opened the back door of the black Sprinter van parked next to him. The interior was packed with electronics. Another man sat inside at a small desk. He was watching the target on the monitors.

He looked over at the man with the rifle. "Why are we watching him? He's not even the target."

"He is the target, Alan."

Alan shuddered. "I don't like you knowing my name when I don't even know yours."

"You know my designation and that's enough."

"Epsilon? It's not even a good code name."

Epsilon slid the rifle case onto the shelf at the back. "Let's get back to work, shall we?"

Alan rolled his eyes. "Work? We're not even following the right target."

"Trust me. It's the right target." Epsilon climbed into the surveillance van. He looked at the other monitors. At the collateral. Watching a target with no set routine had been refreshing. It had been a nice change from the mundane.

Even the rich fell into routines. They might go to different venues. Visit different countries. Try different things. But the routine was still the same. Only the details were different. All the money in the world didn't change that.

Epsilon almost hated for the job to be over. But it was. He had all the information he needed. He'd taken his time. Waited for the target to return from wherever he'd gone. Waited for the target to come back to the single vice he had.

Everything and everyone was in position.

He pulled out his knife kit. Studied the blades. Settled on a small, rusty piece. It felt right for the job. It would send the message that needed to be sent. It would cause the ripple effect that the client wanted.

There were those who would try to cover it up. Try to play it off as a fluke. Their attempts would be unsuccessful. Not because it happened to some random member of the public. But because it happened to an important political leader.

When you want change, you bring it to the doorstep of the politicians. Politicians see their subjects as numbers. Statistics.

Poll numbers. Homicide rates. Burglaries. Robberies. All just percentages on a screen. All happening somewhere out there in the world. Far away from the seats of power.

This would bring it home. Make it very personal.

Epsilon swung the knife through the air. Imagined the savagery of what he was about to do. Grinned.

"You enjoy this a little too much." Alan grimaced. "This is why I don't like freelancers. You people are crazy."

"And you company men are all so predictable." Epsilon put the knife back into the kit. He considered what to wear. What evidence to take with him. The best way to stage the scene.

He'd worked out several scenarios. Settled on three candidates. As usual, he probably wouldn't decide on which one until the last minute. He just hated deciding when they were all so good.

Epsilon sat in a chair. Turned on a computer workstation. He watched CGI renders of the different plans in action.

Alan glanced over at the screen. "I like the second one the best."

"It does have an artistic flair to it." Epsilon switched to the third option. Watched it through.

Alan's gaze flicked to the back of the van. "Did you hear that?"

Epsilon looked up from the screen. There was a sudden rush of heat. A boom. The van flew up into the air. The inside collapsed. A searing inferno burned his flesh to a crisp.

LEON FRY WATCHED THE BURNING VAN.

"Not today, Satan." He slid the remote trigger into his pocket.

The van was in an old, abandoned parking deck. Far away from civilians. Far away from other buildings. It was a good spot to set up a surveillance van. A good place from which to watch unsuspecting targets.

It also happened to be a good place to safely blow up a van. Safe for everyone but the occupants, that is.

Some of the distant civilians were running. Others had their phones out, ready to record. Some saw the rising smoke and were hurrying toward the source. Everyone seemed to think they were citizen journalists these days.

There wouldn't be much for them to find.

There would be an investigation. Police would find surveillance equipment. A pair of burnt corpses. One would be identified by dental records. The other had no records to speak of. Epsilon was an asset. Off the books. Everything about him had been purged by elements of the federal government.

It was a standard part of the NSA playbook. Standard for the CIA too. It had also been standard for Scion and other off-the-books black ops squads.

Leon had discovered multiple assets in the records taken from the Farm. A whole network of people. It spanned from student councils to city councils. Every level of state and local government. Every level of federal government including agencies.

It was vast. But only a tiny number of their resources were listed. Only the ones known to the Farm. And it was just one cell inside a much larger organism. An organization referred to by several names.

Corporate. Central. Downtown. The name used the most in the files was the one he used himself. Enigma.

Enigma was perfectly anonymous. Impossible to track. So, Leon was sticking to the small list he'd taken from the Farm. Disrupting whatever he could. And he was having a little fun doing it.

Epsilon had been assigned to target a politician in Washington state. An important state senator who was a holdout vote on crime legislation. The senator opposed certain aspects of the bill. He didn't like the enhanced surveillance it would grant the state.

The senators from the urban areas wanted more surveillance. They wanted to spread it into the suburbs. Make it so every street corner had a camera. And require all private cameras to link into the government's network.

The rural senators didn't like the idea. They had the votes to prevent the measure from being adopted. And their leader, Paul Nelson, was leading the charge to keep it from becoming law.

Epsilon had been planning to kill Nelson's wife and two daughters. Frame it as a break-in. A tragedy that could have been prevented with enhanced surveillance.

It might have given Nelson the push he needed to advocate for the crime bill. The surveillance addendum was just a small part of the entire package. The rest of it contained things Nelson wanted.

Leon figured it would have almost certainly pushed the senator over the edge. Nelson would have used his personal tragedy to advocate for the legislation. Others would have changed their votes. The legislation would have passed.

But what was most troubling was the man helping Epsilon. Alan Chan wasn't working directly for the Farm. In fact, he probably hadn't even known about it. He'd been assigned to help Epsilon by someone higher up the food chain.

Someone who wasn't listed in the Farm's database.

Leon had only learned about him because of Epsilon. He'd been watching Alan for the better part of two weeks. He'd infiltrated the man's house. Looked into his work. Traced a number of his jobs to the Farm.

Other jobs were legitimate tasks from the NSA. Tasks that Leon personally disagreed with. But they didn't seem to be part of Enigma's agenda. Alan didn't seem to have been a double agent. He was just following orders.

It meant the Farm had hooks higher up in the organization. Hooks that hadn't been affected by the Farm's sudden demise. Leon had blown the place sky high. Stolen all their data. Most of their personnel had been offsite. Most would have survived.

But the infrastructure was demolished. Their medical, armory, and most importantly, their tech modules were rubble. If an asset like Epsilon was still active, still coordinating with the NSA to alter domestic policy, it meant one of two things.

Either the Farm was so compartmentalized that it never ceased functioning, or there were other elements in the government utilizing Epsilon and the NSA for their own purposes. Purposes not authorized by the feds.

It was interesting. Real interesting.

Leon jogged around the corner of the parking deck. Slid into his compact white sedan. It was a Toyota. Just another plain car in a sea of them. It got good gas mileage. Ran quiet. And it was reliable.

Most importantly, no one looked at it twice. He'd been tracking Epsilon and Alan for the better part of two weeks. It was a good thing Epsilon liked to take his time. Enjoyed playing with his food before killing it.

Otherwise, Nelson's family would have been killed the week before Leon discovered the plot in the Farm's files.

Neither Alan nor Epsilon had noticed the white Toyota always trailing in the distance. Mainly because it fit right in with countless others just like it.

Leon pulled out of the parking deck. He circled around the long way. Ended up in a line of cars exiting a busy parking deck about a quarter of a mile down the road.

He lost himself in the retail traffic. Drove to a hotel down the street. Parked in the deck there. He took the elevator to the top floor. Stepped off and into a small lounge.

A hostess greeted him. "Can I help you, sir?"

"Rooftop, please." He pointed to the north side. "Over there, preferably."

"Absolutely, sir." She took him outside. Led him to a table at the corner of the roof. The building was twenty stories high. It offered a breathtaking view of the city. It also gave Leon a perfect view of the smoke pouring from the abandoned parking deck.

"Your server will be with you shortly." The hostess left him.

Leon used a small monocular to watch the growing activity around the van. He heard footsteps. Kept the monocular tucked in the palm of his hand. Turned and smiled at the young man approaching him.

"Sir, if you'd like a menu, you can scan the barcode on the table."

"Do you have Macallan?"

"We have a twelve, a fifteen, and an eighteen, sir."

"I'll have the eighteen neat, please."

The server nodded. "May I see your ID, please?"

Leon chuckled. Showed him a fake ID given to him by the late owner of the company he'd inherited. The name on the ID was Chuck Bannister. The age was thirty-two. A few years older than Leon actually was.

The server glanced at it. "I'll bring it right out."

Leon looked around the roof. There was a couple tucked into a corner near the door. A pair of women sitting next to the roof's edge about twenty feet away. He was seated with his back to the railing. Positioned to watch everyone on the roof and the scene of his crime.

He peered through the monocular again. Watched the police. The bomb squad. Scores of reporters and civilians. All of them converging on the scene.

Patrol cars arrived. Yellow tape was strung up around the scene. Unmarked cars arrived. Detectives stepped out. Surveyed the scene. Talked to the patrol officers. The bomb squad arrived not long after.

They sent in a small robot. A fast one with a camera. Not the kind designed to disarm bombs. It went inside the parking deck. Probably drove around the van a few times. Circled the nearby area. Scanned for more bombs.

Then the people in the EOD suits went in. The bomb disposal suits were bulky. Green. Heavily padded with body armor. They had large, armored helmets that resembled something an astronaut might wear. Despite that, there was freedom of movement.

Leon had worn one before. It had come in handy at the time. These guys would quickly realize they didn't need them.

The bomb technicians would study the residue. Eventually determine that it came from pentaerythritol tetranitrate mixed with RDX to form a plastic-like mix commonly referred to as C-4. This particular kind was unmarked. It was commonly used worldwide by governments and paramilitary groups alike.

Leon had removed a few crates of it from the armory on the Farm. He'd located other offsite storage dumps thanks to the data from the Farm. Most of it looked like it had been taken from the hands of the federal government itself.

That was because it had been. The Farm's contacts used multiple federal agencies to gather its arsenal. It only seemed fitting to use their own explosives against them.

Leon saw the server returning. The monocular fit into the palm of Leon's hand so to the server, it probably looked like Leon was just leaning his head on his hand. It was important nobody noticed him watching. Important because a detail like that would stick out to even the most unobservant.

"Your Macallan, sir." The server set a coaster on the table. Set the drink on top of it.

"Thank you."

The server remained, an expectant look on his face.

Leon sipped it. Nodded. "Excellent."

"Very good, sir. Would you like something else?"

"I'll have the porterhouse steak. Rare."

The server nodded. "Any sides? A salad, perhaps?"

Leon shook his head. "No. All I need is meat and whiskey."

"Very good, sir." The server left.

Leon returned his gaze to the scene. The women sitting nearby were looking at the smoke. Talking excitedly to each other. They'd probably been here when the explosion went off. Probably recorded everything.

They wouldn't have seen Leon when he was at the scene of the explosion. He'd been standing under the trees.

Nothing much was happening at the crime scene, so Leon took out his phone and scrolled through the recent batch of files he'd been studying. There were more plots. More agents. More assassins.

And he was seeing some missions unfold in real time. Because the Farm had a login to a dark ops bulletin board. A place where off-the-books jobs were posted. A place where a cross section of federal agencies responded to such requests.

And one name of note had appeared on that board recently. A name Leon wasn't even surprised to see.

The name was Amos Carver.

CHAPTER 3

Carver drove across the Golden Gate Bridge.

He followed the 101. Followed it to Market Street. Took a left. Drove slowly through the streets of San Francisco.

Traffic was heavy. There were trollies. Buses. Steep hills. Lots of traffic lights. It was a nightmare compared to the forest. But it was a pretty city. At least some parts of it.

Parking was scarce. A tourist website suggested a few places to park the car. He drove past several but didn't see any open spaces.

He reached the Embarcadero. Found several open parallel parking spaces right near the bay. It looked like a good place to start exploring. He parked. Put enough money in the meter to last the day.

Carver got out. Stretched. He checked the burner phone. He'd forgotten to put it on the charger, so it was almost dead. Still no message from Paola. No update on her new number.

It was time for him to get a new burner too. He put the phone on the charger. Took some cash from his duffel bag. Put it in his pocket.

Bobby said Sally was at the Tenderloin. Probably a steak house. He'd pick up a new burner phone and look for a restaurant by that name. It probably wouldn't be too hard to find her.

He walked across the street. Walked past a park. A small section was covered in tents. It looked like a homeless encampment. He'd seen plenty of those in Minneapolis and Portland. This one was small compared to those.

There were metal tracks embedded in the Embarcadero. They weren't train tracks. They were for electric street cars. He walked past the park to Market Street. The same kind of tracks were embedded in it too.

These weren't for street cars. They were for trollies. Carver heard a bell dinging. Saw one of the trollies coming down the hill. It wasn't a fast mode of transportation, but it was the touristy thing to do.

He stopped at a ticket kiosk. Purchased a day pass for all public transportation. He hopped on the next trolley and took a seat on the side. An older man climbed in next to him. He had a coffee in one hand and a newspaper in the other.

The man looked like a local. Carver asked him a question. "Excuse me, I'm looking for a steakhouse. I think the name has Tenderloin in it somewhere."

The man looked up from his paper. Focused on Carver. "Sorry, I don't eat meat. I'm vegan."

"Okay. Thanks."

The man looked back at his paper. Back over at Carver. "You might have better luck using your phone to find it."

"Battery is dead."

"Ah, I see." The man pointed at a woman who was making her way through the car. "Maybe one of the conductors knows."

"Thanks." Carver waited for the woman to reach him.

She stopped behind them. "Tickets, please."

Carver showed her his day pass. The other man showed her something on his phone.

"Thank you." She started to move away.

Carver held up a hand to stop her. "Excuse me, do you know of a steakhouse or restaurant with the name Tenderloin in it?"

She paused. Tapped a finger on her chin and looked to the side. "A restaurant?" She turned to the trolley operator. "Do you know of a restaurant named Tenderloin something?"

The operator shook his head. "Never heard of it."

Another woman seated in the bench behind Carver looked up from her phone. "How did you hear about it?"

"Some guy said I should look for a friend of his at Tenderloin. Maybe I misheard him."

"Are you sure he didn't mean the Tenderloin District?"

Carver gave her a blank look. "Is that a restaurant?"

She laughed. "No, it's one of the districts. Like the Financial District, Nob Hill, Chinatown, and so forth."

"Ah, so it's not a restaurant."

"Probably not. You can get off at Turk, walk west, and you'll be there."

The man with the newspaper showed him the district on his phone's map app. It was about fifty square blocks. That was a lot of territory to cover. Finding Sally would be like locating a needle in a haystack.

"Just don't wander into the wrong parts," the operator said. "It ain't what it used to be."

The other conductor laughed. "I think he can take care of himself. He's a big boy."

"Thanks." Carver leaned back and enjoyed the ride. The operator called out Turk Street when they reached it. He hopped off. Started walking west.

The Tenderloin looked like a nice place. At least on the outskirts. It didn't take him long to see why the operator warned him about the place.

The sidewalks on some blocks were covered in tents. Covered in trash. Urine. Even feces. There were people outside many tents. Standing. Sitting. Passed out on their faces. Some looked intoxicated. Most looked high.

It didn't take much thinking to realize Sally was probably one of these people. Considering Bobby's lifestyle, Sally was almost certainly living on the sidewalk somewhere.

He saw a guy that looked reasonably sober. Approached him. The man watched him calmly. Carver asked him the question. "Do you know a woman named Sally?"

"Sorry. Don't know a Sally."

"How about a Bobby?"

The man nodded. Pointed to a guy passed out on the sidewalk. "That's Bobby."

"The Bobby I'm looking for has a spider tattoo on his throat."

The man shook his head. "No. Different Bobby."

"Thanks." Carver walked out into the street. The sidewalks were blocked with tents. He kept asking anyone who looked sober enough to answer if they knew Sally or Bobby. He was about ten blocks in when he got a hit.

Carver saw a man was sitting in a foldout lawn chair in front of his tent. He was drinking a beer. Calmly watching a man who was screaming at a tree. He looked different from the other sidewalk residents.

Carver walked up to him. "I'm looking for Sally. Have you heard of her?"

The man blinked. Looked up at Carver. "Crazy Sally or Dancing Sally?"

"A guy named Bobby told me she was around here."

"Oh, Bobby Boy?"

"I guess. Real thin. Long bushy beard. Spider tattoo on his throat."

"Oh, that's Slick Bobby."

"Does everyone have a nickname around here?"

The man grinned. "Hell, it's the only way anyone remembers names around here. Most of our brain cells are dead from drugs or alcohol, so any little thing helps."

"So, which Sally knows Slick Bobby?"

"I couldn't say." The man shrugged. Took a sip of beer. "Crazy Sally is about a block down that way." He pointed north. "She runs around naked in the streets about every other day. Screaming that dogs are after her. Sometimes monsters. Dancing Sally is a couple blocks that way." He pointed west. "She used to be a strip dancer. She'll do just about anything for five bucks."

"Thanks." Carver figured Dancing Sally sounded more promising. And not because of what five bucks would get him. He headed west.

"By anything, I mean anything," the man shouted after him.

Carver tipped an imaginary cap at him. "I'll keep it in mind." He wouldn't.

He made his way down the next couple of blocks. Stopped and asked for Dancing Sally. All the men knew who she was. They pointed him in the right direction. Told him to look for a yellow tent.

He found the tent on a street corner. It was zipped up. He thumped on the material. "Sally, you in there?"

There was no answer for a second. Then a woman spoke. "Give me five minutes."

"Okay." Carver didn't see a place to sit. The sidewalk was crowded with tents. There was a bench nearby, but it was covered in trash and smeared with something suspicious. He found a space between tents and leaned against the wall.

A man emerged from Sally's tent a moment later. He pulled up his pants and walked away. A woman who might be forty but looked sixty crawled out of the tent. She stood and looked around. Saw Carver. Her eyes brightened.

"Sally?"

"Yeah!" She smiled. Showed bare gums. "Wow, baby. I'm tempted to service you for free."

Carver returned the smile. "I'm actually here about something else." He walked over.

Her smile turned to worry. "Hey, I'm paid up. Just ask Dizzy." She backed up a step.

"I'm not here about that either." He held up his hands, palms out. "Bobby sent me."

Sally blinked. "Bobby Boy?"

"No, Slick Bobby."

Her eyes widened. She walked up to him. Whispered. "About the thing?"

He nodded. "The briefcase."

"Oh." She covered her mouth. "I don't have it anymore. I gave it to Herbert."

"Who?"

"My boyfriend." She smiled and shivered in delight. "He came to see me earlier. I showed it to him, and he said it was dangerous keeping it around. He said someone might come looking for it."

"Where is Herbert?"

"I don't know." She shrugged. "He moves around a lot. He's got to stay one step ahead of the MIC because of all the state secrets he knows."

"MIC?"

Sally leaned forward and whispered. "The military industrial complex."

"Does he have a usual spot?" Carver gestured around. "Somewhere near here?"

"No. He said he found a new place. A place nobody knows about. He said it's real green and has a great view of the bridge." She sighed. "All that work he did for the CIA and the FBI made him a wanted man."

"I'm sure it did." Carver cupped a hand to his mouth and whispered. "I'm here to help. That briefcase has important information in it that could bring down the corrupt people leading the CIA and FBI. If you see Herbert, tell him I really need it, okay?"

"Oh, really?" She clapped her hands. "He needs help clearing his name, you know? Him and the other guys in his commando unit were accused of crimes they didn't commit. He told me they survived as soldiers of fortune for a while."

Carver didn't have the heart to tell her that sounded like the intro to the A-Team. "I'm here to help." Carver figured he could give her his burner number. "Do you have a phone?"

She shook her head. "I can't afford it."

"Do you move around much?"

"No, this is my home. Everyone knows they can find me here."

"What does Herbert look like?"

"Oh, he's so handsome and sweet." Sally smiled dreamily.

"How tall is he?"

"Oh, a little taller than me."

Carver held his hand a little higher than her head. "This tall?"

"A little taller."

He went higher. "Here?"

"Yes, exactly!"

Carver figured he was about five feet, seven inches, give or take. "Is he skinny?"

"Oh, he's so thin and fit. Not an ounce of fat."

"Can you see his ribcage?"

Sally nodded. "Yep!"

"Anything else of note? Tattoos, moles, missing teeth, and so forth?"

She pursed her lips. "He's missing a few teeth. And his nose is crooked from when he broke it."

"Hair and eye color?"

She looked up. Like she was thinking real hard. "Brown and gray hair. And his eyes are brown." She snapped her fingers. "Oh, and he has a really thick beard. Nice and bushy and sexy."

Herbert probably looked like most other male addicts. The proverbial needle in a haystack. Although needles would probably be more plentiful in this part of town than hay.

Carver nodded. "Okay. I'll check back again soon. If you see Herbert, tell him I need to arrange a time and place to retrieve that briefcase before the NSA gets it."

"The NSA?" Her mouth dropped open. "They're after it too?"

"All of them are after it." Carver spread his hands. "It's a dangerous world."

"Oh, I know it, baby."

"I just hope it has everything inside that I need."

"Bobby said it had some crazy new drug called Flood in it. He said he overheard people talking about it. Probably something the government wants to use for mind control, if you ask me."

Carver nodded. "I think you're right. Can you describe the briefcase?"

"It was heavy. Real heavy." She held her hands apart about three feet. "It was this wide. Had metal latches all around the seam. I've never seen anything like it."

"Military grade." Carver had seen them before. Probably made from titanium. Even the cheap ones cost ten grand. "Thanks for your help, Sally."

Sally smiled. Showed off her gums. "You want to come inside for a while? I'll service you for free."

"That would unfortunately be a conflict of interest." Carver sighed. "I have to keep this professional."

"Oh, yeah." She looked sad. "I understand. Maybe when this is over, we can have some fun."

"Sally, please tell Herbert what I told you. It's vital to national security, okay?"

She nodded. Saluted. "I will."

Carver blew her a kiss. Walked away. It had been a while since he'd dealt with a crazy conspiracy theorist like Herbert. Winning their trust was an uphill battle. But he was curious about the briefcase.

If it looked like Bobby described it, it wasn't something a civilian could buy. It sounded like it was military grade. And it was obviously worth killing for.

CHAPTER 4

Carver stared at shattered glass.

The glass belonged to his 1990 Dodge Ramcharger. Had belonged to it. Now it was debris scattered on the asphalt. It reminded him why he didn't like having things. Especially not big things like cars.

After visiting Sally, he'd toured the city. Enjoyed the afternoon. Then he'd come back to get his phone. Replenish his cash supply. Because San Francisco was an expensive city to eat in.

But he wouldn't be doing any of that. Because all his stuff was gone. Guns, ammunition, camping gear, all of it. Most importantly, his cell phone was gone.

Normally, that wouldn't be a problem. He'd memorized Paola's number. She might not have switched to a new phone yet. But getting another phone and texting her from it wasn't an option.

He'd insisted on using an encrypted messaging app. It blocked all other messaging apps from working. It required registering a phone's serial number inside the app. Otherwise it would reject all messages.

Carver figured it was a good way to prevent anyone from pretending to be him. It was probably overkill. But Carver felt protective of her. That was why he'd established the monthly number change ritual with her.

It would make it harder for the cartel or anyone with a grudge against her or Carver to find her.

It also meant if Carver didn't have his phone with the encrypted app, he couldn't contact her. It meant that if he didn't get the phone back, he might lose contact with her forever. And that bothered him.

It bothered him a lot.

Paola had wanted a relationship. Carver wasn't the person to give her that. But she'd stuck around for a long time. Enjoyed what they had until she couldn't enjoy it anymore. Then she'd left him.

Carver knew it was for the best. He wasn't the kind of guy she was looking for. Not in the ways that counted, at least. So, he'd watched her go. Figured it was for the best.

But a part of him still hung onto her. It missed her. And that part of him was furious about the stolen phone.

The phone also had an encrypted banking app on it. The app was tied to an anonymous offshore account Leon had given him. Without the phone, Carver didn't have access to money anymore either.

And right now, he barely had two dollars to rub together.

The Ramcharger was cleaned out. His guns were gone. Camping equipment gone. He only had the clothes on his back. And to rub salt in the wound, there was a parking ticket under the windshield wipers.

The meter was still green. Still had another four hours on it. And yet, he'd been given a ticket. He pulled it from under the windshield wiper. A box was checked. *Parking over the line.* There was a note at the bottom. *Also cited for littering.*

Carver checked the positioning of the car. The tires were extra wide. The ones on the left were touching the line. But they were still inside the lines. And the only litter on the ground was his shattered window.

He saw a little three-wheeled electric cart a few blocks down. Saw a meter maid writing a ticket. He hustled down the sidewalk. Reached the meter maid when he was sliding into his cart. The man hesitated. Looked Carver up and down.

Carver held up the ticket. Pointed at the Ramcharger. "Did you write this ticket?"

"I did." The man stepped out. Squared up his shoulders. "You can't argue your way out of it with me."

"I'm not here to argue. I just want you to point out the violations. Make sure you got the right car."

"First of all, you tried to fit an oversized SUV into a parallel parking slot. A big gas guzzler like that isn't meant for downtown. And then there was litter all around the back side."

"My wheels are touching the lines. Not over them. And the litter is broken glass. Someone broke into my car."

The meter maid smirked. "If only you tourists would follow simple procedures and not bring valuables in your car."

"That glass isn't litter. It's evidence of a crime. And my tire is touching the line, not over it."

The meter maid shrugged. "You're trying to argue your way out of it. I told you I'm not your guy for that."

Carver worked his jaw back and forth. "You saw the crime scene and didn't even call the police?"

"It's not my job." The meter maid waved a hand around. "I have a lot of territory to cover."

A man on a nearby bench started laughing. His hair was wild. His clothes were filthy. He looked homeless. But it might just be modern city fashion. Carver wasn't sure.

"He saw your car get broken into," the homeless man said through bouts of laughter. "He always tickets big SUVs. He hates them."

"Shut it, Harold." The meter maid waggled a finger at him. "Don't make me report you to the shelter."

Harold kept laughing. Laughing so hard he held his sides.

Carver stared down the meter maid. Read the name on the plastic name badge. *Reedus Stanislaw.* "Reedus, I think you need to tear up this ticket."

Reedus shook his head. "Take it up with the judge. The court date is on the ticket."

Carver stepped closer.

"Touch me and you're going to jail." Reedus puffed out his chest. "I have your license plate. They'll find out who you are. Where you live."

"Will they?" Carver grinned. "I don't think they'll find out much." He'd never registered the vehicle in his name. They'd just trace it back to a guy named Bill in Montana.

Reedus backed up a step. Put a hand on his holstered weapon. It wasn't a pistol. Wasn't even a Taser. It was pepper spray. "Don't make me use this."

"Where did the thieves go? Which direction? What kind of car were they driving?"

Reedus looked confused. "I have no idea. Talk to the police about your missing items."

"Cops won't do nothing!" Harold howled in laughter. "There ain't enough of them left in the city to do anything!"

Reedus hopped back in his cart. He closed the door. Took off down the street. It was fast for an electric cart. Just about as fast as a car.

Carver was tempted to chase down the man. He was tempted to rip the doors off that cart. Flip it over on its side. Have a nice long talk with Reedus. But that would draw attention to him. Put him on the police radar.

It was best to cut his losses and move on. Get back to the wilderness. But he'd need more gear. More money. He had a couple of bucks left in his wallet. Not enough to do anything. Especially not in this city.

He needed to call Leon. But now he didn't have a phone. Even if he did, he needed the encrypted messaging app to contact him.

The burner phone couldn't be traced. Not easily. It was a cheap phone. It wasn't tied to the cloud. None of the tracking options were enabled. Only the service provider could trace it. And that was only if someone made a call with it.

Seeing as how Carver's thumb was still firmly attached to his hand, the thieves couldn't access the phone. Mainly because they needed his thumbprint. That meant the thieves couldn't make phone calls. And even if they could, there was no way Carver could convince the service provider to trace a burner.

Which meant he'd have to track it down the old-fashioned way. Because he wasn't leaving San Francisco without that phone. He could always get more money. He could always find a way to contact Leon.

But he'd lose Paola's number forever.

The encrypted app also had another feature. It automatically deleted messages after four or five days. Carver couldn't remember which. If the message never reached the target phone, it stayed in the cloud. But the moment it hit the phone it would self-delete if it had expired.

He only had a few days to track it down. He hoped the thieves hadn't thrown the phone away. He didn't even know why they'd taken it. Stolen phones were useless without the credentials to use them.

Carver walked over to Harold. The old man was still laughing. He also stank to high heaven. The odor convinced Carver to keep his distance. "Harold, did you see the people who broke into my car?"

"I seen them all right." Harold stopped laughing. He picked up a brown paper bag. Drank from the bottle inside. "I seen them folks a lot. Same people always circling this place like vultures."

Carver raised an eyebrow. "The same exact people?"

"Same exact!" Harold chuckled. "Lots of tourists park here. The thieves know which cars are parked here on the regular and which ones ain't. They'll break out the back side window. Check the trunk from the inside. Take something and drive off."

The Ramcharger's back window had been broken. The thieves had opened the tailgate from the inside. The bags with the camping equipment and guns would have been too heavy. Sliding them out would have been easier than lifting through the broken window.

"Describe the people."

"Oh, young and skinny, I think. They wear hoodies and masks. Can't even see their faces." Harold took another swig. "Some are black, some are white, some are Hispanic."

"I'm talking about these specific thieves," Carver said.

Harold blinked a few times. "I dunno. They look the same as the folks who operate around Union Square. Might be the same folks. I see these car break-ins so much I just filter it out."

"What kind of car do they drive?"

Harold's wrinkled forehead wrinkled even more. "I never paid much attention."

"A car or a truck?"

"Oh, it's a car."

"Silver? White? Black?"

"Might be white. Might be silver too." Harold downed another mouthful of alcohol. "It ain't my concern, I guess. So, I don't notice things."

"How often do they come through here?"

"One day I saw them three times. Some days they don't come at all. Or maybe they do, and I just don't notice 'em." Harold pointed to a cluster of tents in the park across the road. The same tents Carver had noticed before. "Probably because I'm in my home."

Carver assessed the situation. It was a busy area. Lots of people parking cars. Lots of people going to the ferry. Walking into town. Strolling along the boardwalk. There was lots of public transportation too. Trolleys, streetcars, and buses.

"Mister, you got some spare change?" Harold held out a hand. "I sure could use some food."

Carver gave Harold his last two dollars. "Sorry, that's all I've got."

"God bless you, son." Harold showed him a withered hand. "Got that injury in Afghanistan. I ain't never been the same since."

"Thank you for your service, Harold." Carver walked back to his car. Looked inside. The thieves had missed a couple of bags that were on the back floorboard. One of the bags had clothing. The other had a small tent. It was the first tent Carver had used during his road trip before switching to a larger one.

The clothing bag also had an old burner phone in it. Carver turned it on. The battery was still at fifty percent. The encrypted messaging app was deactivated on the phone.

The app required an encryption key to work. Once Carver used the key to install the app on another phone, this one was deactivated. He couldn't reactivate it without authorization from the other phone.

It was getting toward early evening. His stomach would start rumbling soon. He didn't have money to buy food, but that wouldn't be a problem. There were always ways around the money problem.

Bobby's mystery briefcase supposedly had money. But that was going on the back-burner for now. He needed to find the thieves. Get his phone back. Then he could concentrate on the briefcase.

The thieves would be back through here. No question about it. It also sounded like they weren't the average thieves. They were probably part of something larger. A crime ring, most likely.

They stole items. Took them to a fence. The fence paid the thieves. Took the stolen goods and sold them. Probably sold them online. That was the easiest way to sell merchandise these days.

He'd seen similar rings in other countries. He'd joined one in Ukraine. Not a smash and grab that burgled cars. Not the kind that stole from retail chains either. This one acquired weapons delivered from the United States. Resold them online for less than retail.

Carver had infiltrated the ring. Found out who the leaders were. Turned out they were high up in the Ukrainian military. Turned out the country's president knew all about it. The small arms were being sold. The money was being used to buy other weapons.

It was also being used to buy nice houses. Luxury cars. Enriching the politicians at the expense of the US government. Nothing new there.

In the end, Carver was told to back down. The order came from Rhodes. Rhodes got the order from one of the anonymous leaders up the chain. She figured it came from the President himself.

The crime ring here was strictly a civilian operation. Smaller. Simpler. Maybe easier to infiltrate.

It was just business. Not personal. The thieves did this like any other day job. Their actions hurt people, but they didn't care. It wasn't their problem. But like with any criminal activity, there might be consequences.

It didn't look like being arrested or jail was one of the consequences in this city. And that was just fine by Carver. He didn't mind showing these people the error of their ways. He didn't mind demonstrating just how bad the consequences could be.

It might be business as usual for these people. Just another day at the office. Driving around. Smashing. Grabbing. Wrecking people's cars. Ruining their vacations. Making it very, very personal for the affected people.

Carver would find these people. He'd find out all about them. And then he'd show them just how personal it could be when they messed with the wrong man's stuff.

CHAPTER 5

Leon couldn't reach Carver.

He tried the burner number again. And again. Straight to voicemail. That usually meant the phone was off. That wasn't unusual for Carver. So, Leon left a short voicemail.

"Call me. Got some important intel you'll want to know." He didn't go into too much detail. He was using the encrypted communications app, but he still didn't like leaving voicemail.

He sent an encrypted text message too. Just in case.

In the meantime, he had more cleanup to do. He was still at the rooftop restaurant. Still keeping an eye on the police as they investigated the burned out remains of the assassin's van.

Leon finished off the Macallan. Savored the last bit of porterhouse steak. He dropped cash on the table and left. Took the elevator down. Went to his Toyota. Climbed in and drove several miles to a coffee shop.

Leon pulled a ruggedized laptop from the back seat. A latch held the top closed. He used his thumbprint to unlock it. If anyone tried to bypass the lock, the laptop would fry itself with a small charge of thermite.

He opened the laptop. Used his thumbprint and a PIN to login. Trying to bypass either of those security measures would also fry the laptop. It wasn't that the laptop had anything of value on it.

In fact, it had nothing on it. Nothing but a web browser. A text document with a few notes. That was it. Pressing a button on the left side for fifteen seconds would erase the hard drive. Reformat it back to factory settings. It would change the hardware IDs as well.

It was one of many toys Leon had liberated from Breakstone. Toys paid for by the federal government. There had been literal warehouses full of weapons and high-tech gadgets. An arsenal specifically made for Breakstone. Made for the private military company that was supposed to take over black operations for the US government.

All of that was gone now. Carver had killed Dorsey, Menendez, and Rocker. Left Leon as the only stakeholder in the company. Made him CEO by default. And Leon hadn't wanted to play ball with the big boys in Washington.

So, the big boys shut down Breakstone. Took back all their toys. All except the few Leon managed to squirrel away first.

Leon connected the laptop to the free Wi-Fi in the coffee shop. He opened a special browser. It was called Tor. It didn't connect to normal parts of the web. It connected to the dark underbelly of the internet.

It was a chaotic place. There was no Google there. No Yahoo. No major search engines. But it was still possible to find just about anything or anyone there.

It was a place good for hiding secrets. Secrets like a black operations bulletin board government agencies wanted to keep well hidden.

Tor finished loading. Leon browsed to the hidden site. Logged in with the credentials from the Farm. The page was set up like a web forum. There were multiple discussions. Most required an invite to view them.

Leon didn't have an invite. The only forum he could view was the public one. That was where general jobs were posted. That was where he'd found out about the Nelson job. It was where he'd found the bounty on Carver.

And now there was a new one. *Identify Individual*. He clicked on it. Inside was a short summary. *This man is suspected of terrorist activities. Use facial recognition software and any other means to identify him. Images are attached.*

Below the summary were three pictures. They were grainy. Obviously taken from security cameras. Facial recognition software wouldn't have much success. Not even image enhancement would work.

The man in the image was dressed in black. Wearing a hoodie. Wearing a face mask. Dark sunglasses. There were no identifying features. He was wearing common clothing. Mass produced. No brand symbols visible.

Leon didn't recognize the man in the pictures. But he knew who the man was. It was him. He only knew it because of a minor detail. A rollup garage door he'd stood in front of just before he took out one of the Farm's free agents.

They were on to him. At least remotely. It meant his precautions were working. It meant someone high up the food chain was aware of his activities. That was no surprise. Leon had taken out several valuable assets over the past two months.

The Farm and Enigma were built like terrorist cells. Their loose alliance with federal agencies was coordinated here on the dark web. That made it harder to see a pattern. Made it hard to realize someone was systematically eliminating their people.

An analyst at one of the agencies had probably noticed the pattern. Realized the person in the three images was behind the killings. Or maybe it was a team of analysts.

Whoever they were, they were the greatest threat to Leon. They were the ones who could eventually positively ID him. Locate him using cameras.

And then he'd be the one with a bullseye on his back.

CARVER PAINTED A BULLSEYE.

It was an imaginary bullseye. A nice bright target on the backs of the thieves who'd taken his burner phone and other stuff. And he was going to hit them dead center. Or at least he would if he had a gun.

San Francisco wasn't Montana. It wasn't an easy place to find a gun. Wasn't an easy place to buy one. Even if he found someone selling, he couldn't afford it. It meant he'd need to steal one.

Carver didn't like leaving the Ramcharger where it was. Especially not with a broken window. But he didn't know where else to park it. There was no free parking in San Francisco. There was no free parking in most big cities.

He took his remaining possessions from the SUV. The bag of clothing. The bag with the tent. He walked across the road to the park. To the homeless encampment there. It looked a little different now.

Several new tents that had popped up since he'd last seen it this morning. It looked like a few had also vanished while Carver was touring the city. That was probably normal in a place like this.

The park was a nice green space. There were trees. Shrubs. Park benches. Families enjoying the sunshine. At least on the opposite side of the park. On this side, the grass was trampled. Brown. Patchy.

On this side, there were tents of all sizes. Strewn trash. Blankets and articles of discarded clothing. Human feces. Vomit. There were men and women stoned out of the minds.

Some staring blankly. Some slumped over in the dirt. Some shivering and sweating because they hadn't had their fix yet.

It was a common sight in big cities. He'd seen them in Minneapolis. Portland. Seattle. It was no surprise to find a crowd of homeless people in a Californian city. In fact, he would have been surprised to find none.

The weather here was nice. Real nice. Even on a bad day. It attracted people like flies to shit.

If Carver had to live in a tent for the rest of his life, he'd choose somewhere close to a beach. A beach near San Francisco would be too cold. Further south would be better. But he was stuck in San Francisco, so he'd make do.

He walked around the small tent city. Found a place at the edge. A place that wasn't covered in trash. A place not occupied by an addict. He started setting up the tent.

"What the hell are you doing?" A man walked out from between the tents. "I don't remember you asking permission to build here."

"Probably because I didn't." Carver studied the guy. He looked old. Worn out. Missing teeth. But he wasn't that old. He was probably in his twenties.

"I'm the mayor of Embarcadero City. You need to ask me permission. Pay your taxes to me."

"Embarcadero City?" Carver glanced at the nearby street sign. "Named after the road?"

"Yeah, exactly." The mayor walked closer. Puffed out his chest. "It'll cost you a grand up front."

"I gave my last two dollars to Harold."

"What you got in that bag?"

"Clothes."

The mayor bared the few teeth he had left. "You better find something valuable fast, or I'll tear down your tent myself."

"Is that so?" Carver kept hammering in the stakes. "Are you sure you're the mayor in these parts? Are you sure it's not someone else?"

"Of course it's me!" the mayor screamed. "I'm the mayor around here! Someone come out here and tell this guy!"

A woman crawled out of a tent. She looked woozy. Real woozy. Like she was going to fall over any minute. Somehow, she managed to stand. "Baby, what's happening?"

"This man don't believe I'm mayor!"

"My baby is the mayor. He's the super mayor!" She staggered to him. Leaned on him. "Pay up now if you wanna live here."

Carver finished setting up the tent. It was a nice little dome tent. Big enough for two people. Big enough for two of him to lie next to each other. But it wasn't anywhere near as nice as the tent that had been stolen. That one was tall. Big enough for him to stand up in. Big enough for him to have a whole family inside.

And now this tent was about the only place he could call home. Normally he'd be happy staying in a cheap motel. But he didn't even have the money for that. The tent would do just fine. So long as the mayor didn't tear it down.

Carver strolled over to the mayor. "Do I just call you the mayor, or do you have a first name?"

The mayor's girlfriend jutted out her chin. "You can call him Mayor Tommy."

"Baby, don't speak for me." Mayor Tommy shoved his girlfriend. She staggered into the side of a tent and went down. Someone inside the tent started screaming like it was the end of the world.

Carver evaluated the situation. Junkies were volatile. Unpredictable. The best way to win them over was with drugs. He didn't have any. That left a couple of options. Sometimes the promise of drugs was almost as good. If that didn't work, he could use the second option.

"Tommy—"

"Mayor Tommy!" Tommy shouted back.

"Mayor Tommy, I don't have any money. But I do have a connection who owes me some fentanyl. If I promise to give you some, can I stay here?"

Tommy gave it some thought.

His girlfriend crawled over to him. "Say yes, baby. But make him give it all to us."

"How much will you get?" Tommy said.

"My friend said he got the pharmaceutical stuff. Didn't tell me how much."

Tommy narrowed his eyes. "Okay. You got until tonight to get it. If you don't get it, you're gone. Got it?"

"I'm not meeting him until tomorrow."

"Okay then, tomorrow noontime."

"Thank you for your understanding, Mayor Tommy."

Tommy puffed out his bony chest. Bounced a fist off it. "You got forty-eight...uh, twenty-four hours, big boy."

His girlfriend looked confused. "Tommy, that's a whole day. I thought he just had until noon tomorrow."

"I know my math!" Tommy shoved her away again.

Carver went into his tent. No sleeping bag. No pillow. Just his clothes bag. That would do just fine. He took out the clothes. Some of them were left over from Oregon. They were clean but a little ragged.

He would have trashed them if Andi hadn't convinced him to wash them. But he was happy he still had them. They'd work great for what he had in mind. He disrobed. Pulled on the torn cargo pants. Put on the shirt with the small tears in the front. Put on the black hoodie with the stains.

They were bloodstains. But you couldn't tell that with the dark material.

He pulled on the scuffed boots. They'd looked like that when he bought them from the thrift store. His outfit was complete. And since Carver hadn't shaved for the last couple of days, he already looked scruffy. Already looked homeless.

It was chilly, so he put on his beanie. It still looked new. He took it off. Rubbed it in the grass and dirt. Brushed off the excess. Looked it over. It seemed dirty enough, so he put it back on.

He put his other clothes in the bag. Left the tent. Zipped it and locked the zipper. Anyone with a knife or determination could get inside. But he didn't want it to be easy. He went to Mayor Tommy's tent. Patted his hand on the outside.

Tommy poked his head out. "You got the ivory?"

Carver figured it had to be slang for fentanyl. "No. I just wanted to tell you that I'm going out. I want to make sure you can protect my tent from the others. If it's messed up when I come back, I'm not giving you the ivory."

Tommy crawled out. Got up. "Nobody will mess with your stuff. They know better." His eyes were wide and crazy. His breath smelled like yesterday's underwear stains. "Mayor Tommy owns this city."

"Thanks, Mayor Tommy." Carver stepped back. "Where's a good place to get food around here?"

"If you want to panhandle these parts, you gotta pay me tribute."

"No, I mean is there a food line? A shelter?"

"Yeah. There's one on Market. It's a hike, but the one closest to here always runs out of food. All the damned illegals get to it first."

Carver knew the area. He'd been walking around the financial district for the better part of the morning. "One other question." He pointed across the road. "Have you ever seen the people who break into the cars around these parts?"

Tommy ran his tongue along his gumline. Shook his head. "I don't know nothing about that. I got my own revenue streams."

"Like what?"

"Like none of your business, bitch."

Carver nodded. "Okay, Mayor Tommy. I'll be back."

"Ain't nobody touching your stuff. Not under my watch." Tommy ducked back into his tent.

It wasn't an ideal situation, but it was probably as good as it was going to get. Carver walked through the encampment. Saw a man laid out on the dirt. He was still breathing. Another guy was laying halfway out of a tent a few feet away. A woman and a man were slumped together at the next.

Another guy was arguing loudly. Shaking his head. Muttering like he was talking to someone over a Bluetooth headset. But he was just shouting at himself.

Carver stopped in front of the guy. "Who's the mayor here?"

The guy looked up. Shouted gibberish. Stared at the street and started rocking back and forth.

There didn't seem to be anyone else to ask. It probably wouldn't matter. Tommy and his girlfriend seemed to be the only sober people in the encampment.

He walked along the sidewalk. Found a bus stop. The sign told him which bus went to the market. It wouldn't be along for another twenty minutes. So, he kept walking until he reached Market Street.

He waited on a trolley. The conductor gave him a suspicious look, but Carver showed him the day pass he'd purchased.

Carver rode it down to the public library. He hopped off and started walking. Kept walking until he found a chain link fence. He'd seen it earlier. Seen a horde of homeless people milling around it. Seen them going inside the opening around lunchtime.

The fence was set up like a corral. Like a place used to herd cattle toward a truck or a barn. There were two fences about six feet apart. They made a corridor that spiraled inward. The gate was closed.

The gate was latched, but it wasn't locked. Carver opened the gate. Went inside.

About fifty feet in, he reached an opening. This one led to a long row of tables. The kind of tables used for serving food. The corral kept going past the serving tables. He followed it around a corner. Found a big space with lots of tables and chairs.

Carver walked past them and through the exit. Except it wasn't an exit. It was an entrance to a building. A big building full of cots.

A woman approached. "I'm sorry. You'll have to come back at six when we're open."

"Sorry." Carver turned around and went back the way he'd come. Wound his way back through the corral. Stepped back outside on the sidewalk and closed the gate behind him.

A silver Toyota screeched to a stop near the curb. A female figure hopped out. Smashed a window. Reached inside and lowered the back seat. Looked inside. Reached in and grabbed a suitcase.

She tossed it into her car. Hopped back in. It pulled back into traffic and took off. A few pedestrians looked alarmed. Stopped walking. Looked around. Probably tourists. Others hardly even blinked. Kept walking. Kept following their routine. Probably locals.

The license plate on the car was covered. The woman was wearing a gray hoodie with a Gucci logo on it. She was wearing a facemask with the same logo. She was wearing black faux leather leggings. And to finish off the look, Gucci tennis shoes.

It wasn't subtle, but it hid her identity well enough. The car also didn't stand out. It was a Toyota. A common compact sedan model. A car no one would look at twice. And if they did, it would get lost in traffic in seconds.

But this was good. Real good. These might not be the same people who robbed Carver's Ramcharger, but they might know who did.

And he was going to make their acquaintance at his earliest convenience.

CHAPTER 6

Noah pressed the muzzle of his Beretta M9 to the courier's head.

"Where are my five kilos, young lady?" He pressed harder. "Be a good girl and tell me."

"I dumped them at the border!" The girl tried to pull away, but her back was against the wall.

Noah took a deep breath. "That's disappointing, Haley. I paid you good money to bring the goods across."

"They searched me." She sobbed uncontrollably. "If I'd had the drugs on me, I'd be in jail!"

"Which is worse, Haley?" Noah pulled the pistol away from her head. Stepped back. Titus wrapped his huge hand around her neck. Held her in place. "Jail, or losing the most precious one and a half kilos you own?"

She looked confused. "I-I don't understand."

"Your brain, Haley." He walked over. Tapped her forehead with the muzzle. "The average human brain is one and a half kilos."

"My brain?" Haley shook with sobs. "P-please, Noah. Please don't kill me."

"You're a very lucky girl today, Haley." Noah stepped back. Spread his arms. "I'm feeling magnanimous today. I'm feeling like you deserve a second chance."

She looked at him. Hope lit her eyes. "Please! I won't let you down. I promise!"

Deshawn smirked. Pressed his lips together. Titus kept glaring like he always did. He looked gigantic compared to the girl.

Noah nodded. "Haley, I want you to go back across the border. Get the ivory you dumped. Bring it to me."

"But what if it's gone?"

"Then you will go to the supplier and explain the situation. I'm sure they'll be understanding."

The light of hope turned to horror. "Noah, they'll kill me!"

"No, they won't. Drug cartels are notoriously understanding and kind when it comes to missing product." Noah traced the muzzle of the gun down her cheek. "Just like me."

"I'll go get it!" She struggled pitifully.

Titus lifted her by the neck. She gasped and struggled. He dropped her on her feet. Pushed her down to her knees and held her by the back of her neck. She wheezed for breath.

Noah nodded. "Okay, Haley. I trust that you'll get it and bring it to me. Or you'll go to jail trying."

"Yes!" She sucked in a harsh breath. "I'll get it."

"Okay." Noah nodded at Titus. "Let her go."

He released her.

She slumped. Fell to her knees. Panting and sobbing. She was healthy for an addict. A relatively new user. Perfect to use as a mule. Unfortunately, even the best candidates failed. Except Haley hadn't failed.

Noah was almost certain she'd succeeded. And now he was going to find out for sure. "Your car is outside, Haley." He set a timer on his phone for twenty-four hours. "It's ten hours to the border and back. I'm giving you an extra four hours in case the border crossing is exceptionally busy. Be back before this timer runs out, okay?"

"I will, Noah." She groveled at his feet. "I promise."

"Titus, help her up, will you?"

Titus grabbed her by the back of her neck and yanked her up roughly. She grunted. Cried out in pain.

Noah got closer to her. "Haley, if you don't come back, there will be consequences." He opened a document on his phone. Turned it around to show her. "For every hour you're late, I will kill someone on this list."

Her eyes flared. "My mom? My brother? How did you—"

He grinned. "Haley, I recruited you right out of high school. Do you really think I wouldn't know all about you?"

She shivered with fear. "I'll bring it back." Her face blanched. Her voice changed to a whisper. "Please don't hurt my family."

Noah laughed. "Why are you so concerned about them? I thought you hated your parents. Remember what you told me when we met at that party two years ago?"

She wasn't sobbing anymore. Tears streamed silently down her face. "My brother is only ten. My parents were right. I was being stupid."

"And now we have the truth, fellas." Noah paraded around. Hands up as if a crowd was cheering him on. "Dumb teen realizes parents were right all along."

Titus cracked a smile.

Deshawn laughed. "Stay in school, kids."

"Stay in school." Noah backhanded Haley. It made his knuckles sting. It made her nose bleed. "Kids."

Haley looked at him with a numb expression. Her face was slack. Eyes were hopeless. It was like she saw everything clearly for the first time. Saw every decision that brought her to this moment in time.

Noah loved that look. He remembered his own epiphany. Remembered the exact moment it happened. It had made him change his ways. And now he was the one in charge. "Haley, you can be free of all this. You can go get my ivory. Bring it back to me. And then you can go back home. Beg forgiveness from your parents. Go back to school. Would you like that?"

She nodded vigorously. Started sobbing again. "Yes, please. I want that so much right now."

"Then go. The minute you start that car, I'm starting this timer. You need to be back in time with the ivory if you want to save your family, okay?"

"Okay, Noah." Her teeth chattered. "I'll do it. I promise."

"All right." He nodded at Titus. "Help her to her car."

Titus steered her by the back of her neck. Pushed her toward the door. Noah followed them out. Watched Haley get in her old beater. She gunned it out of the parking lot. Almost hit a car pulling onto the road. Then she was gone.

Noah sighed. Shook his head. "Deshawn, what's our success rate again?"

"Sitting at seventy-two percent, sir."

"And she knows the odds like any of our mules, right?"

Deshawn nodded. "Yep. Sometimes we say eighty percent just to make them feel better."

"That's a good ploy, Deshawn. It's not high enough to make them suspicious and not low enough to make them scared."

Titus chimed in with his deep voice. "Seventy-two is damned good odds, boss."

"It's much, much better than it was a few years ago." Noah stared at the San Francisco skyline. "We were at forty-eight percent."

"Yeah, boss." Titus nodded. "It was hard times."

Noah had been thinking about those odds ever since Haley returned. He'd known something was wrong when he saw the look on her face. She'd been a courier three times before. Three successful crossings. Now a failed one.

You couldn't use a courier too many times. People who crossed more frequently were going to be flagged. Especially those who didn't have jobs requiring them to go back and forth between Mexico and California.

Truckers made the crossing all the time. Some operations managed to smuggle ship-ments across with them. There was so much cargo going back and forth that it was easier than it used to be.

But couriers were the way to go for Noah. They were easy to recruit. Easy to manage. Easy to deal with when things went wrong. And they were American citizens. They could legally go back and forth as much as they wanted.

Everyone thought migrants were being used. Especially illegals. But they were the worst people to use. They were almost always picked up. Searched. Put in a holding pen somewhere.

Coyotes were good at it, but they cost too much. Citizen couriers like Haley were the best. They were cheap and effective. And their success rates were no better or worse than using truck drivers or coyotes.

Noah checked the time. "I'm running behind schedule today, thanks to our little mule."

Deshawn went to his car. Pulled out a tablet. "Inventory is in. Looks like the usual except for a couple of items."

"Let me see." Noah took the tablet. Looked at the highlighted items. Two H&K MP5s with suppressors. One Glock 19 with suppressor. One Colt M4 with night scope. Four cans of various ammunition. One cell phone. One large tent.

He raised his eyebrows and looked at Deshawn. "Who brought that in?"

"Derrick's crew. They said it was in an old truck."

"An old truck?" Noah scrolled down the list. "There's camping equipment listed here. Gas stove, big tent. Even a compound bow and arrow. Did that come from the same truck?"

"They didn't say. I can ask."

"Ask them. That's too strange."

"Real strange," Titus said.

Deshawn shrugged. "Maybe a survivalist?"

"In this city?" Noah laughed. "Doubtful." He tapped a finger on his chin. "The truck wasn't marked safe?"

Deshawn shook his head. "They said it wasn't. You know our people are careful about that kind of thing."

"They better be. I don't want corporate getting in our business again." Noah walked to his car. "I'm going to look at the inventory. What else is on your schedule?"

"Just the usual rounds," Deshawn said. "Going to the schools to see how recruitment is going. Scouting out new targets."

Noah grunted. "Yeah, the stores all closed up downtown. Complaining about crime or something like that."

Deshawn sighed. "It's working."

Noah nodded. "Yep. Working like a charm. Just how corporate wants it." He climbed in his car. Cranked the Hellcat's engine. Revved it a few times. He still enjoyed the roar just as much as the day he bought it. He peeled out of the parking lot.

Bounced onto the road. Headed toward his base of operations.

The route went from Bayview all the way back to Market Street. The area had been thriving a few years ago but now the office buildings were empty. The nearby restaurants had all shut down.

Most of the retail stores were gone. Just a few banks remained. The civic auditorium. A museum. And a coffee shop. The streets used to be full of businesspeople. Walking from offices to restaurants. Drinking their twenty-dollar soy lattes. Eating their avocado toast.

Now all that remained were tourists. Tourists and a lot of homeless people. Both were good for business. The tourists drove into town. Parked their cars. Noah's people broke the windows. Took whatever was inside.

The homeless liked drugs. They bought mostly fentanyl from Noah. Took it right out in the open. On sidewalks. In the middle of streets. It was legal here. Sometimes cops moved people off the road. Most of the time they just watched.

The homeless also helped Noah's retail operations. They shoplifted. Brought the goods to the fences. They were paid in cash. Mainly cash that hadn't been laundered yet.

Then they walked across the street. Walked right over to Noah's other business. Bought ivory or whatever vice they wanted with the cash. It was a nice self-contained economy.

Things were going just how corporate wanted.

Noah was doing all the work and they were taking most of the profit. It wasn't like the old days when he was the undisputed king. When he was pushing good old-fashioned drugs like cocaine and heroin.

His volume was lower, but the profit was better. People were long term customers because they weren't dropping like flies. Now the death rate was sky high. Mainly because fentanyl was fifty to a hundred times stronger than morphine.

That was why it was more popular. Cheaper. Sold in higher volumes. It was mostly made in clandestine labs in Mexico. Those labs were owned by corporate. The drugs were funneled through cartels to hide the true origin.

Corporate hadn't told Noah that. He'd sent his own people south to find out the truth. To dig into the fentanyl drug manufacture. Find out what they weren't telling him. They thought he was just a stupid street thug. A puppet dancing on their strings.

He wanted them to keep thinking that while he found out all there was to know about their mysterious organization.

Noah turned right off Market Street. Drove through an open gate. Into a large parking lot of a three-story building that used to be a department store. Retail crime had driven it out of business nearly four years ago. One of the first casualties of corporate's strategy.

He steered left. Around the side of the building. Pulled into a gated lot on the side. This one was full of cars. Not employees' cars. Most of the people who worked here didn't own one. These were cars Noah had acquired over the years.

Most were nothing special. Just plain cars he could drive anonymously to check in on his city. Others were nicer. Much nicer. But his favorite by far was the Hellcat.

He parked it next to an Audi SUV. Got out. Unlocked the building's side door with a key. Went inside. Entered a hallway. It took him around back to the loading docks. It was a busy place. He went back outside.

There were a dozen cars parked in the spots next to large double doors. People were taking merchandise from cars. Putting it onto carts. Wheeling it inside. Two people with tablets were cataloguing everything brought in.

The people with the tablets stiffened a little when they saw him. It was a conditioned reaction. They'd seen what he did to unproductive workers.

Noah walked past the cars. Looked over the stolen merchandise. Most of it was garbage. Some of it was valuable. All of it would be put to good use.

He went back inside. Went back to the main floor. All the clothing racks and shelves from the former store were still there. Even the cash registers and checkout counters were still up front.

That made this place the perfect warehouse and staging area for selling everything his people took. His people catalogued incoming merchandise. Took pictures. Wrote descriptions. Another department took that and put it online.

The people who catalogued all the incoming items assigned values to them. A computer program calculated the total. The thieves—Noah preferred to call them collectors—were then given a percentage of the haul.

The cash registers dinged. Cash was counted. The collectors took their cut and left. Went back to the streets to do it all over again. Some collected from cars. Others collected from retail businesses. Big box stores were the best.

Noah had five crews working full time. Most people in these parts were working for him. Sometimes freelancers tried their hand at it. Noah didn't like those kinds. He didn't like people interfering with his revenue stream.

His enforcers caught them regularly. Told them the rules of the game. Bring the merchandise to one of Noah's operations. Take a reduced amount. Promise not to do it again without permission.

If they were caught again doing unsanctioned work, they were given a lesson. Most of the time it was nonlethal. It was still enough to put them in the hospital for a few days. That usually convinced them not to do it again.

Noah walked past the shelves. Walked past the people taking pictures of merchandise. Past the rows of computers where people posted the merchandise online for sale. All the way to the back.

He entered a back corridor. There were several offices there. Most were empty. At the end was a large office. His office. He stopped at the office next to his.

Tasha was there as usual. Typing on the computer. Entering the numbers. Keeping the books in order. She looked up. Stared at him long and hard. As if questioning why he was there without saying a word.

"I heard Derrick's crew brought in some interesting merchandise."

Tasha stood. Stretched like a cat. "It's in storage next to your vault."

"You put it on the special inventory list?"

"It's on a temporary list." She pushed her glasses up her nose. Crossed her arms. "I'll wait for your approval and then move things to their appropriate place."

"Okay. Come with me."

She hesitated. "Do I have to?"

"Is that a rhetorical question?"

Tasha took a deep breath. "Let's go."

Noah walked across the hallway to the special holding room. Anything out of the ordinary was brought here so Noah could decide what to do with it. He typed a code into the keypad. The door clicked open.

The newly acquired weapons were on a table. The MP5s were shiny and new. The Colt M4 looked used, but well maintained. The Glock looked like an old beater of a gun. A gun that hadn't been cared for.

He picked it up. Handed it to Tasha. "What do you think?"

She broke it down. Spread the components on the table. "The exterior is rough, but the inside looks good. The suppressor looks functional. The firing pin and springs are in good shape." She pointed to a smooth place on the side. "This thing never had serial numbers. Or if it did, someone made it look like it came from the factory without numbers."

Noah nodded. "Looks like the Glocks our mysterious overlords offered us. No serial numbers."

"Might be one of corporate's." She reassembled the gun. Left it on the table.

"Take it to the firing range. Test it for me." Noah put the gun in her hand. "If it passes muster, put it in the armory."

She pressed her lips together in a tight line. "Not special enough for you?"

"Not by a long shot." He looked over the MP5s.

Tasha lifted one. Looked it over. Set it back down.

"Pretty sweet, aren't they?"

She nodded. "Like new condition. No serial numbers."

"Fully automatic too." He chuckled. "Bet you'd like to have both of these fully loaded."

"Why do you say that?"

"Because you'd love to mow me down. Keep firing until the mags are empty."

"I wouldn't give you a quick death. You don't deserve it."

Noah laughed. "That's why I like you, Tasha. You're raw. Honest."

She sighed. "What do you want to do with the MP5s?"

"Add them to my collection. Can't use them on the streets anyway."

She wrote on a notepad. "Done. What else?"

Noah picked up one of the MP5s. He checked the chamber. Checked the magazine. Both empty. Both clean and well oiled. They didn't look like they'd been used much. Tasha was right. The MP5s were like new.

He moved on to the ammunition. Two ammo cans had 9x19mm parabellum in them. One had regular 9mm. Four cans were evenly split with 556 and 762.

Tasha noticed the 762. "Are we missing a rifle?"

"Looks like it."

"Nothing here uses that ammo."

"You're right." Noah assumed the weapon that did was still in the vehicle. Maybe on the floorboard. Might be an AK-47 or other Soviet weapon. He had plenty of those. They were good weapons but nothing special. Not worth a spot in the vault.

Noah decided to put the MP5s on a shelf in his vault. He'd get some nice holders for them. Put them on display even if no one else saw them. He wanted a mansion of his own one day. A place where he could display all his collectables.

He had the money. He could drop it on a nice house in a good part of town. And then the IRS would notice his lifestyle didn't match up with his income. Maybe corporate could save him from the feds. Maybe not. He didn't want to test that theory.

Tasha wrote on her notepad. "What about the ammo?"

"Put it in the vault, too. You can never have too much."

"Unless it explodes." She stared at him. "Is that all?"

He examined the camping equipment liberated from the same vehicle. It was nothing special. "We can sell this."

"I already put that in common inventory," Tasha said. "Could probably sell it to a homeless aid charity in a heartbeat."

"Okay." He picked up the MP5s. Walked outside the storage room. Walked down the hall to his office. The wall was one large window. The word *Management* was stenciled on the wooden door.

Across the hall was a large metal door. He put his thumb on the biometric keypad. The door clicked. Swung outward. On the other side was his personal vault. A room only he had access to.

The walls were solid concrete and steel rebar. The door was twelve inches thick. It had been here when Noah took over the place. Apparently, the original owner had it built because he didn't like keeping his money in banks.

Noah agreed completely. The vault was perfect for him. Inside was everything Noah had ever collected. Rare books. Comics. Weapons. Paintings. It didn't come close to filling the large space, but he was working on it.

He also kept unlaundered cash, gold, and silver in the vault. If things ever went south, he was ready.

Noah found an empty shelf. Propped the MP5s upright against the wall. He pointed them at each other. Crossed the barrels. They looked good. Real good.

Noah went back to the hallway. Tasha was talking to a man. One of the loading dock workers.

Noah approached them.

The man stared at Noah in awe. "Can I help you, sir?"

Noah pointed to the ammo cans. "Carry those to my vault, please. Then take these tents to general storage."

"Right away, sir!" The man picked up two ammo cans and hauled them into the vault.

Noah watched until he was finished. Then he closed the vault door. Tasha started walking to the office.

Noah grabbed her arm. "Come with me." He led her further down the hallway. Past the offices. Down a flight of stairs. Into the basement.

She shivered. "Not this again."

"It's good for you. A reminder."

She pulled her arm free. Closed her eyes and took a breath. "Fine."

Noah kept going. Pushed through double doors and into what used to be a breakroom. There were people waiting inside. Some of them were his people. Some of them were people who engaged in unsanctioned activities in Noah's territory.

Two of the unsanctioned were tied to metal poles. The third was a repeat offender. He was dangling upside down from his ankles. The rope holding him was tied to a hook in the ceiling.

Noah sighed. He remembered this guy. Remembered the first two times he'd been dragged in here. He waved over one of his enforcers. Nodded at the other two detainees. "First-timers?"

"Yes, sir."

"Good." He turned to them. Smiled. "You get to witness a very important lesson today. A lesson that you don't want to learn." Noah glanced at Tasha. "Be a good girl and stay close, sweetheart."

She glared at him but stayed by his side.

One of the detainees tried to talk. The gag muffled whatever he tried to say.

Noah walked over. Punched him in the gut. "Don't speak unless I tell you to, okay?"

The man grunted in pain. His eyes watered. But he nodded. Went silent.

"See? It pays to be polite." Noah walked to the third guy. The guy hanging upside down. He sighed. "On a scale of one to ten, ten being the absolute dumbest, how dumb are you?" He lowered the man's gag.

"Please, Noah! I need money! I'm desperate."

Noah punched him in the stomach. The man gasped. Flailed like a fish caught on a hook.

"Answer the question."

"I'm a ten, Noah." The man gasped. "A ten."

"Yes, you are." Noah shoved the gag back into his mouth. He motioned toward his enforcers. "Get me a tub, please."

One of them brought over a well-used metal tub. It was big and wide. He placed it under the dangling prisoner.

An enforcer handed Noah a thin, narrow knife with an ivory handle. It was real ivory. The knife was carbon steel. Razor sharp. Technically, it was a stiletto. Used for stabbing, not slashing or slicing.

He held it out to Tasha. "I did the last one. It's your turn."

"Please, Noah." She hugged herself. "No."

"Tasha, I'm ordering you to do it."

"I can't."

He gripped her wrist. "You're left-handed, correct?" He squeezed until she cried out. Opened her fist. He put the stiletto in her hand. Closed her fingers around it. "Tasha, don't make me punish you. More importantly, don't make me punish your sister."

Tears trickled down her cheeks. She approached the man. He was wriggling madly. Eyes wide. Face frantic. Down to the last few seconds of his life. All because of his own bad choices.

Noah gripped her wrist. "Tasha, you know what I said about resisting my orders."

"Fine!" She gripped the dangling man by the back of the neck. In one smooth motion, the stiletto dove into his neck. It slid back out just as smoothly.

Blood poured into the tub beneath the man. He gasped. Spasmed. But not for long. He was too weak to do anything a few seconds later. And a few seconds after that, he was dead.

Tasha gripped the stiletto tighter. She stared at Noah. Her eyes were filled with unrequited rage. He knew she wanted to drain his blood into that tub.

"That's a good girl." He grinned. Held out his hand.

She gave him the weapon. "May I go now?"

He nodded. "You may go."

She trembled with anger. Spun on her heel and left.

Noah looked at the dead man. Another dead idiot. Another person backed into an inescapable corner because he couldn't play by Noah's rules. And unfortunately, he probably wouldn't be the last one to die today.

CHAPTER 7

Carver sat next to a dead man.

At least the man looked dead. He was still breathing. Barely. Stoned out of his mind on fentanyl, most likely. He was lying on his side. Lying on the sidewalk. Right next to someone's front door.

He wasn't the only one. There were at least six people stoned out of their mind all within a twenty-foot radius. Some of them had tents. Some of them had just blankets or cardboard. It was a good place to sit. A good place to blend in.

Carver was sitting on brick steps. His back was against a door. It looked like the door to a small apartment building. No one had come out or gone into it yet, so he didn't know for sure.

A school bus pulled around the corner. It stopped right next to the encampment. The stop sign popped out. The door squealed open. Kids poured out. Most of them looked younger than ten.

A couple of parents were waiting nearby. They got their kids. Walked down the street with them. The others just made their way through the bodies on the sidewalk. A little girl walked up to Carver. Looked at the door behind him.

"This is my house."

Carver got up. Moved.

She punched the doorbell. "Auntie, it's me." A buzzer buzzed. The magnetic latch released. She opened the door and went inside.

Carver went in after her. She looked at him. Eyes wide.

"Don't worry. I just need to ask your aunt a question."

The girl hurried down the hall. Past numbered doors. To a door at the end. She opened the door. Closed it behind her. A lock clicked into place.

Carver went to the door. Knocked on it.

"Go away!" It was a woman's voice. "You're not supposed to be in here."

"I just have a question."

"We don't have money, alcohol, or drugs. Go away! I'm sick of you people barging in here!"

"I don't want any of those. I just have some questions."

"You're lying."

"You can answer me through the door. I just don't want to shout."

The door cracked open. A heavy chain lock kept it from opening wider. An older woman looked out at him. "What do you want?"

"I'm new in town. Looking for a friend who I think is living on the streets."

Her gaze softened. "I'm sorry. There are a lot of lost souls on these streets."

Carver nodded. "Where do they get the drugs?"

"Usually, they steal stuff and take it somewhere for payment."

"Any idea where they take it?"

She shook her head. "I keep my head down. I don't go looking for trouble."

"Mommy used to go to a place," the little girl said from inside. "She took me there a few times."

Her aunt shuddered. Closed her eyes. Sighed. "Where did she take you, darling?"

"The old theater. Down two blocks."

The aunt opened her eyes. Gave Carver a searching look. "What do you plan to do?"

"Find my friend." Carver glanced back at the exit. "Which way is the theater?"

"Go left outside. Two blocks down. The front is all boarded up, so you'll probably have to go to the back."

"Thanks." He turned to go.

"I hope you find your friend before it's too late." A tear pooled in her eye. "It was too late for my sister. She tried her hand at being a drug mule. Then she tried stealing from the local gang. They killed her."

"I'm very sorry to hear that." Carver backed away. "Thank you for your help."

"You're welcome!" the little girl shouted from somewhere inside.

Carver left the building. He turned left outside. Started walking. He didn't want to feel bad. But he did. A little girl. Robbed of her mom. Maybe her dad too. Maybe her mom had already been lost even before she brought that girl into the world.

It was an old story. Happened all the time. Happened in big cities, little cities, and all the places in between. It was just more visible in a big city. Especially in a place that allowed drug use.

What used to be hidden was now in the open. Maybe that was a good thing. Maybe it would bring more attention to the problem. But it was most likely nothing would change. Drug use and addiction were just a normal part of human existence. Some people were just wired that way.

Carver reached the theater. It was boarded up just like the aunt said. He saw people shuffling around the corner. He followed them. Went through an open gate in the back. Found a short line of people waiting there.

There was a large rollup door in the back of the theater. A table inside. A woman sitting behind the table. A pair of men standing next to the door. The men didn't seem to be armed. They might be hiding something under their clothes, but Carver didn't see any telltale bulges.

A man waiting in line had a loaf of bread and a jar of mayonnaise. A woman had two boxes of shoes. Another had several jugs of laundry detergent. The other people in line had various items to sell or barter. Some looked brand new. Others looked like they'd been dug out of dumpsters.

Carver watched a woman hand over a pair of new purses. The woman behind the table looked them over. Typed something into a tablet. Words were exchanged. The seller said something. The buyer responded.

One of the men pulled out a baggie. Handed it to the seller. The seller laughed in unbridled joy. Did a happy dance. Ran past Carver. Around the corner.

Carver had considered one plan. It required finding something to barter. Bringing it here and exchanging it for drugs. But now he had a better plan. A simpler one. He turned around. Followed the woman.

She was still giggling. Crying and laughing like someone just saved her life. That was how excited she was. Those two purses had netted her probably a couple of days' worth of fentanyl. Maybe more.

The woman ran to a group of tents in a back alley. A man was sitting outside. He was half dressed. No shoes. No shirt. A pair of raggedy shorts on. Looked like he hadn't bathed in months. The woman showed him the bag.

He tried to snatch it.

She yanked it back. "No! It's mine!"

"It's ours!" He tried to take it again. "You owe me half."

"No, I don't. I paid for it myself." She laughed. Danced in place. "Took me two seconds to snatch those purses and run!"

"Bitch!" The man lunged. Punched her in the face. Punched her again and again. She went down. Groaning. Rocking back and forth on the ground. Bleeding from the nose.

Carver was almost there. The man wasn't looking at anything except the baggie. He was using his teeth. Trying to open it. Carver didn't want to touch the guy. But he did it anyway. He grabbed the guy's wrist. Squeezed hard.

The man screamed. Dropped the baggie. Carver kneed him in the gut. Shoved him hard against the brick wall. The man's head bounced off the hard surface. He crumpled to the ground.

Carver picked up the baggie. Counted ten white pills. He opened the baggie. He had no idea how much equaled a dose. He took a guess. Figured two pills was enough. He knelt next to the groaning woman. Put two pills in her hand.

He closed the baggie. Stuffed it in his pocket. Hustled away. Mayor Tommy was going to be pleased.

Sure, he could've threatened Tommy. Picked him up by the neck. Punched him. Kicked him. A show of violence usually worked. But that was loud. It attracted attention. And Tommy might try to retaliate. Might try to sneak into Carver's tent and stab him in his sleep.

There was no ideal way to handle the situation. No great way to mitigate the circumstances. But this would do the trick for now. Give him camouflage. A place to live until he got his stuff back.

Someone roared. Carver heard the patter of feet on asphalt.

Carver looked back. Saw a couple of men running after him. They'd probably been in the other tents. Neither of them looked too healthy. Certainly not healthy enough to be running. But they had the wild look of desperate men.

Men who would do anything to survive. And to them, getting these drugs was life or death.

Fighting them wasn't appealing. Not because they might be good fighters. Mainly because they might try to bite. Maybe because they'd bleed on Carver. That was a good way to catch something. Something nasty.

Carver saw a broken pallet next to a dumpster. He leaned down. Yanked a 2x4 from the bottom. Checked it for nails. There was one on the end. He tapped it on the asphalt. Bent it down. No sense in impaling anyone today.

Then he turned toward the runners. "Leave me alone or I'm going to hurt you."

"You stole our stuff!" The one on the right was even dirtier than the guy Carver had put down. His eyes were rolling madly. He looked like he might already be on something. "Give it back or I'll kill you!"

The other guy lunged. Carver held out the 2x4 like a cattle prod. Poked the guy in his bony chest. He grunted. The breath exploded out of his mouth. He fell over backward. The filthy guy tried his luck too.

Carver batted him in the side of the head. Gave him a love tap. Enough to make him fall senseless to the ground. The other guy was back on his feet. Charging again. Carver sidestepped. Knocked the guy on the back of the head when he stumbled past.

His face hit the asphalt. He screamed. Flailed and rolled over. Carver didn't want to kill him, but this was getting noisy. He bonked him one more time. This time the guy took a first-class ticket to dreamland just like his buddy.

Carver watched the pair. Made sure they stayed down. The woman was sitting up. Eating the pills Carver left her. Giggling like she was on top of the world. Her boyfriend was still out.

It looked like no one else was coming. Carver started walking again. He kept walking until he was back in the business district. Near the fenced-in area he'd seen earlier. He hopped on a bus. Took it back to the Embarcadero.

Carver hopped off at his new home. He walked to Tommy's tent. "Mayor, I've got something for you."

No answer.

Carver pulled back the flap of the tent. The smell almost knocked him out. He'd smelled worse, but it was still enough to knock a seasoned vet on his ass. Tommy and his girl were inside. Still breathing. Stoned out of their minds.

It was a miracle they didn't suffocate in all that stink. There were open food cans all over. The smell of rotting food. Of body odor. The air inside the tent was practically a bioweapon. It looked like Mayor Tommy would have to get his payment later.

Later when he was nice and sober. Or at least as sober as people got around here.

Carver kept the pills with him. It was the best currency in this local economy. He walked toward the road. Found a bench across from his Ramcharger. Sat down and leaned back to watch.

It was getting dark when a white Dodge Charger pulled up behind his car. A thin boy wearing sweatpants and a white hoodie hopped out. He opened the rear hatch. Climbed inside. Climbed over the back seats. Unlocked the front door.

He hopped out of the back door. Opened the front. Looked inside. Looked inside the glove compartment. Took out the registration. Pocketed it. Closed the Ramcharger's doors and the back hatch and got back in the Charger.

It was just a six cylinder, so it didn't roar. It hummed away into traffic. The license plate was covered. But the car had a purple pinstripe down the side. That was different enough to identify it if Carver saw it again.

There were rows of electric scooters and bikes. But Carver didn't have a way to rent them. He could hop in the Ramcharger and go after the car too, but they'd recognize it immediately unless they were blind.

He started jogging down the sidewalk. The traffic lights held up the car. Gave him time to catch up. He kept jogging. Pretended like he was out for exercise.

The light turned green. The car hummed forward. He kept jogging. The car slowed. Prowled along a line of parked cars. They stopped at one. Broke the window. Looted some bags from inside.

They stopped at another car. Broke into it. Carver noticed something in common. Both cars had orange stickers on the side windows. He hadn't seen one on his Ramcharger. Maybe it had been there before.

The thief peeled the orange stickers off. Took it with him. That answered that. The stickers marked the cars. The thieves took the stickers after they hit them.

The thieves had a spotter. Someone who walked the route, probably. Looked inside cars. Saw which ones were ripe. Which ones were empty. Marked the ripe ones. The operation was more complicated than he'd thought.

None of the other cars along this stretch were marked, so the Charger kept going. Carver kept jogging. The car turned down a street. Vanished from view. The street went uphill at a steep angle.

Carver kept jogging. Four blocks later, he was at the top of the hill. He saw the Charger way down at the bottom. It was idling next to a BMW. The guy in the white hoodie was looting it. He took a suitcase. Tossed it in the Charger. Got back in.

The car kept going straight. It turned left. Out of sight. Carver couldn't catch it if he tried. So, he went left. Walked to the next street over. The Charger was on that street. It was coming uphill toward him.

He watched it all the way. It turned into a hotel parking lot. Carver walked across the street for a better angle. He saw the Charger idling on the circle drive in front of the hotel. The white hoodie guy was looting a car. These people were absolutely fearless.

The Charger rolled back onto the street. Started climbing the hill toward Carver. It stopped once to check another car. Continued uphill. Went past Carver at the top. Down the hill. This time it didn't stop at all. It kept going.

It turned right onto Market Street. Vanished around the corner. Carver jogged another block over. He didn't see the Charger. He waited. It never reappeared. That was okay. It would be back. Of that, he was sure.

He sat down on a bench to catch his breath. Leaned back and enjoyed the view from the top of the hill. The city was beautiful. One of a kind. Certainly, unique among U.S. cities. And it was rotting from the inside out.

That was a damned shame. Because he kind of liked it.

What he didn't like was seeing his Ramcharger broken into for the second time. If those were the same perps from the first time, why had they come back? It was like they thought they missed something.

They had missed the tent and bag of clothes, but nothing else of value. And why had they taken the registration? Come to think of it, the title was in the same envelope. Carver hadn't signed it. Hadn't put his name on anything.

The only name on it was Bill Sniderman. The guy who sold it to Carver.

It was likely that the people who took Carver's stuff delivered it to the fence. The fence was probably surprised to find high quality submachine guns with suppressors inside. Maybe he noticed the 762 ammo can. Maybe he noticed none of the stolen weapons used that ammunition.

Maybe the fence sent someone back to see if there was an AK-47 floating around in the car somewhere. Maybe he wanted the registration to find out who in the hell was packing such serious heat.

Carver couldn't wait to meet them and show them.

CHAPTER 8

Noah wasn't in a killing mood.

But he had no choice. It was his job. His duty. No two ways about it. And someone was trying to play him for a fool. They should have known better. They should have learned a lesson. But some people never learned.

There was a knock on the apartment door. "I'm here, boss."

Noah got up. Unlocked three deadbolts and chain. Opened the door. Titus and Deshawn stood outside. He ushered them inside. Closed the door. Latched it. This was a terrible neighborhood. The apartment was a tiny studio. And it still cost four grand a month.

Titus and Deshawn stood in the tiny kitchen space.

"You got the package?"

They nodded.

"Okay." Noah looked through the window. "Any progress on the briefcase?"

Deshawn shook his head. "Our people on the street are asking everyone about it. No leads yet. They all want that ten grand bounty."

Noah ran a finger down the laminate countertop. "I want to know how in the hell a junkie like Bobby got his hands on it."

"There was a lot going on, boss." Titus shook his head. "The little rat must have gotten it during the shootout."

"And he somehow crossed the Golden Gate Bridge and hid in the forest for weeks." Noah tried to imagine how the junkie managed it without a car. "Then he trekked back into town looking for his next fix. Demetrius and Leroy saw him and tracked him back to his campsite."

Titus grunted. "They should've picked him up right away. Brought him back for questioning."

"They probably thought he'd lead them to the briefcase," Deshawn said. "That was the right move."

"That didn't go too well." Titus scowled. "They ended up dead."

"How does a junkie like Bobby come out on top against two enforcers?" Deshawn shook his head. "Leroy and Demetrius were no chumps."

"Detective Duffy said Leroy's arm was cut." Noah imagined the scene in his head. "Leroy was probably right up in Bobby's face. Threatening him. Bobby was hiding a knife. He surprised Leroy. Cut him. Leroy dropped the gun. Bobby grabbed the gun. Ran. Demetrius shot him in the back. Bobby went down. Rolled onto his back. Shot at them. Got lucky."

"A headshot and a neck shot is real lucky." Deshawn scoffed. "I can't believe it."

"I pay Detective Duffy good money to give it to me straight." Noah shrugged. "He said the way the bodies were positioned indicated that was the likely chain of events."

"Do you think he'd tell you if the cops found the briefcase?" Titus asked.

"He's loyal to my money." Noah nodded. "He'd tell me. The cops scoured the area. Didn't find anything."

"That thing was heavy. Bobby was on foot with his tent, a backpack full of food, and his drugs." Deshawn narrowed his eyes like he was envisioning it. "There's no way he hauled that heavy ass briefcase with him. That thing weighs at least fifty pounds. It's more like a safe than a briefcase."

"I agree." Noah had been thinking about it a lot. "He probably stashed it in town. The question is where? Who are his known associates? Who would he go to for help?"

Titus laughed. "Ain't no telling with junkies, boss."

"Everyone needs someone," Noah said. "Ask enough questions and we'll find the breadcrumbs leading to the answer."

"Sounds smart." Titus nodded. "That's why you're the boss."

"First thing tomorrow, I want all the enforcers to meet at the store. I want everyone on the same page."

"I'll send out the text," Deshawn said.

Noah looked through the window. "Okay, we've wasted enough time. Let's take care of business."

Deshawn nodded. "Let's get to it."

They went outside. Climbed into Titus's Prius. Noah took the passenger seat. Deshawn slid into the back. Next to Tasha. She'd been waiting in the car all this time.

Tasha sighed loudly. "Why am I here?"

"Because you didn't do what I told you to do earlier."

"Yes, I did."

"Not immediately." Noah shook his head. "You hesitated. And you did it in front of outsiders. That shows a severe lack of respect."

"Because I don't respect you."

Deshawn barked a laugh.

Titus growled. "That girl better show some respect."

"She wouldn't know respect if it bit her in the ass," Deshawn said. "Why'd you bring her? She's killing my vibe."

"Because she needs to learn to be a better person." Noah glanced back at her. "One who does as she's told."

Tasha went silent. Stared out the side window.

Noah gave Titus the address. He steered onto the road. Started driving.

They crossed the Oakland Bay Bridge. Went south into the Lower Bottoms. It was a diverse part of town. Decent houses right next to rundown old shanties. It was affordable compared to other bay areas. You could find houses for under half a million. Or you could drive a block over and find one for seven million.

That said, it was also a horrible place to live. Close to the interstate. Crime-ridden. Filthy. The streets were full of potholes. The infrastructure was crumbling. Noah would never want an Oakland address. Not even if the house was a mansion.

It was just a shithole pure and simple.

Something thudded. Bumped and banged. Something in the Prius. Something in the trunk. Nobody acknowledged it. Nobody commented. Not even Tasha. Titus kept driving. Following the GPS to the destination.

They turned onto Henry Street. The houses here were close together. Built right on top of one another. They were long and narrow. Most were wood. Some were concrete. Some looked like old frontier buildings. They all looked like they'd seen better days.

One of the houses was lit up. Music was thumping. There were people outside on the lawn. People on the front porch. Despite the music, they weren't dancing. They were sitting on the grass. Lying on the driveway. Slumped against parked cars.

It wasn't the kind of party where people drank themselves stupid. It was the kind of party where most people were on the drug of their choice. In this case, it was easy to see what everyone was on.

Noah's blood boiled. He might not have been in a killing mood before, but he was definitely in one now. This party was a slap to his face. Like someone spit on the ground he walked on. They thought Oakland was a safe haven.

They were about to find out otherwise.

Titus parked on the street. Noah got out. His Beretta was concealed in its shoulder holster, but he wouldn't need it.

He turned to Tasha. "Wait in the car, darling. We'll be back shortly."

She didn't look relieved to stay there. She knew he had something planned for her.

Noah, Titus, and Deshawn walked up the stairs. Went into the house. Everyone in the front yard was too stoned to notice.

He went inside. Two men and a woman sat on a filthy couch. High out of their minds. Eyes vacant and staring. Some were smiling. Most were expressionless.

Someone laughed in the kitchen. Someone else shouted. Whooped. Someone who wasn't on fentanyl. Not yet, anyway.

Noah pushed into the kitchen. Saw a naked girl on the counter. Her body was lined with white powder. Two men and three women were taking turns snorting lines off the girl. It wasn't crushed ivory. It was coke.

Noah's sour mood changed. He was happy. Not because they were doing coke, but because they weren't voided out on ivory. And especially because the naked girl wasn't stoned on it. He could tell.

Because when she saw him, her eyes went wild with panic. She jumped up. Coke dust went everywhere. The rest of her group shouted in surprise. Some of them tried to snort the coke off the floor.

The girl tried to run. Titus grabbed her. His hand went around her whole neck. Swallowed it like a shark eating a minnow.

"Noah!" Haley tried to play innocent. "What are you doing here?"

Noah showed her the timer on his phone. "Darling, you should be most of the way to Tijuana right now." He stopped the timer. "But I guess you don't need to go since you didn't dump the ivory after all."

"I did, Noah!" She gasped. Tried to wriggle free from Titus. The coke was making her hyper. Frantic. "I just need to go get it."

"You don't have time, baby girl."

The other partygoers were staring in confusion at Noah and his companions. They saw Titus holding Haley. But no one was brandishing weapons. Everyone was calm. Quiet. Just how Noah liked it.

He looked at the others. "Whose house is this?"

One of the men raised a hand. "It's mine, dude. You want to party with Haley?"

"As a matter of fact, I do." Noah waved a hand around. "Where are the drugs Haley brought?"

The man shivered with excitement. "Uh, I think we put them in the fridge." He opened a filthy white refrigerator. Inside was a cooler bag. The kind you packed your lunch in so it would keep cool.

Deshawn took the bag. Opened it. Removed several plastic bags filled with white pills. He bounced each bag in his hand. Set them aside. "It's not too light. Most of it is still here. Give or take."

He pulled two baggies from the cooler bag. They contained white powder. Coke. Deshawn put the fentanyl bags back in the cooler bag.

The homeowner grinned maniacally. "We got coke and ivory. Choose your poison, dude."

The coke was probably laced with fentanyl and god knew what else. Noah nodded at Deshawn. "Leave the coke."

"Yes, sir." Deshawn left the coke baggies on the counter. He picked up the cooler bag with the fentanyl. Started to leave the kitchen.

"Hey, that's ours!" One of the other men lunged after Deshawn.

Deshawn spun. Kicked the guy in the chest. The man crashed into the fridge. Slid down the front. Groaned and stayed down.

"Titus, help Haley get dressed."

"Okay, boss." Titus yanked Haley by her neck. "Where are your clothes?"

Haley started sobbing. "Noah, please! I wasn't stealing from you, honest! I got the pills and brought them back. I was going to give them to you tomorrow!"

Noah laughed. "All the way to Tijuana and back by now? Do you own a corporate jet, Haley?"

"I drove real fast!" She was sobbing. "Please, Noah, you've got to believe me!"

Noah rolled his eyes.

The homeowner suddenly realized what was happening. His grin turned to wide-eyed terror. "Dude, I didn't know. I swear!"

"I know. This is all on Haley and her poor life decisions." Noah left the kitchen. Walked past the den. Through the foyer. Into the front yard. One of the people on the couch was covered in vomit. They were staring at the night sky. Eyes wide with fear.

And they weren't breathing anymore. It was nothing new in the world of fentanyl. It was the downside to selling any kind of drugs. They took a toll on the body. Killed the users. You always needed fresh bodies to keep sales up.

Fentanyl was worse. Much worse. It killed users faster than anything else. Selling it was bad business. Not because of the human cost. But because there was no growth potential. The customers consumed the product. And the product consumed them.

But that was what corporate wanted. It was obvious that they didn't care about long-term growth. They wanted a long, steady slide into chaos. They wanted to rot the city from the inside out.

Noah and Deshawn waited next to the couch. Titus came out a moment later. Haley was dressed in dirty sweatpants and a hoodie. They didn't fit well. They probably didn't even belong to her.

Tasha was standing next to the Prius. She watched quietly. She knew what was coming next. She knew it was inevitable. Unavoidable. Noah couldn't help but smile.

Deshawn hopped into the backseat of the Prius. He kept the cooler bag on his lap. Titus shoved Haley into the backseat of the Prius next to Deshawn. Tasha got in. Squeezed Haley between her and Deshawn.

She was sobbing. Pleading. Deshawn slapped tape over her mouth. "Shut it!"

Noah slid into the passenger seat. Titus dropped into the driver's seat. Put the car in motion. He drove them a couple of blocks. Took a left. Slipped between rusty metal gates into an old warehouse facility near the harbor.

It was a place Noah used from time to time. A place that was nice and quiet. Out of the way. It was a big, empty space. Despite its size, it had become obsolete.

Back in the day, the cargo from ships was taken here for temporary storage. That was before everything was packed into large shipping containers. These days, shipping containers were directly loaded onto trains and trucks. The containers that didn't immediately go anywhere sat in the harbor yards.

The location was undesirable for retail stores. The city refused to rezone it for residential. So, it sat vacant. Unused. It had once been popular for drug users. They could hide inside, safe from the police.

But since drug use was decriminalized, those people were now out and about. On sidewalks. In parks. Right out in the open. Not even those kinds of people came here anymore.

Noah got out and opened the big rollup door. Titus drove inside the warehouse. Noah closed the door. Got back in the Prius. Titus drove until a metal foldout chair appeared in the headlights.

He turned off the car. Left the headlights on. Deshawn dragged Haley out of the backseat. Handed her to Titus. Titus pushed her down on the metal chair. He held her in place by her shoulders.

Her eyes were bugging. Tears and snot streamed down her face. The duct tape on her mouth muffled her cries.

Tasha got out before Noah asked. She walked with him. Kept quiet. Face grim. Resolute.

Noah put a hand on her shoulder. "Good girl."

She didn't react.

Haley kept sobbing. Trying to talk despite the tape over her mouth.

There was another beige metal foldout chair leaning against a steel support beam. Noah unfolded it. Turned it backwards. Sat down facing Haley. "So, you messed up. Thought you could steal from me."

Snot bubbled from her nose. Tears streaked down her face. She nodded. Tried to talk again.

Noah shook his head. "It's too late, baby girl. Too late." He motioned to Titus.

Titus went to the Prius. Opened the trunk. Dragged out a person with a hood over their head. They were wearing long black robes to conceal their clothing. Noah liked the black robes. They added a ritualistic touch to the proceedings.

Noah got up. Turned his chair to face Haley. Titus put the robed person in the chair. There was muffled shouting from under the hood.

Haley's eyes were even bigger. She wasn't breathing. Wasn't moving. She was frozen with terror. Horrified by who was under that hood.

Tasha shivered. Noah grinned and rubbed her shoulder. He let Haley marinate in that fear for a moment. He let Tasha soak it up too. She needed a reminder. That could be her sister if she didn't behave.

The suspense hung in the air. Thick. Tangible. Haley was already suffering. Already frozen with dread. The coke amped her emotions. She was feeling everything tenfold now.

Tasha clenched and unclenched her fists. Trembled. She looked resigned to what came next.

Noah breathed it in. He could smell fear in the air. Smell the pheromonal stench. They were all animals. All driven by instinct. By desire. By self-preservation.

Some animals were superior to others. Some animals tried to better themselves. To create order among the weak. Unfortunately, some animals were incorrigible. Unsalvageable.

It was too late for Haley. Hopefully, Tasha would learn.

Noah walked behind Haley. Put his hands on her shoulders. Massaged them. "You need to loosen up, baby girl. Your muscles are hard as rocks."

Haley struggled. Tried to scream through her gag. It was no use.

Noah ripped off the tape.

"Noah, please! I'll do anything." She shook with sobs. "I'll do anything, I promise."

He knelt in front of her. Booped her nose. "Sorry, baby girl, I can't trust you. It's the byproduct of a bad upbringing."

"I can change, Noah! I can change!"

"Do you know how many times I hear that on a daily basis?" Noah shook his head. "I remember our little talks, Haley. I remember the first time I asked you to be a courier. You were so bright-eyed, and bushy tailed. You were using ivory, but you used it responsibly."

"I still use responsibly."

He shook his head. "Now you're lying to yourself. And that's even worse than lying to others. If you can't trust yourself, who can you trust?"

Titus pounded a fist on his chest. "Nobody, boss man."

Deshawn pounded a fist on his chest. "Truth."

Tasha stared at Noah. Hate plain in her eyes. He relished it.

"Haley, I remember one thing you told me. How much you missed a certain someone in your life. How much you wished they were there to support you in your troubled times." Noah tutted. "But they weren't."

He walked around the other figure. Pulled off the hood. Underneath was a white man. He was well maintained. Perfect haircut. Perfectly trimmed beard. He was young. Maybe late thirties. The gag, the duct tape, and the fear made him look older.

Haley gasped. "No!"

Noah nodded. "I thought you'd be happy to see dear old dad. He left your mom. Never gave you the time of day." Noah mimicked breaking a stick with his hands. "He broke your family, Haley." He walked around her. "And most importantly, he broke you."

Haley's father strained to move, but he was bound securely beneath the robes. He wasn't a big man. Maybe five feet nine inches. And thin. He worked for a tech company. Made half a million a year.

He'd given Haley's mom all the money she wanted. But Haley had told Noah the tragic story of her absent father and broken home. She was angry because her mother had remarried. It didn't matter that her new stepfather made good money.

Haley had never wanted for anything. She'd been spoiled. Raised on avocado toast and silver spoons. And she'd still ended up here. All she'd ever done was complain about what life threw at her. She'd used her problems as an excuse for bad decisions.

Noah knelt next to Haley's father. "Sir, you had a chance to raise a fine daughter. Someone you could be proud of. Instead, you raised a liar and a thief. Or should I say, your lack of raising her led to this. And now the problems you created for society have come home to roost."

Haley's father tried to lunge but Titus held him down. He tried to shout. To roar. But the gag silenced his voice.

"Actions and lack of actions have consequences, sir." Noah gestured toward Haley. "As you can so plainly see. Now, Haley will pay for her transgressions. But I cannot overlook the primary reason she failed. And that reason is the lack of a daddy."

Haley was blubbering. "Please, Noah. Don't do it. Let us go. I promise I'll change. I'll do everything right for you. I'll go to Mexico a thousand times if you want. I'll go to jail. Anything but this, Noah. Please. Anything but this."

Her father was red in the face. Tears in his eyes. He was trying desperately to talk. To wriggle free of Titus. But it wasn't happening.

"I know you want to give me some bullshit excuses, sir." Noah shook his head sadly. "But I'm done with excuses. I'm done with dirty, lying thieves. And I'm done with fatherless behavior."

Noah went to the Prius. Removed a small vinyl case. He unzipped it. Pulled out a small, plastic bottle. The label had been ripped off, but it was Lonadone. Prescription fentanyl. One drop was enough to kill the pain.

Regular usage inevitably caused addiction. Addiction inevitably caused higher usage. Higher dosages. Until the day the user took one drop too many. Then the heart stopped. The brain ceased all function. The user died.

It was all too common in this city. So common that it killed forty or fifty people a month. So common that everyone just accepted it as the new normal. And that was the one thing Noah liked about fentanyl.

He removed the top from the bottle. Handed it to Tasha. "Please do the honors for dear Haley."

Tasha took it. Deshawn grabbed Haley's hair. Pulled her head back.

Tasha looked the girl in the eyes. "I'm sorry."

Haley sobbed. "What is that? What are you doing?"

"It's your favorite drug, Haley." Noah nodded at Deshawn.

Deshawn gripped Haley's chin. Pried her mouth open.

Tasha squeezed the sides of the bottle. Dripped a dozen drops into Haley's mouth.

Titus held Haley's struggling father. Forced open his mouth. Noah gave him the same dosage.

He stepped back and put the bottle away. Sometimes he'd use a syringe. But dripping the liquid fentanyl into someone's mouth was just as effective and it didn't leave marks. He took the bottle from Tasha. Patted her hand. "Good girl."

She didn't say anything. Kept her face cold. Hard. Unemotional.

Noah could respect that. It looked like he was getting through to her. Reminding her that he didn't tolerate insubordination.

He watched the fentanyl take effect. Haley started to slump. She glared at her father. "Why'd you have to be a bad dad?"

Her father tried to reply. The gag stopped him.

Noah felt a slight tinge of pity. "Titus, let the man have a final word with his daughter."

Titus removed the tape. Took out the rag.

"Why?" Haley's father looked woozily at Noah. "It's not my fault."

"Your actions were a ripple in the pond that was your daughter's life." Noah crouched in front of him. Stared him in the eyes. "Every decision you made led to this moment."

"No..." His voice trailed off. Gaze went distant.

Noah watched nature take its course. Watched father and daughter move slower and slower. Like toys with dying batteries. The father went still first. Haley lasted a little longer. Probably because she'd been a heavy user for so long.

Titus put a fist to his chest. "Justice."

Deshawn did the same. "Justice."

Tasha watched in silence.

True justice would have included the mom and stepfather as well, but Noah had to be realistic. Killing an entire family would raise too many eyebrows. Haley and her father would appear to have overdosed. No one would ask questions.

"Let's take them home," Noah said.

Titus put the hood back on the dad. Dumped him in the trunk. Deshawn put Haley in beside the father.

"That's one roomy trunk," Deshawn said.

Titus laughed. "You say that every time we put bodies in there."

"Yeah, because I can't believe how much we fit in the trunk of a Prius." Deshawn shook his head. Got in the back seat. "It's unreal, man."

Tasha didn't say anything. She got in the back seat. Stared out the window. Hopefully contemplating her future choices.

Noah got in the passenger seat. Took a deep breath. Relaxed. He'd recovered his drugs. He'd taken care of the problem. Taught Tasha a valuable lesson at the same time. Corporate would have nothing to complain about. At least nothing more than usual.

And that was good. He didn't want another visit from corporate. They had some scary people working for them. Military people. Assassins. If they knew what he was really up to, nothing could save him.

If they found out about the briefcase, they'd have their people combing the city. He needed to find it first. Because the answer to his problems was inside.

Titus drove them back across the bay. Back into San Francisco. Over to a multiplex right at the corner of Hyde and Lombard. It was a big place. Had an unobstructed view of the city.

Deshawn and Titus unloaded the bodies. Took them inside and upstairs.

Noah got out. Turned to the last passenger. "Tasha, you can wait in the car."

"Okay." She looked ready to get out and run. But she knew better.

Noah went upstairs into the condo. It was big. Had a nice deck. Everything was renovated. Upscale.

Titus and Deshawn staged a scene they'd staged a dozen times before. Nothing over the top. Nice and simple. Then they stepped back and admired their handiwork. It would pass muster. The detectives here were already overwhelmed.

Detective Duffy might recognize the handiwork. If he was in charge, he'd close the case in a week. Chalk it up to accidental overdose. Just like all the others.

Besides, everyone was used to overdoses. Rich, poor, or middle class, they happened every day. This would be sorted and filed. The father's coworkers would be shocked, but not surprised. In a city where most drugs were decriminalized, even nonusers might be tempted to try fentanyl once.

And sometimes, once was all it took.

— • —

CHAPTER 9

Carver walked the streets.

He walked down a row of parked cars. Windows were smashed out on nearly all of them. The sidewalks were covered in tents. It was like everything he'd seen in other parts of downtown were concentrated in one place.

There were people sleeping in the cars. On the sidewalks. In the tents. It looked post-apocalyptic. But it was just the new normal in places like this.

The buildings were nice. There were high rise apartments. Smaller traditional homes. Quaint stores. But it was all tainted. It stank of decay. Just like many urban centers Carver had seen across the world.

And it was the perfect place to sit down. To watch and wait. Because it was getting late. Carver was getting hungry. And he didn't plan on waiting in a bread line.

He spotted his mark not long after sitting down. In fact, he spotted two of them. Two young men. One on his side of the street. The other working his way through the tents on the other side. The tent residents were emerging. Handing money to the men.

Some of them tried to barter. Tried to trade new clothing or packaged items for the goods. But the dealers shook their heads. Pointed down the street. Like they were giving directions.

Probably pointing them toward a local fencing operation. Like the place where the woman had traded purses for drugs. There were probably fences like that all over the city.

The primary source of goods seemed to be shoplifting and larceny. It was essentially a pirate economy. Except it was on land. And most of the pirates were doing it for drugs instead of rum and gold.

The dealer on Carver's side of the street walked past him. Gave him a look. Like he was expecting Carver to stop him. Offer him money for drugs. But Carver slumped. Looked vacantly at nothing.

The dealer continued down the sidewalk. Addicts would give him money. He'd pull a small baggie from the satchel he kept slung over his shoulder. Exchange it for the money. Put the money in the satchel. His partner across the road was doing the same thing.

The dealer kept walking. Kept weaving through the tent city all down the sidewalk. Carver watched him go. Watched the guy across the street. The dealers weren't big guys. They didn't seem to be packing heat.

That was strange. Addicts could be dangerous. Especially if they couldn't afford to buy more drugs. They might become violent. Might attack the dealers to get what they wanted. Unless they were too scared to do it.

Carver kept watching. He saw residents emerging from apartment buildings. Saw people trying to shop at the local grocer. Saw them dodging the addicts lying on the sidewalks. Walking in the street since the sidewalks were covered with tents.

He didn't see anyone suspicious. No one shadowing the dealers. No one waiting to spring into action in case someone attacked the dealers.

Carver had seen a lot of organized crime. Anyone pushing merchandise on the streets was either equipped to defend themselves or they had someone following a distance behind them. Someone ready to surprise any would-be attackers.

That didn't seem to be the case here. It made the task at hand easier. And that was a good thing. Because Carver's stomach was starting to rumble. He'd burned a lot of calories. Hadn't replaced them with anything substantial since lunch.

He stood. Shambled down the sidewalk. Slumped his shoulders. Angled his head so it looked like he was staring at the ground. He squeezed between a tent and a parked car. Detoured into the street to avoid a pile of feces.

The dealer turned a corner ahead. Carver didn't change his pace. Didn't change his gait. He was just another addict. Just another homeless man walking down the sidewalk. Nothing to see here.

He reached the corner. The dealer was stopped at a tent about half a block down. The street population was denser here. There were more tents. More people. It looked like the dealer would be busy here for a while.

Carver scanned the area ahead. Most of the buildings were connected. The few alleys were blocked by tall metal fences and gates. There was no place for him to lie in wait. That complicated his simple idea.

He kept walking. Walked right past the dealer. The man didn't seem to recognize him. Probably because Carver was wearing the same generic outfit a lot of others were wearing. Hoodie. Facemask. Cargo pants.

Carver walked around a large tent. There was another large tent on the other side of it. A space between them. The closest streetlight was broken and dark. It wasn't an alley, but it was close enough.

He stepped between the tents. Cracked his knuckles. Stretched his arms. Crouched and waited.

He heard the dealer. Heard him talking to other tent dwellers. Heard the people in the tent to his right stirring. A woman groaning. Yelling at someone that the drug man was coming. A man answered. Told her to shut up.

The tent shook. Like someone was trying to get out of it in a hurry.

"I got ten," a man said. "Ten right here."

"That'll get you two," the dealer said.

"Two?" The man whined. "It got me three yesterday."

"It's two today."

"Get the two!" the woman shouted. "Get them, you idiot!"

"Shut up!" The tent shook. Someone got slapped hard.

"You better calm your asses down," the dealer said. "Or I'm walking."

"I'm sorry! I'm sorry." The man's voice was shaking. "She's such a bitch. Here. Take the money. Please."

There was silence. A quiet exchange of money and goods. Then the dealer stepped into view. Carver lunged. Wrapped an arm around the man's neck. Yanked him in between the tents. Squeezed the dealer's neck.

The dealer flailed. Legs kicked. Arms swung. But the blood vessels in his neck were being constricted. Carver's arm was applying firm pressure. Reducing blood flow to the dealer's brain. Within a few seconds, he was noticeably weaker.

The man's eyes rolled up into the back of his head. Carver released him. Set him down gently. Checked his pulse. He was fine. Just fine. Only napping.

Carver looked inside the satchel. It was compartmentalized by a sheet of fabric sewn inside. Drugs on one side. Money on the other. The money was loose. Crumpled. Unorganized. Carver pulled out a handful. He sorted it.

It was mostly singles and fives. Piles of coins at the bottom. The dealer wouldn't be out for long, so Carver hurried. There was just enough light coming from the window behind him to see the dollar denominations.

He tossed the singles aside. Grabbed all the twenties he could find. They amounted to about three hundred, give or take. He put the rest of the cash back in the pack. Took a few baggies. Left most of it in the satchel.

The dealer had a knife in the backpack. Some pepper spray. No gun. No other way to defend himself. He was either very confident in himself or he knew no one would attack him because they were scared of his boss.

The dealer had no wallet. No identification. Nothing except a phone in his pocket. The phone was locked. Carver didn't have time to mess with it anyway. The dealer was already stirring. Already moaning.

Carver shambled out of the space between the tents. Performed his addict walk until he turned the corner. Then he straightened a little. Increased his pace. He heard shouting. Heard a man yelling at the top of his lungs.

"You think you can get away with this? You messed with the wrong people!"

Carver wondered if the dealer was shouting at the people in the tents. If maybe he thought they were the ones who assaulted him. A woman shouted in surprise behind him. He glanced back. Saw the dealer standing at the corner. He was shoving through people. Still shouting. Still swearing revenge.

He was furious. Turning in circles. Looking for an unseen adversary. Carver couldn't blame the guy. He'd been mugged before. Robbed. Beaten. It had happened when he was a kid. Even though he knew how to fend for himself there was always someone bigger and badder.

That was just life. Carver had gotten over it. He'd learned. Improved. He'd never be a genius like Rhodes, but he could emulate the best of them. And sometimes that was all it took. Just copy what someone else did. Maybe improve it a little here and there along the way.

Carver could have robbed the guy blind. But it was better to take just a little. See what kind of reaction that provoked. See if it would make it harder to do it again in the future. This was just a poke. A nudge.

Time to see if it would awaken a giant or a mouse.

Carver ignored the shouting dealer. He saw something far more important a few blocks down. A flickering neon sign. A sign of hope. At least for his stomach. He hustled down the block. Went into Uncle Vito's Pizzeria.

They baked him a pie in short order. He ordered a beer too. Sat in a corner with his back to the wall. Kept an eye on the entrance the entire time. It was force of habit. But it was a good habit to have in a city like this.

He polished off the food. Checked the time. Figured it was time to head back to the park. He used the restroom since the tent didn't have one. Went outside. Hoofed it back to California Street. Hopped on a trolley. Took it down the road.

It was dark. Getting well into the evening. That wasn't stopping the tourists. There were still plenty out and about. This was just a few blocks from the Tenderloin but there was a stark difference. It was a lot cleaner. No tents. No homeless. Probably because they tried to keep the touristy parts of town cleaner.

The trolley stopped at Grant Avenue. Right at the entrance to Chinatown. Red lanterns were strung across the street. The buildings looked mostly the same. All except for a few with that distinct Chinese rooftop design.

Most of the shops looked closed. All except for an alcohol store about a block down. Carver stepped off the trolley. He went down the block. Entered the store. It had a decent selection. Mostly domestic. He picked up a six pack of stout beer. Purchased it. Went back outside.

He stopped at a small grocery store half a block down. Picked up some snacks. Just in case he got hungry or needed something to tide him over for breakfast. He also picked up a small satchel. Put his purchases inside and slung it over his back.

The park was a good distance away. He headed back to California Street and the trolley. Something caught his eye when he passed by a small side street. Flashes of rapid movement in the shadows near a streetlight.

Carver paused. Let his eyes adjust. Saw a figure struggling with another silhouette. Heard someone shouting in Mandarin. It wasn't his business. None of his concern. But he turned down the side street anyway.

It was just a narrow little road. Almost an alley between two residential buildings. He heard a cry of pain. One of the figures went down. The taller figure came his way. Running. It passed under a light. Carver saw a face.

It was a man. Maybe middle aged. Maybe just old looking from a drug addiction. It was hard to tell from the brief glimpse. Carver planted himself in the middle of the street. The guy tried to go around. Carver stepped in front. Held out a hand.

"Hand it over."

"Hand what over?" The man hugged the bag. It was decorated with a floral pattern. "This is mine."

"Are those the rules?"

The man looked confused. "What rules? Homey, you'd better get out of my way before I gut you." The man didn't look addled by drugs. He looked thin but healthy. He also had a knife.

Carver kept an eye on the knife. "The rules that say if you can take it, you can have it."

The man thrust the knife toward Carver. "You think you can take it?" He slashed at the air. "Don't matter how big you are, I'll cut you open."

"Okay." Carver walked toward him.

The man's eyes flashed with surprise. He jumped back. Held up the knife. Lunged.

Carver let him lunge. There was no skill to the man's movement. He was just some guy with a knife. He was still dangerous. But the knife was one-sided. It was also serrated. Probably a kitchen knife that he'd stolen from someone.

The man slashed the air. Kept swinging his arm back and forth. Like if he could move it fast enough, he could scare Carver. It'd probably work on most people. They'd see some guy swinging a knife wildly. Back off. Call the police.

Carver let the guy swing it a few times. Timed it. Lunged and grabbed the man's wrist. Squeezed it. Pinched the nerves. The hand opened. The knife fell to the ground. Carver didn't want to bruise his knuckles on the man's skull. Risk cutting his hand on the guy's teeth.

So, he delivered a quick punch to the solar plexus. Right in the center of the chest. Nothing too hard. Just enough to put the guy's internal organs on high alert. Enough to hurt. To shock. Most importantly, to put the guy on the ground.

The man fell hard. He hugged himself. Rolled back and forth. Gasped for breath. Carver knelt. Picked up the knife. It was a table knife, but it was a nice one. There was a brand name on the side.

It was the same brand they'd had at a safehouse in southern Germany. Carver remembered it vividly because Leon had talked about how nice they were. How a set of them probably cost a thousand dollars.

Then Leon had thrown one of them. Impaled a raw chicken from across the room. Rhodes hadn't been happy about it because she was seasoning it at the time. It hadn't even been her turn to cook that night.

Carver put the knife in his satchel. He picked up the bag with the floral pattern. Walked over to the other person. They were lying on the ground. Unmoving. It was a woman. She was small. Asian. Maybe sixty years old.

He put a finger on her neck. She had a pulse. He shook her. She groaned. There was blood on her lip. The man had probably hit her.

Carver wasn't going to call the police. He didn't want the attention. But he couldn't leave the woman here. He scooped her up. Cradled her. Started walking toward the main street.

There was a shout of surprise. Someone came running. Not just someone. A group. At least three but it was hard to tell in the shadows. Carver walked faster. The mugger was still on the ground. Still groaning and hugging himself.

Carver walked past him. Stopped. Turned and waited.

Four men entered the light. They were Asian. Probably Chinese if Carver had to guess. This was Chinatown, after all. The men ranged from young to middle-aged. One of them spoke in Mandarin. He didn't sound happy.

They were looking from the mugger to Carver. Probably trying to figure out what was going on. They probably knew the woman he was holding.

And they looked ready to fight.

CHAPTER 10

The men spoke.

Pointed angrily at the mugger. They started kicking him. Two of them dragged the mugger away. Dragged him into the darkness. The mugger shouted for help. His shouts cut off abruptly.

One of the remaining two men walked to Carver. He nodded.

"You helped her?"

Carver nodded. He held the floral bag out. "He knocked her out. Took this."

The man's face turned angry. "These thugs think they can come into our territory. Terrorize our people. They are protected by the mayor. The police don't arrest them. But they arrest us."

"Two-sided justice system?"

"Yes." The man motioned and one of his companions approached. Held out his arms.

Carver transferred the woman to him. She was stirring. Moaning. Eyelids fluttering. She jerked awake. Started shouting in her native tongue. The man talked to her. Nodded a few times. Set her gently on her feet.

She held onto him unsteadily. Looked at Carver. Started talking rapidly.

"My aunt thanks you for helping her. She wants you to come have dinner with us."

"I just ate a pizza." Carver patted his stomach. "Raincheck?"

"You must allow us to repay you for your kindness. A meal is the least we can do." The man talked to his aunt. "You can come tomorrow evening at seven."

"You really don't have to." Carver knew he shouldn't have gotten involved. "I'm dealing with some things right now. I don't know if I can fit it in my schedule."

"Please, I must insist."

"I'll try, okay?" Carver backed up a step. "What's in the bag, anyway?"

The man opened the floral bag. It was filled with cash. "You see, they know we don't like using banks. That we take the cash to our homes each night. When we try to protect ourselves, we are the ones arrested."

"I noticed this place is cleaner than other parts of the city. No tents. No homeless people."

"Because we don't allow filth here." He smiled. "The instant we see a drug user or tent in our neighborhood, we force them to move."

"You get many car break-ins around here?"

He nodded. "We have tried patrolling. But it's impossible to be constantly vigilant."

"Especially in this town." Carver backed up another step. "I've got to go. I'll try to make it for dinner tomorrow."

"You don't even know where."

"Somewhere around here, I'm guessing."

The man pointed to a door in the apartment building. "Come here, ring the bell. Ask for Zimo."

"That's your name?"

He nodded. "And what is yours?"

Carver didn't want to toss around his real name. Not even with people inviting him to dinner. "You can call me Cutter."

"Cutter is a strange name."

Carver didn't have a response. He didn't even know why he'd chosen a name like Cutter. He kept backing up. "Goodnight Zimo."

"Good night, Cutter."

Carver turned and went back to the main street. Navigated to the trolley station. Hopped on the next one. Those men weren't just regular citizens. They had matching tattoos on their forearms.

Maybe they were all related. A tight-knit family. Cousins or brothers. Maybe they resembled each other. Maybe they didn't. It had been dark, and Carver hadn't gotten a good look at their faces.

It seemed a lot more likely they were in a gang. Family members didn't usually get matching tattoos. Especially not men. But their choice of tattoo was strange.

It wasn't a dragon. Wasn't a tiger. No, their tattoo of choice was a fire breathing panda bear. And it didn't look half bad. If Carver got a visible tattoo, it would be something like that. But getting a tattoo just marked you. Made it easier to identify someone. He didn't need that in his life.

It was already hard enough remaining anonymous. Especially for a guy his size and build. Not that he was monstrously tall or big. But he was enough of both to stand out from the crowd. Or at least the average crowd.

Carver wanted to look up a description of their tattoos. An internet search would probably find something. But he only had the flip phone. Even with the money stolen from the dealer he didn't have enough to buy a smart phone.

The trolley pulled up to the station. Carver got on. Rode it down to the Financial District. Got off and went back to the park. His tent was still there. His belongings were still inside. It wasn't much, but it was something.

Tommy and his girlfriend were sitting outside their tent. Boiling water with a portable gas burner. They were arguing about something. Pushing each other. Tommy was about to trip backwards right onto the boiling water.

Carver sat at the edge of his tent and watched. No reason to intervene. Maybe Tommy would get third degree burns. Maybe he'd stop fighting and start cooking. Or maybe the fight would go on until one of them passed out.

There were a few new tents in Tommy's little city. A few missing tents too. One of the tents was hard to miss. It was big. It was no ordinary tent, either. It was a field tent. The same kind the army used.

There was a row of tents between it and Carver. But the top of it was poking above the others. It was tall enough for him to stand inside. It was as tall as the tent that had been stolen from the Ramcharger.

Tommy punched his girlfriend. "Shut up, Lois!"

Lois screamed. Charged him. Flailed her fists and smacked him in the face. One of them was going to fall in the campfire. Fall in the boiling water. It was anyone's guess who'd do it first.

The field tent shook. A man's head appeared. He exited the tent. Hustled to the fighting couple. He looked healthy. Not muscular, but not scrawny either. His eyes were alive. Not glazed like an addict's.

His clothing looked clean. Almost new. And he had a long beard that looked well groomed. This guy didn't look homeless at all.

"Hey, cool it!" The man pushed between the pair. He almost shoved Tommy backwards into the boiling water. "One of you needs to step away right now."

"But Tommy wants the beef ramen!" Lois jabbed a finger at the boiling water and screamed. "You know beef gives me diarrhea! I want chicken!"

"We never have beef!" Tommy raised his fists like a boxer. Or at least like someone who'd once watched a boxer on TV. "The mayor is having beef tonight."

"I have chicken ramen." The bearded man pointed to his tent. "Just wait there and I'll make it."

"Do you really?" Lois looked hopeful. "I hate beef ramen. I'm allergic and Tommy knows it!"

"It ain't even real beef!" Tommy screamed.

Carver was ready for bed. It wasn't late but it wasn't early either. He could sleep in a war zone, but he preferred peace and quiet. He stood. Approached Tommy. "Hey, mayor, I've got something for you."

Tommy spun around. Hands still up in a fighting position. He looked confused. "You? What do you want?"

Carver held up two of the baggies he'd taken from the dealer. "Payment as promised."

Tommy's eyes went wide. He snatched the bags. Counted the pills. There were only three pills in each bag, but it took him a moment. "This buys you a day."

"A day?" Carver sighed. "Look, Tommy, that's at least a week. And if you don't agree, then I'll take my pills and go somewhere else."

"Where else you gonna go?" Tommy bared his rotting teeth. "You're under my protection. Nobody else can protect you like I can."

"Do you want the pills or not?" Carver snatched them back.

Tommy rocked back. Like he couldn't believe the pills were gone. "Okay, okay!" He put his hands together pleadingly. "Give them back. You've got a week."

"Better not be playing me, Tommy." Carver bared his teeth. "I don't want to get nasty."

Tommy backed up a step. "Hey, I won't cheat you. I promise."

"You are a cheat, Tommy!" Lois was sitting outside the bearded guy's tent. "You told me you'd never make me eat beef ramen because of my diarrhea."

Carver glanced at the boiling water. Most of it had turned to steam. There wasn't much left. Tommy didn't even notice. He was looking at the baggies in Carver's hand. Carver bounced them in his hand.

The bearded guy went into his tent. He brought out a portable gas burner. Put bottled water in a pot. Set it on the burner. He stared at Carver. "What's your deal?"

"I don't have a deal."

"You've got some kind of deal." The guy walked over to him. Looked at Carver's tent. At the pills in his hand. "You don't look like a dealer. Don't look like a homeless guy either."

"You don't look homeless either." Now that the guy was standing next to Carver, he had a better feel for him. "Probably a vet if I had to guess."

The man turned the question back on him. "Are you a vet?"

"Maybe."

"What's your name?"

Carver kept looking at him. "What's your name?"

"Tanner."

Carver nodded. "Cutter."

Tanner raised an eyebrow. "We're going by code names now?"

"It's my last name." Carver handed the pills to Tommy. "That's for one week. Better keep me safe."

Tommy snatched the pills. "Nobody can keep you safer than me." Giggling, he crawled into his tent. Left the rest of the water boiling into steam.

Carver removed the pan from the open flame. Turned off the burner.

"Don't you take none without me!" Lois abandoned all hope of getting chicken ramen and crawled into the tent after Tommy.

They started bickering again. Then the sounds of fighting turned into something else. Sex, maybe. It was hard to tell the difference.

Tanner didn't seem to notice. He was still looking at Carver. "Why are you here?"

"I'm just visiting. And you?"

"Just visiting."

"You must be eating okay." Carver made a show of looking him over. "Either that or drinking a lot."

"Not really your business."

"No, it's not." Carver shrugged. "I'm going to sleep."

Tanner pulled up his long sleeve. Looked at a big watch. A fancy watch. "It's only ten."

"Yeah, long day." Carver couldn't understand why this guy was here. He looked well fed. No sign of drug use. Wore a nice watch. And his tent was big and expensive. Maybe he'd been rich. Now he was down on his luck.

Didn't seem likely. Guys like that had golden parachutes not golden tents. Carver walked toward Tanner's tent. The zipper was open. The inside was big. Real big. There was a table inside. Papers on the table. A cot. A cast iron pan. A portable gas stove. Top of the line everything.

Tanner got in front of him. Pulled the heavy-duty zipper down. "Don't even think about stealing anything."

"I'm not." Carver looked him over. "Just wondering who you really are."

"I told you already."

"I guess you did." Carver's gut told him the guy was mostly truthful. But he was holding something back. Something important. But as long as Tanner stayed out of Carver's way, it didn't really matter.

Carver about-faced. Returned to his tent. Ducked inside. Zipped it. Locked the zipper from the inside. He rested his head on the clothes bag. The ground under the tent was decently soft. Probably because it still had grass. The grass would be dead in a week if he didn't move.

He figured it wouldn't make things look much worse around here. But it probably wouldn't come to that. The car thieves would be around tomorrow. Carver just had to figure out how to follow them.

He could use the Ramcharger. But it was big. Its big beefy frame stood out on these city streets. The car thieves would recognize it in a heartbeat. Even if they weren't the most perceptive people, they'd notice it in the rearview mirror.

There were electric bikes. Scooters. A host of options. But Carver didn't have a way to rent any of them. It boiled down to one option. It wasn't his first choice, but it would work. To beat the car thieves, he'd have to become one. Except he wouldn't be breaking into cars.

He would steal one.

LEON FOLLOWED THE CAR.

He'd been following it all the way from the Atlanta airport. It was going in a familiar direction. A direction he'd once travelled in frequently. Past familiar landmarks. Down familiar streets.

The car went past Breakstone headquarters. The former headquarters. There were government vehicles outside now. There was a commercial realtor sign outside. *Coming Soon.* Leon had handed the keys over to the new owner. The US government.

The property was included in a settlement. One that was supposed to repay the government for breach of contract. A contract Leon had signed along with Dorsey, Rocker, and Menendez. A contract that promised a lot of things.

None of those things had happened. Primarily because Dorsey, Rocker, and Menendez had been killed by Carver. A scandal had been revealed. The government had covered it up. They'd tried to get Leon to continue with the contract.

But Leon had seen what was happening. He'd seen evidence. Evidence that proved Dorsey and the others were up to something. Something that had destroyed his and Carver's former squad.

The car kept driving. Turned into a neighborhood. Like most in the area, it was a mix of old homes and new. A mix of small homes and big ones. A mix of traditional and contemporary designs.

The car stopped. Parallel parked on the street. It hadn't stopped at its destination. It had stopped nearly a block and a half away. Leon only knew that because he knew where the occupant of the car was going.

The driver remained in the car for a few minutes. It was nearly one thirty in the morning. His flight had been a redeye from New York. It had been delayed by mechanical issues. Almost cancelled. But his handlers had found a new plane.

Leon had been monitoring the flight from the comfort of his airport hotel. He'd known exactly when it landed. Known exactly where to wait for the person in question. All he'd needed was the flight number and the airline's website.

The occupant of that car was a professional killer. He'd accepted a job from the dark web bulletin board. The killer's dark web identity was just a number. That number corresponded with information in the Farm's database.

As with Epsilon and other free agents, Leon had deciphered the individual's real identity. Or at least the identity in the Farm's database.

The Farm kept extensive dossiers on assets. They knew Epsilon's real name was Clarence Thompson. They knew where he lived. About his childhood. Everything. They hadn't gathered that information themselves. They'd been given that information by government agencies.

They likewise knew all about this killer. He went by a codename. Nothing fancy. Nothing as pretentious as Epsilon. He preferred to be called Nancy. It certainly wasn't a cool name. And it wasn't even remotely male as far as Leon knew. His real name was Roy. Roy McAdams.

The Farm's records said his codename, Nancy, was the name of the first person he killed. She was sixteen. Rebellious. She'd run away from home. Ended up homeless. The killer had also been sixteen at the time.

Roy wasn't homeless. He was out with friends. Drinking. Partying. Having a good time. He'd been sent to get more beer. There was a corner store that illegally served minors. He'd walked to the store since he couldn't drive.

Nancy was living in a tent nearby. She targeted people going to the store. Begged them for money. She saw Roy. Asked him for money. He told her he didn't have any. Then she held him at knifepoint. Tried to rob him.

Roy had tried to run. She'd chased him. Tried to stab him. He tripped. She fell over him. A tussle ensued. Roy came out on top. He stabbed Nancy in the chest. Watched her breathe her last breath.

He should have been horrified. Most normal people were traumatized when they killed someone. But Roy had discovered a new part of him. A part that enjoyed killing. And that night had given him a high he'd been chasing ever since.

Roy lived in California. He traveled to New York regularly. Not just for business, but for pleasure. The Farm knew all about him. The FBI had given them all the information on file. Cross-referenced it with information from the CIA and NSA. Because Nancy did jobs domestically and abroad.

And now he was just a block and half down from a house Leon knew well.

The house was contemporary. It looked like someone had taken large blocks and piled them together. Cobbled them into a residence. The place was in excess of five thousand square feet. It had a three-car garage. Five bedrooms. Six bathrooms.

It was a massive residence. It could hold two full families, or one large family. But like so many big houses, a family hadn't lived there. It had been home to a single person. A person who'd been given that house by Breakstone.

And that person was Leon.

CHAPTER 11

Nancy was here to kill Leon.

That was obvious. The home had belonged to Breakstone. Chad Dorsey had lived in it for a couple of years. Then he'd purchased a penthouse in Midtown. He'd moved there. The house had sat vacant.

When Dorsey brought Menendez, Rocker, and Leon onboard, he'd given Leon the house. Signed the deed over to him and everything. At least signed it over to a shell company in Leon's name. That shell company had not been hidden.

Apparently, someone thought he still lived there. The home and the shell company had been taken by the government, but the name on the deed was still Leon's.

It looked like they were onto him. Like they knew he was the one behind the recent rash of assassin assassinations. Or maybe he was simply on their list as a loose end. Maybe they knew he was the one who'd blown the Farm to hell. Maybe they didn't.

When the Farm had killed Cliff Barrows, his death triggered an email. That email had gone to a select list. Most of the people on that list were dead. All except Carver and Leon. Enigma was looking for Carver. It looked like they were also looking for Leon.

Nancy wouldn't know why he'd been sent. He was just here to do a job. He wouldn't know if Leon was scheduled for termination because of Barrows' email or because they knew Leon had killed several of their people.

Bottom line? Kill Nancy. Try to find out who was behind this. Try to find out more about Enigma.

That was a tall order. The job listings on the dark web only showed targets and bounties. No reasons were given for the job. No justifications for taking a human life. Just a simple dossier so the killer knew the capabilities of the target.

It didn't take a genius to realize Enigma was coordinating with powerful people. People high on the food chain. They probably owned senators on the Senate Intelligence Committee. They were the only people who could coordinate across so many federal agencies.

Leon put the night vision monocular to his eye. He trained it on Nancy. The man was still in his car. Just sitting. Staring. He didn't even have a line of sight on Leon's former house. He looked to the side. Looked down. Probably at his phone.

It looked like he was typing on his phone. Then he put it down again. Kept sitting. Kept waiting. Almost like he was waiting on something.

Leon had a sudden realization. He turned the monocular on his surroundings. Saw movement on the roof of the house to his left. Movement in the driveway of the house to his right. This was a setup. A trap. They were zeroing in on his car.

He had about ten seconds before they closed the jaws around him.

Leon slammed the shifter into reverse. Hit the gas. The tires screeched. He spun the front around a hundred and eighty degrees. Shifted into drive. Punched the accelerator. A pair of SUVs screeched around the corner in front of him.

He swung a hard right. Hopped the curb. Bounced through a front yard. Smashed a mailbox. Crashed through shrubs. Cut through the yard to the other street. Bounced over the curb again. Glass shattered. Something whined past his head.

Metal pinged on metal. Another bullet whined past. Something rattled in the trunk of the car. He kept going. Kept the pedal to the metal. The SUVs were behind him. But they hadn't been the source of the gunfire.

That had come from the roof of the house. A sniper, no doubt. Which begged the question. Why hadn't they taken him out earlier? He'd been sitting there a full five minutes. Instead, they'd opted to send in a squad.

There was only one answer. They wanted him alive. They wanted to question him. They wanted to know how he was doing what he was doing. Which meant they didn't know he had the Farm's database. They might not even know he was the one who blew the place to kingdom come.

They'd identified him somehow. Spotted him when he killed Epsilon and his buddy, Alan. That was the only answer. Because they would have set a trap there if they'd already known.

It was also possible they'd discovered new footage. There were cameras everywhere. Leon couldn't avoid them all. He usually kept himself disguised. But even that wasn't foolproof.

Maybe Nancy had spotted him tailing his car. It was early in the morning, after all. Not many people out and about. He'd noticed the car. Called for backup.

That seemed unlikely. Someone of Nancy's skillset would opt to kill Leon himself. He wouldn't want backup. He wouldn't want to share a kill. And he certainly wouldn't have requested they take his stalker alive.

Leon hit the brakes. Took a hard left turn. Drove into another neighborhood. This one had traffic calming devices. Gentle humps in the road. The car flew over them. The SUVs turned onto the road behind him.

This was the only downside to using a basic car. It wasn't built for high-speed chases. He'd stolen this car. Taken it off a used car lot. If he had to abandon it, the car wouldn't lead back to him.

Not that it mattered. These people knew who they were chasing. And that led Leon to another thought. Maybe these people could tell him how he'd been found out. It was unlikely. They were probably just foot soldiers.

The off chance that someone in the SUVs might be someone connected to Enigma piqued his interest. He could probably escape. But maybe he could reverse this trap. Capture someone alive.

Chances were slim to none. But that was enough. First, he had to get some distance on them. That would be his only chance to pull this off.

Thankfully, he knew this area well. The first day he'd moved here, Leon had driven through the neighborhood. Studied the nearby streets. Found potential escape routes. Potential places to hide.

After his time in Scion, it was second nature to him. Always know your surroundings. Always prepare for the worst. That was the advice Carver had given him. Carver had told him it was something he got from Rhodes. Rhodes told Leon she'd never told Carver anything like that.

It was good advice. It had saved Leon at least five times. Maybe more. Because even if he was in a foreign country, he made it his territory. Learned it like he'd grown up in the neighborhood.

The same was true for this area. It wasn't really his home. Wasn't really his neighborhood. The place was bought and paid for by someone else. But he'd studied the area. Learned it. Made it his own.

The route he was on had been memorized long ago. He almost took a left on Oak Street. That was the escape route. Instead, he crossed Oak. Took a right on Willow. Hooked into an old neighborhood.

Willow Street was narrower than newer streets. Most of the houses didn't have driveways. Everyone parked on the streets. And that reduced it from a small two-lane street to a single lane. It turned his car from a liability into an advantage.

The cars parked along the curb created an obstacle course. Some of them were almost parked across from each other. Making it tight even for his compact Toyota. He zipped back and forth. Threaded the needle.

The side mirror smacked another car. It went goodbye in a hail of plastic and glass. The SUVs slowed down. They could barely fit between the cars. One of them reversed. Gunned it down another street.

They probably hoped to cut him off somewhere else. But the next five streets were just as tight as this one. And they were going in the wrong direction. Because Leon was taking a left up ahead, not a right.

The SUV behind him persisted. By the time Leon reached the end of the street, they were only half a block back. That was far enough and close enough for his plan to work.

He hooked left. Bounced over railroad tracks. Turned onto a narrow road that twisted into another neighborhood. This road was a little wider. Cars parked on the road didn't constrict it. And that was fine.

Leon reached into his duffel bag. Grabbed a couple of packages. They were already prepped. Ready to go. He slowed. Hopped out. Put the packages in place. Jumped back into the Toyota.

He swerved to the opposite side of the road. Parked behind a large pickup. The SUV screeched onto the road. They'd seen him turn here. The road was too long for him to have vanished already.

They slowed down. Looked in the driveways. Looked at the cars parked along the road. They knew he was here somewhere. That he was trying to trick them. But they thought he was just trying to lose them.

They certainly didn't expect what was about to happen. They didn't expect the hunted to become the hunter. At least that was the plan. Something might go wrong. Leon might get himself killed.

The SUV pulled even with a Jeep Wrangler. Leon pressed a button. The button sent a signal. The signal was received by the packages. The packages were directional breaching charges. They delivered a hard punch in the direction they were placed.

That way the people who planted the charges weren't blasted. In this case, he'd put the charges on backwards. The SUV was right next to them. Right in line with three charges powerful enough to blow open a safe.

The blast punched the SUV hard. Windows shattered. The car rocked up on two wheels. Hung there for a moment. Slammed down on all four. The wheels on the passenger side burst on impact.

Leon hopped out of his car. Wrapped around the pickup. Put his MP5 to his shoulder. Turned on the tactical flashlight. It blinded the car occupants. At least the two occupants on the driver's side.

The ones on the passenger side were alive but completely out of it. Heads lolling. Eyes rolled into the backs of their head.

The driver and the guy behind him were in better shape. They'd been shielded from the worst of it by steel and flesh.

"Out of the car now!" Leon pulled the handle of the driver's door. Pulled it open. Did the same for the rear passenger door. He yanked the guy in the back. The man wasn't wearing a seatbelt. He hit the ground. A pistol clattered next to him.

Leon kicked the pistol away. Shut the door. Yanked the driver out. He wasn't wearing a seatbelt either.

"Make a move and you die." Leon said. "No countdown. No second chances. Just a bullet in the head. Got it?"

The driver was on his back. Hands up. He nodded. The other guy on the ground did the same. The other two passengers in the vehicle were slumped. Unresponsive. Probably alive, but they wouldn't be doing anything anytime soon.

"Why are you chasing me?"

"We were sent to an address. Told to standby."

"It was a trap. Set for me."

The driver nodded. "It was a trap."

"How did they know I'd be there?"

"They didn't say."

Leon trained the gun on the other guy. Raised an eyebrow.

The passenger shook his head. "They didn't say."

"Not even a hint? A dossier?"

They shook their heads.

"What was the mission briefing?"

The driver didn't hesitate. "An asset was leading a target to a trap. We were to capture the target alive if possible."

"No other details?"

He shook his head.

"Who has those details?"

"I don't know. We receive a code via text. It tells us to report for duty. We show up. Get shown a briefing with only need to know information. We gear up. Do the job. Go our separate ways."

Leon mulled it over. "You're all former military?"

He nodded.

"Special forces?"

The man nodded. "Most of us."

"Black ops?"

"Some of us."

"What level?"

He hesitated. "Since you know about levels, then you must have been an SBO too."

SBO stood for special black operations. Only squads like Scion had that designation. Black ops were already illegal. SBO took it to the next level. Not even the chain of command was defined.

"How many of you were in SBO?"

"A few of us."

"Was your group disbanded on criminal charges?"

He blinked. "How did you know?"

"Ours was too. We found out it was planned. Organized by a company called Break-stone."

He blinked again. "I was supposed to go work for them." His eyes widened. "You're Leon Fry."

Leon didn't know how the guy recognized him with the facemask, but then again, he had been in special black ops. "Who are you working for now?"

"I don't know. I was approached. Offered excellent pay and benefits. All under the table."

"So, you're knowingly doing bad shit."

The man nodded. "No different than Archon."

"That's the name of your former unit?"

He nodded.

"Where do you live?"

"Nowhere. I'm always on the move."

"Regionally or nationally?"

"Both. I'm supposed to report to the west coast after this job."

"Why are you telling him so much?" the other guy said.

"Because it's better to keep breathing," the driver said. "So shut up."

Leon frowned. "What's on the west coast?"

"Another job. I don't know the details yet."

"You heard the name Carver?"

The driver blinked. Nodded. "We were sent after a guy by that name. Sent to Oregon. We couldn't find him."

"Where along the west coast are you going?"

"San Francisco."

Leon blew out a breath. He saw the other SUV speeding down the road. It was a few blocks away, but it'd reach him in seconds. He had more questions, but they'd have to wait.

He wasn't sure what to do. Killing these guys might solve an immediate problem, but not the long-term problem. Plus, he already heard sirens in the distance. The explosions had triggered a 911 call.

He backed away. "Take care of your men. Rest up. And think twice before you come after me again. Next time I won't be so forgiving."

Leon backed away. Kept his SMG trained on them. Then he scooted around the truck. Got in his car. Kept the lights off and hit the gas. He watched the rearview mirror. The driver was helping up the other guy.

They were done for the night. Hopefully his pals in the other SUV would take the hint. Decide to keep breathing a little longer. Or they could chase him and die. Because he wasn't going to be in a forgiving mood if they kept coming.

Some people might consider tonight a major setback. Leon didn't. He'd gotten much farther than anticipated. He'd used the Farm's own dark web forum to kill off multiple assets and agents. He'd prevented them from furthering their goals.

But it was just a dent in their overall plan. They'd been at this a long time. They had people in all the right places. They had the resources and manpower to keep going. And now Leon had confirmed something else.

They were going to the west coast. To San Francisco. That could mean a thousand different things. But he was almost positive it was because of Carver. They had a location on him. And now they were sending in their best people.

— • —

CHAPTER 12

Noah slammed his phone on the table.

Titus and Deshawn looked up from their phones. Looked at him expectantly.

"Corporate?" Deshawn asked.

Noah nodded. "They have a problem. A living, breathing problem."

"In our city?"

"Yeah, in our city." Noah shook his head. "And they don't think we can handle it."

Titus grunted. "We can handle anything, boss."

"That's what I told them. They don't believe me." Noah picked up his phone. The protective glass cover was cracked. He'd have to get it replaced again.

"This might cheer you up." Deshawn showed him his phone. The morning news was on. A reporter was outside a fancy home on Lombard.

"Drug overdoses have claimed the lives of a prominent businessman and his daughter," the reporter said. "Jeffery Mansfield and his daughter, Haley, were found dead in his Lombard Street home this morning. Neighbors said they heard loud music and partying during the night."

"Tragic." The news anchor feigned concern. "Alicia, do the police know what substance it was?" As if he didn't already know.

"Fentanyl." Alicia shook her head sadly. "As you know it's very easy to overdose on fentanyl. Even absorbing it through the skin can stop your heart."

"Very sad." The news anchor tried to look sad and failed.

"It is sad, Dan." Alicia motioned toward a police car. "The police say they have no reason to suspect foul play. Just two more lives claimed in the fentanyl epidemic."

"Thanks for the update, Alicia." The news anchor's sad face turned into a cheery smile. "Coming up, how to make some amazing deserts on Baking with Brenda."

Deshawn paused the video. "Too easy."

Noah managed a smile. "Yeah. And I propose we show Enigma how easily we can solve their problem."

Deshawn looked surprised. "We're calling them by their name now? I thought we were keeping that on the down low."

"I don't care anymore," Noah said. "It's not like anyone will know what we're talking about."

"True." Deshawn nodded. "True. Who are they after?"

"Some guy named Carver." Noah pshawed. "They don't even have a description. Nothing specific. Just that he's tall and big."

"That could be Titus." Deshawn grinned.

Titus stood to his full six feet four inches. Flexed. "I'm big, boss."

Noah chuckled. "Are they looking for you, Titus?"

"Better not be. I'll whoop their asses." He pounded a fist into his palm. "I wasn't an ultimate fighting champ for nothing."

Deshawn laughed. "Yeah, they'd learn all right."

Noah got serious again. "Let's keep an eye out for this Carver guy. Let's fix the problem before Enigma does. I don't want them down here." He didn't like their interference. But there were other reasons he didn't want them here. Big reasons that could cause him big headaches if they found out.

The missing briefcase being number one. If his source was right about what was inside that thing, Enigma would kill to get it. Because it would give Noah power to take back what was his.

Enigma had a cause. A system of core beliefs. They used it for recruiting. They'd used it on Noah. But Noah hadn't bought it. Not for a second. He had a saying. *Behind every cause is a rich person.*

People got rich promoting causes. And rich people promoted causes because they wanted more power. That was perfectly fine with Noah. But he wasn't going to be their puppet. He was going to use their infrastructure for his own gains.

So far, his strategy was working better than expected. But it wasn't anywhere close to being enough.

"We need to meet with Duffy." Noah motioned at Deshawn. "Tell him to meet us in an hour. Usual place."

"On it." Deshawn tapped on his phone.

Noah had an old vintage desk in his office. It matched the vintage décor of this old building. He had a matching couch. A table. Comfortable leather chairs. The ceiling was still the original bronzed tin. He'd had it cleaned up and restored.

The floor was the original wood parquet with a large oval rug on it. To the side was a bar with glass shelves and a mirror. The original owner liked to drink. A lot. Noah kept it classy. He stocked it with vintage scotch and whiskey.

Behind Noah's desk was the crowning piece. A vintage wooden bookshelf. It was stocked with the classics. *War and Peace. To Kill a Mockingbird. The Art of War. The Communist Manifesto. Atlas Shrugged. Mein Kampf.*

They were leatherbound. Special editions. He had first editions and originals for most of them inside his vault. He wished he could display them here, but he didn't trust anyone with his valuables.

Noah had read all the books in his collection at least once. Many of them twice. He'd read *The Art of War* four times. It hadn't made him a military genius, but it gave him perspective. Every single one of those books offered perspective. A different way of looking at things.

His life had almost gone a different route. He'd been a philosophy student. Majoring in literature. Then he saw how much that education would cost him. By the end of four years, he'd be nearly sixty grand in the red.

Sixty grand he couldn't hope to pay for. Especially not with a philosophy degree. But it wasn't just the money. It was the people. The pretentious idiots taking the same courses. The people who thought they'd change the world.

Change it with words.

Noah had taken a side gig with a low-level drug dealer. He'd seen the way the guy dressed. How he talked. How he presented himself. It limited him to selling to low class people.

Noah wore business suits. He was well spoken. He knew how to make people like him. And he knew how to reach people with more disposable income.

Those people were afraid to get their product from people like his dealer friend. But they eagerly snapped it up from Noah. That had given him an idea. A targeting strategy that could expand the dealer's market.

The dealer didn't like it at first. He didn't like dressing up. Didn't like changing the way he talked. But it worked. His sales increased three hundred percent.

His dealer's supplier had taken notice of Noah. He'd taken him under his wing. Taught him the ropes about running a drug operation from the top. Noah learned fast. Then he created strategies that leveled up their profit margins.

Noah had started working more. Studying less. Reading only for pleasure. And that was when he realized university was a colossal waste of time.

He could change the world. Not with words. But with his hands. With money. With power. He'd returned home to San Francisco. Studied the local black market. Discovered it was heavily fragmented.

The existing gangs had been fighting for decades. They were weak. Tired. Lacking leadership. Noah had come in and taken over. He'd used his connections to sell massive amounts of product. But he'd kept out certain drugs. Fentanyl especially. He didn't want to kill his customers. He wanted to keep them happy and high for the long term.

Before long, he was the power in San Francisco. He owned cops. Politicians. He owned the streets.

Then Enigma had sent their people for a visit. They already knew he was the king. They knew he was powerful. They knew what they had to do to own him. Enigma rolled into town. Rolled right up to his front door with fully equipped military types.

His street-level enforcers looked like kids with water guns compared to them.

An old white woman had sat down with Noah. Given it to him straight. Told him he had no choice. Join, or die. If he joined, he'd remain king. He'd be paid well. Like some regular employee.

Noah hadn't had a choice. He'd accepted. Everything changed. Gone from boss to employee. Fentanyl became the main product they wanted him to push.

His recruitment strategies were ignored. Instead of finding smart, well-spoken people, Enigma's strategy focused on politics and ideologies. They wanted followers, not independent thinkers.

Enigma controlled people. They preyed on the weak-minded. On fanatics. Drew them to the cause like moths to the flame. Turned the sheep into their flock. Turned the flock into a mob. A violent mob that could be used when needed.

Ironically, they were the same kind of people Noah had gone to university with. Enigma had discovered places of higher learning were fertile breeding grounds for easy prey.

Noah had to admit it was brilliant. But it was also dangerous. Those same people could turn on you in a heartbeat. And God forbid they ever actually got what they wanted. It would destroy the economy and the nation along with it.

Considering how things were going, Noah was convinced that was what Enigma had wanted all along. But with the contents of the briefcase, he might be able to turn it all around. Reclaim his throne.

Tasha entered the office. She had a manilla folder in her hand.

Noah raised an eyebrow. "What's this?"

"The registration for the Dodge. The truck that had the guns in it."

"Derrick and RJ hit it again?"

"I told them about the 762 ammo. Told them to take another look."

Noah grinned. "I love it when you take the initiative, darling. I take it they didn't find another weapon?"

"No. They checked the registration. It belongs to some guy from Montana. I called the number and made contact." She pulled a sheet of notebook paper from the folder. "I spoke to the former owner. A man named Bill Sniderman. He said he sold the car a while back."

"Interesting. The new owner didn't put it in his name yet."

"Apparently not." She tucked the paper back into the folder. "He said he sold it to a big guy. Over six feet tall. Muscular. Looked like he was in the military."

It clicked with what had been found in the truck. Noah wondered if the man had been planning something. Maybe he was a right-wing lunatic looking for a place to go on a rampage.

Or maybe there was something else going on. Whatever it was, it would have to wait. "Good work, Tasha." He stood. Walked across the room. Patted her shoulder. "I think you learned your lesson, didn't you?"

She nodded. "Yes."

"Good girl." He patted her head. Like she was a dog. "You can go now."

She turned and left without another word.

Noah turned to Titus and Deshawn. "Let's go." He left the office. Walked past the heavy metal vault door. Turned left through the main warehouse floor. Passed shelf upon shelf of sorted items.

Runners pulled items from shelves. Took them to the packaging area so they could be shipped to the buyer. They were selling everything from cheap watches to designer clothing.

All of it liberated from brick and mortar stores. All of it sold online through the biggest marketplaces in the world. All of it legit.

Nothing illicit like drugs or weapons. Enigma had federal connections. But it was best not to poke the bear. There were too many feds who could still cause problems.

The warehouse workers waved and saluted Noah. They were believers. They'd bought Enigma's agenda hook line and sinker. They looked at Noah as a leader. As the person who would one day lead to the overthrow of the government.

Some were anarchists. Some were socialists. A few were even libertarian. They all hated the government. Hated corporations. Wanted to kill the rich. Kill the powerful. And here they were working for powerful people. Enigma was probably funded by billionaires.

It was ironic. Funny, even.

He waved. Smiled. Put on a show. He was their charismatic leader. The one who'd take them to the promised land. Except they were already in the promised land and didn't even realize it.

Noah went outside. Climbed into Titus' Prius. He wanted to drive his Hellcat. Roar up and down the roads with it. But not when it came to meeting people like Duffy. It was always better to keep a low profile.

They crossed the bridge. Drove into Oakland. Went to the same warehouse where Haley and her father breathed their last breaths. Duffy was already parked inside. His unmarked black sedan was tucked into the shadows.

Titus parked the Prius. Pulled himself out. The car rocked on its shocks when his weight left it. Noah slid out. Leaned against the car and waited.

A tall, thin man got out of the unmarked car. His face was scruffy. He looked like he hadn't shaved for a couple of days. He had dark circles under his eyes. His hair was unkempt. Oily. That was the way he usually looked.

Duffy nodded at them. "Good day, gentlemen."

Noah got straight to it. "Looking for word about a guy named Carver."

"I've heard the name. Straight from the chief's lips a day ago."

"Context?"

"Person of interest." Duffy shrugged. "He wanted us to pull favors from all our CIs."

Noah whistled. "Burning favors with confidential informants is kind of extreme, don't you think?"

"It is. But you know we can't use force anymore."

Titus smacked his fist into a palm. "Sucks for you."

Duffy nodded. "At least I can trade drugs to seventy percent of mine. Except their drug problem makes most of them useless."

"Not useless. Just unreliable." Noah watched Duffy closely. "Are you holding back?"

"I don't have a reason to hold back." Duffy held up his hands in surrender. "You're the only reason I stuck around this god forsaken place. After they cut our salaries, I couldn't afford to even live in the Bottoms anymore."

"Don't stress." Noah folded his arms. "Where are the orders coming from?"

"The commissioners."

"The commissioners are just puppets. I want to know the origin."

"You know that's out of my reach." Duffy shook his head. "My guess would be the mayor."

"Too obvious." Noah had considered that probability. The mayor showed all the signs of being a puppet. Someone was pulling her strings. She'd come into office with extreme ideas. And those ideas came right out of Enigma's playbook.

"I need anything you can find on Carver. I need your ear on the ground, Duffy." Noah straightened. Walked toward the detective. "We don't want corporate visiting town. It wouldn't be good for me. Wouldn't be good for you."

"You've been good to me, Noah. I'm always doing my best for you."

"I appreciate that. You're happy with the carrot. Some people get spoiled by the carrot. They need the stick."

"I'm happy with the carrot, believe me." Duffy glanced at Titus. "I don't want the stick."

Titus grinned. "I ain't the stick."

Deshawn laughed. "Everyone always thinks you're the stick."

"I'm a sweetheart." Titus's grin grew wider. And somehow more menacing.

Duffy backed up a step. "I'll poke around. I'll risk getting my nose cut off, but I'll do it."

"Maybe there's a better way." Noah went silent. Considered his options.

Duffy was looking at him expectantly. He knew better than to interrupt Noah's train of thought. Titus and Deshawn knew too. They could tell when Noah was looking into the future. Strategizing.

Noah didn't consider himself a genius. He wasn't a prophet, either. But he was educated. Well read. Street smart. Understanding people gave him insights.

Enigma seemed like some distant entity. An entity with all the power. All the money. All the answers.

But like any organization, it consisted of humans. Humans doing human things. And humans were ignorant by nature. They knew what they knew. They were programmed by parents. By society. By themselves.

Enigma was worried about someone named Carver. They were looking for him. All that power, money, and information at their disposal. And they couldn't find one man. And that made them afraid.

Noah knew how to find out just how afraid they were. "Duffy, give me every detail about this Carver guy."

"He's big. Muscular. Might be white. Might be mixed. Might even be Latino or brown."

"Light skinned?"

"Don't know."

Deshawn laughed. "How can they not know a man's skin color?"

Duffy shrugged. "They don't have a picture. Just a basic description."

"Might be a white guy with a good tan," Deshawn said.

Noah held up a hand. "I don't care. It's perfect."

Deshawn looked excited. "Explain for us stupid folks."

"It's simple." Noah thought about the perfect person for the job. "Remember Arty?"

Titus snorted. "That dumbass wanna-be gangster? The one who tried to sell on our turf?"

"Yeah. He's still here in Oakland?"

Deshawn nodded. "He's dealing for us. Still dealing on the side too, but we've been letting it slide like you said."

"He's still dealing tainted goods?"

Deshawn nodded again. "That idiot keeps poisoning his customers. That's why I thought we should get rid of him."

Noah watched Duffy's face. The detective wasn't bothered. He'd vanished three people for Noah. Talking about it in front of him was nothing new.

Titus looked confused. "Are you gonna make him look for Carver?"

"No. I have a better use for him." He turned to Duffy. "I need you to do exactly what I tell you to. Nothing more. Nothing less."

Duffy looked confused. "You want me to kill this guy? I don't know where you're going with this."

Deshawn's eyes brightened. "Oh, I think I see where this is headed."

Noah told Duffy what to do. Told him what time to do it. Where to do it. What to do to prepare for it. Then he leaned back against the Prius again. "I want you to poke the bear. Can you handle that?"

"Absolutely. No problem." Duffy laughed. "Just when I think you can't surprise me again, you give me something like this."

"That's why he's the boss," Titus said.

Noah didn't care about the compliments. About praise. He just cared about winning. "One of my runners will meet you with the equipment. I'll have a tech meet you onsite."

"I'll go right now." Duffy went to his car. Turned it around. Drove out of the warehouse.

Noah watched him go. "Send the order to the department store."

"On it." Deshawn already had a list typed on his phone. "Which tech do you want?"

"Tisha. She always gets it right."

Deshawn sent another message. "It's in the system."

"Let's go." Noah dropped into the Prius.

Titus drove them out of the warehouse. Stopped at the road. "Where to, boss?"

Noah was dropping markers in his map app. Triangulating. He gave Titus an address. Titus plugged it into the GPS. Gently accelerated onto the road.

Deshawn laughed. "We're on a mission and my man, Titus, is still trying to get good gas mileage."

"Gas is expensive," Titus said.

Deshawn snorted. "Bro, you get paid as much as I do. Affording gas shouldn't be a problem."

Titus looked at him in the rearview mirror. "It's a challenge."

"You're still in that Prius challenge group, aren't you?"

Titus looked back at the road. "What if I am?"

"Good for you," Noah said. "If you're not improving, you're dying."

Titus glared at Deshawn in this mirror. "Yeah, boss."

Deshawn shrugged. "All right, then."

Titus reached the address. It was a rundown house in a rundown neighborhood. There was a line of camper trucks and trailers on one side of the road. Most of them looked inoperable. But that didn't matter.

Noah got out. Studied the angles. Studied the area. It was just okay. Not perfect. But it would work. He got back into the car. Gave Titus the next address. They arrived a few minutes later.

This place didn't have any natural cover. No tents. No RVs. It was wide open. He shook his head. Got back in the car.

Titus watched him closely. "What are we looking for, boss?"

"Camouflage." Noah gave him another address. He could look at the area in map view, but the images were usually out of date. The ebb and flow of homelessness in the area changed the terrain significantly.

They reached the last spot. It was no good. But the perfect spot was just down the block. Closer to the target than Noah preferred, but superior to the first place. Lots of RVs. Lots of tents. Lots of people living on the sidewalks.

And even more perfect was the three-story apartment building behind them. It gave him a vantage point over the nearby houses. He just had to get inside. Then he was going to sit back and watch the show.

This Carver guy was going to help Noah catch a bear.

CHAPTER 13

Carver needed a car.

Getting one, even in this city wasn't going to be easy. The movies made it look easy. Like he could rub two wires together. Start the car. Drive off into the sunset.

He could probably do that with an old car. A really old car. Definitely not one of the new ones. There was too much computer stuff under the dash. Too many wires to sort through.

Jericho had been good at it. He'd also had a device that made it easier. Something that let him bypass protective chips. It might have even been a backdoor device. Something provided by a car manufacturer.

Carjacking was another option. Taking by brute force worked in a pinch. But it attracted too much attention. It was also likely the police would respond to a call for that. Or, maybe they wouldn't. At least, not in this city.

It was preferable to take a car that wouldn't be missed for the better part of the day. And Carver knew where to go to make that happen.

He didn't have a pass for the trolley anymore. It was the only form of public transportation they checked for tickets. So, he took a bus. Took it to the expensive hotels on California Street. That was the most likely place to find what he needed.

There were several hotels within shouting distance of each other. Some exclusive clubs as well. He walked uphill. Cased the hotels on that side. Crossed the street. Walked downhill. Checked the ones on that side.

One hotel stood out. There were two valets. They were running like crazy. Grabbing tickets. Running into the parking deck to grab the cars. Handing the next customer a ticket. Driving that car into the garage. Running back to the stand.

There was a line of people waiting at the stand. It was morning. They were eager to get their cars. To go places. They certainly weren't sticking around downtown. If they were, they'd take public transportation. There were plenty of options.

They might be going to the west side of town. The Golden Gate Bridge. The nature parks north of the bridge. Public transportation was plentiful on the east side of town. The west side, not so much.

Whatever the reason, this was the place Carver needed to be. The time was right too. He covered his head with the hoodie. Put on a facemask. Walked toward the valet station like he knew what he was doing.

He walked right past it. Didn't even look at it. He went into the hotel lobby. A concierge greeted him. He greeted her back. He kept acting like he knew what he was doing. Nobody bothered him. Nobody asked him why he was there.

Carver turned around. He'd looked at the line of cars. Saw the one that fit his needs. It was a silver compact car. A Chevy. Nothing special. Probably got thirty miles to the gallon in town. That was a plus. Because he didn't have much money to buy gas.

The silver Chevy reached the valet station ten minutes later. A valet rushed from the garage. Handed the driver a ticket. Hopped inside. Drove it into the parking deck. The other valet ran into the deck to grab someone else's car.

The people in line looked restless. Looked a little agitated. Like they'd been waiting too long for this. Like they couldn't believe their morning was being spent waiting in line for their car.

Carver walked toward the door.

The concierge asked him a question. "Sir, are you waiting on your car?"

"Not yet. Long line."

She smiled apologetically. "Two of our valets are out today. I'm so sorry for the delay."

Carver shrugged. "Not your fault." He walked outside. The valet who'd serviced the silver Chevy ran back. Put the key in the locker. The door was open. No time for him to keep closing and locking it with such a backlog of customers.

The valet ran to the next car in line. The other valet was still in the parking deck. The customers were staring at phones. Talking to each other. Griping.

Carver glanced at the concierge. She was talking to another customer. Nobody inside was looking. He walked past the key locker. Snagged the key to the silver Chevy. Nobody noticed. Or if they did, they didn't shout at him.

He walked into the parking deck. The other valet ran outside. Ran past him to the line of customers. Took another ticket. Grabbed another key. Ran back into the deck. Ran past Carver again.

Carver kept walking. Acted like he knew what he was doing. Most of the parking spots were marked valet only. There was self-parking further back. That meant it wouldn't look odd if someone who wasn't a valet drove a car out.

He found the silver Chevy. It was around the corner. At the start of the ramp leading to the third level. The other valet stopped before the corner. He climbed into a white van. Backed out. Drove away.

Carver unlocked the Chevy. He checked the inside. It smelled like marijuana. Smelled like fast food. There were wrappers on the floor. Trash in the other seat. Crumbs on the upholstery. It wasn't as bad as the minivan he'd bought in Oregon, but it was halfway there.

He found some baby wipes. No baby car seat. No other evidence the driver had a baby. The back seat looked cleaner. Stuff was piled there. Clothing. Crumpled fast food bags. A broken pair of sunglasses.

Carver used a baby wipe to clean off the steering wheel. He started the car. Pointed it toward the exit. Started driving. One of the valets ran past him on his way out. They looked tired. They were sweating. They didn't give him a second glance.

He steered onto California Street. Aimed downhill. Drove all the way to the Embarcadero. He drove down the line of parked cars. Didn't see what he needed. Kept driving. He found what he was looking for closer to the Oakland Bay Bridge. An orange sticker on a car.

Carver found a parking spot. Slid the small car into it. Waited. The white Dodge Charger showed up thirty minutes later. The same guy who'd looted his car twice hopped out. Smashed the rear window with a tap of the hand.

He was holding something between his fingers. Carver got a good look at it. It was a small metal spike. Made breaking car windows effortless. Made the thieves quick and efficient.

The thin guy reached through the window. Lowered the back seat. Grabbed two suitcases from inside. Tossed them in the Charger. He was in and out in thirty seconds. Nice and smooth.

It was impressive.

The Charger took off. Kept going in the same direction. Carver let them get a lead. Then he followed. Kept a comfortable distance between them. The Charger followed the Embarcadero. Followed it all the way to Oracle Park. Hit three cars along the way.

It hooked onto Third Street. Followed it for a way. Hit two cars. It looped onto an adjoining road. There weren't many parking spaces along this road. The Charger stopped next to a Honda that was in a turning lane.

Traffic was stopped in that lane. The thin guy hopped out of the Charger. Smashed the Honda's window. Yanked a backpack and suitcase from the backseat. Hopped back in the Charger. The driver and passenger of the Honda jumped out.

They looked stunned. Like they couldn't believe they just got robbed in the middle of traffic. In broad daylight. And there was a police car right behind them. It was absolutely brazen. Carver saw the looks on their faces and chuckled.

The victims tried to chase down the car on foot. But their vehicle was wedged into the traffic. The Charger wasn't. It took off straight. The license plate was covered. The windows were tinted. The passenger was masked. The cop watched everything with a bored expression.

Carver followed the Charger. It steered back on the Embarcadero. Took a ramp onto Interstate 80. Headed across the bridge to Oakland. It looked like they were done looting San Francisco for now.

There were no signs of pursuit. That cop hadn't cared. He probably saw it happen daily. Maybe he'd arrested the same people before. And then they'd been released onto the streets again a few hours later. Circle of life. Or something like that.

At first glance, Oakland looked nice enough. It looked industrial. Like San Francisco was there to look pretty and Oakland was there to do all the dirty work. Just like San Francisco, the rot was on the surface here in Oakland.

Tents on sidewalks. People overdosing in the streets. And the further Carver followed the thieves, the worse things looked. The thieves stopped outside a house on Ninth Street. The front of the house was blackened. Like it had nearly burned down but been salvaged.

The house was two stories tall. Maybe two thousand square feet. The windows were boarded up. Carver parked a block down. Watched the thieves turn into the driveway. They kept going until they were out of sight.

Carver put on his facemask. Hood over his head. He got out and walked laterally. Followed a broken sidewalk parallel to the house's driveway. The backyards of the three houses between him and the target house were fenced in.

The fences were low. Most of them were rotting. Broken down. They didn't block his view. He could see the backyard of the target house. It was big. There was a large metal garage there.

There was no house on the property behind the building. Just a rotting foundation and burned timbers. The land was overgrown with weeds. It isolated the backyard.

The metal garage was probably where the thieves put their stash. With any luck, that would be where Carver's stuff was. He watched the Charger pull into the garage. It was in there for maybe ten minutes. Then it backed out. Turned around. Drove down the driveway.

It turned onto the road. Came toward him. Carver kept his head down. Slumped. Shuffled down the sidewalk. Walked to the crosswalk at the intersection.

The thieves drove to a red light right next to him. Stopped. The passenger was fanning cash in front of the driver. They were grinning.

Carver walked over to the car. Spit on the windshield. Pretended to polish it. "You gotta dollar? I ain't eat nothing for a day."

The driver's window rolled down. "Get your filthy hands off my car!"

"You got a dollar?"

The driver got out. Brandished a pistol. Put it in Carver's face. "I got a Glock and brass. You want a bullet in your gut? Keep touching my car."

"Oh, please, just a dollar!" Carver was watching the passenger. Looking at the wad of cash. They were mixed bills. Maybe three hundred dollars if he had to guess.

The driver was maybe five feet seven inches. Maybe a hundred and seventy-five pounds on a good day. He shoved Carver anyway. Carver stumbled back. Did his drunken walk. "Please. Just a dollar!"

The passenger laughed. "Shoot him, Derrick! Ain't nobody gonna care."

"Nah, he learned." Derrick got in the car. Revved the six cylinder. Drove off.

Carver went back to his stolen car. Started it. Drove after the Charger. Derrick and his pal went back across the Oakland Bay Bridge. Back into San Francisco. Across downtown all the way to the west side. The car parked in a narrow driveway.

The houses here looked mostly the same. Just different colors. Slightly different facades. They all had single car garages. Stairs to the left of the garage door. They looked small. They looked old and rundown.

Carver parked on the street. He got out. Walked down the sidewalk. Derrick and pal were wrestling something out of the trunk of the car. A big suitcase. They didn't even glance at Carver.

"Gotta be something good in here," Derrick said.

"Noah gonna realize we skimming if we take too much," the passenger said.

"Noah ain't gonna know shit." Derrick finally pulled the suitcase out. "This thing so heavy, it must have gold in it."

Carver walked up behind the passenger. Gripped the back of his neck. Slammed his head into the side of the car. It happened so fast he didn't even have time to shout. He went down hard. Derrick had time to shout. He had time to look surprised.

That was about all he had time for. Carver elbowed him in the face. Derrick went down. Carver dragged him and his friend in front of the Charger so they wouldn't be visible from the street.

He found keys on Derrick. Used them to open the entrance door next to the garage door. He opened it. It squeaked.

"Derrick, that you?" The voice belonged to an elderly woman.

Carver glanced inside. Saw stairs leading up. He didn't bother trying to mimic Derrick's voice. "I'm dropping some things off for him. For Noah."

"Oh, how nice. You tell that nice young man he needs to come by for dinner again real soon." Her voice was distant. Like she was in another room.

"Yes ma'am." Carver liberated the cash from Derrick and his pal. He dragged their unconscious bodies inside the foyer. Put Derrick on his back. Put his buddy on top of him.

She called out again. "I'd get up and help, but my legs aren't the same as they used to be."

"That's okay. I got everything." Carver started to close the door. "You have a good day."

She called back. "You too, young man!"

Carver went to the Charger. He removed the suitcases from the trunk and back seats. He put them in his borrowed car. The heavy suitcase wasn't really that heavy. He opened it and looked inside.

It was filled with women's clothing. With bottles upon bottles of vitamins. Skin care creams. Makeup. Probably worth a lot of money. But definitely not the score Derrick had hoped it was. The suitcases had tags. Tags with names. Names and addresses.

Carver had Derrick's keys. He was tempted to take the Charger. He was tempted to leave a note. *Get an honest job.* But he couldn't really blame the guy. He was making ends meet. Hopefully taking care of his mom or grandma, or whoever it was in the house.

But that didn't exempt him from the consequences. Carver wasn't going to give the guy a pass because he had an old woman in the house. That woman probably bought the house new. Probably paid it off over her lifetime.

Maybe Derrick was just leeching off her. Either way, it didn't matter to Carver. He could be the sweetest kid or the worst. Carver was taking his money.

He drove the Chevy a couple of blocks down. Then he walked back. Got in the Charger. It stank like marijuana, but it was otherwise clean inside. He started it. It had a quarter of a tank. Carver backed it up. Drove it a few blocks.

He found a parking deck. Paid for a slot. Left the Charger there. It was going to help him get his stuff back in a little while. Then he hoofed it back to the Chevy. Drove it across town. Back to the hotel.

The same two valets were busy. He parked the car in the roundabout in front of the hotel. Dropped the keys on the valet station. They still had the original ticket number on them. The Chevy's tank was a few gallons lighter. The trunk and backseat were full of stolen suitcases.

The owner was going to get a surprise. If he was the decent sort, the suitcases would find their way back to their owners. The woman who owned all that makeup was going to be happy at least.

Carver was happy with everything so far. He had some cash. He had a gun. And most importantly, he had a car.

A car that would get him into the garage where his stuff was.

CHAPTER 14

Leon was on his way across the country.

He was driving partway. Chartering a flight the rest of the way. He couldn't risk contacting charter companies in Atlanta. Enigma was watching. Enigma was waiting. Even if he paid cash, they might have people watching for flight plans to be filed. For paperwork with Leon's name on it.

He couldn't just hire a flight without the paperwork. At least not on a jet. There were plenty of light aircraft pilots he could hire. But he'd prefer to drive rather than sit in a two-seater prop plane.

There were probably charter companies in the area that would let him fly without paperwork. But he didn't know which ones. He'd always used legit companies. He'd never asked them about off the menu items.

That was why he was driving. All the way to Houston. That was where an old buddy of his lived. A guy who ran charter flights all over the world. A guy who could fly him under the radar wherever he wanted.

Houston was out of the way. He could have gone through Memphis, up to Kansas City, and across to San Francisco. Instead, he was dipping way south. But it would save him time in the long run. Provided his buddy had availability.

It was a race against time. That was nothing new to him. Nothing new at all. He would either get there in time or he wouldn't. He'd either find Carver or he wouldn't. It was hard to tell. Carver might not even be there anymore.

And if they found Carver. Well, odds were they'd suffer casualties. Maybe a lot. Because Carver on his worst day was better than most on their best day. And despite his size, Carver was a pro at blending in. At infiltration.

Leon buzzed past the outskirts of Montgomery, Alabama. He was in a different car. An old square body Ford pickup. The gas mileage was bad. The suspension was stiff. At least it had power steering.

He would have preferred another compact car. Something that didn't guzzle gas. But this was all he had handy. So, he'd taken it. It didn't have to get him across the country. Only about halfway. And he was only about a quarter of the way to Houston.

Hopefully, he could make it in time.

CARVER WAS READY TO GO.

He had everything he needed. He even had a half decent plan. Rhodes would call it risky. She'd probably shake her head. Give him that look she always gave him when he was about to do something stupid.

And then she'd shrug. Look at the others. Tell them that it'd work with a few modifications. And then she'd turn his dumpster fire of a plan into something elegant.

This plan wasn't elegant, but it'd get the trick done. Minimal noise. Minimal bloodshed. At least, that was what he hoped.

The Charger was the key component to his plan. It was the whole reason it would work in the first place.

It would get him inside. Nobody would realize Derrick wasn't driving. At least for a few seconds. That would give Carver time to evaluate the situation. Let him know what he was up against. And if the odds looked good, he'd take them.

The pistol was a tool of last resort. It'd be better to get in and out quietly. No muss. No fuss. Get his stuff and go.

Carver checked out Derrick's weapon of choice. It was a Glock 45. It wasn't Carver's first choice of Glocks. It was a mix between a Glock 19 and 17. A hybrid. Hybrid was usually synonymous with crap.

But that wasn't entirely true with the 45.

As far as semi-compact pistols went, it did the job. It was also modified. It had a MOS—modular optic system. That was just a fancy way of saying the owner could switch out sights quickly and easily. Whatever they were in the mood for.

Derrick had been in the mood for a reflex optic. It was a little better than iron sights. Just a piece of glass with an LED red light on it. It might be accurate. It might not be calibrated at all. Someone like Derrick probably thought it looked cool. Thought it made him look gangster.

It did look cool. Even Carver could admit that. But he didn't really need it. If he was far enough away from the target that he needed to use it, then he'd probably already lost. Not because he couldn't hit the target. Mainly because he hadn't gotten close enough to take out the target quietly first.

This was going to be a stealth mission. He had no idea how many people were in that garage. He didn't know anything about the house either. But he didn't need to know much if his plan worked.

Carver hopped on a bus. Took it back across town to the parking deck. He got in the back seat of the Charger. Broke down the Glock. Checked the firing pin. The springs. The components.

Everything looked good. Almost like new. Like the gun had hardly been fired at all. Which proved that Derrick wanted it for style points. Not for utility. And that was fine. Everyone liked guns for different reasons.

Carver viewed them as tools. If he was a carpenter, he wouldn't carry around a fancy hammer just for looks. He'd carry around something for utility. Same with guns. Most of his weapons had been well cared for. But no amount of care could keep tools looking new forever.

His guns looked like they'd seen action. They had scratches. Gouges in the metal. Worn grips. Dents. But the insides were well oiled. Everything internal was at peak functionality. And when he pulled the trigger, his guns fired bullets.

And that was about all you could ask for.

He reassembled the gun. Then he searched inside the Charger. Opened the glove compartment. The center console. Looked under the seats. In the trunk. Under the spare tire. He found money. Found fentanyl. Found marijuana. Found a can of glass cleaner.

He had enough drugs to pay off Tommy for a month. But if all went well, he'd be out of Tommy's hair today. Or at least by morning. He wouldn't mind staying another night in the park. Then he could finish touring the waterfront.

It was getting late in the afternoon. Carver considered doing the job at night. He didn't know how many deliveries Derrick made per day. Maybe just one. Maybe as many as he wanted. It seemed likely he was planning on at least one more trip.

After all, Derrick had held onto those other suitcases. He must have hidden them from the people in the garage. Handed a few things over to Noah, whoever that was. Taken his money. Gone home to look through the other suitcases. See if there was anything worth keeping.

The order of events didn't make much sense to Carver. Why not just go straight home? If he was skimming, he'd want to know if there was cash or other valuables he could fence. Then he could take the rest to this Noah person.

Noah was probably just a fence. A person who took stuff the thief couldn't sell himself. He paid the thief a cut based on an assessment of the stolen goods. Then he'd turn around and sell it for top dollar.

Derrick's friend made it sound like Noah expected an exclusive arrangement with them. Like he wouldn't take kindly to them using another fence. Like Noah was someone you didn't want to mess with.

Any way you cut it, it seemed reasonable for Derrick to visit the fence multiple times per day. It wouldn't look suspicious for Carver to drive over there again later. Wouldn't raise eyebrows if the Charger was seen coming down the driveway after dark.

That was the plan and Carver was sticking with it. First, he needed food.

Carver counted his money. Including what he'd found in the Charger, he was sitting at five hundred and twenty dollars. It wasn't much in this town, but it would get him some grub. It would barely be enough for a motel in these parts.

He didn't want one anyway.

Camping life had spoiled him. Sleeping in the forests. Next to rivers. Under the great big sky. It had been almost as good as drinking a beer on the beach. It had certainly been more peaceful.

Once he got his stuff back, he was getting out of town. Avoiding big cities altogether. They were just ratholes. Infested with the worst kinds of people. He should've known better. But he'd decided to play tourist instead.

Carver hopped on a bus. He didn't pay. He didn't think anyone paid to ride them. Nobody checked for tickets or passes. And that suited him just fine. He figured the taxpayers wouldn't mind. They probably paid a king's ransom in property taxes already.

A few more bucks wouldn't hurt.

He hopped off at a diner near Nob Hill. Got himself a couple of breakfast sandwiches. Eggs, bacon, lettuce tomato. Something heavy to tide him over. Then he took the bus back to the parking deck.

Only one hour until dark. With traffic, it would take Carver about that long to get over to the house in Oakland. He slid into the Charger. Fueled up at a nearby gas station. Started driving.

Tonight was the night.

NOAH WATCHED FROM THE ROOFTOP.

He was on the roof of the three-story apartment building. He and his boys had chairs. Beers. Binoculars. They were making a party of it. Nothing loud. Nothing fancy. Just sitting back and waiting for the fireworks.

It was almost dark. Noah's phone blinked on. He unlocked it. Saw a text from Duffy. *Pieces in motion. Happening tonight.*

Noah hadn't been sure if it would happen tonight. He wouldn't have been surprised if it had taken several days. But corporate had pawns everywhere. Pawns at the lowest levels and the highest.

He texted Duffy. *Where did the orders come from?*

The chief said they came from Maryann Lewis. I had a reporter friend call the mayor's office for comment. They had no knowledge. Police will be forming a barricade. A special unit will be making the arrest.

Noah grinned. Maryann Lewis was on the city council. She'd led the effort to reduce the police force. To legalize casual drug use. To forbid the police from removing homeless encampments.

He'd suspected she was directly employed by Enigma. But she'd just been one of many pushing for the same agenda. The mayor had also been advocating for the same policies. It was possible that Maryann was the one calling the shots.

The chief of police didn't take his orders from the city council. Only the mayor had that power. And yet, he'd taken his orders from Maryann Lewis. Duffy had confirmed it. Which meant she might be a link to someone up the chain.

"Looks like the fireworks are starting tonight, fellas." Noah sipped his beer. Leaned back in his chair. Looked up at the dusky sky.

Titus was watching a video on his phone. A video about getting better gas mileage from a Prius. "Boss, I need to get special tires for my car. This guy says they make a big difference."

Deshawn laughed. "Man, tires ain't going to make a big difference. Especially not when you're driving us around town."

"Nah, they'll make a big difference." Titus was already looking at the prices on a website. "Damn, they want three hundred per tire?"

"Those aren't even performance tires." Noah shook his head. "Why don't you just get an electric car?"

"Man, those things are bad for the environment. Lithium batteries are bad news." Titus shook his head. "The Prius is peak economy and it's environmentally friendly."

Deshawn couldn't stop laughing. "Titus, you eat cows, right?"

"I eat beef." Titus flexed. "It's the best protein for muscles."

"Yeah, and cows make a lot of methane. A lot of carbon dioxide."

Noah grinned. "Titus is trying to make up for eating all those methane producing cows by driving a Prius."

"No, I ain't." Titus scowled. "Man, you two need to be more responsible. I can't carry all the load around here."

A car caught Noah's eye. He looked at it with his binoculars. The window tinting made it impossible to see inside. He knew the car. Knew the crew that used it. Their territory was the financial district. The Embarcadero and surrounding area.

What were they doing out here?

The car parked a few blocks down. No one got out. It stayed there until it got dark about twenty minutes later. Then the headlights came on. It started driving. It slowed at the driveway of a house. Turned onto it.

"Those little rascals." Noah tutted.

"Isn't that Derrick's car?" Deshawn said.

Noah nodded. "Looks like him and RJ have been skimming on me."

"There's no way Arty pays better than we do." Deshawn shook his head. "It doesn't make sense."

Noah grunted. "Remember all those drugs Derrick tried to sell us?"

Deshawn frowned. "The stuff he found in cars? The stuff you didn't want because it's not our street stuff?"

"Yeah." Noah pursed his lips. "No quality control. Certainly not enough of it to market to our buyers. And most of our buyers don't want anything except ivory."

"I'll bet Arty buys that stuff. Cuts it with fillers." Deshawn tutted. "Damn, bro. You're about to kill two birds with one stone."

"Best kind of killing there is," Titus said. "Economical."

Noah laughed. "Titus, you're straight up the weirdest gangster there is."

"Hey, I get the job done, don't I?"

Noah nodded. "No complaints."

"Feels nice to get to sit back and watch someone else do the work for you." Titus opened a bag of popcorn. Ate a handful. "I'm going to enjoy this."

"They're here." Deshawn was looking to the west. "Must be thirty police cars."

Noah looked in the same direction. The big black Sprinter vans held his attention. They weren't the same ones used by the police. This special unit was something else. Something he hadn't seen before.

"Whoa, you see those vans?" Titus pointed at them.

"Yeah. Hard to miss." Noah took a handful of Titus's popcorn. Sipped his beer. "Make sure we get it all on camera."

Titus nodded. "I'll get the cameras rolling."

Deshawn leaned his elbows on the top of the roof wall. "Bro, you never cease to amaze me." He shook his head. "How do you figure this stuff out? Figure out how to manipulate the enemy and all that?"

Noah shrugged. "It's simple. Find out what someone wants. Offer it to them. In this case corporate wanted that Carver guy. I wanted to find out who their point of contact is in the local government." He ate more popcorn. "I'll get what I want tonight. Corporate might think they got what they wanted. And maybe that'll be enough."

Titus tapped his temple. "Can't outsmart the boss."

"That's for damned sure," Deshawn said.

Noah couldn't help but smile. Derrick and RJ were good at their job. They hauled in a good load every day. But skimming was disloyal. Selling to someone on Noah's blacklist was outright betrayal.

He just wished they could know that it was him that killed them.

CHAPTER 15

Carver waited until dark.

He noticed some guys on a rooftop down the street. They were drinking beer. Eating popcorn. Watching the area with binoculars. Probably lookouts for the garage. Probably ready to alert the garage if the cops were coming.

It was a good setup. It was smart. But with the dark tint on the Charger's windows, they wouldn't know he wasn't Derrick. And if they had three guys on the roof, that hopefully meant fewer guys inside the garage.

One of the guys noticed him. They looked at the car with their binoculars. Then they talked to the big guy next to them. Another guy looked at the car. Just with his eyes, not binoculars. They started talking.

One of them said something. The others laughed. They were having a good time. They saw the car. Probably said something about Derrick and his pal. Shared a laugh. Nothing suspicious going on here. All was good.

It didn't look like a big operation. He was a little surprised they could spare three guys as lookouts. Or maybe they usually just had one guy. Maybe the others were off duty. That was why they had beer and popcorn.

Carver wouldn't mind beer and popcorn. He wouldn't mind sitting on a roof with a good view. But once he was done here, he planned to put as much distance as possible between him and that roof.

Dusk turned to dark. Carver turned on the car. The headlights came on. He couldn't see the guys on the roof anymore. Maybe they were watching him. Maybe they weren't. He steered into the driveway.

Drove past the house. Into the back yard. The garage was straight ahead. It had three rollup doors. One was open. The lights were on inside. He drove in. The place was maybe thirty feet long by thirty wide.

It was big enough to hold several cars. It was big enough to be a small warehouse. There were cars inside. Both were classics. Maybe late seventies cars. One was a Cougar. One was a Mustang.

Neither looked drivable. One was missing tires. Its engine was on a hoist. Car parts were scattered on a workbench. The Cougar looked closer to being finished.

There were shelves against the back wall right in front of Carver. Shelves to the right. Most of the shelves had what looked like automotive parts. He didn't see anything that looked like it came out of suitcases.

A big man was standing at another workbench. This one was closest to Carver. It didn't have car parts on it. It had vegetation and white powder. He realized the vegetation was marijuana. A big pile of it.

The powder could be anything. Maybe cocaine. Maybe fentanyl.

The big guy grinned. Like he was expecting Derrick. He took off his latex gloves. Wiped his hands off. Started walking toward the car. The big guy had to be Noah.

Carver was looking at the shelves. Looking all around the garage. He didn't see anything that looked like his duffel bags. Either this guy didn't have his stuff, or he stored it somewhere else. He waited until Noah was closer.

Waited until he was ten feet from the car. Then he got out. His hood was up. Facemask was on. He leveled the Glock at Noah.

The big guy rocked back. Eyes flared. "Who the hell are you?"

"Did your boys bring a bag here with weapons in it?"

He frowned. "What did you do to Derrick and RJ?"

"They stole my stuff. I took their car and came to get it back." Carver sighed. "Give me my stuff and I'll leave. Simple as that. No harm, no foul."

"What kind of weapons?"

"Two MP5s. Several cans of ammo."

Noah's eyes flared again. "Man, I ain't seen nothing like that. They bring me normal stuff. Pistols. Rifles. Nothing fancy. Stuff that Noah doesn't want to buy."

"You're not Noah?"

He laughed. "Hell no. I'm Arty. Noah runs this city. He's the one with your stuff. If he knew that Derrick and RJ were dealing with me, he'd probably kill them."

Carver realized something. He realized it later than he should have. "You're a one-man operation."

The man nodded. "Yeah. I used to work for—"

Carver cursed. "You'd better get the hell out of here." He hopped in the car. Slammed it into reverse. He screeched out of the garage. Spun the front end around in a textbook J maneuver. Hit the gas.

He looked in the rearview mirror. Saw the big guy standing in the garage door. Saw him run for another car. Carver hit the end of the driveway. Turned hard right. Then he saw them. Saw the police cars. Saw them lining up to block the road.

He considered gunning it. Trying to make it between them. But they weren't looking for him. They were looking for the guy in the garage. Maybe he could act casual. Drive normal.

Then he saw the cops drawing weapons. Aiming them at him. They'd seen him drive out of Arty's driveway. Saw him gunning it. Now they thought he was that guy. He wasn't talking his way out of this one.

The road was wide. It was built to allow street parking. There were cars parked on each side. That narrowed the street down to normal width. Two cop cars formed a V in the middle of the road. There was no way to squeeze between them.

Civilian cars were parked all along the sides of the road. They formed a wall on both sides. The sidewalks were wide. But there were trees and road signs on them. A small car might fit between them. The Charger wouldn't.

The cops were out of their cars. Hiding behind open doors. Weapons out. Weapons pointed at Carver's car. And that was fine. Just fine.

Because there was another way out.

Carver veered back around. Punched the gas. There was a perimeter around the block now. Two cop cars at each junction minimum. More behind them. Maybe a show of force. Maybe in case his car had turbo jump.

There were black vans coming down the street. They weren't SWAT vans. They were something else. Something that didn't look like normal police. There was no lettering on the outside. No acronyms, nothing.

Maybe things weren't just fine after all.

He gunned the Charger down the driveway. Back toward Arty's garage. There was a narrow space between the garage and the neighbor's wooden fence. He slowed. Tires clawed the dirt. The rear end spun around. Hit the wooden fence.

The fence crumbled. It was more rotten than he'd thought. Carver straightened the car. Wrestled it through the narrow space between garage and fence. He plowed through the wooden fence at the back of the yard.

He was in the backyard of the burned down house. The one with only a foundation left. He pointed the Charger down the side. Bumped over a stump. Over a pile of debris. The rear wheels spun in empty air. The car was bottomed out.

The forward momentum was just enough to keep the car from getting stuck. One of the tires hit a stack of bricks. Propelled the Charger forward. He bounced onto the driveway. Hit the street. Turned right.

Pushed the pedal to the floor. The V6 roared. The tires screeched. Carver hit the end of the block. The blockade was to his right. The extra police cars were right behind the ones forming the blockade.

They hadn't planned this very well. Maybe their plan would have worked flawlessly if Carver hadn't been there. Arty would have been working in his garage. Just doing his thing. Completely unaware of the storm coming his way.

Carver turned left. Gunned it. He didn't know where he was going. Didn't have a GPS. He was just going off memory now. Taking one of the escape routes he'd noted during reconnaissance.

Two police cars turned their lights on. They turned around. Came after Carver. He imagined they weren't the only ones. Others from the neighboring streets would be coming for him. Racing to cut him off somewhere.

The streets were straight. They formed a grid of blocks. There weren't any curves. No rises in elevation. It was unnaturally flat here compared to San Francisco. Unnaturally even. The houses were packed together. Nowhere to hide between them.

Carver took a left. Hooked a right. Raced past a long line of abandoned warehouses. The cops skidded onto the road behind him. The V6 in the Charger wasn't going to outrun them anytime soon. And even if it could, there was no way to outrun the radio.

When the second squad car veered into the road behind him, he realized something. Something he should have noticed right away. The police cars had stars on them. The symbol of the San Francisco Police Department.

Those were SFPD cars. Not Oakland PD. Oakland police cars had shields on them. Even if Carver couldn't see the writing, he knew the symbols. He'd formed a habit of noting things like that.

SFPD didn't have jurisdiction over here. At least they shouldn't. Not unless they had an agreement with Oakland. That didn't seem likely. Politicians and local cops usually didn't like other localities claiming authority on their turf.

They seemed plenty confident. Confident enough to engage in high-speed pursuit. Lights blazing. Sirens wailing. Making a real spectacle. They didn't care who saw them. Most cops would care.

Most cops would be sure to get permission before chasing a suspect onto someone else's turf. They'd engage the local PD. Ask for help. Explain the situation. But there were no Oakland police cars assisting.

As far as these cops knew, they had full authority to be here. They had the right to conduct this operation on foreign soil without a local presence. That was unheard of. Not even the feds would be so brazen.

Which meant someone on high had told the SFPD they could do this. That they had permission. But how? It shouldn't be possible. Carver was sure of that. But knowing that didn't help a bit. He couldn't run to the Oakland PD for help.

They'd just arrest him. Ask the SFPD what the hell they were doing. There'd be some controversy. Some political fallout. But Carver would be in prison just the same. High speed pursuit in a stolen car wouldn't earn him a slap on the wrist. Not even in this part of the country.

That didn't leave him many options. In fact, it only left him one. He had to run. But to where? These flat, straight streets weren't doing him any favors. He couldn't get a lead on the cops. Their cars were faster.

He couldn't take twists and turns and outsmart them. Not in this terrain. That meant finding favorable terrain. That meant getting out of Oakland. Going somewhere with more obstacles. With a gauntlet he could navigate.

Carver cut down Mandela Parkway. Hooked a hard left onto West Grand. Raced up the ramp to the Oakland Bay Bridge. Toward the toll plaza. The Charger had a toll pass, so he whizzed through the Fastrak lane.

Traffic was moderate. It slowed him. Slowed the cops, too. Carver threaded the Charger through the cars. But the other drivers saw the police lights. Heard the sirens. They started pulling out of the way. Giving the police a clear path.

There were two police cars behind him. They were catching up. There was no way to outrun them. No way to use traffic to his advantage. He could start shooting, but that was a last resort. Getting arrested for grand theft auto and high-speed pursuit were still better than attempted murder.

The nearest police car pulled up behind him. Started positioning for a PIT maneuver. He'd steer his front end into the Charger's rear end. Right behind the tire. Cause the Charger to spin. Lose control.

That would cause the car to run into the railing. End the chase real fast. The cops would hop out of vehicles. Guns at the ready. Swarm Carver. Take him into custody. It would be over in minutes.

At least it would be for most people. PIT maneuvers usually worked on civilians. People with no defensive training. People who hadn't trained extensively to counter the tactic.

Countering a PIT was like countering hydroplaning. You had to drive into the skid. Accelerate. Go with the flow, essentially. It felt unnatural. That was why most untrained people spun out. Lost control.

It also depended on how aggressive the cop was. Most of them opted for a nudge. That was usually enough. Some of them simply plowed into the back of the car. Caused a wreck. Sometimes killed the fleeing driver.

So, what kind of cop was this guy?

Carver decided he didn't want to find out. If the cop was aggressive, it'd be very hard to counter the PIT. It would shove the Charger sideways. Probably flip it. So, he opted for the second option.

He let the cop get positioned. Watched him. The cop swung the front end of the car at the rear of the Charger. Carver veered hard to the right. Away from it. The cop swerved wildly. Almost lost control.

That answered the question. He was aggressive. The kind who didn't care if he caused a wreck. That was good. Maybe not so good for normal drivers, but plenty good for Carver.

The cop was already veering back toward Carver. This time, Carver had nowhere to go. The right side of the Charger was near the concrete barrier in the middle of the bridge.

He couldn't avoid the PIT by veering right again. He'd only make the PIT work better if he went left. This time, there was no escape.

That was probably what the cop was thinking. Judging from the aggressive angle of the front of the police car, it was almost certainly what the cop was thinking. He was going to ram the Charger's rear end. Knock it right into the barrier.

And the wreck was going to be spectacular.

CHAPTER 16

Noah watched the police.

Watched them move into position. Form roadblocks. Jump out of their vehicles, guns ready. They circled the block around Arty's house.

The Dodge Charger screeched out of Arty's garage. Spun around. Hit the road.

"What the hell?" Deshawn looked surprised. Maybe impressed. "I didn't know Derrick could drive like that."

"How did he know?" Titus looked confused. "That boy got out of there like he had a sixth sense."

"That sixth sense isn't getting him anywhere." Noah ate a handful of popcorn. Watched Derrick stop at the sight of the roadblock. Watched the car sit there like he was all out of options. Which he was.

"They got him now." Deshawn chuckled. "He almost got out."

"Almost." Noah was having fun. It was like a party. Like celebrating a victory. A minor victory. But it still advanced his agenda. It got him one step closer to the top. Maryann Lewis was a cog in the corporate machine. A decision maker. That was valuable information.

She was powerful enough to get half the SFPD across the bridge and over here in Oakland. Not an Oakland police car in sight. She wasn't even worried about repercussions.

"Oh hell, look at him go!" Deshawn was excited. Like he was rooting for his favorite sports team.

Noah blinked out of his thoughts. Watched the Charger spin around. Duck into Arty's driveway. Arty was climbing into another car. The engine roared to life. It was an old car. A classic muscle car.

The Charger ripped to the side of Arty's garage. Through the yard. Into the neighbor's yard. Down the driveway. It screeched onto the road. Hooked right. Then left. Avoided the blockade and hummed down the road.

Two police cars pursued. Two more came to life. Turned around. Hurried after their comrades.

The special unit operatives were already out of one van. They looked like special forces. All in black. Tactical gear. Night vision goggles. Scoped rifles. They rushed Arty's house. He jumped out of his car. Pulled a pistol. Fired until his magazine was empty.

Titus pulled a police scanner from his bag. He turned it on. Turned it up. There was a lot of chatter. It was hard to understand what they were saying. The plan was coming together splendidly.

The house wasn't in Arty's name. It was in the name of a woman who'd died three years ago. Her children inherited it. They'd had big plans. Renovation. Putting it on the market. Taking the money and moving east where houses were cheaper.

But Noah had seen it as an investment. An investment he didn't want his name attached to. So, he'd talked to the children. Offered them money. Not as much money as the sale of the house. Even this neighborhood had houses selling for half a million or more.

Neither the brother nor sister had been interested. Noah explained things to them. Told them how much better it would be if they accepted his money. The brother got aggressive. He'd died of an overdose not long after.

It was the same kind of overdose that killed Haley and her dad. The same kind that silently killed a lot of Noah's enemies and obstacles. The sister understood after that. She agreed to take the money. To let Noah do what he wanted with the house.

But Noah hadn't been in a forgiving mood. He hadn't given her the money. He'd given her a job instead. Now she was working in one of the warehouses. Making the same wage as everyone else.

She could leave anytime she wanted. Noah wouldn't even bother tracking her down. But he knew where her relatives lived. Where her ex-husband lived with their son. He let her know that. That was all the incentive she needed to keep working.

Noah had given Arty the house as a place to live so he could run the Oakland operations more efficiently. Arty had done a good job. Then he'd gotten overconfident. Gone into business for himself. That was fine. Noah let people have side hustles. So long as they remained loyal and cut him in.

But Arty hadn't done that. Arty had gotten himself in trouble. Noah had given him a second chance. And after a year, Arty had gone back to his old tricks. Noah had once had plans for Arty. Explosive plans.

Deshawn had done the prep work around the house. He'd hidden a cache of ammunition under the floorboards. Inside the cache was a healthy amount of nitroglycerin. The cache was under the floorboards beneath a window on the front of the house.

The exact spot was marked with a dab of white paint. It stood out against the peeling green paint on the rest of the exterior.

It was nothing fancy, but it would get the job done. Noah watched the special police unit advance. They were behind cover. Firing on the front door. The racket was deafening. Lights blinked on across the neighborhood. People were stepping outside. Trying to find out what was happening.

Noah pulled his rifle out of a bag. He rested the barrel on the roof wall. Removed the scope caps. Aimed at the white spot. Waited for the next volley of gunfire. When it erupted, he fired. Nothing happened. He fired twice more. Still nothing.

His angle was wrong. The target was behind the white spot. He was shooting from the side. He adjusted. There was a long pause in gunfire. It lasted ten minutes. Then Arty started shooting again.

Noah fired. There was a boom. The house rattled. Dust exploded from between the wooden siding. The window above the white dot shattered. And then the rest of the ammunition started going off. Crackling like fireworks.

It sounded like a warzone. Well, even more like a warzone than a moment before. The ammunition popped off for a good five minutes. Bullets shot randomly out of the windows. Out of the side of the house. Out of the roof. Then everything went quiet.

The men in black waited. And waited. There was chatter on the radio. They were breaching the rear. Another team went to the front door. Readied a battering ram. There was a countdown. It hit zero. The men in front pounded the door open.

Still nothing from Arty.

The police went in. The radio buzzed. *Subject down.*

Nobody ordered a call to emergency services. Nobody asked for a doctor. The subject was down. Dead. And that was that.

There were still no Oakland PD in sight. No sirens. No signs of anyone coming. If anyone had called 911, the Oakland police hadn't responded. More evidence that Enigma had an inside man high up in the city.

Was it someone on the city council? The mayor? Chief of police? Noah was leaning toward the first possibility. He had the cog in San Francisco. Now he needed to find the one in Oakland. Maybe this situation could be used to kill three birds.

He texted his contacts with Oakland PD. *Do you have orders to stand down this evening?*

It didn't take long for the three to respond. They knew better than to keep him waiting. Two were off duty. They didn't have orders. The third said yes, there was a stand down order. It originated with the city council. She didn't know which member.

Noah texted her back. *Find out.*

Enigma was very protective of their assets. Especially the ones in elected offices. They'd probably spent a lot of time and money getting them there. Probably killed a few contenders to tilt the playing field in their favor. The people who ran corporate were playing chess on a very high level.

But they were still human. They still made mistakes. They could still be revealed. And once he knew enough, Noah had plans of his own.

"Pawn is down." Deshawn grinned. "Just like you planned."

Titus frowned. "Was Arty our pawn? Or their pawn?"

Deshawn laughed. "Hell, Arty was more like a checker piece than a chess piece."

Titus laughed.

Noah chuckled. "What's the news on Derrick and RJ? The police catch them?"

Titus shrugged. "I ain't heard nothing over the radio, boss."

Noah didn't care too much. Derrick and RJ would spend a few days in jail. Then they'd get released without bail. The no bail laws weren't working like the politicians said they would. People were getting out of jail even easier than before.

Which meant the new laws were working exactly like Enigma wanted. Keeping the wheels of justice well oiled. Keeping folks out of jail and on the streets. Sowing chaos.

Derrick and RJ would have some explaining to do when they got out of jail.

And he'd decide whether they kept breathing or not.

CARVER WAS STUCK BETWEEN A COP AND A HARD PLACE.

The aggressive cop lined up for another PIT maneuver. Pulled hard on his steering wheel. Slammed his front bumper into the rear of the Charger. At least he tried to.

Carver saw it coming a mile away. He hit the brakes. The V6 engine wasn't very powerful. It wasn't very fast. But it was lighter than a V8. And the four-wheel disc brakes were good at stopping the lighter vehicle.

The police car slammed into the concrete divider. Bounced off. Carver yanked the steering wheel sideways. Used the police car's momentum. Tapped his front bumper into the rear of the police car.

It spun sideways. The tires gripped the concrete. They gripped it so hard that the rubber couldn't slide. The car was hurtling along at eighty miles per hour. Physics did the rest. The car flipped.

It bounced off its side. Landed on the roof. Started sliding. The other police car was right behind Carver. It hit the other squad car. Clipped the bumper. That was enough to add spin to the other car's slide.

Carver was already around the first police car. He whipped around a civilian car that hadn't pulled over to the side. He was on the downslope of the bridge now. The other police car was close behind. The driver wasn't trying to pull a PIT maneuver. Not after what he'd just witnessed.

They hit San Francisco territory. Carver dove down into the side streets. He avoided an electric bus. Made a hard left onto California Street. Pushed the engine to the limit climbing the hill.

The police car fell behind. Slowed to weave through traffic. Carver was wearing gloves. A mask. A hoodie. Odds were he'd leave behind something identifiable in this car. Maybe hair. Maybe a fingerprint. Maybe some DNA.

He opened the armrest. Pulled out the glass cleaner. Sprayed it on the passenger seat. The dashboard. It foamed up. Filled the car with the stink of ammonia. Dissolved any fingerprints it came into contact with.

It wouldn't do much about hair. Or skin flakes. But there were probably plenty of stray hairs and DNA floating around in this car. Probably enough to camouflage anything he left. Still, better safe than sorry.

He reached Powell Street. Turned left toward the steep downslope. Hit the brakes. Edged the front of the car until it was angling down. Put the car in neutral. He sprayed the steering wheel. The center console. Gave everything a good soaking.

Carver jumped out of the car. Sprayed glass cleaner all over the driver's seat. Closed the door. Gave the car a gentle push. The car started rolling downhill. Powell Street was steep. Real steep. The car picked up speed in a hurry.

There were pedestrians around. People strolling casually. Some of them watching in confusion. Looking from Carver then to the car as it raced downhill.

Carver just stood there. Watched the car. Watched the cop car screech to a halt at the intersection. Watched the cop's face as he looked down Powell Street. Saw the Charger charging downhill. Weaving back and forth. Almost out of control.

The patrol car aimed downhill. Pursued the Charger.

"Dude." A man in dirty sweatpants and a jacket watched the Charger go. His mouth dropped open. "Did you just ditch your car to avoid the cops?"

"Maybe."

The man laughed. Clapped his hands. "That was awesome, man. I hate the cops. They should get rid of them all."

Carver didn't have anything against the police. Some were good. Some were bad. Most were just doing their jobs.

There was a loud crash. The Charger had gone sideways. It was flipping sideways downhill. Bouncing. Sparking. Scattering debris. Making a real spectacle of itself. It slammed into a parked car. Stopped moving.

That was about as good as Carver could have hoped for. The only collateral damage was to property. He hadn't really thought about how it could have killed someone on the way down. It wouldn't have bothered him from an emotional standpoint. But it would have been unprofessional.

He started walking along California Street. Walking downhill the way he'd come. He went to Chinatown. Turned onto the street he'd been on last night. Walked up to the door. Rang the bell. The door buzzed open.

Carver went inside. Zimo was coming downstairs. He saw Carver. Made a show of checking his watch. "You're late."

"Sorry. Got tied up at the office."

"You're two hours late." He motioned Carver to follow. "But we saved you something."

Carver's stomach grumbled. He was hungry. "Thanks."

"Why do you smell like ammonia?"

Carver shrugged. "I was cleaning my car."

"Ah, so that's why you're late." Zimo stopped in front of a door. He opened it. Unfamiliar odors drifted out.

"I mean, it's one reason." Carver followed him inside. His stomach grumbled louder.

The woman he'd helped the night before appeared. She smiled. Said a lot in Mandarin. Carver didn't understand a word of it. He hadn't done much time in any Asian countries. And the closest he'd been to China was still a long way away.

"My aunt said you stink like a janitor."

"It's a living."

Zimo narrowed his eyes. "You don't seem like the janitor type."

His aunt was a small woman. But she pushed Carver into a chair at the table. She set a bowl of thick soup in front of him. He took the wooden spoon she offered. Tasted it. It was thick and meaty. Tasted good. Tasted better than anything he'd had in a while.

"Tell your aunt it's delicious."

Zimo relayed the message. His aunt beamed. She touched his hand. His cheek. Kept talking. Looked at Zimo expectantly.

Zimo smiled. "She says you're very handsome. And very big."

"Is she single?"

Zimo laughed. He kept laughing for a while. "You have a strange way about you, friend. You don't smile much, but you're funny."

Carver kept eating.

"So, Cutter, what is it you really do?"

Carver wiped his mouth. Leaned back in the chair. It creaked under his weight. "What kind of gang has fire-breathing pandas?"

Zimo glanced at the tattoo on his forearm. "It's not a gang. We were just young and foolish and decided to get matching tattoos."

"Like a gang."

"Except not a gang." Zimo sat down across from Carver. "We do have a collective. A group of concerned citizens who want to keep our streets safe. And not all of us are Chinese."

"Well, that's good." Carver smiled and nodded at Zimo's aunt. "Thank you for dinner."

"Surely you're not full yet." Zimo smiled. "That was only the first course."

His aunt brought a plate with noodles. Dumped meat and vegetables on the noodles. Gave him chopsticks to use.

Carver got to it. It was delicious. "Tell her it's even better than the soup."

Zimo told her.

She smiled and talked to Zimo.

"She says yes, she's single. But don't tell my uncle."

Carver cracked a grin. "I can keep a secret."

Zimo got a laugh out of that. Then he grew serious. "Cutter, this area is suffering from a pandemic."

"Like a virus?"

He shook his head. "A crime pandemic. It is systemic. It comes from the top. The police almost never patrol our neighborhoods anymore. They don't do anything about the criminals preying upon our people. The mayor and city council have been unsympathetic."

"I'm sorry to hear that." Carver kept eating. "Maybe people should vote differently."

Zimo laughed, this time without humor. "You cannot vote these people out of office. They are untouchable. It's like a greater power ensures they remain in power."

Carver knew the reason. The organization that controlled the Farm probably had operations in these parts. The area bore all the symptoms. But that was far outside the parameters of his mission.

He just wanted his phone back. It was his only connection to Paola. Everything else was a bonus.

He wasn't here to solve anybody's problems.

CHAPTER 17

It wasn't up to Carver to save anyone.

It wasn't up to any one individual. That was a collective decision. One that required people taking action and making changes. The US government had used Carver to make changes. Changes that probably should have been left to the populaces of the countries he'd been in. That wasn't the life he wanted anymore.

Carver changed the subject. "You know a guy named Noah?"

Zimo flinched. "Not personally. But I know of him. He is what you might refer to as a kingpin in these parts. He keeps the streets flooded with fentanyl. He runs the crime rings throughout the city and probably Oakland. He is to be feared and avoided."

Carver pincered a piece of meat with the chopsticks. Popped it in his mouth. "Where can I find him?"

"Why would you want to?"

"His people took my stuff. I want it back."

Zimo stared blankly at him for a moment. "How did they get your things?"

"They broke into my car."

"You don't look the least bit concerned about what I told you." Zimo leaned forward on his elbows. "Noah is just as untouchable as our political leaders. If you go looking for him, he will find you instead. And he will probably kill you."

"Ah. So that's how I find him."

"Do you not understand me?" Zimo's look grew harder. "You do not want his attention on you. We have already lost enough people trying to put a stop to his activities in our area."

"Lost people?"

"They vanish. Reappear sometimes hours or days later. And they are dead from a fentanyl overdose."

Carver nodded. "It's a very easy way to kill people."

"You speak as if from experience."

Carver continued eating. "You mind if I stop by for dinner again?"

"Cutter, please be serious." Zimo reached a hand across the table toward him. "Don't go after Noah."

"I'm not going after him. Just my stuff. I'm sure I can reason with the man."

"He's not a man. He's an animal!" Zimo stood abruptly. "A very intelligent, very cunning animal. An animal who is very fond of Sun Tzu and has studied him extensively."

"How do you know that?"

"Because all of his Chinese victims were found with fortune cookies in their pockets."

"Seems kind of racist."

"And the fortunes were all quotes from the Art of War."

"Definitely racist."

Carver knew Noah's type. Intelligent. Resourceful. Strategic. The kind of person who rose to power not by force, but charisma. By bringing others to his side. Then again, Carver might be completely wrong. There were plenty of smart street thugs who rose to the top through violence.

He'd save the psychological diagnosis for when he met the man in person.

"Cutter, we need help with basic street crime in our neighborhoods. Your mere presence would be of great aid to us." Zimo took a deep breath. Recovered his calm. "We would be happy to pay you. To feed you. Even give you a place to stay."

The proposition had some appeal to Carver. It would be like Club Periclean. Except he wouldn't just be a club bouncer. He'd be a neighborhood bouncer. A paid patrol officer. But instead of a nice beach to relax on during the day, he'd be stuck in these dirty streets.

Even at its filthiest, San Francisco was still a lovely place. Still scenic. Still beautiful. But Carver yearned to get back to the wilderness. To keep trekking across the nation. The last thing he wanted was to be tied down with a job.

"That's a generous offer, but I can't accept. I have places to go. Places to see."

"Don't you mean people to see?"

Carver shook his head. "Nope. People cause problems."

"That's true." Zimo sighed. "I fear you won't survive to see those places. Not if you go to Noah and demand your things back."

"It's not just the things, it's the principle of the matter." Carver waggled a hand. "And also the things." He didn't want to explain that it was just about one thing. About a burner phone with a number on it.

"What kind of things?"

"Nothing in particular." Carver pushed back his chair. Stood. Nodded at Zimo's aunt. "Tell her the food was amazing."

Zimo did. She talked to him. "Aunt Lin says thank you for her money and her life. You are always welcome here."

"I might take her up on that offer. Haven't found food this good anywhere in the city yet."

Zimo told Mae. She smiled. Rubbed Carver's arm. Patted his rump. Said something in a different tone of voice.

Carver held up a hand when Zimo started to translate. "No need to translate that one." He pecked a kiss on the woman's cheek. Opened the door and left.

Zimo followed him downstairs. "Cutter, if you change your mind, you can find us at the store or here."

"I won't change my mind." Carver studied the other man for a moment. "My real name is Carver."

Zimo bowed slightly. "Thank you for being honest. I know it's hard to trust strangers."

"It's just as hard to trust people you think you know too." Carver shrugged. "Well, so long. And thanks for all the food."

"You are most welcome." Zimo went back inside. Shut the door behind him.

Carver walked back to the junction of California and Powell. The Charger was gone. The car it had plowed into was gone. There was some glass on the street. Some pieces of plastic. That was it.

The same guy in the dirty sweatpants was still there. This time he was sitting on the side of the road. Sitting in front of a brick wall. The wall belonged to a fancy hotel behind it. The man had set up a small tent. It hadn't been there earlier.

He looked at Carver. "Hey, are you the same guy who pushed the car down the hill?"

"What car? What are you talking about?"

"Dude, you wouldn't believe it." The man told Carver the story. He embellished it slightly. Made it sound like he'd helped the man who jumped out of the car. "Four police cars came. Some detective was here. They were asking everyone questions."

"What kind of questions?"

"They were looking for two men." He described Derrick and RJ.

"They weren't in the car?"

He shook his head. "Nah, just one dude. A big guy. A little bigger than you. Like maybe a foot taller and more muscular."

"Sounds like a big guy."

"Huge guy." He spread his arms wide as he could. "Monstrous, man."

Carver found it interesting that the police were automatically looking for Derrick and RJ. At the most, they should have only been looking for the owner of the car. Derrick was not the owner.

Carver knew because he'd looked in the glove compartment. He'd found the registration. It was registered to Monique Jones. Most likely the woman who lived at the address where Carver left Derrick and RJ.

So, why weren't they looking for her instead of two young men?

The police knew about the Charger. They knew who drove it and who rode in it. They already knew more than they should have. Probably because someone in the police department was on Noah's payroll.

"Who asked you about the two men in the car?"

The man was looking blankly down the street. He blinked out of it. "Huh? Oh, um, Duffin? No, Duffers." He looked up. Like he was trying real hard to drag something out of his brain. "Duffy." He snapped his fingers. "Yeah, Detective Duffy."

"He was the first one to ask you this?"

He nodded. "Yeah. The other cops didn't even talk to me. They were standing around the car. Making fun of the cop who chased it downhill."

Carver nodded at the tent. "Do you normally live up here?"

"Man, I live all over." The man grinned. "This is the life, you know?"

"You use fentanyl?"

"Hell no, man." He shook his head. "That stuff is cancer. I stick to the devil's lettuce. Keeps me chill, you know? Keeps me alive. Ivory just makes you dead."

"Ivory is a name for fentanyl?"

"Yeah. That's what most around here call it."

"Why live here? Why not go into the forest north of the bridge?"

"Because I like civilization, man." He pointed at the city. "And where else can you get a view like this for under a million bucks?"

"Makes sense." Carver began to realize something. Something he should have thought of before. There were people like this all over the city. People who weren't insane. People who saw everything happening every day. People who knew the terrain like their own back yard. Because the city was their yard.

He risked a question. "You heard of Noah?"

The man nodded. "Yeah. King of the streets around here. I'd stay away from his people if I were you."

"You know where he's headquartered?"

"Why, man? You suicidal?"

"No. His people took some of my stuff. I want it back."

"You'll catch a bullet dude. Don't go near them." The man shook his head vehemently.

"I just need to know. He has something that's very precious to me. A family heirloom. I want to negotiate for it."

"Aw, man, that sucks." He sighed. "I don't think he'll give it back. If he does, you'll probably have to pay heavy for it."

"I'm prepared for that."

"Well, he's got a lot of headquarters around town. I heard a guy say his main place is in the Financial District somewhere. Or maybe it's in the Tenderloin. Like near that building where all the tech companies are."

"I don't know where that is. I know where Tenderloin is."

"It's the building with the blue bird on it. Twitter, but they changed the name to X."

"His base is inside there?"

"Near there. Not sure where." The man shrugged. "That's about as close as I can get you."

"It's close enough." Carver nodded at him. "Thanks. Dude."

"I would say you're welcome, man, but I'm afraid for your life. Noah is harsh. Real harsh."

"I appreciate your concern, friend." Carver tipped an imaginary hat at him and started walking down California Street. He was tired. Ready for bed. And his tent was a long way away.

NOAH FELT GREAT.

He felt like he'd pulled off a real coup. Arty down. A traitor exposed. And now two of Enigma's political pawns had been revealed.

Titus noticed. "You're grinning like a madman, boss."

"It was a productive night." Noah looked at the latest text from his cop in Oakland. He had another name. Another city council member.

"And we got popcorn." Deshawn sipped a beer. "That was quality entertainment."

Noah leaned back in his chair. His beer was sitting on the roof. Half full. Forgotten. He was moving chess pieces in his head. Playing out multiple scenarios. Trying to find one that wouldn't end with Enigma descending on him like the specter of death.

He didn't control anyone on the city council. He controlled people who were around them. Clerks. Cops. Security. They were controlled by the carrot. Good old fashioned dollar bills. And if that didn't work, there was the threat of the stick.

Nobody wanted the stick. Especially not Noah's stick. Tasha knew that all too well. So did everyone else. They'd heard the stories.

Enigma had other means of control. Money was part of it. Power was another. But they had the most powerful carrot of all. A shared ideology. A desire to transform the world. Noah was fine with transformation. Just not the kind of transformation they had in mind.

He needed control of the apparatus. But that was the sticking point. The enemy had superior numbers. Superior fighters. They had the upper hand in every way. It was a challenge he'd been working on for a year now.

Now he felt closer than ever to cracking that nut. And he would do it Enigma style. Poisoning the target from the inside out. Just like they'd done to his city.

Noah stood and stretched. He picked up his rifle case. He'd already collected the ammo casings. Tucked them inside the case. Deshawn collected their beer bottles. The popcorn tins. Anything they'd touched. He stuffed them into a heavy trash bag.

Then they took the stairs down. Put the bags and case into the Prius' trunk. Got in the car. Titus drove them back to Market Square. Into the warehouse.

Noah put the rifle into his vault. Removed the ammo casings from the case. Locked the vault. Tasha was still in the office. Glasses on, face buried in the computer screen. She was stubborn. Hard to control. But he couldn't fault her work ethic.

"You're here late."

She flinched. Blinked. Looked at him. "I'm behind thanks to the field trips you keep taking me on."

"You need to get out more often. Experience the real world."

She folded her arms. Stared at him. "Need something, master?"

He grinned. "As a matter of fact, I do." Noah handed her the ammo casings. "Refills."

"I'll put it on my to-do list." She took out a cardboard box. The contents rattled. She dropped the casings inside. They clinked against other casings.

He walked around the desk. Looked at the screen. There was a video on the screen. On it was familiar footage. A cluster of modular buildings. "Looking at this again?"

She nodded. "I noticed something."

"Show me."

She resumed playback. Two figures exited one of the buildings. One was medium build. The other was taller. Bigger. Both were wearing dark clothing. Hoodies. Facemasks.

"What's new? Looks the same to me."

"Your contact said these guys were part of the crew there." She froze the image. Zoomed in on the shorter figure. Zoomed in on his hand. There was something there. She switched to a different window. In it was an image.

It was the same image frozen on the screen. But it was cropped. It was enhanced. The thing in the man's hand wasn't blurry. It was clearly a black box with a red switch. A remote detonator.

Tasha switched back to the video. She moved the window to the side. Opened another video. This was a view of the outside of the compound. She played the first video. The two men moved out of view. They walked out of the front gate.

An instant later, the buildings exploded violently. The camera feed went blank.

Tasha rewound the external video. Zoomed in on the shorter man's hand. His arm moved like he was raising it slightly. His hand wasn't visible from this angle. Then his arm moved slightly. Like he was using something in his hand.

"The buildings exploded an instant later." She leaned back in her chair.

Noah sat down in a chair behind her. Enigma had organizations in other cities and regions. He'd sent people to other cities. Had them burrow into the criminal organizations there. Find out if they were affiliates of Enigma.

One of his moles had found one in Oregon. It was called the Farm. It had been massive. It had roots spanning all over the state. It had owned politicians, criminal organizations, and more. And it had still just been a small part of Enigma.

His first mole had found their headquarters. It was quite a setup. Hidden deep in the forest. Trafficking in legal drugs, in weapons, and more. It made Noah's operation look small.

Discovering that had led him to look more closely at his area. Find out if there was something like the Farm controlling his area. But there was nothing. Just a loose confederation of organizations.

All of them reported to a higher power. All of them reported to Enigma.

Noah had once just controlled a part of San Francisco. He'd dealt in soft drugs. In prostitution. In fencing. In chop shops for stolen cars. Things had been good. Business had been profitable.

Customers were happy. Bent cops were happy. The DA was well paid to look the other way. Insurance paid the citizens for their losses. It had been a perpetual economic engine. Everyone benefited whether they wanted to or not.

Crime was a necessary function of society. Black markets, sex trade, drugs, and so forth fueled the underbelly of civilization. Without it, there would be no chaos. No adversity. Nothing pushing for the advancement of humanity.

But too much of anything was destructive. Too much chaos. Too much order. Too much authority. Too much anarchy. All of it was counterproductive. You needed a balance.

Enigma was out to destroy that balance. To tilt the city so hard into chaos that it could never recover. At least, that was what it looked like. And he couldn't understand why.

Enigma's representatives had approached Noah. Given him an ultimatum. Told him he could keep doing business as usual, but the primary drug of choice would now be fentanyl. His people would no longer push out homeless encampments. They would allow them to grow.

Shoplifting would no longer be a penny ante crime. He would organize retail theft rings. Turn it into a major enterprise. They would ensure that state and local laws were changed so it wouldn't be a felony.

They'd done that and more. Changed bail laws. Changed the definition of petty larceny. Changed what was a felony and what wasn't.

Noah hadn't liked the ultimatum. He wasn't used to taking orders. But they were offering complete control of San Francisco. All of it united under his control. And they weren't taking no for an answer.

He found out an entire Chinese gang had been eradicated because they'd refused Enigma's offer. The same had happened in other parts of the town. The gang leaders who refused were vanished or killed violently and publicly.

Noah had accepted their offer. All had been great at first. But here they were three years later. Everything had declined so rapidly that he could hardly believe it. His city was in a death spiral.

He might be a crime boss, but he loved his city. He wanted it to flourish. When the city did well, he did well. If it kept going like this, he would be king of nothing. But to stop it, he'd have to stop Enigma.

How was he supposed to do that? They had resources. Men with military experience. Powerful politicians. All he had were street thugs and a few bent cops. The briefcase was the key. The contents could solve everything.

In the meantime, he saw something else that could help him fend off Enigma. Not something, but someone. The person in the video. Not the short guy. His companion.

The big guy.

CHAPTER 18

Noah knew who the big man in the video was.

He didn't need to be a genius to figure it out. The Farm had been destroyed a few months ago. Now Enigma was searching for a man named Carver. A big man. A tall man. One who matched the description of the man in the video.

Noah pulled his chair next to Tasha's. " Enigma is only looking for one man. Why not this second guy?"

"They're looking for him too. Just not out here. Back east."

"You know this how?"

"One of your people over in Atlanta. Enigma doesn't have a foothold over there yet. They had a major setback with something called Breakstone. A private military company, I think."

"Damned corporate has its fingerprints all over the country." Noah pointed a finger at the big man on the screen. "That has to be Carver."

Tasha flinched. "How—" She stared at him. "You're a smart man. Too bad you are who you are."

Noah smiled. "Keep complimenting me like that and I'll think you like me."

She scowled. "It's an objective fact. Not a compliment."

"Whatever you say, darling." He leaned back. "Tell me what you were going to say."

"The man in Montana sold a Dodge Ramcharger to a big guy. Your mole at the Farm said that at one point they were looking for someone coming in a Dodge Ramcharger."

"Ah." Noah clapped his hands once. "Baby girl, you found the puzzle pieces, didn't you?"

"Yes."

"The question is, why?" He stood up. Walked behind her. Put his hands on her shoulders and squeezed. What he squeezed wasn't soft. Her shoulders were muscular. Taut. And not just because she was tense.

"It was a mystery. I wanted to solve it." She shrugged from under his grasp. Slid out of her chair and stood. "Don't think it's for you. But I don't like Enigma any more than you do. I don't like what it's done to this city or the people. I don't like their end goals."

"What do you think their goals are?"

"They want to destroy the economy. Implement socialism. Gain more power."

Noah nodded. "I can understand why you think that. The peons recruited by Enigma can't stop talking about socialism. But I don't think that's what Enigma wants. I think they're just using ideology and anti-government sentiment to control people."

Tasha blinked. Like it was something she hadn't considered. "Well, whatever they're doing, I don't like it."

"Me either."

"I find that hard to believe."

"You don't have to believe it, baby girl." Noah smirked. "I know you have an ulterior motive for looking into this. I know it's not just because you don't like Enigma."

"It's because I think this Carver guy and his companion might be able to get rid of them." She paused. "And their proxies."

Noah clapped his hands once. "And the truth comes out."

"If you were in my position, what would you want?"

"You're here voluntarily." Noah took her hand. Squeezed it hard enough to make her wince. "Remember that."

"Because my sister—"

"Because your sister stole from me. You voluntarily stepped in to save her." Noah shrugged. "And I magnanimously agreed." He released her hand. "Not only that, but I keep track of her every move. I make sure she's behaving. And, by the way, she is doing splendidly."

Tasha worked her jaw back and forth. "We made a deal. But I never agreed to killing for you."

"You agreed to do what I told you to do. No questions asked." Noah waved a hand. "Enough of this. Carver is supposedly in this city. I want him found. I want him brought to me. And then we will find out if he has what it takes to help us."

"And if he doesn't?"

"I can always use another man on the streets."

Tasha looked skeptical. "He doesn't seem like the type to become a street thug."

"How do you know?" Noah pointed at the frozen video. "That's all you know about him."

"He blew up an entire compound with plastic explosives." She laughed. "What makes you think you can control him?"

"I can control anyone, darling." Noah gripped her shoulder. Gripped it hard. "You've done good work today. Go home and rest. You deserve it."

Tasha stared at him expressionlessly. "Okay."

Noah released her. He left the office. Left the building. Went to the motor pool. Climbed into his Challenger. He couldn't stop thinking about Carver. What drove a man to such lengths? Drove him to find a remote compound in the Oregonian forest and blow it to hell?

Was he a man on a crusade? Had the Farm done something to him or a loved one and triggered the reaction? Why was Carver in San Francisco? Did he know about corporate? Did he know they had operations here?

Or was it something else?

The man was a blank slate. An enigma. Just as mysterious as Enigma the organization. He'd come out of nowhere and dealt a blow to them. But why?

Noah took out his phone. Ran a search on the name Amos Carver. There were a lot of results. None of them about this Amos Carver. Only one story stuck out. One from an independent news website in Miami.

A reporter named Doug Weaver had written a long, rambling piece about assassinations and violence. The name Carver came up twice. Once in regard to a woman who'd fallen to her death next to a popular nightclub.

The second mention was in Morganville, Georgia. About a war between a private military company and a Brazilian drug cartel. It was the name of the PMC that stood out.

Breakstone.

The dots were there, plain as day. Breakstone. The Farm. Maybe corporate had something in Miami too. He had no idea. But it looked like Carver had crossed the entire country just to blow up the Farm.

That explained the weapons in his vehicle. All the ammunition. Carver was planning something big in this city. And Noah's people had stolen his supplies. Which meant Noah didn't need to find Carver at all.

Carver would come to him.

Because Carver would be looking to recover his supplies. He'd be asking all over the city. Trying to find out who took his stuff. Where to find it. And one name would come up repeatedly. Noah.

Noah was excited. He and this Carver fellow had a common goal. The destruction of Enigma. Carver's method was elemental. Destructive. Noah's was more strategic. Together, they could bring down the beast.

But first, he needed answers to important questions.

He didn't know where Enigma was located. He couldn't send someone to blow up a place if he didn't know where it was. Likewise, he couldn't poison an organization he knew next to nothing about.

Tonight's raid on Arty proved one thing. Enigma would use proxies whenever possible. But they would also send in their own men if the threat was considered major. The special unit that accompanied SFPD had come directly from Enigma.

Noah had no doubt they were the best the organization had to offer. And he had lured them out to do his own dirty work. What he had to do next was find out where they came from. Infiltrate their organization.

He had a single contact. An anonymous contact within Enigma. They rarely contacted him unless something wasn't going according to plan. It was also what they hadn't contacted him about that sounded alarm bells.

They had to know about the briefcase. It was possible the briefcase belonged to them. But it was doubtful. Because if his guy was right about the contents, then Noah could deal a pivotal blow to Enigma.

They hadn't requested his help finding it. They hadn't activated any idealists in the warehouse ranks to look for it. They'd done that before. Bypassed Noah and used their recruits to do things for them. Things they didn't want Noah to know about.

Which meant if Enigma knew about the briefcase, they had their own people looking for it. Specialists. Experts. Dangerous people. People Noah couldn't stop.

His street level enforcers weren't cut out for fighting those types. Enigma wasn't like the Farm. It wasn't like Noah's organization. It didn't recruit unskilled civilians to work for it. It was at the center. The core.

Unless and until he put his hands on that briefcase, he'd have to create a contingency plan. He'd need his own person with a special set of skills to infiltrate Enigma. To destroy it from within. And he knew exactly who could do that. The same person who'd destroyed the Farm.

Amos Carver.

CARVER NEEDED HELP.

Cheap help was easy to find. He had plenty of local currency. There were plenty of locals eager to earn it. The problem was most of them weren't up to the task. Years of drug abuse had made them worthless for even the simplest of tasks.

They were fentanyl addicts. Mindless zombies. Just looking for that next fix. Willing to do or say anything to get it. People like the marijuana guy were a better choice. The problem was finding them.

Carver had woken up early. Had breakfast at a nearby diner. Just bacon and eggs were enough to set him back twenty bucks. But a man had to eat, and it was the only place still in business. Most of the other restaurants were boarded up and gone.

The encampment was bustling with activity when he came back. Tommy and his girlfriend were still in their tent. They had plenty of ivory to last them a while. The others were getting ready to hustle for money.

For most of them, that meant shoplifting. Taking it to the local fence. Receiving payment in fentanyl or cash.

One of them was covered in purple glitter. Carver could smell him from twenty feet away. It wasn't a normal dirty smell. It was something else. Something rank.

"It was a backpack!" The man looked at his hands. Tried to wipe off the glitter. But it didn't work. "It started spraying this stuff all over me. And it stank real bad."

The others were laughing. One guy gagged whenever he caught a whiff. There was one sober looking guy in the group. He was covering his nose.

"It's a YouTuber," he said. "I've seen the videos. The guy's name is Rober or Robber. Something like that."

Glitter guy slumped. "Man, I can't catch a break! I need some cash fast."

Carver might be able to help him out. He ignored the stench and walked over. "Anyone here heard of Noah?"

Glitter guy nodded. "Yeah, everyone has. His people buy stuff from us. We take it to a fence down the road. The whole sidewalk is covered in stolen stuff."

"And the cops don't bust it?"

The sober guy laughed. "Cops don't care about it. They're probably ordered not to touch it. It's part of the military police industrial complex."

"Anyone know where Noah's headquarters are?"

They looked at each other. Shook their heads.

"Why would you want to find Noah, anyway?" The sober guy looked concerned. "He's a king in these parts. He even—" He stopped talking. Shook his head like he realized he was about to say something he shouldn't. "I'd just stay away from him."

"Yeah, stay away!" Glitter guy said.

Carver thumped on Tanner's tent. No answer. The heavy-duty zipper was secured with a heavy padlock. A knife in the fabric would bypass the security easily. But Carver wasn't going to do that.

Tommy staggered around the corner. He rubbed his eyes. Looked at Carver. "Is Tanner in there?"

"It's locked up."

"Damn, man. I'm out of food."

"You get food from Tanner?"

"Yeah. Sometimes." Tommy heaved. "I'm on empty, man."

"I can cut open his tent." Carver wasn't serious. But he was curious as to why no one had done it yet.

Tommy waved his hands. "No, no, no. Don't do that."

"Why not?"

"Tanner will put you in the ground if you mess with his stuff, man." Tommy heaved again. "He already put one guy down. Dragged him across the Embarcadero. Tossed him in the bay."

"Right in front of everyone?" Carver pointed to the pedestrian traffic across the road. "Lots of witnesses."

"He did it at night. Made a point to let everyone know what would happen to them if they tried the same thing."

It looked like the violent approach worked with Tommy after all. But Carver didn't mind. "I haven't seen him."

Tommy held his stomach. "You got anything to eat, man? I'm dying here."

Carver didn't like giving handouts. Especially not to people like Tommy. It made them reliant on him. Made them expect things without earning them. "Why would you go to Tanner for food?"

"He goes out to the city every day. Always brings back food and sells it." Tommy shrugged. "Everybody's got to hustle, you know?"

"What's Tanner's deal anyway?"

Tommy shook his head. "I can't talk about it. I ain't got a death wish."

"I have food. I'll trade it for information."

His eyes brightened then saddened. "Oh, man. I'm so hungry. But I don't want to die either."

"Will Tanner really kill you if you tell me about him?"

"He was real open about it when he first came here. Then he got secretive. Told us not to say anything."

"I won't tell him you told me." Carver motioned toward his tent. "Trade, or no deal?"

Tommy pressed a hand to his sunken stomach. "I'll tell you. But don't say a word to him, okay?"

It looked like the real king of this tent city was Tanner. And there was something very strange about him. Carver went to his tent. He grabbed a few ration bars. They weren't a full meal, but they'd do in a pinch.

He held them out to Tommy. Tommy tried to grab them. Carver pulled them back. "Talk first."

Tommy's hands trembled. "Man, I'm gonna die—"

"You're going to die if you don't tell me something and do it fast."

"Okay, okay." He held his hands up in front of him. The universal surrender gesture. "Tanner was looking for someone." He went silent. Stared blankly for a minute. "I think it was a sister." He snapped his fingers. "Yeah. A sister. He showed us pictures."

"Had anyone seen her?"

"No." He blew out his breath. "Man, you know how many people go missing around here? How many people die every day? It ain't as bad as Los Angeles, but it's bad."

"Do you know the name Noah?"

Tommy went pale. "Yeah. Everyone around here knows that name. I'd rather mess with Tanner than mess with Noah."

"Do you know where his headquarters are?"

"Yeah. And you don't want to go near there, man. Not unless you want to die."

"He just kills anyone who goes there?"

Tommy shook his head. "I just mean, come on, man. He runs everything in the city. He's the king. The man literally enslaves people. Forces them to work for him. And if he doesn't like you, you'll end up dead real fast."

Carver gave Tommy the nutrition bars. "Tell me more."

Tommy gobbled down the first bar. Gobbled down the second. Then he took a breather. "He's down near the civic center. There's an old department store. It closed down a few years ago. He took it over. Runs everything out of there."

"How do you know all this, Tommy?"

Tommy laughed. It was a sad laugh. A resigned laugh. "Man, I worked down there. I worked in the tech offices across the road. I was a software coder. Making good money. Over three hundred grand a year."

Carver whistled. "Good money."

"Yeah. But it was stressful. I needed to chill a little." He shrugged. "Marijuana wasn't doing it. One of my friends got some ivory. And it did the trick. Did it good."

"How long ago was this?"

"Almost three years ago." He shrugged. "You couldn't find ivory on the streets here before then. Noah didn't allow it on his territory. Then we had the pandemic. The lockdowns. Everything changed after that. Suddenly, ivory was the only thing being pushed on the streets."

"Strange. Why the sudden about-face?"

"I don't know, man." Tommy peeled the wrapper off another nutrition bar. He glanced at his tent. It was a guilty look. Like he was eating something he should be giving to his girlfriend. "I got hooked. I stopped working. Kept scarfing ivory. In three months, I went from paying off school loans and renting a nice apartment to the streets."

Carver nodded. "Sounds like you know what you did wrong. Like you regret it."

"I do, man. I regret it so much. But I can't stop. I'm too weak." He shivered. "I tried to stop. Tried it twice. It hurts too much, man. I'd rather keep taking it."

"How old are you, Tommy?"

He looked down. "Thirty-two."

Carver thought he looked older. A lot older. Hard drug use would do that to a person. But he didn't say anything. He went back into his tent. Got two more bars. Gave them to Tommy. "These are for your girlfriend, okay? Not for you."

A tear trickled down Tommy's face. "I'm sorry I gave you a hard time, man. But I'm in charge of this place. I have to make sure we don't get any bad people here, you know?"

It was laughable. Ridiculous. And sad. Carver nodded. "I understand. I'm leaving. Keep an eye on my stuff, okay?"

Tommy put a hand on Carver's arm. "Man, don't go looking for Noah. Don't get on his radar. Nothing good will come of it."

"You're right about that," Carver said. Except the nothing good was going to be on Noah's end. Carver just had to figure out how to get in and out with his stuff first.

He went back into his tent. Dug the shoulder holster out of his clothing bag. Put it on under the hoodie. Put his newly acquired Glock into the holster. Zipped up his hoodie. Tucked a facemask in his pocket.

He locked up the tent. Walked to Market Street. Got himself a day pass for the transit system at a kiosk. Hopped on the trolley. The conductor rang the bell and the trolley shifted into motion.

He was on his way to Noah.

CHAPTER 19

Carver hopped off the trolley.

He was a couple blocks from the department store. He would walk around the area. Case the place. Find out what he was up against. If it was anything like the Farm, infiltration wouldn't be a problem.

He was already wearing the official uniform of the Farm. A black hoodie and facemask. Hopefully, Noah's people dressed the same. Hopefully, he could just blend in with the rest of them. Just like he'd done at the Farm.

First, he had to get past the perimeter.

A silver Toyota showed him exactly where to go. It screeched around the corner. Rolled down a street next to the department store. Vanished around the corner. It was the same silver Toyota he'd seen before.

The woman in the driver seat was wearing a facemask with the Gucci logo on it. It hid her face, but it differentiated her from everyone else. Made her stand out. Identified her as one of Noah's roving car thieves.

There was an army of the dead along the sidewalk next to the street. Lots of people in dirty clothes. Ragged coats. Torn pants. They had gaunt faces. Dead eyes. All the signs of homelessness. All the signs of heavy drug use.

Dead men walking.

There were some nicely dressed people among the homeless crowd. Maybe ordinary citizens. Dressed for work. Walking hurriedly down the sidewalk. Eager to get away from the dregs of society.

And then there were the people in hoodies and facemasks. Most of them dressed in black. Some wearing fingerless gloves. Some sporting anarchy symbols. Others displaying the Soviet hammer and sickle. Just like the people working for the Farm.

This was the place.

Carver fit right in with the crowd. He was taller than most. Bigger. He slumped his shoulders to look smaller. Hunched over. A pair of overweight women walked toward him. Their facemasks were pulled down under their chins.

They gave him dirty looks. One of them muttered something to her companion. The other laughed. The first glared at Carver with dead eyes. Flipped him the bird. Held his gaze until she and her companion walked past.

Carver wasn't sure what to make of it. He looked at his clothing. It was plain. Black. Nothing on it. It was like the woman had randomly picked him from the crowd. Maybe it was a prank of some kind.

He glanced back. Saw a thin kid in a gray hoodie and mask behind him. No symbols on his clothing. The kid's eyes brightened. He hurried to catch up. "They really hate you."

Carver frowned. The frown was hidden under his facemask, but it probably reached his eyes because the kid flinched. "You must have me mistaken for someone else."

The kid gulped. "Nah, I've seen you around plenty. You're the big guy who unloads the heavy stuff."

"That's the other big guy. Not me."

The kid laughed. "Oh, my bad. I don't think I've seen anyone's faces ever." He touched his mask. "The mandatory facemask rule. I mean, I know why we have to wear them, but it makes it hard to make friends."

"Those women weren't wearing facemasks."

"Yeah, they keep them pulled down when they leave. Put them back up when they're working." He shrugged. "They're just picking on you because you're in shape."

"Am I?"

The kid looked confused. "I mean, you look like you're in shape. You've got big shoulders and big arms."

"What's your name?"

The kid hesitated. "Uh, you can call me Jeremy. That's my work name."

"I'm Cutter."

"Whoa, that's a cool work name."

Carver assumed a friendlier demeanor. Jeremy was his ticket to finding his things. "I haven't been here long. This place is confusing. Can you give me the nickel tour?"

"Brenda and Janine are the ones who usually give the initiation tours." He pointed a thumb over his shoulder.

Carver glanced back at the women. "Those two are Brenda and Janine?"

"Yeah." Jeremy grimaced. "Maybe I can give you the tour. I just don't have access to a lot of areas. Only the warehouse."

"Sounds good to me." Carver crossed the street. There were several rollup doors in front of loading docks. Most of the docks were raised off the ground. Designed to receive loads from tractor trailers.

There were two extra wide rollup doors. Both ground level. The silver Toyota was parked in front of one. A big guy was unloading suitcases and boxes from the trunk.

Jeremy looked at the other big guy. "That's who I thought you were."

The other guy was several inches shorter. He was bulky. Built like a bodybuilder. Muscles strained against his clothing. Carver wasn't built like that. He didn't want to be built like that either.

Muscles like that reduced flexibility. Made everyday tasks harder. Made it harder to scratch your back if you had an itch. But it looked impressive. At least to an extent.

Carver and Jeremy walked past the silver Toyota. The Gucci girl was talking to the muscular guy. Laughing. The facemask covered her mouth, but her eyes were smiling.

The muscular guy was enjoying it too. He flexed his arm. Let her touch it. Spoke softly to her. They shared another laugh.

Jeremey lowered his voice. "That's Monique. She's one of the top earners here."

"And the big guy?"

"I think his name is Tyrone, but he never talks to me. Just looks at me dirty."

Carver made a show of looking Jeremy up and down. "Where's your anarchy symbol?"

Jeremey laughed. "I'm not part of that crowd. I was a software engineer. Used to work across the street. Then the pandemic closed us down. A lot of us got laid off after the lockdowns ended."

Carver figured there were a lot of people with stories like Tommy's and Jeremy's. "And now you're doing this?"

He looked down. "Yeah. I couldn't afford my rent. I got a loan from Noah. But then I couldn't find another local job. Not even a remote job. Back then the tech companies were fighting over software engineers. Giving us everything we wanted and more. After the lockdowns started, everything dried up."

"Seems strange."

He stopped and turned around. Looked at the giant Microsoft sign on the building across the street. "When everything closed down, most of the people in my department packed up and moved across the country. A lot of them ended up in Georgia, Texas, or Florida."

"Because they could work remotely."

Jeremy nodded. "Yeah. They could rake in California salaries and pay Texas prices for houses."

"Did the layoffs affect them?"

He shook his head. "Apparently, the human resources department had people who regularly combed our social media accounts. They didn't like what some of us had to say about the lockdowns. They didn't like our stances on certain company policies."

Carver raised an eyebrow. "You just put your inner thoughts out there for all the world to see?"

Jeremy sighed. "In retrospect, it was pretty dumb. But I grew up with social media. I never thought stating my opinion in a constructive way would get me fired and blacklisted."

"Never let people know what you're thinking."

Jeremy's forehead wrinkled. "But it's so hard. I just can't let other people keep saying what they're saying unchallenged."

"And where did that get you?"

"Here. In debt to a crime lord." Jeremy's shoulders slumped. "I'm trapped. A lot of the people who work here are."

"You could go beg forgiveness."

"I just can't do that. I refuse to compromise my principles." He looked toward the building next to Microsoft. "I applied at X and Tesla. Still haven't heard anything."

"How much do you owe Noah?"

"Thirty grand and counting. The interest rate is ridiculous. I don't know what the hell I was thinking when I took the loan. I was just so angry and frustrated and determined to make things work, you know?"

Carver motioned toward the rollup door. "How about that tour?"

"Yeah, sure." Jeremy rubbed his eyes. "Sorry, I still can't believe the mess I'm in."

Carver didn't have a response. At least not one the kid wanted to hear.

Jeremy sucked in a breath. Stiffened his shoulders. "What did you do to end up here?"

"Nothing. I just enjoy committing crimes."

Jeremy laughed. "That's funny." He looked at Carver and his laughter died down. "That was a joke, right?"

"Find a job you love, and you'll never work a day in your life." Carver nodded. "I love crime."

"Uh, yeah, sure." Jeremy tugged at his collar. "Um, so this is the loading bay area." He pointed to rows of tables. "That's where everything is sorted and tagged." He walked past the tables to the shelves. "This is where inventory is kept."

"Looks like a smooth operation."

"Yeah. Really smooth." Jeremy brightened a little. "And this is where it gets interesting." He took Carver back past the shelves and inside the store. It looked like it had been a stockroom but now it was filled with cubicles and computers.

Jeremy stopped at an empty computer workstation. "I work here. I do coding for the website. I hook the APIs from our website into merchants and payment processors. All the major online merchants are linked to the merch."

Carver didn't understand most of the terms. But he got the gist. "The stolen items are sold all over the world. Things taken from cars, from retail stores, and so forth."

"Yeah, it's actually brilliant. The bricks and mortar stores are literally making online stores a lot of money." Jeremy laughed. "As if they need the help."

Carver saw offices past the cubicles. "What's down there?"

"Accounting, finance, and Noah's office." He motioned vaguely. "I only went back there once to try to reason with Noah, but he wouldn't even see me."

There were cameras all over the place. Cameras watching the cubicles. Cameras watching the offices. A security guy somewhere was probably trying to watch a hundred screens at once. Or it might be a whole team of them.

"How much is he paying you to work here?"

"He moved me into an apartment building he owns. Said I could live there rent free as long as I kept working."

"And how is that paying off your debt?"

"He deducts from my paycheck." Jeremy made air quotes when he said the last word. "We get paid in cash under the table, of course. But it's barely enough for me to afford food for the month, much less pay off my debt."

"What else is back there?"

"Noah has his personal vault back there. And beyond that is a place you gotta hope you never end up."

Carver stared at the hallway. "Yeah? What place is that?"

"It's where he takes people to punish them. And if you have three strikes against you, you don't come out alive."

"Sounds promising."

Jeremy's forehead pinched. "I can't tell if you're joking or not."

"I take it you can't lead me back there?"

"No way." He shook his head. "Um, what section do you work in anyway?"

"I'm a janitor." Carver started walking. "Gotta empty the trash cans in the offices."

"Wait." Jeremy put a hand on his arm. "Really? I thought you stole stuff since you enjoy crime."

Carver nodded. "Thanks for showing me the offices."

"I hope you're joking." Jeremy shook his head. "Noah doesn't play around."

"He won't be happy if his trash is full." Carver shrugged. "Duty calls. Thanks for the tour."

Jeremy dropped into his seat. He looked confused. Like he didn't know what to believe. He finally nodded. "Good luck." Then he turned to his computer and logged in.

Carver walked past the cubicles. Entered the hallway. Walked to the offices. There was a big office there. A name was stenciled on the vintage door. *Noah*. No last name. Right across from it was a heavy metal door.

It was vintage like everything else. It looked like it was over a hundred years old. Black iron. The lock had been modified. It didn't require a key or a combination anymore. It used modern technology.

More specifically, it used biometrics. A fingerprint. He took out his knife. Jabbed it into the drywall. It struck metal just below the surface. It wasn't just a metal door in a normal wall. It was a real vault.

That was inconvenient.

"What are you doing here?" A woman strode down the hallway. She took off a pair of glasses and put them in her shirt pocket. Unlike everyone else, she was dressed in office clothes. She wasn't wearing a hoodie or a mask.

She had red hair. Green eyes. Pale skin and no freckles. She looked young. Like she kept in good shape. Her forehead was pinched. Her eyes were narrowed. Like she was giving him a death glare.

Carver tucked his knife away. "I'm looking for Noah. Seen him around?"

She tilted her head slightly. Looked him up and down. Her eyes flared. "You need to get the hell out of here now!" She hurried over to him. Grabbed his arm. Pulled him.

Carver resisted. Her strength caught him off guard and he budged a couple of inches. "I'm supposed to be here. I'm the janitor."

"You're not a janitor. You're just looking for trouble." She let his arm go. "Do you have explosives on you?"

He blinked. "Do janitors normally carry explosives?"

"I know who you are," she hissed. "Carver, right?"

Carver was caught off guard again. "Who are you?"

"That's not important. What's important is that you get out of here before Noah arrives. You're lucky he's running late this morning."

"Okay, look." Carver backed up. Held up his hands to show they were empty. "Get me in the vault so I can get my stuff. Then I'm gone. Out of your hair forever."

She laughed mirthlessly. "Really? You're not here to blow us up like the Farm?"

This woman knew a lot. Like that woman who'd been helping Patterson at the Farm. "Are you the resident hacker?"

"No." She rolled her eyes. "Do I look like a hacker?"

"No." He looked her up and down. "You don't look like an office worker either. You're toned. In shape. But not just gym shape. There's something else. You've had training."

She pointed two fingers at her eyes. "My eyes are up here."

"Good to know."

"Are you leaving or not?"

"Not without my stuff."

She flexed her fists and growled. "The only thing in there are a pair of MP5s and several ammo cans. All your camping gear is on the shelves."

"Okay. But what about the burner phone?"

"Burner phone?" She looked confused. "You want a burner phone back?"

"It had some important numbers on it."

"There's a big bin where they toss them. Most phones can't be used because they're locked. We sell most of them to recyclers."

Carver looked at the metal doors. He could replace the MP5s. He could replace the ammo. What he really wanted was the phone. But it was also the principle of the matter. Just letting these people keep his stuff would send the wrong message.

"Take me to the phone bin."

"And you'll go?"

"Yeah, I'll go." It might be a lie. He wasn't sure if he'd be satisfied with just the phone. Probably not. But she probably wouldn't take him if he said no.

She sighed. "Okay. Let's go." She started walking toward the warehouse. Took him past the shelves. Turned left down the main aisle. Walked to the end. There was a large bin. It was piled high with phones, tablets, and even computers.

There was a table next to the bin. There were more phones and devices stacked there. He went through the phones on the table first. The burner phone was small and cheap looking. Most of the phones on the table were of the big expensive variety.

He didn't find his phone on the table. He started digging in the bin. Took out laptops and tablets. Set them on the table. Sifted through the phones. Putting them on the table. "Are you sure my phone is in here?"

"It was listed with the items taken from your truck. A cheap generic phone. Chinese made."

Carver nodded. "That's the one."

"You're about four days deep into the bin now." She frowned. "You should have found it already."

"Then it's not here."

"Is this what you're looking for?"

Carver straightened. Saw a tall black man dressed in jeans and a button-up shirt standing in front of two other black men. One was taller than Carver. Bigger than Carver. He was wearing fancy gym clothes. The other was shorter than the other two. Lighter skinned. Wearing similar clothing to the first.

The first man was holding a cheap Chinese made burner phone. Carver's burner phone. No doubt about it. There was also no doubt about the man's identity. No doubt at all.

It was Noah.

CHAPTER 20

Carver studied the three men.

"Yep, that's my phone. Thanks for returning it."

Noah laughed. His buddies laughed too.

"Tasha, dear." Noah tutted. "What are you doing?"

"I forced her to help me get my stuff back," Carver said. "Told her I'd break her neck if she didn't."

"How noble." Noah put a hand to his heart. "Protecting a woman you don't even know."

Tasha blew out a breath. "I just wanted him out of here. I thought he was going to blow the place up."

"Now that I can believe." Noah nodded. "Because I watched most of the interaction on our security cameras."

Carver motioned at the nearby cameras. "How do you watch so many of them at once?"

"Ah, a tactical question." Noah nodded. "Always looking for information. Always studying your surroundings. And had we not already known you were in the area, you might have slipped by unnoticed."

The big man spoke. "Except he went in the offices, boss."

"True." Noah tucked the burner phone in his pocket. Pulled out another phone. Read something.

Carver cut through the silence. "Noah, how about you give me my phone, my guns, my ammo, and we can peacefully go our separate ways?"

Noah ignored him. Kept looking at his phone. He spoke softly to his shorter companion. The other man nodded and jogged away. Noah looked up at Carver. Pursed his lips as if just now registering the statement.

He shook his head. "I'm afraid you trespassed on my property. Tried to take things that no longer belong to you."

"That's not how it works."

"That's exactly how it works in my city."

The big man spoke again. "What the boss says goes. The whole bay area is his."

"Think what you want. But that's not how it works." Carver folded his arms. Felt the Glock under the hoodie. "We can settle this peacefully, or I'll just make you give me my stuff."

"Why are you so intent on getting a burner phone back?" Noah tucked away his phone and took out the burner. He looked it over. "Maybe you can unlock it and show me what's so important."

"I took a lot of nude selfies. Stuff I don't want anyone seeing."

Noah laughed. "I think it's important to have a sense of humor especially in a tense situation."

"This is a tense situation?"

"You're making it one." Noah held out his hands. "Come to my office. Have a drink. Let's talk business."

"The only business I'm interested in is getting my stuff back and going on my merry way."

"That doesn't jibe with your past activities, Carver." Noah pursed his lips again. "Breakstone. Miami. The Farm." He watched as if expecting a reaction. When Carver didn't react, he kept talking. "I don't know how Miami is connected. Judging from the pieces I've put together it might have just been retaliation for what happened to Breakstone."

Carver said nothing.

Noah kept talking. "Enigma sent assassins after you. To erase you for what you did to Breakstone. Somehow, you found out about the Farm. Took it out. Now you're here in my territory. Ready to take out another of corporate's assets. Except I'm not like the others. I'm different."

"I'm not here to take out any assets. The Farm just happened to be involved in something that required a response. Now I'm on permanent vacation. Touring the west coast. Touring this lovely city of yours. Until someone broke into my car and took my stuff."

Noah watched him carefully. His eyes were bright blue. Piercing. Perceptive. He tilted his head slightly. "You might be telling the truth. But you're a blank slate on the outside. I'm guessing you have military training. Maybe in psyops."

Carver didn't respond.

"Maybe you are in my city as a tourist. Maybe that's God's honest truth." He put a hand on his chest. "But my truth is, I don't care. You're here. You're mine. And you're going to help me with corporate."

The shorter man returned. Jeremy was with him. Jeremy's hood was off. His mask was gone. He looked terrified.

"Deshawn, did you talk to Jeremy?"

The shorter guy nodded. "He says he thought Carver worked here."

"I did, I swear!" Tears poured down Jeremy's face. "I was just showing him around."

"You took a stranger at his word, Jeremy?" Noah tutted. "How dumb are you?"

Jeremy sobbed. "I don't know anyone. Everyone wears masks and hoodies."

The big guy nodded. "That's true, boss. Hard to tell people apart."

Noah nodded. "Jeremy, you're right. I can't expect you to know who's hiding behind the masks."

Jeremy calmed down a little. "I swear I didn't know I was doing anything wrong. I told him not to go to the offices. I warned him."

"Then you did everything right." Noah smiled. "Jeremy, you're clean, right?"

The kid looked confused. "Clean?"

"No drug use."

"No, sir. I need a clear head for programming."

"Clean and smart." Noah mussed Jeremy's hair. "You're a good boy." He sighed.

Carver already knew what was coming. It was obvious as glitter in daylight. "Don't even bother, Noah. He's nothing to me."

Jeremy looked confused. "What's that supposed to mean?"

"Carver is telling us that it means nothing to him if we kill you." Noah nodded at the big guy. "Titus, if you please."

Titus gripped Jeremy by the arms. "Sorry, kid."

Noah removed a case from his pocket. Unzipped it. Removed a syringe. "This is liquid fentanyl. It's a lethal dose to anyone smaller than my friend, Titus."

Jeremy's eyes bugged. "Why? You said I didn't do anything wrong!"

"You told Carver why you're here?"

Jeremy nodded. "Yes, but I didn't think that was against the rules."

"Gave him your sob story?"

Jeremy started crying again. "Yes."

"Now, I don't think your friend, Carver, has heart strings to tug on." Noah narrowed his eyes. Gazed at Carver. "But maybe, just maybe he does. And maybe it's enough to get him to listen to reason."

"Please don't, Noah!" Jeremy squirmed, but Titus held him firm with little effort. "I'm your best coder! I've done a lot of great work for you!"

"Believe me, if I could trade someone else for you, I would, Jeremy. I'd do it in a heartbeat." Noah pulled the plastic cap off the syringe needled. "But you're my only hope."

"Damn it, Noah." Tasha stalked toward him. "He's just a kid. Barely twenty."

"Tasha, be a good girl and stand aside." Noah's smile morphed into a scowl. "I really don't want to have to warn you again."

Shivering with anger, she stopped. Took a shuddering breath. Stepped aside.

Noah inserted the needle into Jeremy's arm. His thumb pressed the plunger.

Carver didn't like how this was going. Jeremy wasn't his concern. Didn't mean anything to him. But there were other ways to handle this. Ways that didn't require letting the kid die. He held up a hand. "Let's go have that drink."

Noah's anger turned to joy. He grinned. Pulled the needle out of Jeremy's arm. Put the cap on it. Put the syringe in the case. Zipped it up. Tucked it away.

"Titus, let Jeremy get back to work." He mussed the kid's hair again. "Good job, Jeremy."

Jeremy was sobbing. Barely able to walk. Titus handed him over to Deshawn.

Deshawn yanked him upright. "Kid, you better start walking on your own, because I ain't dragging you."

Jeremy found his footing. Shivering, he started walking on his own. Shaking with sobs, he glanced back at Carver. Deshawn shoved him hard. The kid nearly fell again.

Deshawn lunged at him. "Speed it up!"

Jeremy ran away.

Tasha stared at Carver. Her rage was gone. Hidden by stone. But it was obvious to Carver she was holding it in. Storing it up. Waiting for the day she could do something about it.

Carver flourished a hand. "Lead the way."

"My pleasure." Noah turned. Started walking. "Carver, what's your poison?"

"Tequila."

"I'm a scotch man myself. Properly aged, of course."

Titus and Deshawn formed up behind Noah.

Carver walked past Tasha. She looked like she wanted to say something. But she kept her mouth shut. Followed behind Carver.

They entered an office. There were several leather chairs. A leather couch. A nice desk. A glass liquor case lined with top-shelf alcohol. A bookshelf lined with classic books. *The Art of War. Atlas Shrugged. The Communist Manifesto. Mein Kampf.* Carver recognized the names.

Rhodes had most of the same titles. But she'd kept hers in a box. A box she kept in a closet. She usually purchased romance novels from a local bookstore. Placed them strategically around whatever building they called home at the time.

She said people who displayed philosophical books were bragging. They wanted to look smart. Wanted people to think they were well read. Maybe that was why Noah had them. But the book covers looked worn on the spine. The edges were dulled. Some had slight tears.

Maybe he'd read the books a lot. Or maybe Noah didn't take good care of his books. It was hard to say. Some folks were smart and wanted everyone to know it. Some folks were dumb and wanted to look smart. He'd figure it out soon enough.

Noah sat behind the desk. Titus and Deshawn took chairs on either side of the desk. That left Carver either a chair across from the desk or the leather couch against the wall. He moved the chair out of the way. Scooted the couch a little closer. Dropped onto it.

Noah grinned. "You're a man who manipulates his environment to suit his purpose."

"I just call it getting comfortable." Carver leaned back. Spread his arms on the back of the couch.

"Tasha, be a good girl and prepare us drinks." Noah pursed his lips. "I'll have two fingers of the Macallan." He leaned his elbows on the desk. "Carver, do you have a tequila preference?"

"I'll just have a beer. Too early for hard alcohol."

"Ah, but an aged scotch isn't just hard alcohol. And neither is the right tequila."

"I'm not that fancy." He considered getting his own beer, but Tasha was already opening a minifridge next to the glass case with the liquor in it. She took out two bottled beers. Handed them to Titus and Deshawn.

She turned to Carver. "What kind of beer?"

"A stout would be nice."

She pulled out a can. It was black and silver with the name TenFidy on it. "Would you like it in a glass?"

He shook his head. "The can is fine."

Tasha opened the glass case. Removed a bottle of Macallan. She poured two fingers into a fancy glass. "Do you want it neat, Noah?"

Noah nodded. He didn't reach for the glass. Didn't even look at Tasha. He just waited for her to set it on a coaster in front of him. Then he took a slow sip. Sighed. "The perfect morning drink."

Carver sipped his beer. Nodded in approval. "Okay, now that we've established how sophisticated you are, maybe we can move on to business."

Noah chuckled. "Is it sophisticated to enjoy something, Carver? Or is it a simple pleasure?"

It was a question that didn't need answering. Carver crossed his leg. Drank more beer. It was nice. Tasted like black coffee. It made him wish he was drinking that instead of beer. "It is what it is, I guess."

"As so many things are." Noah set down his drink. Steepled his fingers. "We have a common enemy, you and me. A problem I call Enigma."

"So you say."

"It's the same organization that ran the Farm. The compound you and your friend blew up a while ago. They also came into my territory. Gave me an offer that I couldn't refuse."

"Because it was so good or because you had no choice?"

Noah's expression soured. "The latter."

"They did to you what you do to others."

"Yes, they do." Noah sighed. "They are formidable."

"In what way?"

"I'll tell you a little secret." Noah paused to sip his scotch. Set it on the table. "When I was forced to accept their terms, I set about to discover all I could about this organization. Their footprint is rather obvious once you know what to look for."

"Let me guess. Retail theft rings. Car break-ins. Drug distribution. Ideological recruitment. Brainwashing." Carver sipped his beer. "Human organs."

Deshawn flinched. Titus frowned.

Noah looked intrigued. "Human organs?"

Carver already knew Noah's operation was already doing everything else. Anyone with eyes could see that. But the organ sales had been a nasty surprise. One Carver hadn't expected to find in the Oregonian woods.

"The Farm was doing everything you're doing. They took healthy recruits and killed some of them for organs. Sold those organs to the highest bidders." Carver sipped his beer. "They'd built a small prefab base of operations in the middle of the forest. They had dozens of departments. Technology that tied them into everything. Highly skilled doctors and operatives."

"I had a mole there. He told me about everything. Everything except the human organs, that is."

Deshawn whistled. "Those people were insane."

Titus nodded. "Amen to that."

Tasha was standing in the corner. Almost invisible. But Carver was watching her out of the corner of his eye. Watching her reactions to the revelations. She was impassive. Keeping her face stony.

She had some kind of training. Military, probably. She looked a little soft on the outside but was probably hard as rocks on the inside. And she wasn't happy to be here.

Noah continued. "You see, Carver, I had my own little kingdom in the bay area long before corporate ever set foot here. I was happy as a pig in shit."

Titus grunted. "All of us were, boss."

"Best days of our lives." Deshawn sighed with regret.

"It's never fun playing by somebody else's rules," Carver said.

"We all play by someone else's rules. There's always someone higher up the chain." Noah sipped his scotch. Set it down. "But corporate isn't interested in making money. They want a breakdown in society. Chaos."

Carver nodded. "They're playing the long game."

"The pandemic hit three years ago. The decline since then has been faster than I could have imagined." Noah put a hand on his chin. "Either all of it was part of their plan, or the pandemic helped them accelerate it."

"Sounds like conspiracy theories to me." Carver didn't think anyone could make something that big happen. "Maybe this mysterious organization has been trying to do this for years and failed. Maybe the fallout from the pandemic is the reason they're succeeding now."

"Maybe." Noah shrugged. "All I know is that my city is in turmoil. In chaos."

"In the midst of chaos, there is also opportunity." Carver had noticed the Art of War book. He'd known it was only a matter of time before Noah quoted from it.

Noah looked like he was going to say something, but he stopped. "I was about to say that."

"Were you?" Carver wasn't surprised. The man had been setting himself up for the quote. Made it obvious.

"That's not the most well-known quote from the book." Noah leaned forward. "Which means you've read it. Which means you know it well."

"Well enough to sound smart," Carver said. "But believe me, I'm not that smart."

"Oh, I disagree." Noah laughed. "He will win who knows when to fight and when not to fight."

Carver nodded. "That's one of the better-known quotes."

"And also, true. I knew better than to fight corporate. The time was never right. I might have raw manpower on my side, but certainly not equipment or training." Noah sighed. "But I do have a template. A path to victory. And you might just be the missing piece."

Carver wasn't interested. But being on the inside was the best way to get his things. He'd play along for now.

"First, I would like to know what's on this burner phone." Noah slid the phone across the desk. "Why someone like you be so eager to retrieve it."

"It has some phone numbers I don't want to lose." Carver shrugged. "That's it."

"Phone numbers for whom?"

"Old girlfriends. Former squad mates."

Titus laughed. "Can't blame a man for wanting that."

"Sounds reasonable enough," Deshawn said.

Noah nodded at the phone. "Unlock it. Let me see it."

Carver started to get up.

Noah motioned at Tasha. "Give the man his phone."

Tasha walked over. Picked it up. Took two steps. Handed it to Carver.

He took it. The screen was nice and clean. The sides weren't scuffed up. "This isn't my phone." He pointed to the screen. "It's missing a hairline crack at the top."

Noah smiled. "I wouldn't give you the real phone. A man like you could glance at the phone numbers and memorize them. I'm surprised you haven't already done that."

"The people I know change numbers frequently." He decided not to mention the encrypted messaging app. And especially not the encrypted banking app. It didn't matter if he memorized Paola's current number. Without the messaging app he couldn't contact her.

"Fair enough." Noah steepled his fingers again. "I want you to find out all you can about corporate. To help me find a way to break their grasp on my city."

"That's a tall order." Carver set the fake phone to the side.

"Keep that phone," Noah said. "It's a new burner for you to use while we work together."

Carver tapped a finger on the phone screen. "This is a lot of work just so I can get my phone back. What else is in it for me?"

"The satisfaction of a job well done." Noah grinned. "And Jeremy gets to keep on living."

So much for a quick in and out. Now Carver was tangled up with the local crime boss. It wouldn't be the first time it happened. Hopefully it would be the last. Because what came next was inevitable.

Violence and a whole lot of death.

Chapter 21

Carver didn't care about Jeremy.

He didn't care about Tasha. About anyone here. But it would be better if he got to pick and choose who kept breathing and who didn't.

He sipped his beer. "Using strangers as collateral isn't the most effective way to make me help you."

"It got you here, didn't it?" Noah rubbed the leather armrest of his chair. "That's how I keep a happy, motivated work force. It's kept Tasha on my payroll too."

"So, you're a slave owner."

Titus pounded his armrest with a fist. "Shut your dirty mouth, boy."

Noah held up a hand. "It's okay, Titus. Carver is close to the truth. But I consider them more like indentured servants."

"We're hostages," Tasha said. "No more. No less."

Noah snapped his fingers. Pointed to her. "Even better. But I treat my hostages very well."

Carver grunted. "Doesn't seem like an effective method. What happens if the collateral dies?"

"Their own lives are collateral." Noah shrugged. "And many get Stockholm Syndrome. They learn to become happy. They learn to love me."

Deshawn looked amused. "Except for Tasha."

"Yeah." Titus snorted. "She's always grumpy."

Tasha didn't respond. She stared at them with dead eyes.

"So, Carver." Noah smirked. "You in or out?"

Titus bared his teeth in a grin. Stared Carver down.

"Looks like I've got no choice." Carver tucked his new burner phone in a pocket. "What, exactly, do you want me to do?"

"That's complicated." Noah finished his drink. Tapped the glass and looked at Tasha.

She took the glass. Put two more fingers of scotch in it. Set it on the coaster. Went back to her corner of the room.

Noah sipped. Rapped a finger on the desk. Like he was thinking about where to begin. He nodded to himself. "Tell me a bit about yourself, Carver. You were in the military. That much is obvious. But how did you get from there to here?"

"There's not much to it." Carver considered how much detail to go into and decided little to none was best. "I was in the military. Got out after a few years. Hit the beach. Enjoyed the quiet life."

"It hasn't been that quiet. I can connect you to Breakstone and the Farm. I want to know more."

"A former squad mate wanted to reconnect. I went to visit them in Morganville. Then a private military company and a local drug gang started a small war." Carver shrugged. "I just happened to be there."

"That's what the news reports said." Noah gave him a discerning look. "But is that what really happened?"

Carver nodded. "Some guy attacked me. I guess he thought I was with the cartel. I defended myself. Got the hell out of Dodge. Moved to Miami. But they followed me there. Tried to kill me. So, I moved again. They found me again. Sent a kill squad. I decided to go pay them a visit. See if I could get them to leave me alone."

Noah barked a laugh. "And you blew them to hell."

"They just happened to have an armory full of explosives." Carver twirled his beer can. "I put it to good use. Nothing fancy."

Tasha stared at him from her corner. Like she couldn't decide if this was truth or fiction. It was a little bit of both.

"A modest pro." Noah nodded. "I like that."

"Yeah, but why are you in San Francisco?" Deshawn said.

Carver didn't need to lie about that part. "I bought some camping equipment and a truck. Figured I'd put them to good use while I was on the west coast."

Noah smiled. "You parked your car on the Embarcadero. My people took your stuff."

Carver nodded. "And here I am."

"Oops. My bad." Noah's smile grew wider. "It seems lady luck and good planning have brought you to me."

"I'd call them a series of unfortunate events." Carver sipped his beer. "However you want to cut it, we're here. In this room."

"And I have something you want very dearly for you to stay here."

"It's not that dear to me. But you mentioned Enigma. The people who controlled the people at the Farm. The people who keep chasing me. And that interests me." That felt close to the truth. Carver was interested. Maybe not interested enough to track them down but interested enough to learn more about the shadowy organization that wanted him dead.

Noah nodded enthusiastically. "You see? We have a common enemy. A common cause. We can be partners. Not enemies."

"That depends," Carver said.

"On what?"

"On how much of this partnership I have to carry. How much risk versus reward."

"Then I'll start with our first targets." Noah glanced at Tasha. "Get my tablet, darling."

She left the office. Returned a moment later with a tablet. Set it on his desk. Noah turned it on. Tapped on the screen. Turned the screen to Carver. There was a picture of a middle-aged woman on the screen. It said Maryann Lewis below her picture.

Noah turned the tablet around. Set it flat on the desk. Tapped on the screen. Turned it around to Carver again. The picture was of a younger woman. Pamela Harris. The rest of the text was too small to read from a distance.

"They're with Enigma?"

Noah nodded. "City council members. One from here, the other from Oakland."

"You want them dead?"

Noah shook his head. "I want to know all their connections. Who they talk to. Who they meet with secretly. Everything."

"You could hire a private investigator for that."

"I could. But I have you."

"I was just a grunt in the military. I'm not good at stalking people."

Noah chuckled. "I had a friend at the federal level run a background check on you. There's nothing. Absolutely nothing."

"I grew up in a military family. We were all over the place. And I kept out of trouble."

"That doesn't explain the void." Noah leaned forward. "My contact told me there was evidence your records were purged. That it was done from the top. And the only reason they would do that is because you were a dark asset."

"Your friend sounds like he's reaching." Carver didn't want to deny it too hard. That would cast doubt on the other parts of his story.

"I have no doubt you were special forces of some kind. Doesn't really matter." Noah flicked his hand as if dismissing it. "What's important is that you have a certain set of skills. Infiltration is certainly among them. And I want you to investigate these two women. Find out everything you can. And I want this within a week."

Carver whistled. "A week? That's a tall order for even the best of investigators."

"And I have no doubt you can make it work."

Titus bared his teeth in a grin again. Like he was underlining Noah's point. Implying a threat if Carver didn't comply. Deshawn looked uninterested. But he wasn't. He was sizing up Carver. Evaluating his responses. They were a team for a reason.

There was something else about Deshawn that tickled Carver's gut instincts. He had a furtive look about him. Like he was doing something he shouldn't be doing. A nervous tic in his right eye. He had no reason to be nervous. Unless he was doing something Noah wouldn't like.

Carver watched him out of the corner of his eye. It might be something. Might be nothing. Just a gut feeling. Nothing more.

He put his thoughts back on track. Back to the matter at hand. Maryann Lewis and Pamela Harris. Provided these women were ordinary civilians without extra security, he could probably get this done in less than a week.

But there were other factors that could make it harder. A lot harder. He'd just have to see.

"You know where they live? Where they work? Their schedules?"

"I only know what's public."

"What about your friend who ran a background check on me?" Carver raised an eyebrow. "Can they tell you more?"

"This friend will get nervous if I start asking for background checks on politicians." Noah shook his head. "I'm afraid you'll need to gather intel yourself." He waved a hand at Tasha. "She will provide you with any resources you need, within reason."

"This isn't something I can just do on my own," Carver said. "I need a team. I need someone who's good with computers."

"Then why don't I assign Jeremy to help you?" Noah grinned. "Let you two get to know each other better."

"So he can have more value as collateral?" Carver shook his head. "Someone anonymous will do just fine."

Titus barked a laugh. "He's gonna fall in love, boss."

Deshawn tossed in his two cents. "He acts like a tough guy, but he's not."

"It's Jeremy or no one, Carver." Noah sipped his scotch. "You, Jeremy, and Tasha will either make an effective team, or Jeremy is going to suffer."

Tasha shuddered. Clenched her fists. But she kept her mouth shut.

Carver finished off his beer. Set the can on the table. Right next to the coaster. Condensation dripped on the wood. "Fine. Get me a space to work in. And I'll need Tasha and Jeremy exclusively. No interruptions."

Noah snapped his fingers. "Tasha, get Jeremy in here."

She hesitated. Opened the door. Left.

"Let me be clear, Carver." Noah stood. Stretched. "Jeremy is counting on you to succeed. His loved ones are counting on it. Just in case you think you can spirit him away and save him."

Carver tapped the beer can on the table. "I'll have another."

Titus seemed to think the request was aimed at him. He stood. Straightened to his full height. About six feet five inches, give or take. "Get it yourself, boy."

Carver leaned back. "But you're already up."

Titus punched a fist into the other palm. "Maybe I'll put your head through the refrigerator."

"Rude." Carver shook his head. "Hard to find good help these days."

Titus stomped forward. Noah snapped his fingers. "Titus, don't let him goad you."

The big man clenched his fists. He looked like he wanted to break something to prove a point, but apparently smashing Noah's nice furniture wasn't a good idea. He backed up. Sat back down.

Deshawn looked amused by the interaction. Like he was repressing a laugh. He kept glancing at Noah. Gauging his facial expressions. His reactions. He was observant. Maybe he was smart too.

The tic in his right eye was gone. He was feeling more confident. Maybe he'd been nervous about Carver earlier. Maybe that had been all it was. Maybe there was something else going on. Either way, Carver would keep an eye on him.

Deshawn and Titus were Noah's inner circle. Trusted. At least as much as any gang leader trusted anyone. Maybe they were childhood friends. Maybe they'd only known each other for a few years.

Carver decided to prod a little. See what he could discover. "At least your attack dog knows when to heel."

"I ain't his attack dog." Titus looked ready to get up again. But he glanced at Noah first. Stayed in his seat when he saw the warning look.

"If you keep trying to stir up Titus, I might just let him teach you a lesson," Noah said.

Titus cracked his knuckles. "I'd love to, boss."

Deshawn was looking at his phone. He had it angled toward Carver. It looked like he was reading something. But Carver saw him tap the screen. Like he was taking a picture.

He didn't want anyone else to know he was doing it. That seemed obvious. It made Carver think Deshawn was up to something behind Noah's back. Why else would he do something like that?

Tasha returned with Jeremy a moment later. The kid looked terrified. Like he was reliving a nightmare he thought was over.

Noah stood. "Jeremy, I'm promoting you."

Jeremy was shivering. His eyes were red. Face was sheet white. "Please, Noah. I don't know this guy at all. I was just trying to be helpful. I don't want to die because of some stranger."

Noah walked around the desk. Put a hand on the kid's shoulder. "Calm down, Jeremy. If you do well, then you might earn complete forgiveness for your debt to me."

Jeremy's eyes brightened a little. "I'd be free?"

Noah nodded. "You'd be free."

"Wow, Noah." Jeremy nodded fervently. "I won't let you down. Just tell me what you need."

"Carver will tell you that. You, Carver, and Tasha are a team now."

Jeremy looked confused. "A team?"

Noah nodded. "You can use the old break room as a workspace. I want you to get it set up with computers, a whiteboard, and anything else Carver needs."

Jeremy shivered. "The old break room?"

Noah grinned. "Yes."

Jeremy gulped. He looked at Carver. "Yeah, just tell me what you need. I'll get everything setup in there."

"Really, Noah?" Tasha huffed. "The break room?"

Noah stared at her. "Don't make me repeat myself."

Tasha pressed her lips together. "Why me, Noah? You know I can't work the books while I'm doing whatever the hell this is."

Noah smirked. "You hate working the books."

"Yeah, and you love making me do things I hate." She held out her hands questioningly. "What's your point?"

"Just be a good girl and do this. I have someone else who can take care of the books while you do this." Noah motioned toward the door. "Go get started. The clock starts ticking in two hours. That will give you time to set up your workspace."

"Two hours?" Jeremy looked concerned. "Wait, why is there a ticking clock?"

"Because we have one week to do what needs doing." Carver got up. Opened the minifridge. Took several more beers. Closed it. "Lead the way."

Tasha left. Carver followed her. Jeremy hurried after them. Noah and his pals remained behind.

"The old breakroom?" Jeremy caught up with Tasha. "He's playing mind games with us, isn't he?"

"Yep." Tasha stopped at her office. She picked up a laptop. A charging cord. There was a whiteboard against a wall. It was covered in numbers. "Clean that off and bring it with us."

Jeremy grabbed a dry eraser. He cleaned off the board while Tasha grabbed some other items.

"We could just use this office," Carver said. "No reason to cart stuff somewhere else."

"He wants us to use the old breakroom because there are cameras in there," Tasha said. "So he can watch and listen whenever he wants."

"That's not the only reason," Jeremy said. "I've heard rumors about what happens to people in there."

Tasha sighed. "Yeah, there's also that."

Jeremy pushed the whiteboard into the hallway. "Carver, what else do you need?"

"You any good at hacking or cracking?"

He frowned. "I can use scripts and tools like anyone else. If you expect me to hack into a computer, then no, I'm not good at that."

"Do you have access to covert surveillance gadgets?" Carver spread his hands. "Anything like that?"

"No. But there's a guy not too far from here." Jeremy waved a hand in the general direction. "Everyone's real interested in security these days. Noah gives protection to the store so people will buy from there."

"And he gets a commission for it." Tasha shook her head. "I've got what I need. Let's go."

Carver followed her. She left the office area. Went down a long, winding ramp. Into the basement. It was a big, empty space. Concrete columns. A musty odor.

There was a pile of old mannequins in the middle. They were piled so high they reached the ceiling. Someone had positioned other mannequins in a circle around the pile. It had a ritualistic look about it.

Jeremy shuddered when he saw it. "They bring us down here during orientation. Tell us every mannequin in that pile represents someone who tried to betray Noah."

Carver liked the display. Noah knew how to use psyops to his advantage. It even made Carver feel a little uneasy.

Tasha ignored the pile. She kept walking past it. On the other side was a heavy metal door. There was a deadbolt on the outside. Some blood on the concrete. It was old and black. Like it had soaked into the pores a long time ago.

Tasha slid the deadbolt to the side. Opened the door. The hinges creaked. She flicked a light switch. Old florescent lights hummed. Flickered on. Cast the room in a dim yellow light.

Inside the room were two metal poles. They were attached to the concrete floor and to a metal beam in the ceiling. There was an old rope hanging from the ceiling. Blood spatters under the rope.

They looked fresher than the ones near the door. The place had a coppery scent. Smelled like pennies. A place didn't get that odor unless it had soaked in a lot of odors over the years. From the look and smell of this place, it was definitely a kill room.

"Oh, God." Jeremy gagged. "This is worse than I thought."

Tasha didn't say anything. She shivered a little. Didn't look at the rope or the poles. She knew what happened in this room. She'd seen it before. Maybe even recently. Noah seemed to enjoy mentally torturing her.

Jeremy looked at the poles. The rope. He shivered. He looked at Carver. At Tasha. Then he took a deep breath. Rolled the whiteboard into the corner. "I'll go get my stuff." He hurried away.

There was a small table in the corner. Carver put the beer bottles on it. Then he leaned against a wall. Studied the room. Noah was heavy on mental gameplay. He was a smart guy. Cunning. A little cocky, but not overly so. Probably a tough nut to crack. But there was always a way.

There were plenty of other places in the department store for them to set up shop. Noah wanted them here. Next to a pile of fake bodies, in a room that served as a constant reminder. Fail Noah and die. Simple as that. It was nothing Carver hadn't seen. Carver had, in fact, used the tactic before.

Sometimes it worked. Sometimes it didn't. In this case, it was just background noise. Carver already had plenty of motivation. He'd gone from being annoyed to angry. Noah had backed him into a corner.

It was a corner Carver could leave anytime he wanted. He could let Jeremy die. He could lose his burner phone. Then he'd lose Paola forever. He wouldn't know if she was safe. If she was living a good life or if the cartel caught up to her.

He should walk away. Paola would be fine. There was no need for him to worry about her. Everything else was just material possessions. He could replace it all eventually. Even without the bank account Leon had given him.

But there were other reasons he was going to stick around. Personal reasons. The events of Morganville, Georgia were still following him. Still harassing him like vengeful ghosts. He could dig into Enigma. Find some weaknesses. Exploit them.

Maybe then he could put a stop to this. Finally find some real peace.

It put things in a different perspective. Made it seem worthwhile to do Noah's dirty work for the time being. And once Carver had what he needed, he could leave.

A week was short for planning and executing an operation. He'd made do with less before. He'd also had Rhodes supplying the brain power. Now he had to do it. Plan it all. Rise to the challenge.

Find a way to keep three people alive.

—·—

CHAPTER 22

Carver wrote two names on the whiteboard.

Maryann Lewis

Pamela Harris

Two women. Both supposedly contacts for Enigma. Carver had heard that name before. He'd heard it from Leon. Probably in a text. It sounded a little dramatic. A little pretentious. It sounded like a name politicians would give one of their special programs.

Maybe it had started out like that. A program politicians dumped billions of dollars into. Then it grew. Morphed into something else. Gained a life of its own. Turned into a monster they couldn't control.

It wouldn't be the first time.

It could also have started somewhere else. Could be a byproduct of someone wealthy. Someone with a vested interest in destroying business as usual in the United States. Someone who knew that attacking the US from the outside was a losing proposition.

Attacking a developed nation from the inside was the only way to go. The CIA had been doing it to other countries for decades. Taking out important people. Inserting moles in governments.

Enigma was taking that to a whole new level. They were turning the populace against itself. Fomenting civil unrest at levels not seen since the sixties and seventies. Carver hadn't been alive then, but he'd seen the videos.

They weren't attacking from the top down. They were attacking from the bottom up. A grass roots effort, so to speak. And it was working.

The goal seemed to be to tear apart the fabric of society. Sow division. Chaos. Cause the citizens to hate each other so much that they were ready to kill each other.

It was somewhat admirable. Enigma was infiltrating local governments. Creating laws to favor criminals. Using those criminals to fund its activities. A part of Carver wanted to meet the people behind it.

Maybe someday he'd have that opportunity.

Carver stared at the whiteboard. At the two names on the board. It wasn't much, but it was a start.

Tasha walked over. Looked him up and down. "What's wrong with you?"

"Nothing."

"You've been staring at that board without moving for five minutes."

"I'm thinking."

"What's there to think about? We need to dig into these women's lives. Find out how they're connected to Enigma."

He shook his head. "I don't think we'll find much. They probably just take orders and don't ask questions."

Tasha looked up at the two cameras in the room. They were modern Wi-Fi cameras. Complete with infrared. They could rotate to look around the room. Not that they needed to. They were mounted in opposite corners. Able to cover each other's blind spots.

Tasha looked at the rope. The blood beneath it. She looked away. Back at the whiteboard.

Carver erased the names on the board. "You know what happens in here, don't you?"

"Yes."

"He makes you watch?"

"Yeah."

He wrote Enigma at the top. Drew diagonal lines. Put Maryann Lewis at the end of one. Pamela Harris at the end of the other one. He put a question mark on each line.

"You don't think they're connected to Enigma?"

"They're connected, but it might not be a direct connection."

"You think there's a middleman."

"There's definitely a middleman. But are they a handler who works for Enigma or an independent contractor who handles multiple assets?"

"In which case these women are insulated." Tasha pursed her lips. "They wouldn't know anything about anything."

"Exactly." Carver kept staring at the names. "And how were they recruited? Bribes or are their ideals aligned with Enigma?"

"Okay, so we pay them a visit and find out for sure."

Carver raised an eyebrow. "Beat it out of them?"

"No. Spy on them."

"That kind of work takes weeks. Months. Years."

"Not if we break into their phones and computers."

"Still might be a waste of time." He put the cap on the marker. Set it in a holder on the side of the board. "We need to know more before we concentrate on them."

"How do we find out more without spying on them?"

"That depends."

She stared at him as if expecting more. "On what?"

"On how much of a head start Jeremy can give me." He selected a beer. Knocked the cap off using the side of the table. Normally he respected people's property. Even if it was in bad shape. But none of this belonged to Noah.

Carver turned to Tasha. "Want a beer?"

She shook her head. "You're awfully cavalier for someone in your position."

Carver noticed one of the cameras rotating. They were being watched. He sipped the beer. "You sure? It's good beer."

"I don't want any damned beer, Carver!" She strode over to him. Put her hands on his chest. Pushed Carver's back against the wall. She was as strong as she looked. Stronger maybe, considering she was a head shorter than him. "You've got Jeremy's life and my life in your hands. You'd better start taking this seriously or I'll gut you myself!"

Carver set down the beer. Kept his hands to his sides. Looked at her hands on his chest. "Violence doesn't solve anything."

Tasha laughed without mirth. Backed away from him.

"Uh, I'm back." Jeremy stood outside the open door. He had a pushcart loaded with equipment. He'd seen the interaction between Carver and Tasha. "That was intense."

Carver patted the table next to him. "Set up here."

Jeremy pushed the cart to the table. Started unloading items.

Carver helped him. "You have a phone?"

Jeremy nodded.

"Run some searches on the names on the board. See if we can get home addresses."

He ran the searches. "It's easier to do this with a keyboard."

"I just want to see what comes up." Carver looked over Jeremy's shoulder. He pointed to a news story. About protestors lining up outside the home of Maryann Lewis. "Did they give an address?"

Jeremy shook his head. "I can call the group that organized the protest. Find out the address."

"Do that." Carver pulled the rest of the stuff off the cart. He untangled some wires. Put the computer monitor in the center. A keyboard and mouse in front of it. The workstation was decent sized. He put it on the right side of the table.

Jeremy made the call. Spoke with someone. Carver hooked up cables. He wasn't a computer genius, but the cables were pretty self-explanatory. They wouldn't fit in the wrong slots. At least not most of the time.

He powered on the setup. Backed up.

Tasha gave him a confused look. She pushed past him and logged onto the workstation. Connected it to the Wi-Fi. Then she ran searches for Pamela Harris. She and Jeremy had home addresses for the two women in about fifteen minutes.

Carver wrote the addresses on the board. He leaned over in front of the computer monitor. Ran another search. Read the news stories he found. A news reporter named Elena had taught him that a lot of answers could be found that way.

Tasha left. Returned a few minutes later with a couple of rolling office chairs.

She scooted one behind Carver. He dropped into it. "Thanks."

She didn't respond.

Jeremy sat next to him. "What are you doing?"

"Gathering information."

"From reading news stories?"

"Yeah." He clicked back to the main search. Pointed out several stories. "What do these have in common?"

Jeremy peered at the headlines. "Um, something about the San Francisco district attorney?"

Carver opened a story. "The voters wanted to recall the DA. The city council had to file a resolution backing it. But two council members refused. The recall vote never went through."

"What does that have to do with anything?" Tasha said.

Carver switched to another browser tab. Ran his finger down a list of headlines from the Oakland area. He leaned back and let Jeremy and Tasha read them.

Jeremy clicked on a story. Read it. "There was a similar recall effort in Oakland. It didn't require a council resolution. But then Pamela Harris and another council member refused to back a bill to put a special recall vote in the budget. So, the recall vote can't take place until the next general election in two years."

Tasha sat on the corner of the table. Folded her arms and looked down at Carver. "Are you insinuating that the other council members who voted with Harris and Lewis have something to do with this?"

"Maybe. But look at this." Carver clicked another tab. Displayed news stories about Bret Bushner, the San Francisco DA. "This is why he's being recalled."

Tasha read the headlines. "He refuses to prosecute most of the drug dealer and robbery crimes. But he's prosecuting people who go vigilante and try to stop crimes."

Carver switched to another browser tab. "Lacy Andrews, Oakland DA, is doing the same thing. Letting criminals go and punishing people who try to protect their own property."

"The voters want them out, but the council can't do it because they don't have the votes."

Jeremy whistled. "So, the district attorneys are the ones we need to go after?"

Carver pushed back his chair. Walked to the whiteboard. Wrote four more names on it. Descriptions next to them. The two district attorneys, Bret Bushner and Lacy Andrews. Then Carl Ortez, the San Francisco council member who voted with Lewis. Megan Chao who voted with Harris.

Jeremy looked at the names. "You think all of them are with Enigma?"

"Some are leaders. Some are followers." Carver finished writing the names in their respective places. "We need to separate the sheep from the wolves."

Tasha laughed. "I can't wait to hear how you plan to do that."

Carver turned to Jeremy. "Did you find some gadgets for me?"

"We have to go pick them up." Jeremy scrolled through the search results. "We can go now if you want."

Carver nodded. "Let's go."

They went back upstairs. Down the hallway past the offices. Noah's door was closed. The windows were covered. Carver could hear people talking inside. Whatever they said was muffled.

Jeremy led them outside. They walked down the sidewalk. Kept going a couple of blocks. Stopped outside a little shop. A bell tinkled when he opened the door. The inside was small. It smelled moldy. Musty. Like an animal had urinated on the floor.

There were a few shelves. Most had normal networking stuff. Cables. Adapters. The kind of things you used to find at Radio Shack. None of it looked particularly useful for Carver's purposes.

A young Asian man emerged from a door in the back. He walked behind the counter. "How can I help you?"

Jeremy cleared his throat. "Noah sent us."

"Oh, okay." The shopkeeper walked around the counter. Motioned them to follow him through the back door. There were monitors in the back. Nearly a dozen against a wall. A large monitor in the middle.

It reminded Carver of the setup at the Farm. The screens were filled with images of everyday life in the city. Not just in and around the shop, but all over the nearby area. The man had seen them coming from two blocks away.

The shopkeeper ignored the bank of monitors and headed upstairs.

"What's with all this?" Carver stopped in front of the security station. "You monitor everything?"

"No, of course not." The man shook his head. "I just record and upload. The data stream is analyzed with facial recognition software and other tools."

"For Noah or for Enigma?"

The man frowned. "I don't know if I should be answering your questions."

"What's the harm?" Carver said. "We're here to do some heavy lifting for Noah. I assume you're his guy. Not Enigma's."

"That's true."

"What's your name?" Tasha said.

"Lee."

"Lee, we need your best surveillance equipment. We have to squeeze every bit of information out of someone that we can within a week."

Lee's eyebrows shot up. "That's quite a short time frame."

Carver knew what he wanted. "Do you have a leech?"

"Those are extremely hard to come by in the civilian world."

"Okay, but do you have one?"

Lee looked reluctant to answer.

Carver prodded harder. "Noah won't be happy if you're holding out."

"Yes, I have one. But I thought I could make a good profit on it." His shoulders slumped. "Noah doesn't pay market prices."

"Does Noah even pay?" Carver asked.

Lee waggled a hand. "Not very much."

"He lets you survive and that's about it." Tasha grimaced. "I hate to do this to you, Lee, but we're going to need a lot of equipment."

Carver shook his head. "Just a couple of cameras. A couple of parabolic mics if you have them. Some recording equipment too."

"Really?" Tasha gave him a look. "We've got at least two people to watch. We can't be there all the time."

"Don't need to be." Carver motioned toward the stairs. "Let's see what you've got."

Lee led them upstairs. It ended at a wire metal door. A combination padlock hung open next to the door. He opened it. Led them into a room that was large by San Francisco standards. Maybe six hundred square feet of shelves. The windows were barred off. Metal shelves sat in front of them.

Lee opened a black metal chest. Rummaged inside. Pulled out two parabolic microphones. Small digital recorders. A variety of cameras. Some were pinhole cameras. Others were the normal Wi-Fi connected kind.

They would be handy. But they weren't going to be the most useful things. Not in this day and age.

Lee slid a small case from inside the chest. He cradled it. Like it was his baby. Then he reluctantly gave it to Carver. "This is the leech. If possible, I would like it back. This one was taken directly from the company that makes them for the CIA and NSA."

"It's bidirectional," Carver said.

Lee nodded. "It's a masterpiece. Worth fifty thousand on the open market."

"At least." Carver opened the case. Studied the small black device inside. It used a variety of wireless signals to connect to any device it was set next to. Then it used backdoors built into device software to bypass security.

Those backdoors had been required by government agencies. The big companies had fought them. The courts agreed. Told them they didn't need to do it. Their customers cheered them on. Felt safe. Happy that their private data was protected.

Criminals were part of that fanbase. They thought they were safe too. That everything was protected behind a wall of encryption. Just to make things more secure, they used encryption apps to erase everything.

The Farm had used that on their devices. Plus, their phones were locked down. The users couldn't modify anything on them. Couldn't use the regular encrypted apps. And the phones tracked the owner wherever they went.

Despite the big court win, despite the public loss, government agencies came to an arrangement behind closed doors. The big companies had to submit, or the Federal Communications Commission would take control of the frequencies they operated on.

Other federal agencies would regulate them more. Cost them more money. Reduce profit. Cause them all kinds of unwanted problems.

The companies capitulated. Backdoors were created. The keys were given to government agencies. The public was never told.

Rhodes had told Carver all about it. He didn't know how she knew things like that. She just knew. She was the kind of person who dug into a mystery until she knew everything.

That was what got her killed.

Now Carver had to dig into a big mystery. An enigma. The Farm had been a hell of an operation. They'd used advanced tech. Controlled important people. Amassed a small army of idealists. But what they'd had in those areas, they'd lacked in military expertise.

Enigma was different. It was a combination of Breakstone and the Farm. High tech. High skill. Extremely dangerous.

Where the Farm had sent half-baked amateurs, Enigma was sending full paramilitary units. Just like the ones who'd assaulted Arty's home. And Enigma controlled the people who controlled the police.

There were a lot of layers to Enigma. He had to be careful to peel the outer layers slowly. Make sure nobody noticed. Because if they did, the response would be swift and deadly.

Carver looked in Lee's storage chest. He found a few more items. Lower tech items. Stuff that had served him well in the field before. He put everything into a duffel bag Lee provided.

The leech was a small square device. There was an LCD screen on the front. A rotating dial on the side. Pressing it opened a menu. Pushing up or down navigated the menu. Lee showed him how to operate it.

Carver tested it on his burner phone. It connected. Entered through the backdoor. Downloaded a clone of the phone within twenty seconds. It was fast, but only because the phone had nothing on it.

He turned to Tasha. "Let me test with your phone."

She shook her head. "Mine is a burner just like yours. Nothing on it."

Jeremy handed Carver his phone. "Try it with mine."

Carver did. It took almost ten minutes to download half of the contents. "How much do you have on this phone?"

"I make a lot of videos. Take a lot of pictures." Jeremy looked at his feet. "I thought I'd get into content creation. Find a way to earn more money on the side."

Carver aborted the download. He had an idea of what to expect. He returned the phone to Jeremy. Tucked the leech into the duffel bag. "This will do."

"Thanks, Lee." Jeremy was checking out some items on a shelf. "Your shop is amazing."

"Yes, well if you want to spend money, please come back." Lee turned to Carver. "Please return in one piece."

"I'll do my best." Carver went downstairs. Exited the shop. Stood on the sidewalk outside. It was getting late in the day. He turned to the others. "I'm going to go. I'll meet you tomorrow morning."

Tasha checked the time on her phone. "It's not that late. We can do more planning."

"Yeah, but I'm hungry." Carver stretched. "A little tired too. It's been an eventful day."

"Where are you staying?" Tasha asked.

"Nowhere in particular."

"There are facilities onsite. You can stay at the department store."

"I'd prefer to sleep somewhere Noah can't find me." Carver flashed a grin. "See you in the morning." He started walking. Hopped on a bus. Sat in the back.

There was a laptop in the duffel bag. It wasn't ruggedized. Wasn't hardened like the one he'd had before. It couldn't be erased at the touch of a button. But it would do just fine. He opened it. Turned it on.

Carver took out the leech. Pulled the tip off the case. Beneath it was a small USB cord. He plugged it into the laptop. Uploaded the contents he'd taken from Jeremy's phone. Like the kid said, there were a lot of videos.

He watched one. Jeremy walked around the city. Recorded activity around a large homeless encampment. Talked to drug users. Asked them if they needed help. If they wanted to kick the addiction.

Sometimes they said yes. Asked him to help. Most of the time they chased him off. Some threatened violence. One guy tried to gut him with a knife. Apparently, Jeremy was quick on his feet because he was still alive.

There was a video of Jeremy working a food line. Feeding homeless people. Another of him recording long lines at the shelter. He walked down the long line. Most of the people waiting weren't locals. They were migrant families looking for a place to stay.

He seemed like a good kid. Like he wanted to help people. It would probably be the death of him.

Carver got off in the financial district. Stood at the entrance to a side street between permanently closed stores. He looked around. Side to side. Pulled up his hood. Entered the alley. The service door at the rear of an old coffee shop had been broken open.

There were homeless people inside. Drug users. The usual. Carver walked past them. They were too stoned to notice. He entered an empty closet. Closed the door to a crack. Waited.

Because someone was following him.

CHAPTER 23

Carver didn't have to wait long.

A hooded figure entered the shop. Stopped in front of the addicts. Looked them over. The figure was wearing a facemask. The hoodie was bulky. Covered their features. The contours of the body were hidden.

But there were some things that couldn't be hidden. The slope of the shoulders. The height. The eyes. Most importantly, the color of the eyes. Small details. Small, but hard to miss.

At least to someone who hadn't met them before. Seen them without a mask.

They stood there for a minute. Looked around the room. It was dim inside. Crowded with maybe a dozen addicts. A few of them had even set up tents inside. Then the figure walked around the room. Checked out the stairs.

Carver waited until they went upstairs. Then he walked up after them. There was a ruckus upstairs. A man shouting in alarm. Someone else shouting at him to shut up. Carver walked faster. The shouting covered any noise he made.

He saw his stalker walking past the shouting man. Saw another man shouting at the original shouter. Both trying to drown each other out. Carver sneaked up behind the stalker. He gripped their arm. Twisted it behind their back.

They twisted with the motion. A knee came up fast. Carver released his hold on the arm. Blocked the knee from his crotch. Hooked a hand beneath it. Swept the other foot. The stalker went down with a grunt.

He knelt. Pinned the legs beneath his own. Lowered his hood. His mask. Grinned. "Hello, Tasha."

Tasha's green eyes burned with anger. She struggled. "Let me go!"

He stood. Took his weight off her legs. "Noah send you after me?"

She stood. Brushed off her jeans. "No. I wanted to keep tabs on you. My life and Jeremy's depends on it."

"Jeremy's maybe. Not yours."

"That doesn't mean Noah won't torture me."

Carver figured it didn't matter if she knew where he was. He had a tent. He could move anytime he wanted. "You hungry?"

She frowned. Blinked. Looked confused at the sudden change of subject. "I could eat. Why? You buying?"

"Not exactly." He walked downstairs. Went outside. "Let's take a walk."

Tasha frowned even more. "Where?"

"Does it matter?"

She sighed. "I guess not. Just no fast food."

Carver started walking. Led her away from Market Street. Down Grant Avenue. Toward California Street. Tasha walked alongside him. At first, she didn't look happy. The frown faded away after a few blocks. Melted into something neutral.

That was probably about as good as it would get with her.

"Carver, where in the hell are we going?"

"Chinatown."

"Chinatown?"

"That's what I said." He kept going. Walking up steep hills. Crossing trolley tracks. Ducking through side streets.

Tasha kept up. She was in good shape. Maybe from walking the hills of San Francisco a lot. But probably because she trained with weights. She was strong. He could tell from the brief tussle in the abandoned coffee shop.

"Why didn't you pull your gun on Noah when he was threatening Jeremy earlier?"

It took Carver a second to process the question. He'd kept the Glock under the hoodie. Positioned it so it didn't show as a bulge. "What makes you think I have a gun?"

"I felt it when we wrestled in the coffee shop."

Carver knew she hadn't come close to touching the gun. Her hands had been too busy cushioning her fall. They'd never touched his upper body. "I know that's not true." He kept walking.

She kept quiet. Like she expected him to answer after a pause. When he didn't, she let out an exasperated sigh. "I saw the bulge, okay?"

"Pretty sharp eye to see it." He patted the spot beneath his arm. "A trained eye, even."

"Does it matter?"

"It matters."

She threw up her hands. "Are you going to answer my original question?"

"I didn't pull the gun because the situation was easy to deescalate." He shrugged. "I just agreed to their terms."

"You could have pulled it in the office. Shot them all dead."

"Doubtful." Carver shook his head. "Noah probably has a gun under his desk. A gun on a swivel. Aimed right at me the entire time. I couldn't pull the pistol from the holster before he took me out."

She blew out a breath. "You're right. How in the hell did you know that?"

"See? You already knew the answers before you asked the questions."

"Yes, but I needed to hear your answers."

"You're evaluating me."

Tasha nodded. "Yes. And I still want to know how you knew about Noah's gun."

Carver stopped outside Aunt Lin's grocery store. It was still open. He went inside. Lin was there behind the counter. She saw him and beamed. Motioned him to follow her. He followed her down an aisle. The shelves were full of ramen and other packaged goods.

Lin went into the back room. Zimo was there with two other men. One of the men was older. Maybe Lin's age. He was cooking noodles and vegetables in a large pan.

Zimo stood. Looked curiously at Tasha. "Carver, you're back! Does that mean you've changed your mind?"

Carver sniffed the food. "No, I just got hungry."

Zimo slumped a little. "You are welcome to share a meal with us."

Lin said something in Mandarin. The cook laughed. Replied. Gave a thumbs up to Carver.

Zimo and the other man laughed. "Uncle Feng says he approves of you as his wife's new boyfriend."

"Tell him I'm honored." Carver returned a thumbs up.

Feng spoke in heavily accented English. "Thank you very much." He bowed. "You save her. You are good man."

Carver bowed back. "My pleasure." He motioned toward Tasha. "This is my guest, Tasha. Tasha, this is Zimo, Aunt Lin, and Uncle Feng."

Lin spoke again.

Zimo grinned. "She wants to know if this is your second girlfriend."

Tasha grimaced. "Hell no."

"Just a new acquaintance. I hope you don't mind if she joins us."

"Yes. My pleasure." Feng bowed toward her. "Please sit."

There was a table with chairs. Carver sat down. Tasha hesitated. Shook her head. Sat next to Carver.

She leaned over and whispered. "You saved that woman?"

"More or less."

"Carver is very modest," Zimo said. "He prevented a mugger from harming my aunt. He protected her life and her hard-earned money."

Tasha didn't look convinced. "You sure we're talking about the same guy?"

Zimo looked confused. "Yes. Why?"

She shrugged. "I just didn't think he was that kind of guy."

Feng set bowls in front of them. Piled noodles inside. Dropped vegetables on top. Piled chicken on top of that. Lin placed chopsticks in front of them. Poured them both tea.

"Well, he must have done something right to get treated like this." Tasha picked up the chopsticks. Plucked a piece of chicken with them. Ate it. She moaned. "Wow. This is the best Chinese food I've tasted."

"Because it is authentic." Zimo smiled proudly. "All natural. Unprocessed whole food."

Carver picked up a pile of noodles and meat. Shoved it in his mouth. It was every bit as good as the last meal. He polished it off quickly. Feng served him another heap. He ate that one slower.

Lin returned to the front of the store. Feng served Zimo and his male friend. It was the guy from the other night. The one with the matching panda tattoo. He didn't talk much. Just ate and drank his tea.

"Carver, are you sure you won't reconsider?" Zimo held out his hands imploringly. "There were two more muggings last night."

"Why don't you escort people home at night?" Carver said.

"We don't have the manpower."

"One more guy isn't going to make a difference." Carver sipped the black tea. It wasn't sweet but it was a good palate cleanser. "You need a dozen more people to even make it work."

"You could help with that. Lead the effort." Zimo looked desperate. "We need a leader."

"I'm not a leader." Carver folded his arms. Gave it some thought. "Are there hotspots? Places where this happens frequently? Or is it random?"

Zimo nudged his friend. "Oscar has made a chart. Overlaid it on a map."

"Oscar?" Tasha frowned. "What kind of Chinese name is that?"

"It's the American name he chose."

Oscar nodded. "I choose. I like better."

Carver didn't think it would help much with such a heavy accent, but he didn't say anything.

Oscar pulled out a tablet. He opened the maps app. Tapped the screen a few times. Dots overlaid the map. They were red, yellow, and orange. Some places had more dots than others.

Carver took the tablet. Studied it for a minute. "The incidents are happening near the perimeter. He pointed to the two major hotspots. "Are there homeless encampments near these places?"

Zimo shrugged. "Not inside our territory."

"Yeah, but outside?"

Oscar's forehead pinched. He nodded. "Yes. Homeless."

"Okay, so those are the main sources." Carver zoomed out. Pointed to the areas where there were hardly any dots. "Probably no encampments near these places."

Zimo nodded. "What can we do about it? If they're not in our territory, we can't force them away."

"You don't need to. Just put a couple of people here." Carver tapped a street to place a marker. He put down two more markers. "Here and here as well. Then you can see the trouble before it happens."

Zimo nodded. "We'll try that."

"What have you been doing up until now?" Tasha said.

"We patrol the streets. Walk around and make sure everything is safe."

"That's a waste," Carver said. "You need to stop them at the border. Then you won't have as many incidents inside. Some will still slip through, but there's not much you can do without more people."

"Thank you," Zimo said. "We will try this and let you know next time you come for dinner."

Carver pushed back his chair. Stood. Bowed toward Feng. "Thank you for the meal."

"Very welcome." Feng put a hand on Carver's shoulder. "Very, very welcome!"

Carver left by the back door. Started walking back toward California Street.

"You're strange, Carver." Tasha shook her head. "You're like a hero to them."

"I just did what anyone would do." He shrugged.

"You don't seem like the kind of person to help anyone unless it serves your interests."

"True. But sometimes I mess up and help someone for no good reason." He stopped at the trolley station. Leaned against a light pole.

Tasha stood with him.

"You following me all the way back to my place?"

She nodded. "I'm not letting you out of my sight. I don't trust for a minute that you won't run."

"I'm not running."

"Why not?" She looked genuinely curious.

"I have my reasons."

"Tell me those reasons."

"I already did." He heard the trolley bell ringing in the distance. Saw the trolley car appear at the bottom of the hill.

"This can't possibly be just about that cell phone. Not unless there's something valuable on it."

"Just a few nude selfies."

She didn't laugh. "Tell me the truth."

"I already told Noah the truth. There are people I'll lose contact with forever if I don't get the phone back." He shrugged. "Simple as that."

"I have a hard time believing that."

"You don't have to believe it." Carver pretended to watch the trolley. But he was really watching Tasha's facial tics. Trying to gauge her. "I also have a vested interest in learning more about Enigma."

Her eye twitched. Then she stared blankly at him. Like she wasn't sure what to believe or how to respond. "You say that so casually. Like it's no problem that there are dangerous people after you."

"It's a problem." The trolley stopped in front of them. He climbed on. There were wooden benches to sit on. The ones next to the operator faced outward toward the street. The ones further back in the car faced inward. Carver sat on a bench facing outward.

Tasha got on after him. There was space for her to sit next to him. She held onto a pole next to the bench instead. "Of course, it's a problem. It's a huge problem."

Other passengers glanced at her. Probably wondering if there was about to be an argument. Some of them got off the trolley in a hurry before it started moving again.

Carver spread his arms on the back of the seat. No one else was sitting there and he wanted to stretch. He'd chosen this seat because it gave him an open view of the road. Turn his head ninety degrees in either direction and he could see everything.

He wasn't just sightseeing. He was checking on something else. Specifically, to see if someone was following them. And more noticeably if no one was following them. The latter seemed to be the case.

That rang alarm bells in Carver's head. Noah wasn't just going to let him go. He wasn't the kind of guy to let an important new asset out of his sight. That might be why Tasha was here. She wasn't following him for her own sake. She was following him on Noah's orders.

That didn't seem likely. Tasha was looking out for herself. Noah was keeping tabs on Carver somehow.

It was also almost guaranteed that the phone Noah gave Carver had location services enabled. Noah could go on a website and find the location of the phone anytime he wanted.

That possibility was easier to eliminate. The solution was in the duffel bag he'd gotten from Lee.

The trolley stopped at an intersection next to the hotel Carver had borrowed the car from earlier. He hopped off. Tasha followed him. He walked down the driveway. Past the valets. Inside the lobby.

The woman at the desk smiled. "Welcome to the Stanford!"

Carver smiled back. Waved. "Thank you. I'm enjoying my stay here."

"We're so glad to hear that! Can I help you with anything?"

Carver shook his head. "Not now, but I might have some friends stop by. Can you send them to my room, fifty-one zero two?"

"Absolutely, sir."

"Thanks." Carver continued toward the elevators.

Tasha whistled. "This is where you're staying? It's five hundred a night."

"Yeah, it's not too bad." He past the elevators. Found the restrooms. Tasha didn't follow him inside. Carver went into a stall. Closed the door. Took out Noah's phone. Turned on the screen. He removed an identical phone from the duffel bag.

Lee had a variety of burners to choose from. Carver had taken three to be safe. He manually copied the three contacts from Noah's phone to the new burner phone. Then he dropped the phone into the trash. Covered it with paper towels.

Carver used the bathroom. Went back out to the lobby. Tasha was there.

"That took a while. Stomach problems?"

He nodded. "Constipation. Thanks for asking."

"Why didn't you wait until you got to your hotel room?"

"I don't want to stink up my own room." He walked back through the lobby. Left the building.

Tasha grabbed his arm. "Did you seriously just go in there to use the bathroom?"

"Better than using the street." He walked down the driveway. Reached the sidewalk. Crossed the street. There was a bus stop across the street. He went there. Sat down. Pulled his hoodie over his head.

Tasha sat next to him. "We're taking the bus now? Where in the hell are we going?"

"Nowhere for now." Carver leaned back and waited. It took less time than he'd expected. A Prius pulled up. It was loaded down with three men. Carver couldn't see the faces but he knew who they were.

Carver took another item from the bag. Another item Lee had provided him. A monocular. He put it to his eye. Toggled on night vision. Watched the Prius enter the roundabout in front of the hotel.

Deshawn got out of the backseat. Went inside. He spoke to a concierge. Showed her a picture of Carver. It had been taken while he was helping Jeremy set up the computer in the breakroom. Taken from the security cameras.

It wasn't the picture Deshawn had taken in Noah's office. Maybe he hadn't been taking a picture after all. Either way, Someone had finally gotten a clear picture of him. He didn't like it. Not one little bit. It was something he'd have to take care of. Not now, but later.

He'd burn down the entire building if he had to.

CHAPTER 24

Carver kept watching Deshawn.

The concierge looked a little confused. It wasn't normal to show someone a picture and ask if they were staying there. But Carver hadn't given her his name. Just a room number. She stared at the picture for a moment nodded. Wrote something on a slip of paper. Probably the room number.

She pointed at the elevators. Deshawn nodded. But he didn't go to the elevators. He walked back outside. Slid into the backseat. Handed the slip of paper to Noah. Noah said something. Carver wasn't great at reading lips but it looked like he'd repeated the room number.

They sat there for a time. Watching and waiting. Noah looked at his phone. Carver could only see the side of the phone from his position. He figured Noah was looking at a dot on the map.

The trash had been almost full. A nice hotel like this wouldn't let it stay full for long. It would be taken out. Probably thrown in a dumpster out back. The dot would move then. Not by much, but maybe enough to arouse curiosity.

He tucked away the monocular. "Guess that answers that."

Tasha looked from the Prius to him. "Is that Titus' car?"

"Yep." He stood. "Where do you live?"

"I'm not telling you."

"Fair enough. I'll see you tomorrow." He started walking.

Tasha followed. "I told you I'm not letting you out of my sight."

Carver stopped. "Then let's go to your place. My house is a mess."

"I'm not showing you where I live."

"My thoughts exactly." Carver stared at her. "You've got two choices. Stop following me or take me to your place if you want to keep an eye on me all night."

"And if I don't?"

"Then I guess we'll be sleeping on a park bench."

She stiffened. "Then let's sleep on a park bench."

"You're that afraid I'll run?"

She nodded.

"And you're on orders from Noah to keep an eye on me?"

"Noah doesn't know." She narrowed her eyes. "He was tracking the burner phone, wasn't he?"

"Yep. I'm surprised he's not tracking yours."

"He's not worried about me."

"Because he has your sister as collateral."

Tasha nodded.

"Does he physically have her?"

"No, but he keeps tabs on her."

"How old is she?"

"I'm not telling you anything else."

"Fair enough." Carver started walking again. Tasha was telling the truth as far as he could see. She was concerned he would run. She wasn't doing it for Noah. It looked like he could take her to his residence, such as it was.

"That looks like a comfortable bench." Tasha pointed to a bench across the road.

Carver stopped at the next trolley station. Tasha looked at him but didn't say anything else. The trolley stopped. They climbed on. Rode it until it stopped at Market Street. Got off. Walked toward the park next to the Embarcadero.

The tent city was a little bigger than last time. Three more tents had gone up at the perimeter. Tommy's little city was growing fast.

Carver walked between the tents. Walked toward Tanner's tent. It was locked.

"Someone put up a field tent?" Tasha laughed. "That's practically a mansion by tent standards."

Carver was almost embarrassed to show her his tent. He unlocked it. Ducked inside. She ducked in after him. He sat on the sleeping bag. Turned on the camping lamp. Spread his hands. "Welcome to Casa de Carver."

Tasha wrinkled her nose. "It stinks."

He took off his hoodie. Unstrapped the holster. Slid out the Glock. Set it next to his clothing bag.

Tasha wrinkled her nose again. "Ew. A Glock forty-five?"

Carver popped out the magazine. Cleared the chamber. "You know your Glocks."

"I know my guns. Period." She took the Glock. Broke it down. Put it back together. She wasn't the fastest, but she was fast enough.

"Military?"

She shook her head. "Military dad and brother."

"Older brother."

"Yes."

"That's nice." Carver put the loose bullet in the magazine. Clicked it into the pistol. Put it under his makeshift pillow. "Real nice."

He took off his shoes. His socks. His shirt. He lay down on his back.

"Your feet stink."

He didn't respond.

Tasha stared at him long and hard. "You're going to sleep?"

"Yep." He turned off the camping lamp. "Sweet dreams."

Tasha sighed. Polyester rustled. Shoes thumped off. "It's cold. Do you have another blanket?"

He picked up the hoodie. Held it out until he felt her hand. She took it. Didn't even say thanks.

Carver closed his eyes. Went through his relaxation ritual. Fell asleep fast.

Something woke him up. It was dark outside. He heard traffic. Heard distant trolley bells. He checked the burner phone. It was almost nine.

He hadn't been sleeping long. Something had woken him up. He reached out slowly with a hand. Felt his hoodie. Tasha wasn't there. He reached under his clothes bag. The Glock was still there.

Carver sat up. Put on the hoodie. Pulled on his socks and shoes. Felt for the tent zipper. It was closed but not locked. He unzipped it. Crawled out. Crouched and listened.

Had Tasha decided to go home? Or was she just going to the bathroom?

The tent city was quiet. All except for conversation drifting up from somewhere in the middle. He trained his ear on it. It sounded like it was coming from Tanner's tent.

He crouch-walked along the backside of the tents. Stopped and listened. The conversation was louder now. He continued along the tents. Reached the tent closest to the sidewalk.

Carver went around it. Peered down the alley between the tents. Saw a light glowing in one tent. Tanner's tent.

He went past the tent alley. Around the back of the tents on the other side. Kept going until he was behind Tanner's tent. He listened. Heard loud whispering. It was too muffled to make sense of.

There was a space between Tanner's tent and the one next door. Carver crept between them. Went to the front of the tent. It was zipped closed, but it wasn't locked.

Carver stepped to the side. Bent down. Pinched the large zipper between his fingers. He yanked it up. The conversation died immediately. The canvas fell open. Carver looked inside. Saw Tanner holding a rifle. Bringing it to bear.

"Housekeeping," Carver said.

Carver pushed the other flap to the side. Saw who Tanner had been talking with. It wasn't Noah. Wasn't any of Noah's lieutenants. Wasn't Mayor Tommy either.

It was Tasha.

Tanner lowered the rifle. "That's a good way to get your head blown off."

Carver nodded at the rifle. "You have good trigger discipline. Almost like you were in the military or something."

Tasha was standing on the other side of the table. She glared at Carver. Didn't look guilty at all. Like she wasn't ashamed that he'd found her in here. Almost like she hoped he'd find her.

Carver walked in. Looked at the table. There were flyers on the table. There was a woman's image on the flyers. Some text above and below the image. *Missing Woman: Tasha Silverman. Please call this number with any information.*

"This is strange." Carver noticed a foldout chair. He sat in it. "Real strange."

Tanner removed the magazine from his rifle. Cleared the chamber. Put the rifle in a case. "I thought he was asleep."

"Obviously, he woke up." Tasha sighed. "Carver, you can't say anything about this to Noah."

"Wasn't planning on it." Carver wriggled in the seat. "This is comfy." He looked around the tent. Noted specifics. One cot. One sleeping bag. Multiple rifle cases. Multiple ammo cans. He looked at Tanner. "Planning on taking down Noah's entire organization?"

"I don't owe you an explanation, Carver." Tanner unfolded another chair. Sat down.

"It's up to you," Carver said. "I can draw my own conclusions."

Tasha sat on the edge of the table. Faced Carver. Glanced at Tanner. "I really don't think we can trust him. It's not worth it."

Tanner nodded. "I agree. But we don't have much of a choice."

"I think we do." Tasha sighed. "Carver, just go back to your tent."

It was classic psyops. Simple reverse psychology. They wanted him to resist. To tell them he wasn't going anywhere until they told him what was going on. To insist that they let him help them.

There wasn't much resemblance in Tasha and Tanner's features. Maybe it was because her hair was red and his was brown. Her eyes were green, and Tanner's were brown. She was pale. Tanner had olive skin.

Their noses looked similar. That was about it. But that didn't mean anything. Carver had met plenty of siblings who looked nothing alike. Tanner, it seemed, was the military brother who'd trained Tasha in weapons.

Out of all the tent cities in San Francisco, how had Tanner ended up in this one? How had he ended up in the same one as Carver? It wasn't a coincidence that Tanner had appeared a day after Carver.

This was planned. It had to be. The odds of it occurring naturally were astronomical. He wanted to ask how they did it, but he didn't. He wasn't going to play their game. They were going to play his.

Carver stood. "I'm going back to sleep. Try to keep it down, okay?" He headed for the exit.

Tanner and Tasha exchanged looks.

"Carver, wait." Tasha grabbed his arm. "Maybe we do need to explain some things to you. I don't want this getting back to Noah."

"Why would I tell Noah anything?" Carver feigned confusion.

Tasha threw up her hands. "Screw you, Carver. You already figured out that Tanner is my brother, didn't you?"

Carver glanced at the flyers. "Why haven't I seen a single one of those around town?"

"Because Noah's men warned me to stop." Tanner worked his jaw back and forth. "They told me to stop looking."

"I knew Tanner was looking for me. I called him. Came and talked to him." Tasha pressed her lips together. "I told him that I couldn't be free until Noah was dead. Otherwise, Enid would always be in danger."

"Tasha, Tanner, and Enid?" Carver frowned. "Who in the hell named you kids?"

"Enid was our grandmother's name on our dad's side." Tanner fiddled with the magazine he'd pulled from his rifle. "He died a while back. All we have left are our mom and sister."

More pieces were sliding together now. Carver saw a more complete picture. "You want my help to take down Noah."

Tasha nodded. "Tanner saw potential the moment he met you. He sent me a picture. I put two and two together along with the Dodge Ram and realized who you were."

"It's a Ramcharger. The Ram is the truck."

She looked confused. Like she couldn't understand why that mattered.

Carver kept talking. "So, you knew where I lived all along?"

She nodded. "You're such a pain in the ass. I hated playing along. I just wanted to punch you in the face and tell you to go back to your dirty little tent."

"Rude." Carver studied their faces. They seemed sincere. Dumb, but sincere. "You're telling me Tanner ended up here by chance?"

"I've been moving my tent around town. Trying to keep off Noah's radar." Tanner shrugged. "Just so happened I ended up here and saw you."

Carver wasn't sure he believed it. But it seemed plausible enough. "Okay."

Tasha folded her arms over her chest. "Now that we've settled that, can we get to the meat and potatoes?"

Carver grunted. "You want me to help you get rid of Noah."

She nodded. "After what you did to the Farm, this should be a cakewalk."

"It's never a cakewalk." Carver looked at Tanner. "If your brother really was former military, he can tell you that."

"I don't need to prove my credentials to you, Carver." Tanner thumbed a bullet out of the magazine. Pushed it back in. "If you agree, we'll have two people on the inside."

Carver raised an eyebrow. "And we what? Bum rush Noah and gang while they're chilling in his office and ice them?"

Tasha shook her head. "We can't do that. Noah claims he has a failsafe if something happens to him. Someone else will kill Enid."

"We need to find out what that failsafe is," Tanner said. "Once we know, then we can take action."

"Okay. So, I have to find a way to take down Enigma, find Noah's failsafe, and then kill Noah and gang?" Carver brushed off his hands. "Easy."

"The two of us can pull it off," Tasha said. "You're smart. You already sent Noah on a wild goose chase tonight."

"A failsafe like this isn't something you write down on a scrap of paper." Carver tapped his temple. "You just know who it is and what they're going to do."

"Provided Noah isn't bluffing," Tanner said.

"The only way to know for sure is to interrogate Noah."

"Deshawn might know too," Tasha said.

Carver noticed she didn't mention Titus. Probably because Titus didn't seem like the brightest of the bunch. Titus was the brawn. Noah was the brains. What did that make Deshawn? Certainly not an advisor. There might be something deeper there. A friendship perhaps? Maybe they grew up together.

Carver posed the question. "Who is Deshawn to Noah?"

"They're friends," Tasha said. "They go way back from what I can tell. Titus has been around a long time too, but I don't sense the same connection between him and the others."

"He used to compete in ultimate fighting," Tanner said. "He had a bright career, but it stalled out for some reason."

"Good to know." Carver considered that. If Noah shared anything with anyone, it would be Deshawn. But would either of them bend under interrogation? Would they bend under torture? Or would Noah just taunt them and refuse to talk?

The latter was most likely. Because Noah would know if he gave up that information his life would be over. It didn't seem possible to solve the failsafe issue and unravel Enigma at the same time.

Those were two different objectives. Diametrically opposed. Carver needed Noah to fight Enigma. The man and his organization were assets, not liabilities. This was like any poison pill operation.

Use the enemy to take out another enemy. Then kill that enemy from the inside out. Rhodes had been a master at planning those kinds of operations. It was like running a long con except you weren't doing it for money.

Noah knew who Carver was. Sometimes that would be a bad thing. In a case like this, it was a good thing. Because Noah fancied himself a brilliant strategist. He was also smart enough to know he didn't have the manpower to achieve his goals.

Carver decided a litmus test was in order. "We help Noah with Enigma first. Then we finish off Noah."

Tanner shook his head. "We don't have time. And screwing with Enigma only puts us all in more danger."

"Why don't we have time?" Carver tapped a finger on the table. "Why don't you move Enid far away?"

"We tried that once. He tracked her down in twenty-four hours." Tasha shook her head. "He must have someone watching her. Must have multiple ways of tracking her."

"I want her current location. I want pictures of her. Of her school. Her home. I need to know what I'm dealing with."

Tanner nodded. "I'll give you a file."

"Why do you want all of that?" Tasha said.

"Because I don't know you. I don't know any of you." Carver didn't trust them either. They were playing a long con. He could sense it. He had to smoke it out. Reveal it.

Before his ignorance got him killed.

CHAPTER 25

Leon was stuck in Arizona.

His plans for a charter flight out of Houston had gone out the window. His buddy in Houston hadn't answered his texts or calls. He'd finally gotten through to someone at the charter flight company. They told him his friend was overseas for the next month.

Now Leon was here.

The old Ford had taken him to Flagstaff. It had breathed its last breath of carbon monoxide just inside town. Trapped him in a fast-food restaurant parking lot. Now he was faced with a decision. Steal a car, or risk using funds to buy one.

He'd used the last of his cash on the Ford and other necessities. He could probably get away with using an ATM. The account he was drawing from was supposedly secret. Unconnected to him. But it wasn't foolproof. If Enigma had dug into his financials, they'd see the shell companies. See the money funneled to other accounts.

They could have eyes on them. The moment he used one, it would raise a red flag. Send an alert to someone. The location would be known an instant later. A jet would warm up. A response team would hurry to the runway.

Within an hour, they'd be on the way.

Maybe he was being paranoid. It had kept him alive so far. No good reason to stop now. Stealing a car came with its own set of risks. The theft might be noticed immediately. An APB would be put on the license plate.

He wouldn't be safe until he crossed the state border. Which was why he needed to find something that might not be missed for a while. Airports were good places to find cars like that. Cars that were left in long term parking while their owners traveled elsewhere.

But the airport was a good seven miles south. He didn't have cash for transport. Couldn't use a card to pay for ride share. Which meant he'd have to get there the old-fashioned way.

Walking.

NOAH WALKED THROUGH the hotel lobby.

This hotel usually charged four to five hundred a day. It was the tourist off season, so the rates were lower. But it was still a fancy place for someone like Carver to stay. A real fancy place. The shoe didn't fit.

Deshawn walked out of the restroom. He held up a cell phone. The same one Noah had given Carver.

Noah grinned.

Deshawn frowned. "He obviously doesn't respect the rules."

"I gave him the phone. I didn't tell him he had to keep it." Noah shrugged. "It's that kind of trickery that's going to get us Enigma."

"Except now we don't know where he is, boss." Titus scowled. "You ought to let me put some fear into that boy. Knock him down a peg or two."

"I agree," Deshawn said. "It's like bringing a pit bull into the house to get rid of cats. And then the pit bull is the biggest danger."

"Naw, ain't nothing I can't handle." Titus flexed a meaty fist. "He might think I'm just a street fighter. I say we let him play around and find out."

"For now, we're going to let Carver do his own thing." Noah took the phone. Pocketed it. "I'll see how things are going in a couple of days. Then I'll take action if necessary."

"Whatever you say, boss." Titus cracked his knuckles. "I'm aching to teach that boy some respect."

"You might get that chance." Noah left the lobby. Went to the Prius. "For now, let's go relax. Take the night off."

Titus drove them back to the office. Noah got in his Challenger. Revved the engine. Closed his eyes and listened to the rumble. He watched Titus drive out of the parking lot. Turn and leave.

Then he drove out of the lot. Onto the road. Circled to the backside of the building. Pulled into a service area. It was a place where utility vehicles could park. A place where electricity, water, and sewage came into the building.

It was a nice hidden spot. His own private motor pool.

Noah parked the Challenger next to a row of plain cars. He chose a white sedan. Backed it out. Exited the service area. Then he went back toward the front of the building. Deshawn was just pulling out of the parking lot.

Noah got behind another car. Slowed down. Waited for Deshawn to leave. Let him get a few car lengths ahead of him. Then he followed him.

Deshawn was his best friend growing up. His most trusted advisor and ally. Someone he could tell anything to. And that made him extremely dangerous.

He'd been acting strange lately. Vanishing for long periods of time. Noah had considered tracking his car. But Deshawn was a paranoid type. He swept his car for bugs regularly. Did the same for Titus's car too.

There was nothing wrong with that. It was smart. But it also meant Noah couldn't rely on technology to track him. He'd have to do it himself. Deshawn wasn't telling him something. That something might get Noah killed.

Or it might be something harmless. Maybe Deshawn was a sex freak. Maybe he had a harmless secret. A secret he was afraid to tell Noah.

But if it was something harmful. Something that could hurt Noah's enterprise. Then Noah would have no choice. He'd have to end a long friendship.

End it with a bullet to the head.

CARVER DIDN'T TRUST ANYONE.

There were too many interests competing for his time. Too many people with lofty goals. Goals that required a lot more than just one man and a handful of amateurs.

Carver went to his tent. Picked up a few supplies. Then he zipped the tent. Locked it. Tasha and Tanner were still talking inside the field tent. He would have spied on them if he thought it would be helpful. But they weren't going to talk openly. Not when they knew Carver could be just outside.

That was just fine. It gave Carver a chance to slip away. To leave Tasha behind. Because he had a few things to take care of. Things he didn't want the others knowing about. He found a lonely cab idling on Market Street. Hopped in.

He gave the man an address. It was a place on Steiner Street. Carver hadn't had a chance to see that part of town before his car was burgled. The dead of night seemed as good a time as any.

The driver put in the address. Drove to the destination. Stopped at the corner of the block. About a hundred feet from the Painted Ladies. The driver didn't even glance at them. He'd probably seen them so many times they were nothing special anymore.

They were famous houses. Also called the Seven Sisters. Each one painted a bright pastel color. And one of them just so happened to be home to one of the people on Carver's list. That person wasn't Maryann Lewis, the city councilwoman.

Carver had looked at the addresses for each of the people on the list. He'd singled out people who matched a profile. A profile that demonstrated living beyond their means. Or at least at the very edge of their means.

The San Francisco district attorney, Bret Bushner, matched that profile to a T. Carver had looked up his salary. Public record told him it was just north of two hundred grand. That was good money in most parts of the country.

In San Francisco it was a living wage. Something that would put a roof over your head. But any of the Painted Ladies were more than just a house. Not because they were big or modern. But because they were rare. Because they sold for nearly four million each.

Carver had looked over news articles. Gleaned useful information. Bret Bushner had been a newcomer to local politics. He'd been in a tight race until a car accident killed his opponent. His net worth at that time had been negligible.

In fact, Bushner had been living with his parents when he ran for office. Now a scant two years later he was living in a four-million-dollar home on a two-hundred-thousand-dollar salary. That was a big red flag. One that the IRS usually noticed real fast.

But this guy was in a protected class. He was a politician. Unless he made an enemy of someone powerful, he wasn't going to get into trouble.

At least not with the typical authorities.

Carver pulled up his hoodie. Put on the facemask. Got out of the taxi. He was about a block down from the house in question. Aside from the fresh paint and the whimsical colors, Carver didn't know what made these houses any better than the ones around them.

The one on the end had scaffolding outside. It looked like it was undergoing renovations. Carver walked alongside it. Studied the house behind it. There was a wall. Behind the wall was a narrow space. A small alley.

He continued studying the area. Looked at the trees. The poles. The porches. The sides of the houses. Every little detail mattered. A single missed detail could get you captured or killed.

There was a camera mounted on the porch of the house in front of him. Nothing on the back or sides of the Painted Lady at the corner.

The camera on the porch was pointed at the stairs. Angled to view anyone who came up there. The alley between the houses was a blind spot. It was also pitch black. The nearest streetlamp was on the opposite corner.

Carver jumped. Caught the top of the wall. Muscled himself up and over. He was behind the first Painted Lady. The target home was in the middle. He used his monocular to study the area.

It was dark so he turned on the night vision. There was a fence. No cameras on the back of the next house. He climbed the fence. Dropped onto the other side. Studied the next hurdle. Another fence. No cameras.

He climbed over the next fence. Crouched. The target house was next. There was a camera on the back. It was angled down. Watching the back yard. Carver stayed in its blind spot. Put his back to the corner of the house.

He peered around it. Saw another camera in the narrow alley between the houses. It was angled to watch the street. No one could come that way without being seen.

There was a blind spot between the side and rear cameras. It might be enough for Carver to slip under the rear camera. But the rear door was covered with a heavy iron gate. He wasn't going to be jimmying it open anytime soon.

Lights were on upstairs. Dim light spilled out of the back windows. Probably because the lights were on in the front room. Bushner was single. He was probably inside. Probably alone.

Carver knew the interior layout. A realtor had recorded video tours of the Painted Ladies a few years back. Aside from a few renovations, the interior was probably largely unchanged.

But the exterior had been beefed up. There were iron bars on all the windows. Security cameras. Heavy iron exterior doors. It looked nice. Probably made Bushner feel nice and safe. But it was just an added layer of annoyance to Carver.

Carver hopped back over the fences. Went back to the sidewalk. Walked around the corner. Looked up at the front of Bushner's house. The first story windows were barred. The second story windows were bare. The attic window was also unguarded.

There was no way Carver was getting access this way. Not unless he got a sixteen-foot ladder or a grappling hook. And that was just fine. Because he wasn't planning on scaling the front of Bushner's house.

He went back to the house at the corner. Looked up at the scaffolding. There was cloth wrapped around the outside. Probably to hide the renovation work. Plywood was laid over the metal bars to form a platform.

Someone had removed the first level scaffolding ladders. That wasn't an obstacle. Carver jumped. Gripped the plywood platform. Pulled himself up and on top. Rolled onto the platform. The ladders to the second and third levels were still there.

No one seemed to be living in the house. It was the dead of night so they might also just be asleep. Carver climbed as quietly as he could.

He could afford to go slow since the scaffolding canvas hid him from any pedestrians. But if they heard someone climbing it at this hour, it would raise suspicions.

The top was level with the roof. He stepped onto it. It was pitch black up there. No one would see him from the street. The house was narrow. Maybe twenty feet wide. He crossed the distance in a few steps.

Stood at the edge. The gap was less than a foot at the narrowest point. He stepped across it. Tread lightly on the next roof. Crossed it to the third house. The next house was Bushner's. He went prone and studied it.

No cameras. Nothing on the roof except a chimney stack.

He walked to the front of the roof. Went prone. Looked over the edge at the attic window below. It was identical to the one on Bushner's house. Looked like it had been upgraded to a vinyl window sometime in the past.

Carver crept to the edge. Stepped over to Bushner's roof. He studied the attic window. It looked the same as the neighbor's. There was no curtain on the window. No light on in the room.

There was a small decorative ledge beneath it. He lowered himself to the ledge. Silently dropped in front of the window.

Looked inside with the night vision monocular. There were boxes piled inside. A treadmill. Other various odds and ends. No cameras.

Carver checked the sides of the window. Looked for wires or telltale signs of alarm sensors. He didn't see any. There also didn't appear to be motion sensors inside. This was the perfect point of penetration.

Provided the window cooperated.

He put on his gloves. Put a hand against the window. Pushed it firmly up and down. It wiggled. That was a good sign. It gave him a couple of options. He went for the option that made the least noise.

In this case it was a slim jim. A slim piece of metal that could fit into cracks. Unlock car doors. Jimmy open house doors. It was an excellent all-around tool for getting you into places you weren't supposed to be.

The window lock was a curved piece of metal. There was nothing for the slim jim to catch onto. Friction was key here. Pushing the slim piece of metal between the frame and the curved metal would hopefully cause it to rotate slowly but surely.

He slid the slim jim between the panes. Pushed it sideways. It rubbed against the back of the locking mechanism. Friction did the rest. Caused the mechanism to rotate ever so slightly. It wasn't much, but it was working.

Carver pulled out the slim jim. Slid it back in on the left side. Pushed to the right. Friction nudged the lock a bit more.

He washed. Rinsed. Repeated.

It took a few tries. The lock finally rotated enough so the edge protruded. The slim jim caught the edge. Rotated the lock the rest of the way.

He put the slim jim back in his bag. Pushed the window up. It resisted. Probably hadn't been opened in years. It finally broke free and slid open. He climbed inside. Closed the window behind him. Then he stopped and listened.

A voice drifted up from below. A male voice. Talking urgently. Dishes clinked. A water faucet turned on.

Carver eased to the edge of the stairs. He looked down. Tested the first one with his weight. It didn't creak. He tested the next one. And the next. It creaked slightly but the clinking dishes and pouring water drowned it out.

He made it to the first landing. Looked around the corner. He could see the den from this point of view. Bushner was sitting on a couch. Typing on a laptop. He was on the phone. Talking and looking annoyed at the noise.

Carver leaned out a little more. Saw a woman cleaning the dishes. She was an older woman. Asian. Probably a house maid or a cook. Maybe both.

Bushner looked exasperated. He put a hand over the phone. "Rosie, can you please wash the dishes tomorrow? I'm on a very important call."

The woman turned off the water. Spoke with a light accent. "Yes, Mr. Bushner." She dried her hands. Put some items in the refrigerator and trash. Wiped off the counter. A few moments later she was out the door and gone.

Bushner was alone.

— · —

CHAPTER 26

Carver waited in the shadows.

Without the maid, the house was quiet. Too quiet. It gave Carver time to think about strategy. He could handle this rough or smooth. Violently or stealthily. The second choice was usually the best.

It just required a lot more waiting around. It wasn't like Carver had anywhere to be. He backed up a little. Moved himself out of sight in case Bushner happened to look up at the stairs. It was dark, but he might sense something. Might see a shadow that wasn't supposed to be there.

Bushner was still on the phone. He nodded. Grunted. Said yes a handful of times. It seemed like a one-sided conversation. Carver wanted to know who was on the other end of that call.

The leech could download the phone's contents. There might be answers in the data. Or it might have the same protections as the phones from the Farm. Their texting app was encrypted. It deleted messages after a few hours.

The leech couldn't download what wasn't there. That would be bad for Bushner. Very bad. Because then Carver would have to resort to interrogation. Possibly torture.

It wasn't ideal, but it would do the trick. In the end, results were all that mattered.

Bushner looked stressed. The phone call wasn't going well. He finally got a few words in. "I told you a radical shift too quickly would do more harm than good. I can't stop the recall. I don't have the power to."

His face went from red to starch white in an instant. He shivered. Nodded. "I understand. Yes. Absolutely. Whatever it takes."

He'd been given an ultimatum. That could be used to Carver's advantage. But it probably wouldn't work. Bushner was too scared of his employers to betray them.

Carver retreated back upstairs. The old carpet smelled a little moldy. But it was soft. Softer than the ground, anyway. He lay down on his back. Crossed his hands over his body. Rested his eyes.

His internal clock woke him a couple hours later. The house was dark. The climate system was running. Pumping out heat. The blower was somewhere below him. Maybe on the first floor. The rattling was loud even two floors away.

That was good. Real good. It gave him plenty of cover for walking around. He stood. Used his phone's flashlight to orient himself in the darkness. He reached the top of the stairs. The heater stopped running.

The house went dead silent.

Carver grinned. Fate would give you a gift then rip it away. Par for the course. He was glad he'd opted for soft soled shoes instead of boots for his tourist adventures. Otherwise, he'd have to take off his shoes.

He crept downstairs. Stopped about halfway down. Took out his monocular and swept it across the den and kitchen. He didn't look for the phone. Didn't look for a laptop. He looked at the home's layout. Looked for motion sensors. Cameras.

He knew what the house looked like from the tour videos, but it was better to confirm the details. The den was on the second floor. The kitchen and bedroom were too. The garage and basement were on the first floor.

There were IR cameras in the corners of the room. It looked like they were meant to watch Bushner, not intruders. There were no motion sensors. Probably because the cameras had them built in. Sneaking around the house unseen was going to be difficult.

Difficult, but not impossible.

Carver zoomed in on a camera. There was a low-voltage wire running into the ceiling. It was a common setup. Wired directly into the home for power and networking. It was hard to tell where the wiring went.

Carver lowered the monocular. Turned on the phone flashlight. He examined the paint on the wall next to him. It was older paint. It looked thick. Like layers of it had accumulated over the years.

The material was drywall, not plaster. These homes originally had plaster, according to the tour video. The plaster had been replaced a long time ago. He raised the monocular. Examined the wall around the camera.

The paint on the wall around the camera looked the same as the rest of the paint. No sign of repairs. No sign the drywall had been cut out so wires could be run through the wall. There was just a small hole in the ceiling. The wiring ran through it.

The wiring was coming up to this floor. To the attic.

Carver went back upstairs. Back to the attic. He walked between the piles of boxes. Found a closet door. The space around it was clear. The door was heavy duty wood. Maybe oak. There was a biometric reader on the lock.

Thankfully, the door opened outward. He slipped the slim jim into the crack. Worked open the latch in a few seconds. Opened the door. Inside was a table. On the table was a small computer.

A small network switch was next to it. There were several network cables running into it. Carver looked at the switch. Confirmed it was POE—power over ethernet. That meant the network cable also delivered electricity to the camera.

It was a nice little setup. Probably recorded everything in the house and uploaded it to a server controlled by Enigma. Bushner was theirs in every sense of the word. Lock, stock, and barrel.

He wondered if anyone was actively watching, or if they simply reviewed the footage later. The cameras only recorded when they sensed motion, so there wouldn't be a lot of footage. Which meant the cameras were inactive right now.

Without motion, the cameras went to sleep. Unless someone remotely activated one, they would be dormant. Waiting for something to wake them. Which was perfect.

Carver unplugged the power from the switch. It killed the local network and the power to the cameras. With the house quiet and asleep, no one was expecting footage at this hour anyway. Unless Bushner had a stalker who liked to watch him sleep, Carver was in the clear.

The heater came back on. Although it was already stuffy inside the house, Carver welcomed the noise. He went downstairs. Waved a hand toward the first camera. The IR lights didn't activate. It had no power.

That was no excuse to get sloppy. He ensured the other cameras were off. Counted each one in turn. There were two in the den. One in the kitchen. Even one in the guest bathroom. That was five.

The bedroom door was open. Sleeping with an open door was like sitting with your back to the door. Bushner was ballsy. Carver could give him that. Then again, his handlers might have told him to sleep with the door open.

Carver stepped inside. Looked through the monocular. Found the sixth and seventh cameras. The eighth was in the master bath. The shower was enclosed in glass. The camera was lower to prevent condensation from forming on the lens. But it could still see everything.

Bushner's phone was on the nightstand. Connected to a charging cable. Carver turned on the leech. Set it next to the phone. He looked around the room. Didn't see a laptop. It was probably in the office across the den.

The leech connected to the phone. The screen showed him what to expect. Two gigabytes of data. Time to download, five minutes.

Carver left the leech to do its thing. He went to the den. Found the ninth and tenth cameras in the office. Which meant if there were cameras downstairs, they were on a different system. Because there had only been ten cameras attached to the switch upstairs.

It made sense. They hadn't cut into the walls. They'd just drilled up through the floor. Fished the wires through the space between the attic floor and the second-floor ceiling.

The laptop was on a minimalistic desk. The kind with a motor that raised it to standing height. It matched the rest of the décor in the house. Nothing fancy. Nothing traditional. Just open spaces and simply designed furniture.

The laptop was the kind with a detachable keyboard and a touch screen monitor. He tapped the power button. A lock screen appeared. Prompted him for a password. The username was a string of numbers and letters.

The profile picture was a globe of the world. But the continents were black, and the oceans were red. The only thing it was missing was a sword piercing the middle of the planet. As if it had been designed with a science fiction angle in mind.

Carver wondered if that was Bushner's choice or his handlers'. It might be the official symbol of Enigma. It might be something Bushner downloaded from a website. Carver took a picture of it.

He went back to the leech. It was done. He took it to the laptop. Let it do its thing. The leech connected. Examined the contents. It subtracted system files. Focused on documents, images, and so forth. The important stuff.

Most computers saved logins and passwords. The leech could access those records. But it was unlikely Bushner was allowed to save his passwords. Carver had the leech look for them anyway.

The total download was small for a laptop. Only a little larger than the phone's. Carver took what he could get. Went back upstairs to the attic. Took the tablet from the duffel bag. Connected it to the leech.

It took a few minutes to upload. Then he went over the contents. There were a lot of images and videos. Harmless stuff. Pictures of Bushner with other attorneys. Selfies. Videos of Bushner talking about his views on crime.

Carver put in headphones so he could listen to the audio. There wasn't much to it. Just political talk. Nothing that he probably couldn't find in the public domain.

There were texts between Bushner and other officials. Not a lot. Just reminders about events. Tasks. The usual. He skimmed them. Didn't find anything remotely incriminating.

The encrypted messaging app had what he was looking for. The last text was twenty-four hours old. Older texts had been automatically deleted. The last one told Bushner to expect a call. Didn't say from whom. Just said when. The sender was labeled as Dad.

Carver knew a little about the call. He'd overheard Bushner's side. What little he'd said. He knew what it had been about because it was all over the local news. The voters wanted to recall Bushner. They thought he was too soft on crime.

If only they knew who he was really working for.

Carver noticed another folder from the phone. *Recovered*. He opened it. Found four folders. One was named Dad. Another Jenny. The names of the other two were garbled. He opened the one from Dad.

There were more text files inside. The texts that had supposedly been deleted. Texts the leech had recovered. Apparently, the leech was everything Lee advertised. Maybe even more. The one he'd had in Miami couldn't recover deleted files.

Jericho had once explained how file recovery worked. Only the file locaters were deleted. Not the actual files. Some programs could rebuild the directory. Find the missing files. Just like this leech.

He opened the first file. The date was yesterday. *Their funding is from individuals not corporations or rich donors. Unable to shut it down. Moving to next phase.*

Carver dug through the files. Some were garbled. Only bits and pieces were legible. The only thing that stood out was what looked like a name. *Fannie*. The last name was garbled symbols.

He went through the other folders. Read the other text files. They were sufficiently vague. Nothing useful unless he found greater context. But it was still better than nothing.

The laptop had nothing except duplicates of the image and video files from the phone. The only difference were official documents and memorandums. One memo named *Recall Effort* was addressed to staffers.

It had guidelines for all messaging and communications. A list of responses. When to not comment. Another memo was about a prosecutor who refused to follow orders. Bushner had pressured her to drop criminal charges against several defendants.

The attorney refused because they were violent crimes. Bushner retaliated by suspending her and anyone who didn't toe the line. Apparently, that was one of the reasons Bushner was being recalled.

Carver finished skimming the data. Concluded there was very little of use. The only clue was the name Fannie.

Carver opened the search page on the tablet. Searched for *Fannie*. It was too vague. He added Bushner's name to the term. Several local news stories appeared. Most were behind paywalls.

He found one that wasn't. Fannie Myers was a local activist. A chapter leader for multiple anti-crime organizations. An organizer for neighborhood watches. And she was also leading the recall effort for Bushner.

She wasn't the only one. There was another major figure in the effort. Susan Cullen. The prosecutor who'd been suspended. The mayor was strongly considering her as a replacement for Bushner.

It sounded like an uphill battle. A battle Bushner and Enigma were going to lose. Maybe they wanted Susan Cullen. Maybe that was Phase Two. It seemed doubtful. If it was true, Bushner wouldn't have been so upset during the phone conversation.

Carver had a thought. Maybe it wasn't a great thought, but it might be something. He put the leech next to the small computer in the attic closet. The same computer that was connected to the cameras.

The leech linked to it. There were gigs of data to download. It was going to take an hour. Gave him some time to kill. Not literally, of course. That wouldn't solve anything.

He started the download. Considered his options. Maybe Bushner would be willing to talk. There were ways of doing it. Ways that protected Carver's identity. Maybe kept Bushner from talking about it too.

Carver gave it some thought. He lay on the floor. Rested his eyes for a few minutes. Let the leech work. He thought about what Rhodes would do. He compared it to similar operations in the past.

There were always parallels. Always useful lessons from the past. Most of the time Carver or one of his squad mates would infiltrate a place. Steal information. Leave the target blissfully unaware they'd been compromised.

But sometimes there was nothing to find. Only an interrogation would do the trick.

Carver heard noise downstairs. A subtle creak. Probably Bushner going to the bathroom. There were more creaks. Someone walking. Everything went silent. The heater kicked back on and washed out the sound.

He crouched. Went to the stairwell. Didn't see anyone. He hadn't heard a toilet flush either. Or heard someone getting a cup of water. Those were the typical things people got up for in the middle of the night.

Maybe Bushner didn't flush. Maybe he liked to conserve water. *If it's yellow, let it mellow.* Whatever the reason, it put a crimp in Carver's plans. He'd have to wait for Bushner to settle down again.

The download finally finished. Carver waited for the heater to turn on again. When it cut on, he made his way downstairs. Glanced at the thermostat. It was set to seventy-eight degrees. Bushner apparently liked it hot.

Carver went to the bedroom doorway. He listened. Couldn't hear anything over the rattling heater. He stepped inside. Dim light came through the window. Enough to highlight a silhouette. Someone crouching right next to the bed.

The figure lurched upright. Lunged at Carver. It was dark. Difficult to see what he would hit if he swung his fist. Carver met the fist with his elbow. Heard a loud crack. A man shouted in pain. Carver reached out. Grabbed thin air.

Footsteps thudded. Carver followed them out of the bedroom. The figure ran out the front door. Slammed it shut behind them. Carver tried to yank the door open, but it was locked. The only way to open it from the inside was with the biometric reader.

He looked through the window in the door. Caught a glimpse of someone running down the sidewalk. He was dressed like Carver. Dark pants. Dark hoodie. Facemask. He was medium height. Thin.

That was all Carver got before the figure ran out of sight.

Carver went back to the bedroom. He turned on the light. Found Bushner in his bed. He was lying on his back. Eyes closed. Drool pouring from his mouth.

He was dead.

CHAPTER 27

Noah followed Deshawn across town.

His best friend wasn't going home. He was going somewhere else. Somewhere to the north. His home was in Parkside. The clubs he liked to spend his free time in were in the same area. It was too early to go to the clubs anyway.

They crossed the Golden Gate Bridge. Passed Sausalito. Took the Richardson Bay Bridge into Strawberry. The houses here were nothing to look at. But many of them cost as much if not more than similar sized homes in San Francisco.

Noah knew because he'd considered getting a place out here. A retreat when he needed a break from the city. It was quiet out here. No trolleys. Few tourists. Less traffic. It turned out the suburbs were too quiet for him.

He'd rented a place on the bay. The view was amazing. The location was perfect. But without all the sounds of the city, he hadn't been able to sleep a wink. Turning on a television with the volume set to low didn't even do the trick.

Deshawn pulled up to a gated driveway. He stopped. A moment later, the gate rolled open. He drove inside.

Noah whistled. "What the hell, Deshawn?" He looked at the gate. At the tall iron fence around the property. There was a camera at the gate. Noah didn't see any along the fence.

The property on the other side of the fence was nothing special. A small house on a small rise. A few scrubby trees tried to block the view but didn't do a good job of it. He rolled the car forward for a clear view of the driveway and front door.

He opened the glove box. Took a pair of binoculars from inside. He rolled down the window. Looked through the binoculars. Deshawn knocked on the door. A tall blonde woman answered. They hugged. Kissed.

A little girl ran outside. Hugged Deshawn's leg. He picked her up. Kissed her cheek. Laughed and smiled. The girl was maybe two. Just a toddler.

"Holy shit." Noah watched them go inside. "My man has a whole family he didn't tell me about." A family hidden in the hills.

Deshawn had a secret family living in a multimillion-dollar house. He could afford it. Hell, Noah could afford a mansion if he wanted one. But it was all about keeping a low profile. Keeping off the fed's radar.

Noah watched them go inside. They walked past the front window. The woman closed the curtains. Their shadows were still visible on the other side.

He wasn't angry. Wasn't surprised. If he had a family, he wouldn't tell Deshawn about it either. The less everyone knew about his business, the better. And there was something else to consider.

Deshawn loved his hookups. He loved finding women at the bar. Taking them home. And he had a type. Tall blondes. It was possible he'd knocked this girl up. She'd wanted to keep the baby.

He'd talked about starting a family before. Maybe he'd turned an unwanted pregnancy into a family. It certainly didn't look like anything nefarious. It also explained why Deshawn disappeared sometimes. He was trying to live two lives.

Noah put the binoculars away. He leaned back in his seat. Gave it some thought. It was getting late, but he made a call.

A man answered on the first ring. "How can I help you, sir?"

Noah gave him the address of the house. "I want to know who owns it, when it was bought. Everything."

"Yes, sir. Just give me a moment and I'll call you back."

Noah ended the call. Watched the house and waited. His man called him back in fifteen minutes."

"It belongs to Diana Young. Her maiden name is Sanders. She was formerly married to Bryce Sanders."

"The baseball player?"

"Yes, sir."

Noah whistled.

"Her net worth with alimony is north of five million."

"Kids?"

"Yes. Abigail Young. Born well after her divorce from Sanders. Birth records show she is two years of age."

Deshawn was definitely batting out of his league with this one.

"The father is listed as unknown."

"You can have a birth certificate without listing the dad?"

"Yes, sir. Happens all the time. A woman sleeps around after a wild night at a club, finds out she's pregnant weeks later. Father unknown."

"Thanks. That's all I need for now." Noah moved to end the call.

"Sir!"

Noah put the phone back to his ear. "Yes?"

"There is something else that's very interesting about this woman."

"I'm listening."

"She is apparently also an off-brand Marshall."

"I don't know what that means."

The man cleared his throat. "As in, she was conceived out of wedlock to a woman named June Young. A woman who was believed to be a long-time mistress of real estate mogul Henry Marshall."

Noah chuckled. "An off-brand Marshall. Clever."

"Sorry, I should just stick to the facts and not try to make jokes."

"No, no, no, Barry. This one works. I approve."

Barry cleared his throat. "Thank you, sir."

"And this is very interesting." Noah thought hard. The name June Young sounded familiar. But he couldn't put a finger on it.

Barry already had the answer. "June Young was the California state school superintendent for two terms. She supported Tony Yates, the current superintendent."

"And her campaign was funded by Marshall?"

"Her campaign was funded by a political action committee that is linked to Marshall and several other billionaire donors."

Now this was interesting. Deshawn was playing family with a billionaire's illegitimate daughter. A woman who had top level political connections. Possibly access to vast resources. The exact kind of person Enigma had in its bullpen.

The most important question was, did Deshawn know? Or was he being played? Getting the answer to that question would be tricky.

"Got anything else for me, Barry?"

"No, sir. That's everything in the FBI database. There might be more elsewhere, but I wouldn't have access to it."

"You're a good man, Barry. Call me if you find any other bombshells, okay?"

Barry cleared his throat. "Yes, sir. My pleasure."

Noah ended the call. He stared at the house for a long while. Ideas danced through his head. Should he go to the gate? Ring the bell and demand answers? That kind of straightforward action would just put him in the crosshairs.

He needed a safer method to get to the truth. Maybe a third party. Someone who possessed the necessary skills to get to the truth of the matter. Because in this business, there were no coincidences.

Billionaires were exactly the kind of people who'd fund something like Enigma. Marshall might be a major backer of the organization.

Deshawn might be a fish on a hook. He might have been set up. Lured in by his own male weaknesses. And he might not even know it. Or there was a more sinister possibility.

Deshawn was working for Enigma.

It didn't seem possible. Not after all they'd been through. They'd grown up together. Gone to school together. Even got the same scholarships for a paid ride through university.

It was the time at university that made Noah rethink the current situation.

Deshawn had met a girl. A blonde, of course. And she was heavy into political activism. He was always out with her. Always protesting. Doing sit-ins. Hanging out with radical student groups.

Noah had been a philosophy major. He knew plenty of radical types. The types who wouldn't do a single day's work if they could get paid for free. That turned Noah off to university.

That was the time he started pushing drugs. Stopped going to school. Stopped accumulated debt for a worthless degree.

While Noah was working hard to make bank, Deshawn was out posting flyers. Threatening professors. Doing sit-ins at the dean's office. Then an opposing group had come to counterprotest them.

Fights had broken out. Weapons had been used by both sides. Deshawn's girlfriend had been struck in the head with a bat. One of her own people had accidentally hit her. She'd been permanently disabled, mentally and physically.

Campus security was increased. Protests were shut down. Dozens of radical student groups were forced to disband.

Noah convinced Deshawn to quit school. To come work with him. University was a waste of time and money. And it was a hotbed of political activism.

They returned home to San Francisco. Noah started building his black-market empire. But he was running into problems with the local cops and politicians. Many were owned by other local gangs.

Deshawn was supposed to grease the political wheels. His disabled ex-girlfriend had family in high places. He tried to use them to his advantage. Then he'd been pulled back into politics by another woman.

This woman had helped Noah put more politicians on his payroll. The rival gangs couldn't outbid him. He'd used the power of local government to get rid of the competition. It was no different than what corporations did.

If the law was against you, pay off politicians to change the law. If the cops were after you, pay off politicians to keep the cops away from you. Money was the answer to everything.

Deshawn's new connections had helped their enterprise succeed. They'd consolidated power. Noah had become the king of San Francisco. The politicians and everyone else benefitted from his success.

Then Enigma came. Everything changed. Now Noah's mighty empire was decaying. Turning to dust right before his very eyes. Because Enigma beat him at his own game.

And now Deshawn was in bed with another powerful woman. A woman connected to someone who might be at the heart of Enigma. Which meant one thing.

Deshawn might be his enemy.

CHAPTER 28

Carver checked for Bushner's pulse.

There wasn't one. His gloves were thin. He'd feel a heartbeat if it was there. There was something on the floor. A small plastic bottle. Carver picked it up. There was liquid inside. Not much.

The top of the bottle was designed like a dropper. Squeeze the bottle, a drop comes out. Except it didn't contain eyedrops. This stuff was prescription. Stuff called Lonadone. The kind of stuff the VA hospitals once prescribed as pain medication.

They didn't prescribe it anymore. Mainly because it was highly addictive. Easy to overdose on. Anything more than a few drops could stop someone's heart because it was nothing more than liquid fentanyl.

Apparently, killing Bushner was Enigma's Phase Two. Or maybe it was an intermediary phase. Insurance. They wanted Bushner silenced. Dead men tell no tales.

Whatever the reason, it seemed wasteful. It probably cost hundreds of thousands if not millions of dollars to get someone elected here. That made Bushner a very expensive asset. Someone worth preserving. Maybe not at all costs, but certainly more than this.

Carver decided not to waste the opportunity this presented. He went into the closet. Found Bushner's wallet. Took the cash. He rifled through the drawers. Did it in a hurry. In case the killer came back.

He found a manilla envelope in the sock drawer. No address or name on it. But it was thick and heavy. No one hid an envelope like this unless it contained something important. Carver took it. He turned off the closet light. Turned off the bedroom light. Kept the Lonadone.

He went to the attic. Picked up the leech. Plugged the power back into the network switch. Went to the window and left via the rooftops. He kept thinking about what had happened. About why it had happened.

Something struck him. Something important. The killer hadn't gone upstairs to disable the cameras. The man was masked and hooded, but footage of him killing Bushner would have been recorded if Carver hadn't disabled the cameras.

Maybe Enigma could remotely delete the footage. That made sense. They could have also disabled the cameras remotely. Except if they'd tried, they would have discovered the cameras were offline.

If the killer was connected to Enigma, they most likely would have gone to the attic. Looked at the cameras to find out why they weren't operating. Maybe the killer didn't know about the room. He'd have to be blind not to know there were cameras everywhere.

Carver put himself in the killer's place. He might be working for Enigma. He might be working against Enigma. If the latter were true, who was the killer working for? Why had he killed Bushner?

To keep him quiet? To send a message to Enigma? Maybe it was simpler. Maybe a victim of a violent crime wanted Bushner dead because he released the perpetrator back on the streets.

There were a lot of possibilities. It might be a third party. It might be a competing organization. One that didn't like what Enigma was doing. Or he might just be a single disgruntled citizen. Maybe he'd killed Bushner to prove that he was too soft on crime.

The latter didn't seem likely. The killer had gotten past the heavy iron door with biometric locks. That pointed to a pro. Possible someone with inside connections.

Carver reached the scaffolding. Climbed down the ladder. Dropped over the side to the sidewalk. The nearby streets and sidewalks were empty. He took one of the remote cameras from the duffel bag. Secured it in one of the small trees growing along the sidewalk.

It wasn't very well hidden, but it would do. He angled it toward Bushner's house. Turned it on. He opened the camera app on the tablet. Made sure it was working. It was high resolution. Motion activated. The battery should last most of the day even if it was constantly recording.

With that done, it was time to get home. Carver started walking. It was a long way back to the Embarcadero.

There was a hostel nearby. He'd noticed it on the way here. They didn't normally ask for an ID. He tested the theory. Found out he was right. Rented a bed with the cash he'd taken from Bushner.

He went to the shared bathroom. It had stalls inside. He sat on the toilet. Locked the stall door. Pulled the manilla envelope from the duffel bag. Inside it was a stack of documents. Some were printed on legal paper.

The first document was dense reading. Something about the sale of real estate. Signed by someone named Nora Henry. Witnessed by Bushner. Carver plugged the addresses into the map app. Some were in the Financial District. Some were in Market Square.

They were all big buildings. Formerly owned or leased by big corporations. Most were clustered around the same general area. One company had owned several of them. Then they'd sold them.

The sale prices were phenomenally low. Carver knew that because the appraisals were listed next to the actual amount paid. They were discounted nearly sixty percent.

The next item of interest was the purchaser—the city of San Francisco. That was unusual. Especially since there was nothing in the document indicating the mayor even knew about the deal.

There were more real estate documents behind the first. Commercial real estate sold for heavily discounted prices to the city. There were letters attached to the documents. Letters detailing why these prices were justified.

They cited economic facts. The pandemic had ended the era of bricks and mortar. People were working from home now. And if companies wanted to force a return to the office, they'd face several new taxes implemented by the city.

The first was a new payroll tax on employees making over a hundred thousand a year. Companies would pay six percent of gross salary for each of those employees.

The tax was intended to create more affordable housing in the area. It was touted as a cure to the homelessness problem.

The second was an environmental impact tax. Two percent of gross revenues would go to preserving nature within the city limits.

The third was a tax on the sale of corporate real estate. Sellers would face up to a forty percent tax on the proceeds of a sale if they couldn't prove the sale would increase affordable housing and reduce the environmental impact of whoever purchased the property.

The first two taxes affected the companies that would normally lease the buildings. Most companies opted to find locations outside the city limits to avoid the taxes. That left the property owners with empty buildings.

The commercial buildings that were once cash cows became anchors around the necks of their owners. No one wanted to buy the buildings. And even if they did, the owners would have to face the new real estate tax if they sold to them.

San Francisco magnanimously offered to bail them out by purchasing the buildings at pennies on the dollar. The property owners were taking what they could get. The city took full advantage of it.

Some property owners tried to hold out. But without tenants, they had no income. They still had plenty of expenses. Maintenance, property taxes, and so forth. They couldn't pay the bank and went into foreclosure. The city bought those too.

It was quite a racket they had. Perfectly legal too. Because the city made the laws in the first place.

Carver couldn't figure out the end goal. By driving out businesses the tax base was being annihilated. It was going to put the city into a death spiral. What good was all that real estate if you didn't have businesses operating inside the city limits?

The next page was a memorandum. It was from Bushner to the mayor. Explaining how greedy landlords were causing a housing crisis. He claimed the high prices were creating poverty. Poverty was creating crime. It was a cycle that needed to be stopped.

The next memo was from Maryann Lewis, the city council member. She had a plan to make sure big business and landlords paid their fair share of taxes. The new payroll and environmental taxes were part of a larger package of initiatives. There was also a new tax on renting buildings. The tax was supposed to increase availability of affordable housing.

The next memo was from Carl Ortez, another city council member. He added an amendment to the bill that allowed the city to purchase buildings and rent them to companies or individuals without needing to rezone them.

It was quite a scheme. Create laws to drive out businesses. To decrease property values on corporate property. To snatch up the now cheap property. To turn around and fill the city coffers with money from rent. All while claiming it was for the public good.

It was also how the city could destroy the corporate tax base without running out of other people's money.

The last sheet was a printed email. It was a chain of three conversations. It was from a name Carver knew on sight. A name many would know without an internet search.

Carver started at the bottom of the printed email. The first in the chain. It was an angry email. It asked Bushner why the city government was buying land the sender had wanted to acquire at bargain basement prices.

The sender was a real estate mogul. Henry Marshall. A guy worth billions. It made sense for him to be upset. He'd seen the dip in corporate real estate. Probably thought he could turn a healthy profit.

Marshall's company had put in offers for various corporate buildings. Offers much higher than anyone else. Then the sellers had chosen instead to go with San Francisco. Because the new real estate tax would have made them lose money even if the sale price was higher.

The next email in the chain was a response from Bushner. It said simply, *It's an Enigma, isn't it?*

Marshall replied with one word. *Understood.*

It was interesting. Very interesting. Marshall seemed to know about Enigma. Maybe he was even connected to them. Or maybe he worked for a competing faction. Maybe that was why Bushner was dead.

It was certainly another mystery. A new enigma. One that was too large for Carver to unravel. It only underscored a simple fact. Noah's quest to destroy Enigma was too much for him to tackle.

The food chain was a lot longer than Noah thought. It reached a lot higher too. If people like Marshall were involved, the stakes were astronomical. The Farm had been extremely well funded and equipped. It had also only been one venture started by Enigma.

Only someone worth billions could have funded it. The same went for San Francisco. It took a lot of money to own politicians. To ensure their chosen people got into office. To kill or ruin the opposition.

It was way more than Carver wanted to get involved with. Which meant he was going to do what he usually did. Carve his own route through the mess. Get back to living life.

He considered abandoning the phone. It was his weakness. An anchor holding him down. But he couldn't bring himself to do it. He didn't want to lose touch with Paola. Lose contact with her forever.

That was exactly why he should forget the phone and get out of town. His attachment to her was a weakness.

On the other hand, he could put another dent in Enigma's operations. Maybe dissuade them from coming after him. It was doubtful, but it was worth a try.

The phone was probably in Noah's vault. The vault could only be accessed with the proper biometric reading. Probably with Noah's fingerprint.

Maybe it would be easier to follow Noah home. Kill him. Take his hand. Then that would result in Noah's failsafe kicking into action. Tasha's sister would die. Jeremy too. Titus or Deshawn would make sure of that.

But that wasn't his problem. Was it?

Maybe not, but there was no reason to get people killed over his burner phone. For now, it was better to play along. To learn more about Noah. Find his weaknesses. To wait for the right opportunity to present itself.

Carver certainly had enough new information to keep Noah happy for the time being. But he still wasn't closer to finding out how to dismantle Enigma. That was a goal he was unlikely to achieve.

He tucked the documents into the envelope. Tucked the envelope into the duffel bag. Zipped up the duffel bag. Left the bathroom. Went to the room down the hall. At least four people were sleeping there. He could tell by the snoring.

He'd been assigned a bed near the door. That wasn't to his liking. He used the dim light of the phone screen to find an empty bed at the back. He took off his shoes. His socks. His shirt and pants. Slid the duffel bag and clothing under the bed. He slid under the covers. Went through his relaxation routine.

The nap at Bushner's house made him less tired. The snoring from the other sleepers was loud. He still didn't have a problem drifting off within minutes.

It was still dark outside when he woke. He instinctively checked the room. Looked for any suspicious shadows. Everything looked the same as it had when he'd gone to sleep. He checked the time. Zero five hundred.

He put on his clothes. His hoodie. His facemask. It was nice being anonymous. He got his things and went outside. Took a detour parallel to Bushner's home. There were no cops outside. No indication anyone had visited since he and the killer had been there.

Bushner's absence would be noticed quickly. There would be texts to his cell phone. Calls. Someone would eventually be sent to knock on his door. They'd look inside the garage window. See the car parked inside.

A call to the police would be made. A wellness check requested. Since he was a high priority citizen, they'd arrive in no time at all. Bushner might even make the afternoon news. His death would be a big story. It would be front page news for the next few days.

It was supposed to look like an unintentional fentanyl overdose. But Carver had taken the evidence. That threw a nice wrench into the works. It would raise questions. Suggest foul play. All because of one missing bottle.

It brought a grin to his face. There was something fun about screwing with the best laid plans. Probably because that had been one of his functions in Scion. The only difference now was that he wasn't getting paid for it.

Carver sat at the bus stop. He'd missed the first bus by a few minutes. The next one would come around in twenty minutes. He took the time to upload the camera data from the leech to the tablet.

It finished about the time the bus arrived. He boarded the bus. Sat in the back. Put in the earphones and started watching video clips. The oldest was from a week ago. The system probably purged videos after a certain time. Otherwise, the hard drive would run out of space.

Carver watched the first video. The nightstand lamp turned on at six. Bushner showered, ate, brushed, and was out the door by seven. The video ended. The next video showed Bushner arriving home at nine in the evening.

His maid arrived shortly after he did. Cooked a meal. Cleaned up. Left. Bushner talked on the phone. Did some work on his laptop. Then he went to bed at eleven.

The next videos showed the same schedule over and over. The only difference was the time Bushner arrived home in the evening. Sometimes it was at eight. Sometimes it was later. The maid would always arrive moments later, do her work, and leave.

There certainly wasn't anything incriminating in the videos. Bushner was usually talking DA business when he was on the phone. When he was off the phone, he would often complain about the noise the maid was making.

In one conversation he was trying to convince a judge to reduce bail for a violent offender. In another conversation he was strong-arming another prosecutor into dropping criminal charges. It would make some people angry, but none of it was breaking the law as far as Carver knew.

The bus had almost done a complete circuit of its route by the time Carver reached the halfway point of the videos. He was just skimming the contents. Watching them on double speed without audio.

He started the next video. It was from two days ago. It started the same as the others. Then it got interesting. Bushner was eating breakfast. He flinched. Looked at the front door. Carver slowed the video to normal speed.

Someone knocked at the door. Bushner frowned. Got up. Wiped his mouth. He went to the door. The camera rotated to follow him. The door opened. Carver couldn't see them because Bushner was in the way.

Bushner threw up his hands. Shook his head. Glanced back at the cameras. Then he backed up and shut the door.

Carver paused. Reversed the video in slow motion. There was a single frame where the person at the door was visible. Just a glimpse of the face. The person was wearing a hoodie, but not a facemask.

And Carver couldn't believe who it was.

CHAPTER 29

Carver stared at the face on the screen.

He pulled a backup drive from the duffel bag. Saved the video file to it and erased it from the tablet. It was a weapon he could use later if necessary. For now, it was best to keep it to himself.

He watched the rest of the videos at triple speed. There wasn't anything else useful on them. He would still give them to Noah. Make him think he was working on the Enigma task. It wouldn't get him a time extension. That much was clear.

Noah wasn't the kind of guy to give extensions. He was a hardliner. Someone who followed his own rules for better or worse. That might be useful to Carver. It depended on how things panned out.

Carver didn't need an extension. He needed his phone back well before the end of the week. More specifically, within two days.

If he didn't get it back by then, it wouldn't matter. The message from Paola would expire. Even if the message with her new number was still waiting in the cloud, it would self-delete the moment it reached the phone.

One way or the other, he'd get the phone back by then. No matter what the cost.

Carver got off the bus at the next stop. Took a trolley to the department store. He walked down the street to Lee's store first. The shopkeeper was there behind the counter.

"I have a question about biometric locks."

Lee blinked. "I don't have a way to hack them open if that's what you're wondering."

Carver took out the tablet. He opened the folders taken from the phone. Went to the app folders. Looked over the names. Pointed to the one named Guard Dog. "This is the app that controls a biometric lock. Is there any way to find out what fingerprints are registered with the lock?"

Lee turned the tablet to face him. "The prints are registered in the app and the data is uploaded to the cloud."

"Can two people with the app control the same lock?"

"Depends on the manufacturer." Lee tucked the tablet under an arm. Walked to the stairs. "Let me try something."

Carver followed him upstairs. Lee went into the storeroom. Sat at a desk. Plugged the tablet into a computer. He ran a program. A simulated smartphone screen appeared on the desktop.

Lee dragged the Guard Dog folder to the smartphone screen. The folder turned into an icon. A red outline of a growling dog. Lee used the mouse cursor to open the app. It opened with an error.

Phone not registered with app.

"It's hardware locked?" Carver said.

Lee nodded. He opened another folder downloaded from Bushner's phone. Dragged over several files. "These will allow it to use the digital ID of the other phone." The simulator processed the files.

He opened the Guard Dog app again. This time it worked. It showed the registered fingerprints. One had Bushner's name next to it. There were two others. No names, just numbers next to them.

"Can you run those prints through a database?" Carver asked.

"I have someone at the police department who can."

"Do it and let me know." Carver gave him his burner cell number.

He walked downstairs. Left Lee's shop. Went to the department store. Went downstairs into the basement. Circled around the pile of mannequins and into the break room.

Tasha and Jeremy were already there. They were just sitting around doing nothing. Tasha looked angry. Jeremy looked worried. About as expected, considering what Carver knew about them.

Jeremy jumped up. "Oh, thank God. I thought you'd abandoned us."

"Nah." Carver nodded at the computer. "Anything on the news?"

Jeremy frowned. "Why?"

Carver just nodded at the computer. He pulled up a chair and sat down. Jeremy turned on the computer. Pulled up several local news sites.

"I don't see anything major."

"I guess it'll take a while." Carver looked up at one of the cameras. He figured Noah was watching them. "Might want to come down here and see what I found."

Tasha's mouth dropped open. "You don't tell Noah what to do. I can go get him if you'd like."

"Sure, whatever works."

Tasha's phone buzzed. She looked at it. "He's on the way down."

Noah and his entourage arrived later. Noah looked a little tired. Like he'd been up all night. Deshawn didn't have that bored frown carved on his face. In fact, he seemed to have a spring in his step.

Titus looked like he had yesterday. Eyes narrowed and glaring at Carver. Playing the intimidation game. Like they were scheduled for a cage match. And they probably were if things went the way Carver figured.

Noah yawned. "You have something for me already?"

Carver nodded. He motioned at the table and chairs around it. "Make yourselves comfortable."

"Boy, don't you take that attitude with the boss." Titus bared his teeth.

Noah patted the big man. "It's okay. I'm curious to know why he dragged us down here. If it's not good, then..." He paused as if for effect. "I think Jeremy will lose a toe."

Jeremy gasped. His face went white. "B-but why me? Carver doesn't even care about my toes!"

"Your toes are safe with me, kid." Carver stood. Pushed his chair to the head of the table. He didn't sit down, though. He pulled the manilla envelope from his bag. Set it on the table.

Noah's eyes flashed with curiosity. Deshawn raised an eyebrow. Titus kept staring down Carver.

Noah sat. Opened the envelope. Took out the legal documents. Read them from start to finish. Looked over the photographs of the other documents. His face remained impassive. Only small twitches gave away his surprise.

He read the memos. Nodded to himself. Like something he'd wondered had finally been answered. Then he read the email. His eyes flared. Darted to Deshawn. Back to the paper.

Carver saw something deep in that glance at Deshawn. Saw something that confirmed a few things.

Noah pushed the paper into the envelope.

"Hey, I want to look at it," Deshawn said.

"It's a lot of legalese. I'll sum it up." Noah's fist clenched and relaxed. "Enigma is using the city to buy up a lot of very valuable real estate at criminally low prices."

"Using the city?" Deshawn frowned. "How?"

"How do you think?" Noah stared at Carver. "Let's step outside and have a word."

Carver motioned toward the door. "After you."

Noah walked to the door. Titus started after him. He shook his head. Held up a hand. "Wait here."

"But, boss—"

"I'll be okay." Noah stepped into the hallway.

Carver went out after him. They walked down the corridor. Around the corner.

Noah stopped. "Where did you get those documents?"

"Bushner, the DA."

"The DA?" Noah's eyebrows arched. "How did you get the documents?"

Carver shrugged. "Standard spy work."

"Don't be coy with me. I want details."

"I used the spy stuff Lee gave me. Got into the house. Downloaded stuff from his computer and phone. I found the documents in his sock drawer."

Noah pursed his lips. "You did this without him knowing?"

"More or less, yeah."

Noah's eyes narrowed. "What's that supposed to mean?"

"Let's just say Bushner won't know much of anything anymore."

"You killed him?"

"No. My plan was to get in and out without him knowing."

"And?"

"Someone else paid Bushner a visit while I was there. They killed him in his sleep."

Noah whistled. "Holy shit." His gaze went distant. Like he was imagining the scenario. "Did you get a look at them?"

Carver shook his head. "They were hooded and masked. And it was dark."

"Damn."

"What's interesting is that they entered by the front door. A heavy iron door with a biometric lock."

"So, it was someone with a key?"

"Maybe. But they might have registered their fingerprint with the door too." Carver was pretty sure he knew who it belonged to. But he wasn't ready to tell Noah yet. It was better to time it just right for maximum effect.

"Are you being straight with me, Carver?" Noah stared Carver down. "You sure you didn't kill him?"

"Why would I?" Carver shook his head. "It would've been better to get in and out without him being any wiser. If this guy was working for Enigma, then his death is going to sound all kinds of alarms."

"And make our job harder." Noah pursed his lips. "You might try to use that as an excuse."

"I've got no reason to. I can leave anytime I want."

"Yeah? And then Jeremy dies painfully."

"Sure, but at least I don't have to be around to see it."

Noah chuckled. "You've got a dark sense of humor, Carver."

"Wasn't supposed to be funny."

"Well, it is." Noah crossed his arms. "Let's assume the alarms are ringing at Enigma. What happens next?"

"Nothing yet. They don't know where to send their kill squad."

"True. They don't have any reason to suspect me or my people."

"It's also possible there's a rival faction." Carver pointed to the manilla envelope in Noah's hand. "Henry Marshall."

Noah took out the documents. Pulled the printed email from the stack. Showed it to Carver. "It looks like he knows about Enigma. He didn't even argue with Bushner. What makes you think he isn't involved with them?"

"They might have a gentlemen's agreement." Carver tapped the paper. "Stay out of each other's way."

"True. Respect each other's turf." Noah tucked the email back in place. "Bushner signed the legal paperwork. Served as legal counsel on the sale. But he's still a small fry. Why kill him?"

"Because he knew a lot."

"They would have been better off kidnapping him. Interrogating him."

"Or, there's another possibility. Enigma thought he was a liability. They thought it was better to kill him." Carver didn't think that was the answer, but he was happy to muddy the waters with another theory.

Noah bit his lower lip. "What I find strangest of all is that they sent someone to kill him the same night you were there."

Carver didn't find it strange. Not if he was right about who the killer was. "Stranger things have happened."

Noah didn't look convinced. He had the look of a man with inside information. Information he didn't want to share. He took a breath. Released it. "What's next? You going to break into the mayor's house?"

"I don't know yet. I need to see how this plays out."

"This doesn't buy you more time, Carver." Noah tucked the envelope under his arm. "I don't care if Enigma is on high alert. You're going to do the job by the end of the week."

That gave Carver an idea. A way to find out for sure who knew what. He shrugged. "Yeah, we'll see." He turned and headed for the breakroom.

"Where are you going?"

"To get back to work." Carver went into the breakroom. Titus and Deshawn were staring down Tasha. Jeremy was in front of the computer. Doing his best to stare at the screen and make himself small. As if that would keep them from noticing him.

Everyone looked at Carver when he walked in. He nodded at Tasha. "Let's go. We've got work to do."

Jeremy stood. Rubbed his hands nervously on his jeans. "What do you need?"

"A car. You got one?"

"No."

Carver looked at Tasha. She shook her head. He turned to Noah. "Got a car we can borrow?"

Noah nodded. "I'll have one brought around." He made a call.

Titus looked curiously at Carver. "Where did you go? What did you talk about?"

"Your boss can fill you in."

Deshawn was leaning against a wall. Staring at his phone like he was bored with the whole thing.

Noah got off the phone. "It'll be out back in a minute. Where are you going?"

Carver backed up. Put his back to the wall so he could see everyone in the room. "To Oakland. I want to check out the city councilwoman over there before news of Bushner hits the streets."

One person didn't react. They just frowned. One person flinched. Surprise flashed on their face. Another person stiffened. The last one just looked confused.

Carver had expected one person to react. Not two. That muddied the waters. But the person he'd expected to react had. Maybe the other one was a fluke. He'd have to let it play out. See where the chips landed.

Noah nodded. "Give me regular updates."

"News of Bushner?" Tasha frowned. "What are you talking about?"

"We'll talk in the car." Carver left the room.

Everyone left the room. Noah and his entourage split off from them. Went toward his office. Jeremy and Tasha stuck with Carver.

Jeremy was quiet. He kept looking at his phone. Glancing at Carver.

Tasha grabbed Carver's arm. "Bushner, as in Bret Bushner, the DA?"

"Yep."

"And?" She looked expectantly at him. "What does he have to do with this?"

"I paid him a visit last night."

Jeremy's mouth dropped open. "Y-you went to his house?"

"You what?" Tasha stopped walking. "Are you serious?"

"Yeah." Carver kept walking.

"Did you interrogate him?" She hurried to catch up.

Carver shook his head. "Just downloaded some stuff from his phone and computer. Didn't touch him."

"Really?" Tasha didn't let go of Carver's arm. "What did you find out?"

"Nothing in particular."

She stared at him. "Then what, exactly, did you mean by news of Bushner?"

"Someone else killed him while I was there."

"They what?" Jeremy's mouth dropped open. His face went pale.

Tasha stared blankly at him. "Someone killed him. Not you?"

"Why would I kill him? I needed him to remain blissfully unaware that I was ever in his home."

"I don't believe you."

Tasha hung back. Like she was too shocked to keep walking.

Jeremy was clenching his phone now. Looking at the screen. "I need to go to the bathroom. I'll meet you outside." He rushed off.

Carver watched him go. Tasha stared at him. Eyes narrowed. Like she was trying to see through him. Trying to figure out the truth.

She finally talked. "Killing Bushner doesn't help us."

"It helps someone. Just gotta figure out who." Carver went outside. A late model Honda was idling in the parking lot. Carver climbed in the driver's seat. He waited for the others. Tasha finally came out of the building.

She climbed into the front seat. "I need you to be honest with me."

"I didn't do it."

She pursed her lips. "I don't know if I can believe you."

Jeremy came outside. Saw the car. He climbed in the back. "Sorry, my stomach was killing me. It really stresses me out when Noah talks about cutting off my toes."

Carver plugged an address into the GPS. Started driving. The address was in Oakland. "Jeremy, can you find real estate transactions online?"

Jeremy was staring at his phone. He blinked. "Real estate?"

Carver nodded. "Find out if anyone's been buying up corporate properties in Oakland."

Tasha wrinkled her nose. "Why would anyone want to buy business properties in Oakland?"

"Because they were using Bushner to buy them in San Francisco."

Jeremy shook his head. "How does a DA have the power to buy real estate in the city's name?"

"Because the city council gave him the power to sign legal documents," Carver said. "Can you find out if the same thing happened in Oakland?"

Jeremy nodded. "I'll look through public records." He pulled a laptop from his bag. Opened it.

"Waste of time." Tasha looked at the GPS. "Where are we going?"

"I just want to get a look at downtown Oakland. See the current state of the city."

"Your plan is to go sightseeing in Oakland?"

"Something like that." Carver turned left even though the GPS wanted him to go straight. He got on Market Street. Followed it southwest.

Tasha looked confused. "We're going the wrong way."

"I need to pick up something along the way." Carver looked at Jeremy in the rearview mirror. "Any indication Bushner's death is public yet?"

Jeremy tapped on his laptop. Shook his head. "Nothing yet."

The morning was getting long in the tooth. It was surprising no one from the DA's office had gone to check on the man. Or maybe it wasn't all that surprising. Maybe most of the city attorneys were still working from home.

But if Carver was right, that was going to change soon. He took a right on Franklin. A left on Fell. A right on Steiner.

"Carver, where in the hell are we going?" Tasha looked from the GPS to Carver.

"I need to pick up something." He pulled into a parking space on the side of the road. It gave him a clear view of the place he'd visited last night. Bushner's house.

"Why are we wasting time?" Tasha threw up her hands. "There's nothing here but houses."

"Yeah, it's a nice neighborhood, isn't it?" Carver kept waiting. He figured it wouldn't take long.

Maybe two minutes passed. An unmarked black van skidded around the corner. It screeched to a halt in front of Bushner's house. Two men got out. Former military for sure. Wearing black suits, no ties.

One of them pressed a fob to the front door. It clicked open. They ran inside.

"You came here to see this?" Tasha shook her head. "Why?"

"Just curious to see how fast it happened after I told someone Bushner was dead." Carver put the car in gear. Pulled out of the parking spot. He didn't really need to be here. The camera he'd put on the tree had enough battery power to keep recording.

Besides, Carver already knew what he needed to know. Another piece of the puzzle had revealed itself.

CHAPTER 30

There had been six people in the breakroom.

Noah, Titus, Deshawn. Tasha, Jeremy, Carver. One of them had notified Enigma their boy, Bushner, was down when Carver mentioned him.

It wasn't Noah. And Carver had one other suspect he could remove from the equation. It boiled down to three people. And he had a pretty good guess as to who it was.

Jeremy was still tapping on his laptop. "Carver, there haven't been any corporate buildings sold. But a big investment firm purchased a lot of smaller strip malls and surrounding neighborhoods. Most of them were damaged or burned down in the riots a few years back."

"What investment firm?"

"Slipstream." Jeremy scowled. "It's nothing new. They control billions in retirement funds and use them to buy up homes and other properties so they can turn them into rental properties."

"How much land do they own in Oakland now?"

Jeremy went quiet for a moment. "Ah, here it is." He turned the laptop so Carver could see the screen. Carver pulled over to the side of the road and looked. It was a map of Oakland. Areas owned by Slipstream were shaded blue. There were a lot of blue neighborhoods.

Jeremy asked a question. "You think Slipstream is in cahoots with Enigma?"

Carver gave it some thought. "Are there other big companies like Slipstream? Ones that buy houses?"

"Yes." Jeremy turned the laptop around. "I think I know what you want."

"See if something similar is happening in San Francisco. And add in corporate properties too."

"Might take a little while."

"We've got time." Carver pulled back onto the road. Headed north.

"We're still going in the wrong direction," Tasha said. "Are you intentionally confusing us?"

Carver cancelled the GPS route. He opened his window. Hung an arm out. Enjoyed the cool weather.

"Are you going to answer me?"

He glanced at her. Her cheeks were red. Flushed. She was angrier than usual. He saw something else in her eyes. It wasn't anger. It almost looked like embarrassment. "No need to go to Oakland if Jeremy can do everything on his laptop."

Tasha sighed. Leaned back in her seat. Stared out the side window at the passing scenery.

Carver drove all the way to the Golden Gate Bridge. He parked at the welcome center. Got out. Stretched. There was a path leading down to a scenic viewpoint. He walked down it. Jeremy and Tasha got out of the car. Hurried after him.

He reached the spot. It had a real nice view of the bay and the bridge. Looked like a postcard. He sat on a bench and got comfortable. Jeremy sat next to him. Opened his laptop.

"Are we staying here for a while?"

Carver nodded. "As long as you need."

Tasha sat on the other side of Carver. It was chilly out. The sky was a little gray. She was wearing a thin jacket, but the weather didn't seem to bother her. She sat upright. Shoulders straight. Legs not crossed.

Carver didn't like sitting between them. But he spread his arms along the back of the bench. Leaned back.

Tasha glared at him. "Do you mind not manspreading?"

"There's another bench if you want to move."

She didn't move.

Carver enjoyed the view for a while. Then he got up. Walked along the path. It circled back to the top of the hill. Gave him a good view of an old Civil War fortress. He returned. Found the others still sitting on the bench.

Jeremy looked up from the laptop. "I've got it."

"Show me." Carver sat next to him.

Jeremy handed him the laptop. The map had sections shaded blue. Others shaded green, brown, or orange. There was a legend explaining the different colors.

Slipstream was blue. Forefront Investments was orange. Brown were city owned properties. Marshall Investments was green. There was a lot more shaded blue and orange than green. Large sections of San Francisco were brown.

The city owned a lot of corporate properties. Which meant Enigma owned them by proxy. But there was almost nothing owned by the major investment firms in San Francisco. Most of their properties were in Oakland and surrounding areas.

The blue and orange shaded areas were often connected. The green areas were dispersed among them. It looked like Marshall Investments hadn't had much luck buying entire swaths of land.

There was one area shaded green north of the Golden Gate bridge. Carver pointed to it. "Why'd you include this area?"

"I compiled the available data and correlated it into the maps app." Jeremy clicked on separate browser tabs. "There are independent groups that track these companies. I just included whatever information they had. Then I added in the city-owned properties from a local homeless advocacy group that wants the city to use these properties as shelters."

Carver zoomed in on the green blip north of the city. "It's a single house."

Jeremy clicked on another browser tab. He typed in the address. A dollar amount appeared over it. "That's a five-million-dollar home."

"You think Marshall lives there?"

Jeremy clicked a button and a street view appeared. The house had a black iron fence and gate. It looked okay but wasn't anything special. Not a place a billionaire would live.

"What's the point of this?" Tasha said. She gave Carver a sour look. "Is this getting us closer to our goals?"

"We're putting together the big picture," Carver said. "Then we can drill down to the smaller stuff. Figure out how to handle it."

"Smaller stuff?" She looked incredulous.

Jeremy put another layer on the map. Prices of the properties inside the shaded areas.

"Are those purchase prices or estimates?" Carver said.

"Estimates." Jeremy clicked on another browser window. Dragged another overlay onto his map. More dollar signs appeared. "These are estimates versus the actual purchase prices. Some of them are lumped together."

Carver whistled. "Pennies on the dollar."

"Except for the properties purchased by Marshall Investments." Jeremy hovered the mouse cursor over the prices. "They paid much closer to the appraised prices."

"That can't make Henry Marshall very happy," Carver said.

"I think I see what's happening." Jeremy panned across the map. To the areas that hadn't been touched by the investment firms. "These areas have the more expensive Oakland real estate."

Carver saw where he was going. "They're buying up the cheaper stuff. Turning them into rental properties. Driving up overall home prices."

"Exactly. Pricing people out of the market." Jeremy looked confused. "But, why?"

"To ramp up the homelessness situation. Create more problems. Break down the economy."

"I still don't understand why they want to do that." Jeremy stared at the map. "It's like destroying the city from the inside out."

Carver glanced at Tasha. "Thoughts?"

"They want to depress real estate as much as possible, buy it all up, then resell it later after the economy recovers." She shrugged. "Simple investment stuff. Buy low, sell high."

Carver wasn't sure that was their goal. But it made sense. Only if Enigma was a capitalist venture. Judging from the Farm, he didn't think that was the case at all. The people recruited by the Farm were mostly socialist fanatics.

Noah's operation was filled with the same kind of people. They wanted to destroy capitalism. Replace it with a socialist utopia. But maybe the people who controlled Enigma didn't believe the same thing.

Maybe they knew that it was much easier to control fanatics if they pretended to align with their beliefs. They could use them to destroy the economy. Drive prices into the gutter. Then buy everything at bargain prices.

Then they could rebuild the economy. Drive prices back up. Sell the acquired real estate for sky-high prices. Except real estate prices were already sky high because of housing shortages. Because the investment firms were buying up all the single-family homes.

It really didn't matter. It wasn't Carver's problem. These were problems on a scale he couldn't deal with. Not even if he had a list of names and addresses. Noah's assertion that he could destroy Enigma from the inside out was a pipe dream.

Carver had known that from the start. But this information gathering hadn't been so much about fighting Enigma as it had been about sussing out the players. Figuring out who really worked for whom.

He had a loose idea by now. Maybe not enough to show his cards, but enough to make some bets. There were some details that needed confirming. Some facts that needed finding. He'd get to that later.

Tasha stood. "Can I talk to you alone, Carver?"

Carver nodded. Got up. Followed her down the path to another overlook. He knew what she was going to say.

She didn't disappoint him. "You're focusing a lot on Enigma when you should be focused on Noah."

"I'm not making a move on Noah until I can get my stuff back."

"It's all in his vault, okay? You kill Noah, and we can use his body to get inside."

"Yeah, but we have to find the failsafe first, right?"

She nodded. "That's the whole point of the exercise."

"I still don't know how we're going to do that."

Tasha pressed her lips together. "I was hoping a person with your skillset would have some ideas."

Carver thought of something else. "What if my phone isn't in the vault?"

"Then we'll find it." Her eyes narrowed. "You still haven't explained why that burner phone is so important to you. Just that it has some woman's phone number on it. And that doesn't make sense, because a person like you would remember the number."

Carver decided he had to deploy the truth. He needed Tasha to understand why the phone was so important. "That woman is on the run from a cartel. I told her to change her number every month. To text me the new one. I'd do the same when I switched burner phones. If I lose that phone, I'll probably lose touch with her forever."

"How do you not remember her number?"

"Because it's in an encrypted messaging app hardware locked to the phone."

Tasha's gaze softened. "Oh. That makes sense."

"It's all I care about. And until I know exactly where it is, I'm not going anywhere." Carver didn't like opening up to her like this, but sometimes it was necessary.

"Look, I'm sorry I keep pushing you, but we don't have a lot of time." Tasha sighed. "Noah will kill Jeremy. He'll torture him first. Make you watch. Maybe even make you put him out of his misery."

"And then what?" Carver said.

She frowned. "What does that mean?"

"He kills Jeremy, and then what? I'm still going to want my phone back."

She laughed. "You're cold."

"I'm just being practical."

Tasha nodded. "Okay, so we've established that Jeremy is not effective collateral. Only the phone is."

"That sums it up."

"If I promise to find the phone, will you promise to do your part? Kill Noah and his two stooges?"

"What about the failsafe and your sister?"

"Assuming we find out who his failsafe is."

Carver shrugged. "I'm not making any promises. But find my phone and we'll negotiate."

Tasha shook her head. "Not good enough."

Carver raised an eyebrow. "You expect me to take out three people alone?"

"Can you?"

He nodded. "Sure. Anything is possible in the right circumstances."

Tasha put on a sad face. "Carver, I need your help. My sister needs your help."

"I don't do murder for hire. I don't kill people for favors." Carver waggled a hand. "But I'd probably kill someone to get that phone back."

"Then we'll go from there." The wind blew her hair into her face. She sputtered. Used a hair tie to get it under control. "God, I hate my hair."

"Why don't you just shave it off?"

She flinched. "Why would I do that?"

"You said you hate it."

"I don't want to cut my hair." She ran a hand through the length of it. "It took me forever to grow it out this long."

"You had it shorter before?"

She nodded. "I wore it buzzed."

Carver imagined her with buzzed hair. She had a good face for it. Not everyone did. "Just keep it in a ponytail then."

"I don't like ponytails."

"Yeah, but they do the job, don't they?"

"They give me a headache."

"Don't wear them tight, then."

Jeremy walked over. "Are you two talking about hair?"

"Yeah." Carver nodded at Jeremy's long locks. The wind was blowing his hair in his face and everywhere. "That doesn't bother you?"

"I don't really think about it anymore." Jeremy closed his laptop. "What's next?"

"I want to find out who lives in that house north of the bridge." Carver started walking up the path. There weren't many tourists out. The weather was probably keeping them inside. Fog was already rolling in, hiding the bridge.

He noticed a couple of guys coming down the path. They were midsized. Stocky. Wearing gym pants and nice jackets. Both sporting Giants ballcaps. Probably in their mid-thirties. They looked like ordinary citizens out for a stroll.

It was their eyes that threw Carver off. They were serious. Dead serious. And searching. Searching for someone in particular. One of them stopped. Locked eyes with Carver. Looked away. Laughed and said something to his friend.

His friend laughed. But the laughter didn't reach their eyes. The laughs were fake. They were just acting. Playing it cool until they could get closer. Carver felt certain of that. Not just because of the laughs. Mainly because he could see telltale bulges under their jackets.

Carver kept a poker face. He kept talking to Jeremy and Tasha. But the men knew. They could tell that he was suspicious. They unzipped their jackets. Started jogging. Coming straight for them.

And there was no way past them.

CHAPTER 31

There was no way past the men.

But the path circled around under the bridge. There was another way up into the parking lot from there.

"Start walking." Carver prodded Tasha and Jeremy. "We've got company."

Tasha glanced at the men. Her eyes flared. The men saw her response. Started running. Jeremy sucked in a breath. His mouth dropped open.

Carver prodded them. "Run!"

Jeremy seemed to turn in slow motion. Started flailing his limbs. He looked like he was trying to run in a dream. Carver prodded him again. Gave him a boost. He glanced back at the men.

One of them had a pistol. The other was reaching into his jacket. The fog was rolling in fast. There weren't many tourists on the trail. The conditions were ripe for killing. The men could unload on them.

The sound would attract attention. Some people would come running. Others would turn tail and run the other way. That didn't matter to these gunmen. With the fog and face masks they could commit murder and get away scot-free.

Tasha was off like a shot. Jeremy finally got moving. Carver outpaced the two of them. Reached the curve in the path. It went uphill from here. Back to the parking lot. Back to the car. But there were two more men coming down the ramp.

They saw Carver hoofing it. They stopped abruptly. Reached into their jackets. Carver yanked the Glock 45 from under his jacket. Dropped to a knee. Aimed. Fired. The bullet hit right where he was aiming.

Right on the man's kneecap. Bone splintered. The man screamed. Went down holding his leg. The second guy was pulling a pistol from under his jacket. Carver fired again. The bullet struck the man's arm.

He dropped his weapon. Shouted in pain. Carver stood. Ran straight at the second guy. Rammed him with his shoulder. Sent him toppling over the railing. Kept running for the parking lot.

"Oh, God!" Jeremy shouted. "Oh, God!" He sounded scared out of his mind. Stuck in a loop.

Tasha didn't say anything. She kept running. They reached the top of the path. A black BMW sedan was sitting in the no-parking zone. A man was in the driver's seat. He was looking in the direction of the other path entrance.

His gaze flicked toward Carver. His eyes flashed surprise. Carver aimed the pistol at him. He ducked out of sight. Carver tucked the pistol into the holster under his jacket. Tourists were milling around outside the welcome center.

They'd heard the two gunshots. Two pops. They looked confused. Like they didn't know if they'd heard gunshots or something else. There was a lot of traffic in the area. A lot of noise from the bridge.

They were like sheep. Staring in the direction of perceived danger. Looking for a wolf. Not seeing anything. Because the wolves were already among them.

The other two men appeared at the top of the path. It didn't look like they'd stopped to help their companions. Their pistols were hidden again. The sheep watched them. Confused. Decided they were just more sheep running from danger.

Some of the tourists ran into the welcome center. Others grabbed the hands of kids or spouses. Dragged them away. Out to the parking lot.

Carver went straight to the car. Got in. Started the engine. Flipped the transmission into reverse. Slammed the gas. A minivan was backing out behind him. Carver hit the brakes to keep from hitting them.

The two men hopped in the BMW. Tires screeched. It launched down the drive. Headed straight for the row Carver was parked on.

Carver spun the steering wheel. Angled the car sharp right. Backed up. He missed hitting the minivan by a few inches. Slammed the car into drive. Hit the gas. The minivan bounced to a stop. The BMW veered around it.

The parking loop was one way. Carver went the wrong way. Bounced over a concrete median. Made a U-turn in the middle of traffic. Cars screeched to stops. Horns honked. Angry drivers waved fists at him.

He drove under the 101. Hooked a left. Gunned it onto the entrance ramp. The BMW wasn't far behind. It was made for performance and handling. It had wide tires. The kind with soft rubber meant for gripping the road. The kind of tires that might last twenty thousand miles if you were easy on them.

The Honda was nice enough. But it was made for utility. For economy. The tires were probably fifty-thousand-mile radials. They gripped the road okay. But they didn't hug it. Didn't give him confidence to take a sharp turn at high speed.

The engine was okay too. But it wasn't going to outrun a BMW on a straightaway. Traffic was light. That was going to give the BMW a big advantage.

And that was fine. Just fine.

The Honda was doing all right. It was doing eighty miles per hour in a thirty-five zone. That was bound to attract some attention. The BMW was dodging around cars. Gaining slowly but surely. It was probably going north of ninety miles per hour.

"Is this car connected to Noah in any way?" Carver asked.

Tasha shuffled through the glove compartment. Dug out a paper. "It belongs to some guy in San Diego."

Carver glanced in the rearview mirror. Jeremy was white-faced. Clutching his seatbelt. Starting to look a little green around the gills.

The highway went into a tunnel. Under the Presidio. Emerged on the other side. Kept going straight. There were traffic lights ahead. Heavier traffic. That might be good. Might be bad.

It depended on how far the men in the BMW were willing to go. They'd been willing to draw their guns at the welcome center. Maybe they'd been willing to use them. Maybe they thought brandishing them would be enough.

If the gunmen had been waiting in a van, it would've meant they wanted prisoners. Pulling up in a BMW sedan sent another message. There were five of them. A full load for the BMW. The trunk might hold Tasha and Jeremy, but Carver wouldn't fit.

Carver wouldn't fit inside the car either. That told him they hadn't planned to take anyone for a ride. It could also mean they were just bad planners. Or maybe they had to leave in a hurry and didn't have time to get a bigger vehicle.

The light ahead turned red. Carver positioned the Honda in the left lane. Gave himself some room in case he needed to drive into oncoming traffic. There were two cars between him and the light.

He stopped.

Tasha looked alarmed. "Why are we stopping?"

Carver watched the BMW in the rearview mirror. It slowed down. Bumped over the concrete median. Drove into oncoming traffic. "Finding out how far they're willing to go."

She twisted around in her seat. Glanced back. "Looks like they're willing to go all the way."

"Yep." Carver bounced the Honda over the concrete median. The bottom of the front bumper scraped. Metal screeched. The median wasn't that tall, but it was tall enough to cause some damage.

The BMW sat a little lower. It was probably taking more damage. Not enough to take it out of commission. Not unless it hit a median like that when it was going fast.

Cars screeched. Veered out of the way. Drivers honked horns. Shouted. Waved fists and extended middle fingers at Carver.

He swerved around the stopped cars. Cut through the intersection. Yanked the car back into the right lane.

He considered cutting onto one of the side streets. But they were just two-lane streets. Jammed with traffic. This street was still four lanes. It gave him some wiggle room.

Carver kept straight. Dodged through the traffic. Cars were bunched up at the next traffic light. He cut across the median again. Weaved between oncoming cars. Dodged back into his lane. But the medians ahead had shrubs. The concrete was higher. It was going to be harder to do that again.

The BMW wasn't far behind. It cut across the median. Swerved through the intersection. Cut back and forth between cars. The driver was decent. Nothing special. Not as far as Carver could tell.

Leon had been the expert driver on the team. Carver had filled in for him a few times. He'd had to make a few getaways by himself on tight European roads. The roads here were wide by comparison.

That was good and bad. It was good when you had the superior car. But when the other guys had the better car, it was bad. It was going to be okay, though. Because the 101 turned into a different road in this part of town.

It had been Richardson Avenue a few blocks back. Then the highway curved and changed names again. Now it was Lombard Street. There was one thing Lombard was famous for, and it was coming up in a couple of miles.

Carver just had to make it there.

He kept threading through traffic. The BMW followed him with ease. It was just ten car lengths back now. This straightaway played right into its strengths. It could handle just about anything thrown at it, provided the driver was up to the task.

Carver bounced over the median again. Crashed through small shrubs. The front bumper scraped concrete. It sounded like it was about to come off any minute.

He guided the Honda through oncoming traffic. He flashed his brights. Honked his horn. Surprised drivers veered out of the way. Jeremy shouted in alarm. Tasha gripped the door handle. Held on tight.

He stayed in oncoming traffic. The BMW lost some ground. Fell back a few more car lengths. The driver didn't have the nerve to go faster. Didn't have the reflexes to dodge oncoming cars.

Carver went back to his lane. Sped up. Fifty miles per hour felt like a hundred in tight quarters. He scraped past another Honda. Took out the passenger side mirror on his car. The driver's side mirror on the other car shattered.

The 101 took a sharp right ahead. Carver kept going straight. Straight on Lombard. It went from flat and level to a steep hill. The Honda climbed it. Bounced over the hump at the next intersection. Scrambled up the next hill.

There was almost no traffic on this section of road. The BMW was catching up again. Racing uphill after him.

The Honda hit the next intersection. The place where Lombard and Hyde intersected. Just across Hyde was the famous part of Lombard. It turned into a steep winding brick road. And there were tourists standing right in front of it.

Carver honked. Flashed the brights. People screamed. Scattered left and right. The Honda raced through the gap. On the other side was the brick road. It winded and twisted steeply downhill.

He accelerated. Drifted right around the first switchback. Left at the next one. The back wheels hit the curb. Jolted the car. Carver nearly lost control. He hit the brakes. Got the car back on course.

He hit the next switchback too close to the inside of the turn. The front tire bounced off the curb. A pedestrian on the sidewalk shouted. Jumped backward and tripped into the shrubs. Carver grimaced. Wrestled the car back into the middle of the street.

Jeremy was shouting nonstop.

Tasha was shouting too. "Slow down, you maniac!"

Carver couldn't see if the BMW was back there. The steep angle and twists made it impossible to see anything in the rearview mirror. All he could see was Jeremy's head bobbing back and forth with every turn.

But he was almost there. Almost to the bottom. Just a few more switchbacks. Leon probably would have been at the bottom already. But Carver thought he was doing pretty well. Good enough to give them a chance to lose the BMW.

Carver hit the last turn. He caught sight of the BMW. But it wasn't behind them. It was coming from the right. The driver had decided not to take the twisty part of Lombard. He'd cut right instead.

Gone around the block. Taken a left. Driven down the straight roads. And he was closer now than he'd been before.

Tasha saw the BMW too. She laughed. It wasn't a funny laugh. It was a crazy laugh.

Carver could admit when he'd been outplayed. The other driver knew he wasn't up to the task. So, he'd skipped the scenic route. Taken the longer but faster way around.

A man leaned out of the rear window. Aimed a pistol Fired.

Carver hit the accelerator. Bounced across the street. The front end of the car dived downhill. It was steep. If the car had been going any faster it would have gone airborne for a second or two.

A bullet punched through the window next to Jeremy. It whistled through the cabin. Shot out the window on the other side. The windows spider-webbed. The safety glass held on for a few seconds. The next hard bounce was too much. They crumbled.

Jeremy wasn't screaming anymore. Not because he was dead. His eyes were wide. His mouth was clenched tight. Like he'd just seen his life flash before his eyes.

Carver kept the car aimed downhill. He hit the brakes. Veered right on the next street. It climbed uphill for several blocks. There wasn't much traffic in the way. But that would play to the BMW's advantage.

Things would go sideways if this chase kept going. Carver would wreck. The cops would get involved. A stray bullet might punch a hole in his skull. The odds weren't in his favor.

Stopping wasn't an option. There were three armed men in the car. Carver only had the Glock 45. He wasn't going to win a gun battle with that. But maybe he didn't have to.

The BMW was half a block behind. It had almost caught up. Somehow it had fallen behind on the downhill section. The driver must have been hoping to ram the Honda. He'd been going too fast. Overshot the turn onto Lombard.

That gave Carver a possible option.

He slowed. Turned left off Jones and onto Greenwich. Accelerated. Hit the brakes and turned onto a narrow street. It wasn't much more than an alleyway. It curved sharply ahead. He drifted around the bend.

Carver gunned it to the end of the road. Turned back onto Jones Street again. Cut left to put his car perpendicular to the road he'd just left. He stopped. Lowered the window. Drew the Glock. Aimed it down the alley.

The BMW reached the curve. Slowed. Turned toward them. Carver aimed. Fired. The BMW's windshield cracked. The driver panicked. The car lurched forward. Slammed into the building at the curve.

Carver tucked the Glock back into the holster. Hit the gas. He cut down another street. Drove a few blocks. Kept an eye on the rearview mirror. Didn't see the BMW. It was probably out of commission after hitting the building.

He started making his way back to Noah's.

"I have to admit, that was pretty smart." Tasha smiled. It looked genuine. "You're not much of a driver, but you know how to improvise."

"I think I peed in my pants." Jeremy wiped tears off his face. "And I think I pulled a back muscle."

Tasha laughed. Glanced back at him. "You held it together okay."

Carver gave her a sideways look. "At least I know how to get on your good side."

She snorted. "What, with a high-speed chase?"

Carver didn't answer. His mind was racing. He thought he'd figured everyone out. Knew about their loyalties. But now he was questioning what he knew. Just like he was questioning his driving abilities.

He wasn't as good as he'd thought. Maybe he was just out of practice. He just didn't know. Maybe he was wrong. Wrong about everything.

And it was going to get him killed.

Carver had connected the dots. But the lines between them were all crossed now. Tangled up. There were several sides to this. Noah's side. Enigma's side. Tasha and Tanner's side.

Carver had poked the lines. Waited to see who reacted.

He'd let slip that Bushner was dead. Watched the faces of everyone in the breakroom. Then he'd driven to the house to see if anyone would go there to investigate. Someone had. They looked a lot like the people who'd gone to Arty's house. Militarized. Definitely not cops. Almost certainly Enigma's people.

Which meant Enigma hadn't known Bushner was dead. They hadn't killed their own guy. Someone else had. Someone with a different agenda. Tasha and Tanner wouldn't gain anything from it.

Noah, however, would. He'd acted surprised when Carver told him the news. But maybe he wasn't. Maybe he was playing games with Carver.

Carver was starting to lean toward Noah being behind Bushner's death. Which meant Carver didn't have an ace up his sleeve anymore. He'd hoped to use a bombshell revelation to his advantage later. But now it seemed that it wasn't such a bombshell after all.

It was all about the man in the security footage. The man who'd come to see Bushner just a few days prior. Judging from the build of the man, it was almost certainly the same guy who'd killed Bushner.

That man was Deshawn.

— • —

CHAPTER 32

Leon was hoofing it down the road.

He was doing this the hard way. Unless he wanted to risk being tracked by Enigma, this was the only way. The Flagstaff airport wasn't much further. Once there, he'd have his pick of cars from long term parking.

At least that was the plan.

Even though he was on foot, he was avoiding major highways. Keeping to the back roads. Staying off the radar. It was highly unlikely that Enigma had agents in town. Even less likely one of them would happen to drive past him.

The interstate was almost the only way to reach the airport. Almost. He'd found a route that avoided the interstate. State Route 3 had taken him to a web of neighborhoods. A single road led from those neighborhoods and to the airport.

The neighborhoods were nice. Pristine. Few of the yards had grass. Most were covered in gravel. Probably because the arid climate didn't provide much rainfall. Water conservation was key in these parts.

Lack of water was probably why the houses looked so clean too. No mold. No damp rot. Just sunshine bleaching every surface all day long.

Leon was glad it was dark. Even without the sun, the air was so dry it parched his skin and his throat. He'd gone through two bottles of water, and he'd only walked five miles.

He was on the home stretch now. He'd left the neighborhoods behind. Entered a long empty stretch of road with nothing but scrubby pines and scraggly grass.

An engine rumbled a distance behind him. He turned and saw headlights approaching. Only a single car had passed him in the last twenty minutes. This road probably wasn't used much by locals unless they were going to the airport.

Leon angled further off the shoulder of the road. He wasn't in the mood to accidentally get run over.

The loud car was getting closer fast. Probably speeding. The engine sounded old. Like something from the sixties or seventies. Probably a Ford or Chevy big block, if he had to guess.

Headlights lit the road. He wouldn't have to guess for much longer. The headlights were dim. Old school halogen lamps. They should have been replaced ages ago with something modern. Judging from the rectangular shape, they belonged to an old Chevy. A truck or van.

The vehicle passed him a moment later and answered the question. It was a van. California plates. It screeched to a halt. Reverse lights came on. It backed up. The passenger side window rolled down the old-fashioned way.

A young woman smiled at him from inside. "Where you headed?" She was pretty. Latina. Had a slight Mexican accent. She had a stunning day of the dead tattoo on her upper arm. A woman with red hair and the face of a skull in vibrant color.

"The airport."

She smiled. "Hop in. We'll give you a ride."

Leon couldn't get a good look at the driver. The inside light was off. All he could see was a silhouette. Even if it had been broad daylight, he would've declined. Like his mother always said, don't accept rides from strangers.

"Thanks for the offer, but I'm just walking there and back." He made a show of stretching. "It's good exercise."

"Oh, okay." She touched her tattoo. "I noticed you looked at it. Do you like it?"

"It's beautiful. A work of art."

"Aw, thanks." She bit her lower lip. "You're cute."

Leon adjusted his stance. Smiled. "Aw, thanks."

The van's sliding door opened. The interior light came on. A young man, early twenties, was sitting on the floor. He grinned. Brandished a knife. It was a survival knife. Sharp on the front, serrated on the back. The handle was thick. Wrapped in leather.

"Sorry, cutie, but we need some gas money." The woman pursed her lips like she was sad. "Empty your pockets for my friend, please."

With the interior lights on, Leon could see the driver. Another young guy. A little bigger than the guy in the back. A little older. A little more masculine. His hair was long and straight. His jaw was chiseled.

Leon nodded at the guy in the back. "Is that your brother, or your boyfriend's brother?"

She looked confused. "I'm sorry. Why are you asking questions instead of emptying your pockets?"

The driver joined the conversation. "Hand over your backpack, hombre. Everything."

"Yeah, sure." Leon took off his backpack. Handed it over to the guy in the back. The young man reached for it. Leon gripped his wrist. Yanked him out of the van. Twisted his arm and took the knife. He had him face down on the ground before the woman and driver could even look surprised.

Leon flipped the knife. Caught it by the tip. Balanced it on his finger. Flipped it the other way. "I don't appreciate you trying to take my things."

The driver pulled a gun. Aimed it at Leon. He was also aiming it right near the woman's head. "Drop it!"

Leon laughed. "Are you going to risk putting a hole in your girlfriend's head to get me?"

The woman looked from Leon to the driver. Gasped. "Pedro, get that thing out of my face!"

Pedro climbed out of the van. Ran around the front, gun waving in front of him. "Drop the knife, gringo!"

Leon threw the knife. The hilt smacked into the driver's forehead. It was a thick hilt. Made of metal. Pedro grunted and stumbled back. He dropped the gun. Grabbed his head. Cried out in pain.

Leon picked up the gun. It was a Glock 19. Looked like it hadn't been cleaned once in its life. It was scratched and banged up. Probably kept in a glove compartment or under a seat.

There was blood on the muzzle. Blackened and old. Like someone had been shot point blank and the gun was never cleaned.

The woman was shouting in Spanish. Fumbling with something in the glove compartment.

Leon pointed the gun at her. "Get out."

She froze. Stared at him.

The young guy was moaning. Trying to stand. Pedro was rolling over. Also trying to stand. Leon raised his boot. Slammed it down on the back of Pedro's head. His face slammed asphalt. He went still.

"You killed him!" The woman screamed and jumped out of the van.

"No. I just put him to sleep." Leon motioned her over. "Besides, he's killed before, hasn't he?"

She whimpered. Looked at the gun. Nodded. "Don't kill him. He's my boyfriend."

"And that guy?" Leon motioned at the younger guy.

"His brother."

"Pedro is a bad influence." Leon tutted. "What's your name?"

"Flora."

"Where did you get the van?"

She looked hesitant to answer.

"Don't make me ask twice, Flora." Leon pressed the muzzle of the gun to her forehead. "I'm not the kind of person you want to piss off."

"It's stolen!"

"Is the owner dead?"

She whimpered. Nodded.

"Who killed the owner?"

"Pedro."

"Are you lying to me? Was it you?"

She shook her head. "I tried to shoot someone. I couldn't do it."

"What's Pedro's body count?" Leon pressed the muzzle harder to her head.

"I don't know. He did a lot before we left Mexico. He worked for the cartel."

"And his brother?"

"He hasn't done anything. He just does what Pedro says."

Leon thought it over. Nodded. "You're lucky I'm on a tight schedule." He motioned her around the side of the van. Looked inside. There were no seats in the back. There was a fridge and some camping tools.

He saw what he needed. "Put the brother back in the van. I'm going to get Pedro."

Tears trickled down her cheeks. "What are you going to do?"

"Oh, you sweet summer child." Leon tutted. "If you live a life of crime, you'll one day mess with the wrong person. Today is that day."

"Please don't kill us!" She dropped to her knees. Clasped her hands. "I'll do anything. Anything!"

Leon backed up a step. "Flora, I'm not going to kill you, as long as you do what I say. But I am going to take your van."

She shivered. Looked forlornly up at him. "Are you lying?"

"No, Flora, I'm not." Leon motioned to the brother. "Get him in the van. Now."

She struggled. Lifted him from under his arms and dragged him toward the van. Leon put the gun on the hood of the van. He dragged Pedro by his feet. Hefted him into the back of the van.

There was rope inside with the camping gear. He bound Pedro and the brother. Tied them up nice and tight. Gagged them. Then he closed the sliding door. Got the gun off the hood. "Flora, get in the passenger seat."

She did what he said. Didn't argue. Just sat down.

Leon got in the driver's seat. The van stank. The inside was dirty. Smelled like cigarettes and weed. It was nothing new to him.

He turned the van around. Headed north. Drove back through the pristine neighbor-hoods. Drove to Interstate 40. Got on the road. Headed west. Toward San Francisco.

Flora was still shaking but she looked a little relieved. "Where are we going?"

"I have a friend who's being hunted by a shadowy organization named Enigma. They're also after me since I killed some of their assassins." Leon smiled at her. "I was going to the airport to steal a car, but then you guys came along and voila." He wave a hand around. "Here we are."

"You're insane."

Leon sighed. "Flora, I wish I was. I wish it was all in my head. But it's not." He glanced at her. "Please tell me you swapped the license plates on this van after you killed the owner and stole it."

She nodded. "Jaime did."

"That's the brother's name?"

She nodded.

"Similar make and model?"

"Yes, of course. It wasn't hard to find in Los Angeles."

"Good."

She went quiet for a while. "What are you going to do to us?"

There wasn't much of anything in these parts. No thick forests. No lakes. Nothing. He'd just have to make do. He took the next exit. Drove north. Out in the middle of nowhere. It was dark, but he didn't need to see far to know that he was surrounded by scrubby pines and grass.

He turned onto a dirt road. Kept going.

Flora started shaking. "You promised not to kill us, remember?"

"I made you a promise." Leon turned off the dirt road. Drove between the trees far out into the scrub. "But tell me this. You've aided and abetted a murderer. Hell, you're dating him. What makes you think you deserve to live?"

"I haven't killed anyone!"

"You have by association. You've probably distracted people so he could get the drop on them."

She hugged herself. Started sobbing. "Yes."

Leon stopped the van. Put it in park. Turned off the headlights. "Okay, so you bear some guilt." He got out. Opened the sliding door. Jaime was awake. Staring wide-eyed at Leon. Like he couldn't understand how he went from robbing Leon to being his prisoner.

Pedro was bleeding from the nose. His face was scratched up. But he was groaning. Trying to wake up.

Leon went through the camping equipment. Found what he was looking for. He pulled out the shovel. Grabbed a flashlight. Walked to the passenger door. Motioned Flora out.

She was still sobbing. Still shaking. She got out. Looked at the shovel. "You're going to kill me, aren't you?"

Leon shook his head. "I made you a promise. But you are going to dig Pedro's grave."

"But you said you wouldn't kill us!"

"I said I wouldn't kill you, Flora." Leon motioned the flashlight toward a bare patch of land. "But you are going to suffer some consequences for your actions, okay?"

"Please, no. Please don't make me do this."

"Flora, if you don't do what I say, then I won't be able to keep my promise. I told you I wouldn't kill you if you did what I said." He held out the shovel. "Now, start digging."

She started digging. Really put her back into it. It was hard going at first, but then she started making progress. After about an hour she had a hole four feet deep, two feet wide, and five feet long. Pedro wasn't tall, so that made it easier.

Leon went to the van. Pedro was awake. Dried blood covered his face. He stared furiously at Leon. Leon removed the gag.

"Do you know who I am, gringo? You know what I've done?" Pedro spat blood. "I'm going to kill you."

"I appreciate your honesty." Leon got the gun. He beckoned Flora. She was filthy. Covered in dirt.

Pedro's forehead pinched. "What in the hell?"

"Untie him, Flora."

She got to work. Loosening the knots. Freed her boyfriend.

Pedro rubbed his wrists. He touched his face. Winced. "Que merde. You gringo asshole, I'm going to beat you before I kill you."

"Get out." Leon motioned with the gun. Backed up a step.

Pedro slid out.

"Flora, take your boyfriend's hand. Lead him to the campsite."

She was crying again, but she took his hand.

Pedro yanked it away. "What the hell, Flora? What's going on?"

"Just follow her, Pedro."

She shook with sobs. Took his hand again.

Pedro scowled. But he followed her into the trees.

Leon followed with the gun and flashlight. Kept them in sight but didn't follow too close. Then the light hit the hole in the ground.

Pedro shouted. He ran. Leon shot him in the leg. Pedro went down squealing.

"Flora, stand clear."

She backed away. Stood to the side.

Leon walked around the squirming man. Stood over him. "You've really put me in a spot, Pedro. I hate playing judge, jury, and executioner, but I think it's about as clearcut as it could be in your case."

Pedro put up his hands. "No, please! I have money! You can have Flora and do what you want with her! Anything!"

Leon leaned down. Kept the flashlight on Pedro, blinding him. "You know what? You've changed my mind."

"Really?"

"Nope." Leon jabbed the survival knife into the man's neck. Blood spurted.

Flora screamed.

Pedro shouted in surprise. He put his hands over the wound. Tried to stop the bleeding. But nothing would save him now.

Leon watched him bleed out. Watched the dry ground drink it in. Pedro finally went still. His eyes stared blankly at the night sky.

Flora was huddled on the ground. Crying and shaking.

Leon tossed her the shovel. "I really should make his brother help you, but I have a feeling he'd try to run."

She looked up at him. Tears tracked through the dirt on her face. "You're evil."

"No, this dirtbag was evil." Leon kicked Pedro's body. "Get him in the ground, please."

She took a deep breath. Stood. Grabbed Pedro by the feet and dragged him into the hole in the ground.

Once she finished, Leon led her back to the van. He pulled out the rest of the camping equipment. Dragged the brother out but left him tied up. They had bags of food. He put it outside the van.

Flora watched him. "What are you doing?"

"I'm leaving you out here. You have food and water. You can camp, or you can hoof it back to civilization."

"Don't leave me here. Take me with you."

He frowned. "You want to come with the monster?"

"No, but I don't want to be abandoned in the middle of nowhere!"

"Oh, I get it." Leon nodded. "At least it's better than being dead and buried, though."

She shivered. Stared at him. It was cold at night. The body heat from digging the grave was wearing off. She had warmer clothing in a suitcase. Leon had seen it.

Flora finally spoke. "Yeah, it's better."

"Okay." Leon looked at Jaime. The young guy was staring at him with pure hatred. He knelt next to him. "Your brother was a bad dude. I'm giving you a chance to turn your life around. I've killed a lot of people in my time. Government leaders. Special forces soldiers. Regular civilians. I left that life behind because it was wrong, you know?"

Jaime looked confused. Maybe a little concerned. But he was still gagged so he couldn't talk.

Leon kept talking. "I just want you to know that if you don't straighten up, I can and will hunt you down. I'll put you in the ground like your brother."

"You're either insane, or..." Flora trailed off.

"Maybe I am a little insane, Flora." Leon shrugged. "I've seen some crazy things. Done crazy things. All because some faceless person up the chain of command ordered it. Now I'm on my own and I'm trying to help a friend." He walked to the van. "So, I'll bid you adieu and get on my way."

He got in the van. Started it. The old engine rumbled to life.

Leon got back on the dirt road. Followed it to the highway. Followed that to the interstate. Then he turned west. Toward San Francisco.

And hoped he reached Carver in time.

CHAPTER 33

Carver knew who killed Bushner.

He was almost dead certain it was Deshawn.

Carver had watched Deshawn's face when he mentioned Bushner in the break room. Deshawn had been surprised. Not surprised that Bushner was dead. He was surprised to discover it had been Carver he'd encountered in the house.

The man who killed Bushner had come in through the front door. That meant he had a key. Or it meant his fingerprint was registered with the biometric lock. Why would Deshawn have that kind of access if he wasn't with Enigma?

Maybe he was playing both sides. Maybe Noah had told his friend to play both sides. That seemed like something Noah would do. Maybe they'd planned to kill Bushner and pin it on Carver.

Noah was watching everything they were doing. He knew Carver had named other possible Enigma affiliates like Bushner. Maybe he thought Carver would go after Maryann Lewis, the San Francisco councilwoman, first. He didn't think Carver would go after the DA right away. So, he sent Deshawn to kill him.

The plan was to send Carver to visit the DA the next night. Carver would arrive. Find the dead man. The cops would bust in. Pin it on Carver. Then one of Enigma's top guys would be dead and none of the blame would fall on Noah.

Carver nodded to himself. That felt right. Noah loved mind games. He loved outsmarting everyone around him. Carver had foiled the game by skipping a step. Now Enigma knew their man was dead.

Deshawn might be playing double agent on Noah's orders. Pretending to be a loyal Enigma operative. Pretending to work with Bushner and other agents. In reality, he was spying for his best friend, Noah.

Enigma would review the security camera footage. Find Deshawn in one of the images. It wouldn't raise any alarm bells because that was normal.

Enigma's people would review the footage from the night of the killing. Find nothing because Carver had disabled the system. They wouldn't know who did it. But maybe they'd suspect Noah. Maybe someone else.

Carver imagined a corkboard in his mind. There were pictures and names of organizations pinned across the top. More pictures pinned below. Threads connected from one pin to another. Some had only one thread. Some had at least two.

Noah was just below Enigma. Connected with a red thread. He was working for them but working against them. An unwilling participant. A green thread connected Noah to Titus. Titus wasn't connected to anything else.

Deshawn was more complicated. Connected to Noah by a green thread. Connected to Enigma by a red thread. His connection was different from Noah's. He was a double agent. Faithful to Noah but pretending to be on Enigma's side.

Tasha was connected to Noah by a red thread. She was connected to Tanner by a green thread. She was forced to work for Noah but trying to work against him. Trying to use Carver for that.

Jeremy was connected to Noah. Another unwilling participant. Another hostage Noah enjoyed playing with. Disposable collateral.

Enigma was connected to lots of players. Bret Bushner. Maryann Lewis. Too many to list in his head. There was a big red X through Bushner's picture now. One agent was out of the game.

But Carver had identified another possible Enigma agent. That agent was sitting in the car with him right this moment. Technically, everyone working for Noah was working for Enigma. But some were working more directly for them. Keeping an eye on Noah.

Jeremy was directly helping Enigma. Carver felt certain about it. It wasn't purely by choice. Noah threatened his life. Jeremy went to someone higher up the chain for help. Told them what Noah was forcing him to do.

They found out about Carver. Sent men after him.

That was why Jeremy had been looking nervously at his phone after Carver leaked news of Bushner. That was why the kid went to the bathroom. So he could message his handlers at Enigma. Let them know about Bushner.

And that was why Enigma's people had showed up so fast right after Carver spilled the beans.

There was one other player at the top of the whiteboard. Henry Marshall. He was as enigmatic as Enigma. Was he connected to them? Was he working with or against them? Carver couldn't answer those questions yet.

There was also the question of the men at the welcome center today. Had they followed Carver there? Or had Jeremy told them where to find Carver?

The latter seemed most likely.

If that was the case, they certainly considered Jeremy disposable. He'd nearly been shot during the car chase. It would have been smarter of Jeremy to go hide somewhere and not get into the car.

Carver kept thinking about it. He came up with more questions than answers. How had Jeremy contacted Enigma? Noah was supposedly the only person who had direct contact with them.

It was possible Jeremy used someone like Maryann Lewis to contact Enigma. He might have told her he had valuable information he could trade for protection.

Carver nodded to himself. That seemed most likely. Instead of getting protection, Jeremy had found himself caught between a rock and a hard place. He was working for Noah and Enigma.

He'd told Enigma about Carver. Maybe told them Noah was working against them. Once he'd given up his most valuable information, he'd become disposable again. The car chase surely drove that point home.

It put Carver in a predicament. His whereabouts were compromised. Enigma knew he was working with Noah. They knew where to find him. But they weren't ready to attack him at Noah's compound. Not yet anyway.

That was why they'd tried at the Golden Gate Bridge.

Tasha broke the silence. "You've been really quiet."

"Just thinking." Carver needed to test something. He thought about talking to Jeremy, but he wasn't ready to let the kid know that he knew about his Enigma connection. Maybe the car chase taught him a lesson. Maybe Jeremy would just wait until he was well away from Carver before giving him up again.

Besides, if he confronted Jeremy, the kid would just lie. It probably wouldn't be hard to break him, but it was too much work when he could just use it to his advantage.

Carver pulled into the department store parking lot. Parked the Honda out front. His stomach grumbled. It was well past lunchtime.

"What do we do now?" Jeremy asked.

"Get some lunch. Take a breather." Carver opened his door. "I need to figure out who sent those men before we go back out again."

Jeremy nodded. "Yeah. Do you think Enigma sent them after you?"

"Seems most likely."

Tasha shook her head. "How would they even know where you are? Noah definitely wouldn't tell them."

Carver shrugged. He kept an eye on Jeremy. The kid was doing a good job looking confused.

"Um, maybe we can go grab pizza?" Jeremy said. "There's a good place around the corner."

"I don't want pizza." Tasha stretched. "I'm going to get lunch at home."

"Oh, okay." Jeremy slumped. "I'll see you guys in an hour?"

Carver nodded. "See you then." He started walking toward the gate. Food first. Tell Noah about the car chase afterward.

Jeremy walked in the opposite direction. Went inside the building.

Tasha caught up to Carver. "Where are you going to eat?"

"Don't know. Somewhere close."

"I have some steaks at my place. Wouldn't take long to cook them."

Carver raised an eyebrow. "All it takes is one car chase to make you friendly?"

She smiled. "I'm just coming around to the idea that you're not who I thought you were."

"Maybe I am the guy you thought I was."

She shook her head. "I'm good at reading people, Carver. After seeing that little old lady cook for you, and then seeing how you handled the car chase, I'm starting to think you're not all that bad."

Carver stopped walking. "I'll take my steak medium rare. Do you have potatoes and beer?"

"Yes."

"Does Noah have your place under surveillance?"

She shook her head. "Tanner sweeps it for me once a week."

"Okay." Carver motioned for her to lead the way. "Let's go."

Tasha led him down the sidewalk. Around the corner. They went past the civic center. Past tall corporate buildings. Past small stores and restaurants. Most were permanently closed.

She took a left at a small brick building sandwiched between two newer, modern buildings. Went in the front door. Up creaking wooden stairs to the third floor. She stopped in front of room 311 and unlocked it.

They went inside. It was small. Cozy. A studio apartment with one door leading into a bathroom. A television was mounted on a wall. There was a small couch. A bed folded into the wall.

A countertop separated the kitchen from the rest of the room. There was an old white fridge. An old electric stove and oven. A microwave. A few cabinets for storage. There were two stools at the kitchen countertop.

"It's not much, but it's better than sleeping at the store." Tasha opened the fridge. Removed a paper-wrapped package. She opened it. There were two steaks inside. She put them on a plate. Seasoned them with salt and pepper.

She pulled a couple of potatoes from the fridge. Poked holes in them with a fork. "You care if they're microwaved?"

"Fine by me." Carver sat on one of the stools.

Tasha put a pan on the stovetop. Turned the power up to max. She looked at the steaks. The potatoes. "Tanner was supposed to eat these with me tonight. But he's not coming over later."

"His loss."

She pulled a couple of domestic beers from the fridge. Opened them. Set one on the counter in front of Carver. He took a draw from it. It wasn't bad. Wasn't good either. It was adequate. Either way, it was a good excuse to sit at the counter. It was also a good excuse to go to the store.

He pulled a small device from his pocket. Stuck it to the bottom of the counter.

Tasha noticed his expression. "You don't like the beer."

He shrugged. "I've had better. Is there a store nearby?"

"There's a package store just around the corner. You can get something more to your liking there while I cook."

"I'll be back, then." Carver left the beer on the counter. Exited the apartment. Closed the door behind him. He turned on the receiver for the bug he'd planted under the counter. Put the earbud in his ear.

He couldn't leave it there. Not if Tanner swept the apartment for bugs. But he was curious to see what happened when he left.

Carver heard steaks sizzling. Heard the microwave running. Heard Tasha's voice. She was talking to someone. Probably Tanner. He couldn't quite make out what she was saying over all the background noise.

He plugged a finger in his other ear. The conversation became clearer.

"I didn't think it was you, but I wanted to make sure." Tasha blew out a breath. "Who was it, then?"

There was a long silence.

"I'm doing my best, but there are a lot of people after this guy. I'm going to get killed in the crossfire."

Carver grinned.

There was more silence.

"Please do." A huff. "Okay. Okay. Fine." It sounded like she slammed the phone on the counter. She growled. Sounded like she pounded the counter with her fist. Then she cursed a few times.

Carver reached the store. He went in and picked up some stout beer. Paid. Left. Walked back toward the apartment.

His phone vibrated. There was a message from Lee. *Bushner's biometric lock kept a logfile in the cloud. I was able to check the access log. There were two instances of a remote fob being used last night. Then another instance late this morning. I found no matches for fingerprints registered with the app except for Bushner's. The others aren't in any federal databases.*

The killer had used a fob, not a thumbprint. That made sense. He'd probably been wearing gloves to keep from leaving fingerprints.

Another text from Lee popped up on the screen. *The Guard Dog app was made by Guard Dog Security. Guard Dog was acquired by Parabellum Industries two weeks ago. There is a maze of shell companies between Parabellum and the real owner of the company. I'm digging through them to find the real own. Probably associated with Enigma.*

Carver replied. *Seems likely. Let me know as soon as you have something.*

The bug picked up Tasha talking again. It sounded like she was on the phone again. "Hey. I can't talk now." A pause. "Yes. I'm working on it. I'll come see you tonight and we'll talk about it."

Silence again.

Carver figured the first person she'd talked with was Noah. The second was Tanner.

He entered the apartment building. Climbed to the third floor. Went back inside Tasha's apartment. She looked up from the steaks. Smiled. "Almost ready."

Carver sat back at the counter. He considered leaving the bug there. It was tiny. She probably wouldn't see it. But if Tanner swept the apartment, he'd find it.

"Did Tanner ever find anything when he swept the apartment?"

Tasha shook her head. "Noah never bothered to bug it. He could probably have demanded I install cameras. But I think he likes knowing I'm under his thumb." She bit her lower lip. "That's why we need to come up with a plan to find the failsafe. Protect my sister so we can take out Noah. Then we'll all be free."

Her voice didn't have the same conviction as it had the night before. Like she was just reminding Carver that she wanted something from him. Something important.

"As soon as someone can tell me how to get this information, I'll formulate a plan." Carver pulled the bug off the bottom of the counter. Slid it back into his pocket. "I can't just kidnap Noah and torture him for the information. He's too proud. He'll hold out just to spite me."

"There is a way."

Carver opened a stout beer for himself. "Want one?"

She nodded.

He opened one for her. Set it on the counter. "What way is that?"

"Noah lost something very valuable. Something he might be willing to trade anything to get it back. Including giving you the failsafe information."

"Maybe I could just trade it for your sister's freedom."

"Maybe. The problem is, someone stole this item. We have no idea where it is."

Carver sipped his beer. "Well, now, that's a problem. How do you even know about it?"

"Because Noah ordered me to text all his street people. Told them to look out for it."

"I'm having a hard time understanding what could be that valuable to Noah." Carver watched her cook the steaks. They looked great.

Tasha used tongs to turn the thick steaks onto their sides to sear them. "I don't know exactly what it is either. He didn't tell anyone."

Carver's stomach growled. "Awfully hard to recover something if you don't tell people what it is."

"Let me clarify." She rotated the thick steak slowly. Searing the sides evenly. "This valuable thing is inside a briefcase. He described the briefcase, not whatever is inside it."

Carver stopped thinking about the steaks. About eating. His attention was solely focused on one word. *Briefcase.* He kept his face emotionless. Pretended to watch the steaks. "Yeah? What's so special about this briefcase?"

She started working on the other steak. Searing the sides. "It's made from titanium. Latched all the way around. Needs a six-digit code to open it."

Carver sipped his beer. Acted nonchalant. But his mind was racing. "Briefcases like that aren't cheap. It must have something valuable inside."

"Yeah. It's like a spy briefcase."

An image of a reinforced briefcase popped up in Carver's mind. He'd seen countless variations. Even ones designed to look like leather on the outside to draw less attention.

More specifically, he knew exactly which briefcase Tasha was talking about. It was the briefcase Bobby had stolen. The one that got him killed. The one with a special new drug inside it. The Flood.

And now he knew who it belonged to. Who wanted it badly enough to kill for it. Who might want it badly enough to trade anything for it.

Noah.

CHAPTER 34

Noah wanted the briefcase.

He might trade anything for it. Carver's phone. His stuff. He might even take a package deal including Tasha and Jeremy. Provided it was as valuable as Tasha claimed.

Flood must be some kind of wonder drug if it was that valuable. Carver wondered why Noah couldn't just make more. Maybe it was too expensive. Maybe there was more than just the drug in the briefcase.

It might contain the formula. Maybe Flood wasn't even Noah's drug to begin with. Maybe he stole it from someone else. Someone like Enigma. Anything was possible.

Carver felt like he should have connected Noah to the briefcase earlier. But it hadn't exactly been at the top of his mind. Not with everything else going on. And if Tasha knew about it all this time, why hadn't she mentioned it sooner?

She should have mentioned it when she and Tanner first asked him to team up with them. He could have turned his focus on finding the briefcase.

He wanted to ask her the question. But his gut told him not to. Tasha and Tanner were playing their own game. They'd known about the briefcase. They knew it might be the best way to free Tasha and her sister from Noah. And yet, they hadn't mentioned it until now.

It was best to play dumb. Hold his cards close. Find the briefcase. It had been three days since he'd spoken with Sally. Maybe she'd heard from Herbert by now. Hopefully she'd relayed Carver's message to her boyfriend.

"What are you thinking about, Carver?" Tasha was holding the last steak to the heat. Searing the final edge.

"Food." He sipped his beer. "I'm starving."

She smiled. It was a nice smile for a change. No sarcasm detected. Her red hair fell across her face. Almost made her look girlish.

The microwave beeped. Tasha turned down the heat on the stove. Opened the microwave. Put the potatoes on separate plates. "You like all the fixings?"

"I do."

She opened the fridge. Pulled out sour cream, butter, shredded cheese, and bacon bits. Set them on the counter. "Come make it yourself."

Carver finished off his beer. Walked around the counter. Sliced open the potato and loaded it up. Finished it off with salt and pepper.

Tasha put a steak on his plate. Handed him a steak knife. He went back to the stool. Sat down. Cut into the steak. It was nice and red inside. Juicy. It had been a while since he'd enjoyed a steak.

He cut off a chunk. Put it in his mouth and chewed it. He sighed. Nodded. "Perfect."

She grinned. "Steaks and baked potatoes are a staple in my family."

Carver nodded. "As they should be. The four major food groups all on one plate."

Tasha looked at the potato. Laughed. "I guess you're right." She sat on the stool beside him. Ate in silence.

He opened another beer. Chased the steak with it. It complemented it perfectly. When he finished, he rinsed his plate in the sink. Opened the dishwasher. It was empty.

Tasha shook her head. "I just handwash my dishes. You can leave it in the sink."

Carver took the sponge. Turned on the water. Washed his plate. Set it in a dish rack next to the sink. It was strange seeing something so domestic in Tasha's apartment. She didn't seem like the kind of person who would hand wash dishes.

She didn't seem like the kind of person to have a cabinet full of spices either. Even after all his experiences, people could still surprise him. That could be a good thing. But it was mostly a bad thing in his line of work.

Paola had surprised him all the time. She was nice when she could have been mean. Forgiving when she could have been angry. Always quick to smile. Quick to hug him if she thought he was unhappy.

She was unlike anyone Carver had ever met. Despite all the horrible things she'd suffered, she was mostly good. It seemed too good to be true. Like she was putting on an act. Doing whatever she could to make him happy, so he'd be more open to a relationship.

Then she'd had enough and left. She wasn't angry. Just sad. Carver still remembered the tears rolling down her cheeks. That silent look of resignation on her face. That last kiss when she said goodbye.

Carver cleared his throat.

"You went real distant there for a minute, Carver." Tasha was watching him from the other side of the counter. "I take it you don't do dishes that much?"

He shrugged. "I do dishes all the time. It's a requirement when you're camping."

She brought her dishes around. Carver took them. Washed them. Set them in the rack. He dried off his hands and turned. Tasha was standing right behind him. Her hair was hanging in her face again.

"I know I haven't been exactly pleasant to be around." She sighed. Her shoulders slumped. Like the tension left them. "I just don't trust anyone."

"That's a good policy." Carver leaned back against the counter. "It'll keep you alive."

"Yeah, but it's not a very fun policy." She stepped a little closer. Touched his arm. "I actually have faith in you, Carver. I'm starting to believe you can help me get my family out of this mess."

"No promises, but I think so too."

She closed the gap. Hugged him tight. She was a strong woman. He could feel the hardness of her muscles. Not bodybuilder kind of muscles. These were the kind of muscles earned through high intensity training.

Despite that, she was soft on the outside. Lean and toned. Carver put his arms around her. Gave her a squeeze that wasn't quite a hug. It just wasn't his thing.

She backed up suddenly. "I'm sorry. I don't usually do that."

Carver pushed her hair away from her cheek. Ran his thumb along the scar. "What happened here?"

"I brought a gun to a knife fight."

He raised an eyebrow. "Were you out of bullets?"

"Something like that." She closed her eyes. Sighed. "It's so ugly."

"I like scars." Carver noticed a fainter one on the side of her neck. He touched it too. "They tell me something about a person."

Tasha looked up at him with her big green eyes. "What do they tell you about me?"

"That you need to stay away from knife fights."

She laughed. It was a full-throated belly laugh. The first genuine one Carver had heard. Then she stood on her tiptoes. Grabbed Carver by the back of his neck. Pulled him down for a kiss.

She had nice, soft lips. Strong hands. Carver pulled her closer. Kissed her back. His hand ran up under her shirt. He felt the small of her back. Ran his fingers up her spine.

Tasha shivered. Backed away. She hesitated a moment. Took his hand and led him around the counter. She pulled the bed down out of the wall. Turned around and kissed him again. Her hands slipped under his shirt. She pushed it up and off.

Carver decided he liked where this was going.

It was getting dark outside when Carver slid out of Tasha's bed. He went to her bathroom. Found a towel and took a nice, hot shower. There was a bar of purple soap there. It smelled like lavender.

There were more hair products than he could shake a stick at. Conditioner. Toner. Shampoo. Oil body wash. It looked like too much for someone like Tasha. Hair care didn't seem to be her top priority.

"I'd join you, but that shower is ridiculously small." Tasha peeked around the shower curtain. "We can't tell Tanner about this, okay?"

"It's not something I usually bring up in conversation."

"I didn't think you would." Her eyes lingered on his chest. "I just wanted to say."

Carver rubbed soap on his chest. "My eyes are up here."

She laughed. Another genuine laugh. Met his gaze. "Looking never hurt anyone."

He sniffed the soap. Nodded at the array of hair care products. "How long does it take you to shower?"

Tasha blinked. Like she was confused by the question. Then she looked at the products. "Oh, uh, those are my sister's. She brought them when she stayed with me a few times."

Carver remembered all the products Paola used. Remembered that it took her an hour sometimes to do her hair. He was usually in and out of the shower in five minutes. She took twenty minimum.

He nodded. "I figured you were the sort that took about fifteen minutes to get ready, start to finish."

"Yeah, that's me." Tasha ran a finger along her scar. Her eyes went distant. Like she was remembering the day she got it.

Carver felt like there was a lot more to that scar than she let on. It wasn't his business. He wasn't going to ask. She could tell him if she wanted.

She blinked. Looked guilty, like he'd caught her doing it. He didn't think she realized how often she did that when there was no apparent reason for it.

He'd noticed other scars. One along her right knee. Another on her hip. It was the puckered circular scar on her leg that caught his attention. It was a gunshot wound.

Some of the scars might be from childhood accidents. Easily explained. But the gunshot wound wasn't something she got as a kid.

It was still raised up on the edges. She'd gotten it as an adult. Probably a few years ago. Probably before Noah.

It was hard not to notice all those things when she was naked and there was plenty of light in the room. It led Carver to think she'd lied about never being in the military. It was also possible there was a more innocent explanation.

A hunting accident. Maybe someone hadn't cleared the chamber on a gun, and it went off. She came from a military family. A family that probably had a lot of guns. Accidents happened even with the most careful people.

Carver turned off the water. Grabbed the towel. "Jeremy probably thinks someone killed us."

Tasha's eyes widened. "Oh, I forgot all about him. I'll text him and let him know we're okay."

"He's going to know we slept together if you do that."

"I'll just tell him something came up. I'll see him in the morning and leave you out of it."

Carver nodded. "Good strategy."

She walked away, still naked. Carver was tempted to stay a little longer. But he had work to do.

He stepped out of the shower. Dried off. The bathroom was tiny. A small vanity with a sink and mirror was sandwiched between the shower and toilet. The shower was barely three by three. Roomier than a lot of showers he'd used over the years, but not by much.

He crouched. Opened the vanity to look for deodorant. There was an assortment of household cleaners. A package with several boxes of the purple soap. More bottles of hair care products.

There was also a three pack of women's deodorant. He reached for one then noticed more packages behind them. They were men's deodorant. Men's disposable razors. Shaving cream. One of the men's deodorants looked used.

He took it. Remove the lid. It was worn down almost to the nub. He used it. Put the lid on. Tucked it under the sink. He hesitated. Couldn't help himself from opening a box in the back of the cabinet. Looked inside.

What he saw didn't make sense. Or, maybe it made perfect sense in the right context. Maybe it was an anomaly. Maybe it was nothing out of the ordinary.

Carver closed the cabinet. Stood and looked at himself in the mirror. He combed his hair to the side with his fingers. It wasn't that long but he wanted to get it cut again. He left the bathroom.

On the way out, he tested the doorknob to the closet just outside. It was locked. He kept walking.

Tasha was sitting on the bed in the den. Typing on her phone. She smiled when he came in. "Want to stay the night?"

"Can't. I'm helping Zimo tonight."

She frowned. "With what?"

"I told him I'd help with some neighborhood patrol strategies. Simple stuff." He found his underwear. Pulled it on. "Believe me, I'd rather stay in bed with you."

Tasha reached out. Stroked his leg. "Yeah, I'd like that."

He pulled on his pants. His shirt. His socks and shoes. "You texted Jeremy?"

She nodded. "He said he wasn't worried. I think he went home. Probably had to shower since he wet his pants."

"Then, I guess I'll see you tomorrow."

Tasha stood. Pulled him in for a kiss. She was still naked. She inhaled deeply. "You smell great."

"It's the lavender soap. Brings out my manliness."

She laughed. Ran her fingers along his back. "You can come by later if you have time."

"I'm afraid this will be an all-nighter."

She sighed. "Okay. I guess I'll go talk to Tanner. Let him know about everything from today."

"Yeah, good idea." Carver left. Went downstairs and outside. It was dark and chilly. The trolley was still running, so he hiked down the street to a station and sat on a bench.

He was thinking. Thinking hard. He sniffed an armpit. Confirmed that it smelled familiar. That was no big deal. A lot of deodorants had a similar smell. This one was nothing special. Just a *Shower Fresh* scent that was probably available from multiple brands.

Maybe the men's toiletries belonged to Tasha's sister too. Maybe she had a boyfriend. Maybe Tasha had an ex-boyfriend who used to stay with her. There were plenty of explanations.

It was the things Carver hadn't seen that concerned him the most. There were small holes in the walls. Small squares where the paint hadn't faded as much from sunlight. Pictures had been hanging there for a long time. Now they weren't.

The place was clean. Almost too clean. Carver wondered if he'd opened the closet in the back of the room if he would've found the missing pictures. Found other things that had been hastily removed.

He took out his phone. Downloaded a real estate app. Looked at Tasha's building. All the rooms were rented, but there were prices listed. Over three thousand dollars a month for a six hundred square foot studio.

Was Noah paying Tasha anything? Did he own the apartment and let her live there for free? Something didn't add up. Maybe it didn't matter at all. Maybe it mattered a lot. Carver didn't have time to look into it.

Besides, if he found the briefcase, none of it would matter anymore.

CHAPTER 35

Carver reached the Tenderloin District.

The night crowd didn't look much different from the day crowd. People were sitting outside tents. Some were slumped over. Others were walking in slow motion. One guy was laid out flat on the sidewalk. Pants down, feces trailing from his backside.

Carver walked in the street. He didn't want to get any closer to the addicts than necessary. They were unpredictable. The odor wasn't too pleasant either.

He spotted Sally's dirty yellow tent in the same place as last time. Another tent had squeezed onto the sidewalk nearby. The tent city seemed to have grown longer even though it had only been three days.

A bearded man was sitting on the sidewalk next to the new tent. He was shouting. Like he was arguing with someone over the phone. But there were no earbuds in his ears. He was just cursing at his invisible demons.

Carver walked between the tents. The stench hit his nose. Body odor. Feces. Urine. God only knew what else. He crouched outside Sally's tent. It was zipped up. He scratched the fabric. "Sally, you in there?"

The man looked at Carver. Kept shouting. "Killers! Monsters! Leave us alone! Leave us alone!"

Carver couldn't tell if he was shouting at him, or just repeating what he'd been saying earlier. "Is Sally home?"

"Killers! Killers! Go away!" The man kept repeating it over and over again. No one else was paying him any attention. The people who looked sober were huddled around small fires. Staring blankly. Probably wondering when, where, and how they'd get their next hit.

Carver unzipped the tent. The odor grew even stronger. But this was something different. Something rotten. He looked inside. It was dark. He used the flashlight on his phone. A dark hump became visible.

Sally's wide eyes stared at him. She was propped into a sitting position against a mound of clothing. Her mouth hung open. Her tongue was swollen and lolling. There was no light in those eyes. Only the haze of death.

Her hands were stretched out to either side. There was a bottle next to her fingers. A small empty plastic bottle. Identical to the one he'd found at Bushner's house. There was nothing left in it.

Her arms were cut up. There were cuts on her face too. The fingers on one hand were crooked and broken. She'd been tortured. Then she'd been killed. Fentanyl overdose.

Carver backed out of the tent. Zipped it shut. Wiped off the zipper tab with his jacket. He turned to the shouting guy. "Did someone come see Sally?"

The man kept shouting the same thing.

Carver got closer. Snapped his fingers in the guy's face. "Hey! Answer me."

The man flinched. His eyes seemed to focus on Carver. "I ain't got nothing."

"Did someone visit Sally recently?"

"The killers." The man nodded. "She was screaming a lot. Said she didn't know anything. Said Herbert took it. She hadn't seen him since."

"What did the men look like?"

"A thin guy. Black. Not real tall. He was with another guy. A white guy who looked all business. Like military or something."

"The first guy didn't look military?"

"No, no, no." The man's eyes started to go distant. "He was dressed too nice."

"Did Sally say where Herbert was?"

"She didn't know." He gasped. "Her screams. "Nobody noticed. Everyone here screams. Everyone here is crazy." He grabbed Carver's jacket. "We ain't safe, man. The killers are us. We're killing ourselves!"

He shivered. Released Carver slumped. "Go away. Let us die in peace."

Carver stood. He walked away. Acted casual. Like nothing had happened. But he was looking. Looking hard. And he saw what he thought he'd find. A black Audi parked just down the road.

It was facing him. Positioned with a clear line of sight to Sally's tent. There was a shadowy figure inside. A person. It was hard to tell what he was doing. But he was probably watching Carver. Probably texting someone right now.

Sally had a visitor.

Someone on the other end was sounding an alarm. Sending more people. At least, that was what Carver thought they would do.

He cut between tents. Went into an alley. He took out his monocular. Focused on the car. Turned on the night vision. The car was empty. What he'd thought was a person was the seat and headrest.

The other cars along the street were empty too. Then Carver saw something else. A camera attached to a streetlamp pole. It was high up. Small. About the size of a trail camera. And it was aimed right at Sally's tent.

That made more sense. Watching remotely was smarter. It didn't require much manpower. Whoever was on the other end had probably alerted his people that someone had visited Sally's tent.

If they were Noah's people, they'd soon know it was Carver. If they were with Enigma, they'd also know it was Carver, not Herbert. It had been stupid not to look for surveillance beforehand.

Then again, Carver hadn't expected this. He'd thought Sally was off the radar. Bobby hadn't given up her name as far as he knew. She'd given the briefcase to Herbert. Kept her mouth shut.

But someone had found out. Sally must have talked to someone. Must have said something that got back to Noah's people. Or maybe someone had seen her with the briefcase. It probably wasn't easy to hide.

Noah's enforcers had found out. They'd come here. Tortured Sally for information. She'd given up Herbert's name but didn't know his location. Then they killed her. Maybe to keep news of the briefcase quiet.

They didn't want their new street drug publicized until they were ready to market it. At least, that seemed like the most logical reason to kill Sally. Then again, they could have done it for fun.

Carver hadn't seen many of Noah's enforcers. He'd seen a few. Enough to know he hadn't seen any white military types among them. That didn't mean there wasn't one. But the ones he'd seen were typical street thugs. All street smarts. No military training.

If Noah found out Carver was poking around in Sally's tent, he'd want to know why. The question practically answered itself. Carver had no real reason to be here. No reason to visit a random homeless person in the Tenderloin District.

It would compromise Carver's search for the briefcase. Or would it? If Noah confronted him about it, he could say Tasha told him about it.

He could tell Noah that he'd find it. And if he did, Noah would promise to give him back his phone. He'd also promise to give Tasha and Jeremy their freedom.

It wasn't ideal, but it would work.

But he wasn't any closer to finding Herbert. For all he knew, the man wasn't even in town anymore. Sally had said that Herbert had found a new place. A great place he didn't want anyone to know about.

Carver replayed the conversation in his head. There was one part that stuck out. Herbert had told Sally it was real green and had a view of the bridge. He hadn't said which bridge. It was either the Golden Gate Bridge, or the Oakland Bay Bridge.

He thought back to the drive to the Golden Gate Welcome Center. There hadn't been any homeless encampments on the west side. The area was a lot cleaner. More upscale. Maybe there were some back in the neighborhoods, but none of them had a view of the bridge.

Carver opened the map app on his phone. He studied two areas in particular. One thing he noticed was the lack of public transportation on the west side near the Golden Gate Bridge. There were no trolleys, street cars, or electric buses.

He searched for homeless shelters. They were clustered in the downtown area near the bay. He ran an internet search on the term *homeless encampments San Francisco*. Someone had made a map overlay showing dozens of them. Color coded them by size.

The Tenderloin was full of red-colored camps. Meaning they were the biggest. Smaller camps were scattered throughout the city. There were none anywhere near the Golden Gate Bridge. There was a small one near Fisherman's Wharf.

Another small one near Pier 39. Right in a park. It was almost on the water. That had to be the place. It had a view of the bridge and it was green.

The rest of the encampments were clustered further back into the city. None of them in green areas. None of them with a view of the Oakland Bay Bridge.

Carver cut through the alley. Took it around to the other side. He hadn't seen any signs of people coming to investigate his presence. He didn't plan to hang around and wait, either.

He hopped on a trolley. Took it as far as he could. Took an electric bus the rest of the way. He got off a few blocks later. Went into a dark alley. Waited twenty minutes to see if anyone was following him.

It didn't look like anyone was. He hadn't seen any cars following the bus. Hadn't seen anyone suspicious board the bus after him, either.

He gave it an extra ten minutes to be sure. Then he strolled down Beach Street. Across the Embarcadero. Into Plaza de California. It was a nice spot. Nice and green. Oceanfront property. There was a small cluster of tents nearby.

A man and woman sat on plastic milk crates outside one tent. They were huddled in front of a fire. Eating something out of cans. There were two milk crates across the fire from them. Carver sat down on one.

They looked calmly at him. Like strangers sitting at their fire was a common occurrence. It probably was.

The woman paused with a spoonful of baked beans halfway to her mouth. "Hey, man. Welcome to Commune City."

"Thanks." Carver looked around. "My friend Herbert told me all about it."

"Herbert?" She looked confused. "So far, it's just ten of us. Nobody named Herbert for sure."

"Oh, I think he just heard of it from a friend." Carver wondered if maybe Herbert was just going by a different name. "He's about five foot seven, skinny. Missing some teeth. Brown hair. Brown eyes. Crooked nose. Long bushy beard."

"Missing teeth?" The woman shook her head. "Sounds like an f-head."

"A what?"

"Fentanyl user," the man said. "We don't allow that here. Weed only." He held up two fingers. "Peace and love. Not deadly drugs."

"That's a good rule." Carver knew right then that this was the wrong place.

"We don't have many rules, but that's one," the woman said. "We want to tear down the old city. Build a new one with no landowners, no landlords. Just the will of the people, you know?"

The man nodded. "Perfect harmony."

"Sounds great." Carver nodded at the tents. "Do I get to choose where I live?"

"Newcomers have to bring their own tent. They have to contribute to the community first."

Carver nodded. "Makes sense. I'll go get a tent."

"Yeah, awesome!" The woman clapped. "Bring food if you have it. You can trade it for art, or music, or anything here."

"Do you take money?"

"No way, dude." The man shook his head vehemently. "Keep that capitalist venom out of here. We trade in labor and goods only."

"Barter."

"We call it moral currency here." The woman held up her can of beans. "Food is pure currency, you know?"

"I'll bring some, then." Carver stood. "Thanks for the information."

"See you soon!" The woman said.

Carver went back to the Embarcadero. He started to rethink the conversation with Sally. Maybe Herbert had tried to move into this encampment and been refused. Maybe he was talking about a different place altogether.

He looked at the custom map overlay. The encampment markers relied on people's firsthand reports. It wasn't updated in real time. There was a timestamp at the top. It had last been updated a week ago.

That was plenty of time for new encampments to appear. Maybe Herbert had found a place not listed on the map.

Tanner might know more about new encampments. He'd been all over the city. Searching homeless encampments for Tasha before he found out she was with Noah. He might remember something.

And it might not be a bad idea to bring Tanner and Tasha into this. It directly involved them, after all. Tasha was probably still talking to her brother in his tent.

It was a pretty good hike back to his encampment, so Carver rode a streetcar down the Embarcadero and to his stop. He got out. Walked into the park. Went straight to Tanner's tent. It was closed up tight. Locked.

Carver thumped the fabric. "Tanner, you in there?"

No answer. He put an ear to the fabric.

Tommy came around the corner. "He left a while back."

"Did he leave with the redhead who was here last night?"

Tommy frowned. "Who?"

"Never mind." Carver figured the two might have gone somewhere else to talk. Maybe in a warm building since it was a little chilly out. He walked back toward the Embarcadero. Looked at the Ferry Building. There were some small shops inside. They might be there.

Then he noticed something else. Something that was clear as day even in the middle of the night. He stared at it for a moment. Turned slowly around. Walked back inside the tents. He found Tommy sitting in a lawn chair outside his tent.

"Tommy, do you know a guy named Herbert?"

Tommy blinked slowly. It looked like he'd just dosed himself. "Herbie? Yeah. Over there." He pointed to a row of tents. The same row Carver's tent was in. "At the end."

Carver walked to the row. He looked out at what he'd seen earlier. A picture-perfect view of the Oakland Bay Bridge. A view from a nice green park. Tommy's little tent city wasn't on the homeless map. But it fit the description.

He walked down the row of tents. A skinny woman sat outside one. She was staring blankly ahead. Probably high. He went to the last one. The grass around it was still nice and springy. No dead patches underneath it.

It hadn't been here long. He thumped on the fabric. "Hey, Herbie, Tommy wanted me to ask you something."

There was rustling inside. A head poked out. There wasn't much hair on the top. But it had a bushy beard. The man looked up at Carver. His mouth hung open. He was missing several teeth on the top and bottom.

"Hey, I gave Tommy my rent."

Carver crouched. Looked inside the tent. A small battery powered lamp lit the inside. There was a sleeping bag. Several bulging garbage bags. And one bag with something square inside of it.

"Hey!" The man crawled out of the tent and stood. "Don't invade my privacy!"

Carver stood up. Looked the man over. "Herbert, Sally sent me."

He blinked. "She did?"

Carver nodded. "She's dead. They killed her. If you don't give me the briefcase, they're coming for you next."

He went pale as a ghost. "No, not Sally!"

"I'm sorry."

"I loved her. She gave me good company when I needed it."

Carver shook his head. Spread his hands helplessly. "I'm sorry."

"Oh, God!" Herbert started crying. "Not my Sally."

Carver didn't want to touch Herbert's filthy clothing, but he patted him on the shoulder anyway. Herbert took that as an invitation. He buried his face in Carver's jacket and sobbed.

Carver let the man have a moment. Then he backed up a step. "Herbert, I need the briefcase."

The other man nodded. Sniffled and wiped his nose with his jacket. "Yeah, I never could get into it anyway. I was afraid to ask anyone for help." He ducked into the tent. Pulled out the trash bag with the rectangular object in it. "Take it and run, man. I don't want to die for some stupid briefcase."

Carver took the bag. It was heavy. The corners of whatever was inside strained against the plastic. He looked inside. Saw a metallic case with latches all the way around. Saw a combination lock on the front and sides.

This was it. Simple as that, Carver had the briefcase.

CHAPTER 36

Carver tucked the bag under an arm.

"Herbert, don't breathe a word of this to anyone, okay?"

"I won't, I swear." He started sobbing again. "Why did they kill my Sally?"

"Don't say anything about her, okay? It's important. And change your name. They might already be looking for someone named Herbert."

The other man gasped. "I didn't think of that. What name should I use?"

"Frank is good. And you might want to find someplace where no one knows your real name."

Carver left him with that advice. He went back to his tent. Zipped it up. Took the briefcase from the bag. It was heavy duty. Solid. It was more like a safe with a handle than a briefcase. It looked a lot like the ones the techs from his secret unit used for their sensitive equipment.

He knew what it took to open one of these without the combination. No amount of prying worked. Cutting it required special tools. Welding it required special high heat welders. The seams were tight, making it nearly impossible to cut or saw through the latches anyway.

A high heat welder could cut through the metal, but it was likely to burn or destroy the contents. Diamond tipped sawblades or drills might eventually breach the case, but it would take hours and burn through the blades or bits.

Hacking the combination was also next to impossible. There were six combination dials. Each dial went from zero to nine. That made for a lot of possible combinations. It was possible for him to eventually find it just by elimination, but it would take a very long time.

Jericho had figured out a way to crack these briefcase safes. It wasn't exactly an easy method, but it worked without damaging the contents. And Carver knew just the place that could do it.

Arty's garage had a machine shop inside. It had a hydraulic press, welders, metal cutting blades, and more. Provided the cops hadn't carted everything away, Carver could use one of those tools to open the case.

It would be best to get Tanner and Tasha to help. If someone was following him, he'd need backup. Those two could handle themselves. Then Carver could negotiate with Noah. Get his phone back.

Everyone would have a new lease on life by morning.

He left the case in his tent. Locked the zipper. Walked across the road to the Ferry Building. Even though the lights were on, most of the shops inside were closed. No sign of Tanner and Tasha.

He went outside. Passed by his Ramcharger. It had a boot on the back wheel now. A thick stack of tickets under the windshield wiper. It boiled Carver's blood to see his truck treated that way.

He might have to bring a tool from Arty's workshop to remove the boot. Because he hoped to get the hell out of this city by tomorrow morning. And he wasn't going to pay any parking tickets. Not a single one.

Carver gave it some thought. Maybe Tanner and Tasha had gone back to her apartment to talk. Maybe she hadn't come down to see him here since it was getting dark out. Maybe he'd gone to her.

He considered what to do about the briefcase. It was probably safe inside the tent. Maybe safer than him publicly lugging around a plastic trash bag with a suspicious object in it. There were two options. Take it or leave it.

There was too much at risk to leave it. So, he decided to take it. He went into his tent. His clothing bag was big enough to hold the case. He removed most of the clothes but left a layer on the bottom. He put the case inside.

He stuffed more clothes around the case and on top. When he held it up, the square shape wasn't visible anymore. Carver tugged on a beanie. Put on a facemask. Went outside.

He slid the bag's shoulder strap over his shoulder. The briefcase made it much heavier. But it was nothing compared to carrying around a bag of guns.

Carver headed to the trolley station. He looked like he could be homeless. But he might also just be a regular homeowner toting his laundry bag around. And his identity was mostly hidden. He couldn't do much about his height or size except slump.

The trolley took him back uptown. He got out one block past Noah's compound. It felt awfully risky to be this close to that place with the briefcase. But the store looked empty this time of night.

Carver followed the sidewalk. Found his way to the front of Tasha's apartment building. The entry door was locked. He tried a few buzzers. No one let him in. Sometimes it worked. Most of the time people checked before letting anyone in.

He decided to resort to modern methods and texted her.

You home?

Her window faced the alley. There was light coming from the window, so she was probably home. He checked the phone. No response.

Maybe he should go old school and toss a pebble against the window. That seemed like a dumb idea, so he went into the alley. There was a fire escape on the side of the neighboring building.

The ladder was retracted. He jumped. Pushed it up. The latch folded. The ladder dropped. He climbed it. Walked quietly up. It was right next to the windows of the other building. Most of them were dark. Nobody home.

He reached the third level. Got a clear view into Tasha's apartment. She was there. Tanner was there too. They weren't talking. They weren't eating or watching television, either.

They were going at it on the bed.

Carver used his monocular to make sure it was Tanner. It was. And he definitely wasn't treating Tasha like a sister. Which explained a lot of things. It explained why they looked nothing alike.

Because unless they were heavy into incest, they weren't related at all.

Carver sat down. He should have felt more confused, but he wasn't. His initial gut reaction to Tasha and Tanner had felt off. Like they were keeping something from him. And now he knew for sure they had been.

They weren't brother and sister. They were a couple. So, why in the hell had they lied to him? And why had she bedded Carver when she had a boyfriend?

It also explained why so much stuff was hidden. Why the pictures on the wall were missing. They'd hidden Tanner's stuff. Made the place look like a bachelorette pad. Maybe they'd planned this out.

Sleeping with an asset was as old as time. It was a way to make someone like you more. To soften you up. Make you more eager to please. Tasha's entire act toward him was a textbook salt and sugar approach.

Start off salty. Make someone think you don't like them. That you don't trust them. That you want nothing to do with them. Then come up with a reason to suddenly like them. Turn on the sugar.

The sudden one-eighty change in attitude would make the target think that they'd won you over. The target would feel happy. They'd feel gratitude. They'd want to keep pleasing you. It was a con game, plain and simple.

She'd even slept with him to seal the deal.

Tasha and Tanner told Carver that they were related just to make their sob story even stronger and more emotional. He might have more sympathy for a brother and sister trying to save their little sister as opposed to a boyfriend helping his girlfriend with the same problem.

And it also meant they could use the romance approach on Carver as well.

Carver clapped his hands silently. "Well played, you dirty bastards."

He wasn't mad. He wasn't happy either. But at least he knew the truth. He would play dumb for the time being. It seemed best.

He was happy he'd trusted his gut and not told Tasha about the briefcase. He was happy that his first instinct was always to distrust everyone.

Tasha and Tanner finally finished. Tanner rolled off the bed. Went into the bathroom. Carver texted Tasha.

Hey, I decided to come over after all. I'm a few blocks away.

He kept watching. Tasha stretched. Sat up. She stood and walked over to the counter. Picked up her phone. Panic lit her face. She said something. Ran into the bathroom. Tanner came running out a minute later.

He tugged on his clothes fast as he could. Tasha ran into the bathroom. Tanner hightailed it out of the building a moment later. He climbed into a small silver car. Carver watched with the monocular as Tanner lowered the driver seat so he could be out of sight.

Tasha texted back. *Sure, come on over.*

That confirmed it. Carver and Tasha's fling hadn't been a secret. Tanner knew. Either he wasn't the jealous type, or there was something else going on. They might be a couple. They might just be friends with benefits.

It was almost certain they weren't related. If they were, it wouldn't be the first time Carver had seen something like this. In the end, it didn't really matter. He'd been ready to throw a little trust their way. Not anymore.

They would have been watching his back tonight. Now they wouldn't. There might be a whole lot more to their deception. Might be something worse to discover. As usual, Carver was on his own.

He considered having some fun at their expense. Decided it wasn't worth the trouble. He had a lot to do tonight. He texted her again. *Zimo has an emergency. I can't come after all.*

Tasha was staring at her phone. She saw the message. Put a hand on her chest. Breathed a sigh of relief. She typed out another text.

It arrived on Carver's phone. *Aw, I was looking forward to more fun.*

She kept typing on her phone. Tanner got out of the car a moment later. Came back inside. The two of them started talking. Carver wished he had the parabolic microphone with him. He'd left all of the surveillance equipment at Noah's compound. He didn't trust leaving it in his tent.

Tasha's and Tanner's faces were serious. Businesslike. Carver didn't see any affection. No hugs. No kisses. No reassurance. Carver had been trained to read body language. He felt like he got it wrong more often than he got it right.

He was more inclined to trust his gut. His gut told him there was a lot more to these two than what his eyes told him. Provided everything went as planned tonight, he wouldn't have to worry about them much longer.

Carver made his way down the fire escape. He walked across the road. Looked inside Tanner's car. It was clean. Nothing on the seats, floorboards, or in the cupholders. He walked to the back. Saw a rental car tag.

Tasha never said exactly where her family was from. He'd assumed they were local. The sister was somewhere Noah could reach her whenever he wanted. Maybe not in the city. Maybe somewhere else.

It was irrelevant now. Just another mystery that didn't need solving. Time to get to work. Time to find out exactly why this briefcase was so valuable.

He took a trolley back to the department store. The Honda was still parked in the carpool behind the store. Carver noticed something about the other cars parked nearby. Each one had a small green decal on the bumper.

Carver backed up. Studied all the cars. They all had the same decal. Nothing printed on them. They were just one-inch green squares.

They reminded Carver of the cars marked with orange stickers. Marked for Noah's car bandits.

Those cars were marked as targets. These green decals had the opposite purpose. To tell the bandits to leave them alone. After all, Noah didn't want his own vehicles vandalized.

The Honda was pretty shot up. He dumped the bag with the briefcase into the backseat. The rear windows were both smashed from gunfire. He didn't want to drive around in a car that might be recognized by the people who chased them earlier.

Carver looked around the parking lot. There were plenty of cars to choose from. There was probably a box with the keys in it somewhere. He decided to text Tasha.

We need a new car for tomorrow. Any idea where Noah keeps the car keys for the carpool?

She texted back a moment later. *There's a lockbox on the wall near that door. Are you planning on getting a car tonight?*

I might get one so I can drive back from Zimo's. Transit won't be in service later.

She replied again. *The combination to the box is 41004. Just don't take a nice car or you'll piss off Noah.*

Thanks.

Carver noticed a text had arrived from Lee. He clicked on it. Lee had traced the real owner of Guard Dog and Parabellum. The controlling corporation had been at the top of a pile of shell companies.

He'd dug through the list of major investors and singled out several names. One name stood out in particular. That name made it clear who owned Guard Dog and how the killer had gained entrance. It also made the motive clear.

It wasn't who Carver had thought it was. But he also wasn't surprised. He tucked his phone back in a pocket and got back to the business at hand. Choosing one of Noah's cars.

He looked around. There were about twenty cars to choose from. Most were ordinary midsized and compacts. There was a row with an Audi Q5, a Lexus RX, and two BMW midsized sedans.

These were probably the nice cars Tasha warned him about. The ones he shouldn't take. He settled on the Audi. Screw Noah and his rules.

The back door to the department store was locked. Carver walked around to the front. The doors were open. That wasn't surprising since some of Noah's workers lived here.

He cut left. Made his way past the tables and shelves where illicit goods were sorted and into an open space filled with cots and sleeping bags. Workers were carrying on with their daily night life here.

Some were sleeping. Some were reading. Others were playing board games. There were kids here too. Presumably kids of the workers and not child laborers. With Noah, anything was possible.

He caught some looks as he walked past. Mostly looks of fear. They probably figured he was one of Noah's enforcers. The place reminded Carver of a refugee center. One of those places governments tossed together last minute to shelter people fleeing war zones.

These people looked every bit as hopeless as the refugees he'd seen. Each one of them was bound to Noah in some way. Probably owed him money. Might even be addicts who were paid with drugs.

Carver walked on past them. Reached a corridor leading to the back door. He found the lockbox on the wall. It was heavy duty. Made of thick metal. Tasha's combination opened it right up.

He found the Audi keys. Took the keys to one of the BMWs as well. He put the Honda keys back in place. There was a small box of green decals at the bottom of the lockbox. He took one for his Ramcharger.

He closed the lockbox. The department store's back door was bolted shut from the inside. The handle didn't unlock it from the inside. He retraced his route back to the front of the store.

The break room was nearby. He decided to swing by to get the duffel bag of surveillance gear.

There were no plans to use it tonight, but now he had a car. With the green sticker on it, it was safe from thieves. Hell, the meter maids might even leave it alone.

The duffel bag was where he'd left it. He grabbed it and headed back upstairs. A voice echoed from the hallway. Sounded like someone was arguing. Probably arguing with themselves because he didn't hear another person replying.

Carver eased down the hallway. Looked around the corner. Someone was standing outside the door to Noah's vault. A medium sized person. Thin. Wearing nice sweats and tennis shoes. A hood covered the head.

They were holding a phone to their ear. Talking in a low voice. Carver took out the parabolic mic.

Put the earbud in his ear. Aimed the mic at them.

"It's impossible. Besides, I don't think he has it. Ain't no way he's just pretending not to have it." He stopped talking. "He's the only one with access. How many times I got to tell you that?"

The figure stiffened. Nodded. "Okay. Tomorrow." He ended the call. Turned in Carver's direction.

Carver ducked back around the corner. But he got a clear look at the face beneath the hood. It was exactly who he thought it was.

It was Deshawn.

CHAPTER 37

Deshawn was trying to break into Noah's vault.

That wasn't something a friend would do. Wasn't something an ally would do. Which meant Deshawn was working against Noah. He was working for whoever he'd been talking to on the phone.

That changed things. Changed them a lot. It meant Carver's theory about Bushner's death was completely wrong. Noah hadn't sent Deshawn to kill the man. He hadn't planned to pin the murder on Carver.

Deshawn had done it for the person on the other end of that phone. The text from Lee about the owner of Guard Dog told him exactly who that person was. Or it might be a representative for that person.

Carver put the parabolic mic back into the bag. He shouldered the bag. Peered around the corner. Deshawn was gone. Carver hurried to the corner. Looked around it. Deshawn was headed out front.

He let him get out of sight. Then he hoofed it down the hall. He kept his distance and waited until Deshawn left through the front door. Carver went out after him. Watched him get into a white Camaro.

The engine rumbled to life. Carver hurried around the side of the building. He grabbed the bag with the briefcase from the back of the Honda. Unlocked the Audi. Tossed everything into the back floorboard.

He wheeled out of the carpool. Out onto the street. Rounded the corner. Saw Deshawn's taillights turn a few blocks ahead. Tailing him was probably a waste of time. Time better spent opening the briefcase.

It might also be time well spent. Carver might find something he could use to his advantage. It seemed like he'd need an arsenal of advantages against Noah. He was strong on his home turf. But if his most trusted guy was exposed, that would put a major chink in his armor.

Deshawn headed west on the 101. It was the opposite direction Carver needed to go. But traffic was light, and he was going fast. He crossed the Golden Gate Bridge. Kept going north. Past Sausalito. Across the Richardson Bay Bridge. Into a place called Strawberry.

He stopped in front of a gated house. The gate rolled open when he approached. Carver kept driving. An Audi wouldn't draw any attention in this area. There were plenty of them parked in driveways.

Deshawn was already pulling into the driveway by the time Carver drove past. Carver parked across the road. Looked through the iron fence at the house beyond. It was decent. Nothing special. The tall iron fence and gate seemed out of place.

He checked the real estate app. Whistled at the price tags on the nearby homes. There wasn't anything under one and a half million in the vicinity. This house was probably worth three to four million at least.

The neighborhood was nice enough. A mix of mini mansions and ordinary ranch homes. The main surprise was that Deshawn was willing to buy such an expensive place.

A lot of criminals were caught living above their apparent means. It was usually the IRS that did them in. Nailed them for tax evasion because their income said one thing and their lifestyle said something else.

Carver watched Deshawn get out of his car. Watched him go inside. There was a big picture window in the front of the house. A little girl ran past the window. Deshawn picked her up and kissed her. Spun her around.

An attractive woman walked into view. Kissed Deshawn. Kissed him long and hard. He wrapped his arm around her back. Held her close while the little girl wriggled in his other arm.

Carver had seen those kinds of kisses before. Two people deeply attracted to each other. Two people in love.

Deshawn and the woman grinned at each other. Talked while he held her up against him. He kissed the little girl. Nuzzled his nose against hers.

This was a bonafide relationship.

Carver rolled down the window. Turned on the parabolic mic. Aimed it at the happy couple.

"You had a good day, baby?" The woman said.

"I'm having a good day now." Deshawn kissed her.

She laughed. "You look stressed. I could give you a back rub."

He laughed. "Baby, you know what happens when you give me a back rub."

"It's all part of my evil plan." She waggled her eyebrows.

"I'm in." Deshawn kissed the little girl. "But first, someone needs their bedtime story so they can go to sleep."

The girl giggled. "I want a backrub too, Daddy!"

"Sorry, sweety. You've got to be a lot older for that." He nuzzled her nose with his. "Maybe when you're thirty-five."

The woman laughed. "Daddy's little girl."

Deshawn kissed the woman. He took her hand, and they walked out of sight. The mic couldn't pick up anything through the brick exterior.

Carver put the mic away. Sat and stared at the house. It looked familiar. He suddenly knew why. It was the house Jeremy had looked up earlier in the day. The house that belonged to Henry Marshall.

The puzzle pieces clicked together nicely.

Lee had identified Marshall as the majority owner of the corporation that controlled Guard Dog and Parabellum through a chain of shell corporations. This information cinched it.

Deshawn was working for Marshall. He was trying to get into Noah's vault. Deshawn had been talking on the phone with Marshall or one of his people. He'd told them Noah probably wasn't pretending not to have something.

Not to have what? There was only one thing it could be. The briefcase. Marshall wanted it. But why would he want samples of a street drug? The money in the briefcase was nothing to him.

He was a billionaire. A real estate mogul. But he might also have some underground enterprises.

Carver ran an internet search. Saw the same information Jeremy had shown him earlier. The man was an investor and owned a ton of real estate all over the country. He was worth billions. Street drugs seemed way below his pay grade.

This revelation was the bombshell Carver had hoped for earlier. Noah had no clue about this. Maybe he knew about the wife and kid. Maybe he even knew the home was owned by Marshall. But did he think his best friend was working for Marshall?

Maybe, maybe not.

Noah didn't seem like the type to let traitors keep breathing. Not even if they were childhood friends. Then again, Noah fancied himself an intellect. A strategist. He might think keeping his enemies close was good policy.

Knowing his friend was working for Marshall was valuable information. Noah might think he could use it to his advantage against Enigma.

It wasn't safe to assume anything with Noah. The man was smart. Maybe even brilliant. He could probably think circles around Carver. It was best to go into this armed with the contents of the briefcase and Deshawn's alliance with Marshall.

Carver thought about infiltrating the property. Planting some bugs. But he didn't have time for that tonight. Besides, using Deshawn against Noah was just a backup plan. The briefcase should be valuable enough to pay off multiple debts.

He turned the Audi around. Aimed south. He plugged Arty's address into the GPS. It told him to go north. To take the Richmond bridge east. To go south into Oakland from there.

It took him about forty minutes to reach Arty's place. He parked a couple of blocks down. Used the monocular to sweep the area. The house was in ruins. A blackened skeleton.

Yellow police tape hung limply in front of the driveway. It was strung up outside of the house too. The workshop looked okay. The rollup doors were closed and padlocked. Carver used night vision to hunt for cameras.

He didn't see anything. It was unlikely they cared to surveil the place. They'd thought Arty was Carver. They'd been wrong. There had been no one of interest at the house.

Carver kept the headlights off. He drove to the other street. Took the driveway of the derelict house behind Arty's workshop. Drove through one backyard and into the next. The same route he'd taken to evade the cops.

The SUV handled the stumps and bumps better than Derrick's Charger had.

He parked behind the workshop. Took the lockpick set out of the toolbox. It took him a few minutes to work open the padlock on the first rollup door. It popped loose. He pushed up the door slowly. Quietly.

He turned on his flashlight. Looked around inside. All the tools were still there. A battery charging dock glowed dimly. That meant the shop still had electricity. It was a small miracle since the house was halfway burned down.

Carver went back to the car. Pulled the briefcase from the bag. Carried it into the shop. He closed the rollup door. Turned on the lights. There were no windows in the shop. Some light might escape under the doors. Not enough to alert a neighbor that someone was in here.

There would be loud noise. But the closest neighbor might not hear it or might think it was a truck.

He found the drill press. Found a toolchest with diamond tipped drill bits in it. This would be the backup plan. It would be slow and tedious. But it would probably work. His primary hope was the bigger machine further back.

The hydraulic press.

The shop had special welding machines. It had cutters. But they'd just destroy anything inside the case. Jericho had systematically tested methods for opening cases like this one.

Most low-end cases didn't need extreme measures. They could be picked open, jimmied open, or the latch could be cut. But this was basically a safe with a handle. Reinforced inside and out.

A drill press with carbon or diamond tipped bits worked. You had to drill into the seam right where the latches went through. The titanium quickly dulled the bits. Each one took several minutes to penetrate.

Hopefully, Carver wouldn't have to resort to that method. He went to the hydraulic press. Turned on the power. Raised it as high as it would go. He put the briefcase into the press. Set it on the edge so the sides were on the top and bottom.

The press had a cylinder of solid steel. There was a tool chest with different plates that could be used with the press. Some were flat. Some were wide. Others were narrow. He chose a wide one with a wedge tip.

He lowered the press. Lined up the wedge with the seam. He lowered it again. The press whined. The air compressor hummed. The wedge pushed unrelentingly into the seam.

Carver backed up behind a plexiglass shield. Kept his finger on the down button. The case bent. Bowed. Metal groaned. Snapped. He raised the press. Flipped the case onto the other side. Lined up the wedge again.

Repeated the process. The case bowed out further. The latches resisted but the press snapped them to pieces.

Carver lined up the top of the case with the wedge. He could almost see inside the case through the bent sides, but it wasn't wide enough yet.

The wedge lowered into the front seam. The case bowed out further. Bending rather than breaking. The front latches finally gave. The case fell open with a thud.

There was a rectangular box inside. It was sealed inside a plastic sheathing. Carver used a utility knife to slice it open. The box was heavy cardboard. It slid open without further trouble.

Inside was a booklet. The exterior was unmarked. There was a rectangular plastic box on top of the booklet. It was maybe three inches wide, four inches long, and a couple of inches tall.

Carver opened it. Inside were several vials of fluid. The vials were plastic, not glass. He set aside the box with the vials. Opened the booklet.

The first interior page was titled.

Study Results

A positive case for

Fentanyl X

And

Antifen

Fentanyl X caught Carver's attention. It sounded like a more potent version of fentanyl. He didn't know how much more potent it could be. It was already deadly in small doses.

He kept reading. There were a lot of big words inside. Most of them looked made up on the spot. Probably by scientists.

The study took twenty rats. Divided them into two groups of ten. One was given Antifen. The other was given Fentanyl X, also called Fex for short. From what Carver could tell, Fex was like ten doses of fentanyl concentrated into a single drop of liquid solution.

The rats that took a drop of Fex died in minutes. The rats that took a drop of Antifen were also given Fex. Eight of the ten rats survived. Two died. One rat exhibited signs of being high. The other seven showed no signs of impairment.

Carver examined the vials. Some were labeled Fex. Some were labeled Antifen.

He kept reading.

The next section was human trials. A group of ten fentanyl addicts. A group of ten non-drug users. They weren't volunteers. They weren't being paid anything. They were taken right off the streets of San Francisco.

That explained the lack of company names or scientists in the study. Normally, scientists were clamoring to be front and center in studies. Success got them more grant money. Better status in the science community.

This was a black lab. Anonymous. The kind of labs the government used to keep nasty research secret. These kinds of clandestine labs were usually in Mexico.

The addicts were given Fex. None lasted more than five minutes. Most died within two. The study was considered a success. Fex was too powerful for even the heaviest Fentanyl users to survive.

They gave the non-users Antifen. Waited two days. Studied their brain activity. Observed them for negative effects. One subject claimed he lost his sense of taste and smell. Another said she had dry mouth.

They were put through CAT scans and other tests. No other side effects were reported. Then they were all dosed with a drop of Fex right under the tongue. The subject who lost taste and smell from Antifen died in minutes. The one who had dry mouth got high as a kite.

The rest of the subjects didn't have any reaction to Fex.

More tests were run. Scans. Bloodwork. The whole nine yards. The Fex was in their system, but it wasn't affecting them. That was because Antifen blocked the opioid receptors in the subjects' brains.

That meant the fentanyl wasn't chemically reactive in their bodies. It couldn't make them high. Couldn't kill them.

Another dose of Antifen was given to the subject with dry mouth. Nothing changed. They concluded there was an anomaly with this individual's receptors that didn't bond completely with Antifen.

They did an autopsy on the subject that died. It turned out that subject had a genetic predisposition for Alzheimer's. Dementia. It caused a problem with Antifen binding to their opioid receptors. The subject with partial binding had once been a heavy drinker.

They concluded alcohol abuse might have affected their brain. Caused the receptors to not allow perfect binding.

The surviving subjects were tested again six months later. It didn't say if they were kept imprisoned the entire time. Sometimes these labs released them and had them come back later.

Sometimes they paid them. Let them think they were volunteers. Sometimes they threatened them or their families.

Either way, the same subjects were tested again. The dry mouth subject got high again. The others didn't react to Fex. They didn't react to other opioids either.

They were tested again and again over a period of two years. The receptor blocking seemed to be permanent.

Another group of ten addicts were brought in. This group was given Antifen. They were thoroughly scanned and tested. One of them reported loss of taste and smell. The others didn't have any side effects.

All ten subjects showed signs of withdrawal during the dry phase of testing. That meant three days without fentanyl or any other drugs. On the third day, they were given Fex.

The one with loss of taste and smell got high, then died in under five minutes. The rest kept going through withdrawal. The extreme dose of fentanyl did nothing to them.

They were given morphine. Heroin. Two of them had a placebo effect. They thought they were high, but they weren't. The rest kept going through withdrawal.

Carver set the booklet aside. Looked at the vials. There was no money in the briefcase. There didn't need to be. This thing was worth more. A whole lot more. Billions to the right person.

Because whoever took Antifen could never use Fentanyl again. They could never use any opioid again.

It would absolutely destroy a billion-dollar drug market.

Chapter 38

Antifen would wreak havoc on the black market.

It would destroy pharmaceutical companies that marketed opioids as painkillers. That begged the question—why would anyone make something like this? More importantly, who would?

There were too many major interests tied up in fentanyl and opioids. Too many black markets. Too many big pharma companies. Too many governments.

Some countries like Afghanistan relied heavily on the opium trade. It funded their government. Funded terrorists. It was sometimes referred to as Afghan Crude. And it was valuable.

Someone was trying to disrupt the entire opium economy. Fentanyl was the biggest target. It was essentially synthetic morphine. Or something like that. Carver wasn't a scientist. He only knew what he'd read.

He hadn't seen Flood mentioned anywhere in the study. He hadn't seen any cash in the case either. Odds were good that Bobby had overheard someone saying those words. He'd assumed they had something to do with the briefcase.

Carver couldn't figure out how a low-level addict had gotten his hands on this briefcase. There were a lot of missing puzzle pieces on that side of the puzzle. None of them really mattered.

What mattered was that Carver knew what Noah wanted. Why Noah wanted it was anyone's guess. Maybe he figured by flooding the streets with Antifen, he'd destroy the drug trade. That would hurt Enigma financially. Hurt them big time.

Enigma had multiple revenue streams. The Farm had been selling human organs on the black market. They'd been dealing in drugs too.

But fentanyl was probably a major part of their operations. It probably accounted for billions while the rest was in the paltry millions.

Carver suddenly understood where Bobby got the Flood name from. It was biblical. Noah and the flood. And now this Noah wanted to flood the streets with Antifen. The booklet had all the formulas. Everything someone needed to make more of the stuff.

All it took were a few drops of Antifen. It could be injected or taken under the tongue. Just like fentanyl.

It was interesting that all of this was on paper. There was no digital copy in the box. Probably because whoever published it didn't want it digitally transmitted. They thought keeping it on paper was safer.

Paper was safer. But only marginally. Making copies was just as easy as taking a photo. Carver took out his phone. Used the camera to scan all the pages. He took pictures of the vials as well. Then he considered what to do next.

The answer was simple. He hid the booklet and vials in Arty's shop. No one would be coming here anytime soon. He'd take the broken briefcase. That would be proof enough that Carver had what Noah wanted.

He found spare keys to the garage padlocks hanging on the wall. He turned off the lights. Left the shop. Locked it up. Got in the car and went back out the way he'd come in. He drove across the Oakland Bay Bridge.

Exited into the city. Made his way back to the Embarcadero. He parallel parked down the street from his Ramcharger. It was probably safe to leave everything in the car since it was marked.

He didn't feel like taking the chance. He stuffed the broken briefcase back into the clothes bag. Took it and the duffel bag with the surveillance equipment to his tent.

He went to Tanner's tent. Thumped on the side. "Tanner, you in there?"

No answer. He was probably still at Tasha's. Carver still hadn't decided what to do about them. He was starting to doubt everything they'd told him. Other theories were forming in his head.

Theories that made more sense in light of what he'd found. He hoped he was wrong, but as Rhodes always told him, it was better to shoot first than to be shot first. Rhodes had been in a bad mood at the time. But the advice checked out.

He went back to his tent. Locked the zipper. Lay on his back and gave thought to what he needed to do. He came up with a simple plan. One that was so simple, it might not work. But it was all he had to go with.

The most important thing was that he got his phone back. Nothing else mattered. Not Tasha and her sister. Not Jeremy.

Only Paola.

Carver flinched. He didn't know why he'd thought of it like that. He wanted the phone. The option to contact Paola. The thought of losing the phone made him a little sick inside. Because it meant he'd lose contact with Paola, probably forever.

It was definitely about Paola. About his feelings for her. It was fine to have feelings. Perfectly fine. Just as long as Carver remembered what happened when you had feelings for someone.

It was a risk. A big risk. But he was a big boy. He could handle it. Well, he could handle some things. Relationships, not so much. And that was okay.

He closed his eyes. Put his hand slightly to the side. Remembered what it was like feeling Paola in bed with him. Feeling her curl up against him. Hear her little moans as she fell asleep. Her little cries of terror as the nightmares haunted her.

Then he'd turn on his side. Put an arm around her. The shivering would stop. The cries would stop. She'd settle down and go to sleep.

And it made him feel good. Made him feel human. Like he hadn't killed more than twenty people to make her safe. Like he hadn't committed mass murder to save one life. One life that was worth more than all those cartel killers combined.

Tomorrow was the last day. If she'd sent a message the day he'd arrived in San Francisco, it would expire tomorrow. It would be gone forever. And he'd probably never find her again if he didn't get the phone back.

But now he had the briefcase. He had the collateral that would get his phone back. Carver would be able to text Paola again tomorrow. It was reassuring to know that. And it helped him doze off in minutes.

Carver woke up early the next morning.

He stopped by Tanner's tent. Thumped on the fabric. There was no answer. He just wanted to see the man in the flesh. See if Tanner could act naturally face to face since Tasha had slept with them both.

He went across the street to the Ferry Building. Got coffee and breakfast. He ate just enough to be full. He didn't want to go into this feeling bloated.

The next thing he did was text Noah. *I've got information. Can you meet me at this diner in an hour?* He added an address that was a good twenty blocks away from Noah's compound.

He texted Tasha. *Hey, mind if I shower at your place?*

He crossed the street. Noticed Herbert's tent was gone. The man probably cleared out soon after Carver's warning. Hopefully, he'd survive. If he was halfway smart, it wouldn't be a problem. Plus, the briefcase location was about to become known. They wouldn't care about Herbert anymore.

Carver got everything and put it in the Audi. He checked his texts. Tasha had replied.

Sure, come on over.

He took a route that detoured him away from the department store. He arrived in front of Tasha's. The silver car Tanner had been in was gone. The parking spot where it had been was open.

Tanner had probably just left.

There were two reasons for taking a shower here. Carver could have gone to a hostel or a public shower. But he wanted to get a good feel for Tasha this morning. He needed a gut feeling as to where her chips would fall.

Carver chose fresh clothes from his bag. He went to the main door. Hit Tasha's buzzer. The door opened. He went inside. Upstairs. She answered the door in a bathrobe. Her hair was wet.

She smiled. It looked genuine. She put her arms around his neck Pulled him in for a deep kiss. "Good morning."

"Good morning." Carver figured he had time to spare, so he took her to the bed. She seemed happy to oblige. Genuinely happy.

When he was finished, she curled up next to him. "I've been thinking. Maybe we could get my sister and just make a run for it. Noah's powerful here, but he's not all over the country, you know? We could be safe somewhere else."

"What about Tanner?"

She stiffened a little. "Oh, he'll be fine. He's a survivor."

It sounded like a genuine offer. "Sounds risky for you."

"Sure, a little risky. But with you around, I wouldn't be afraid of anything. Plus, I can take care of myself and watch your back."

"What about your sister?"

"Tanner has a plan to hide her. I could tell him to do that."

"Why didn't he do that before?"

"Because it's risky. Noah found her the last time we tried that. We still don't know how."

Carver didn't detect any lies in her body language. "You still hardly know me. I'm not exactly relationship material."

"I know. But we don't have to be in a relationship, you know?" She traced a finger down his bare chest. "We could cohabitate and have fun. You do your thing and I do mine."

That sounded and felt like the truth. It was probably exactly what she had going on with Tanner. Maybe she'd conned him into helping her like she was doing with Carver.

He nodded. "I like the idea. Let me think it over."

She put her hand under the blankets. Lowered it until she found what she was looking for. "We can have a lot of fun, Carver. "

"Yeah, we can." He got out of bed. "I'm tempted. Really tempted."

She gave him a sultry look. "Redheads are good at temptation."

"So, I'm learning." He flashed her a grin. Went into the bathroom with his phone. He checked the messages. Noah had responded.

We can meet here discreetly. I'm not dragging my ass halfway across town for you.

Carver was disappointed but not surprised. He'd have to negotiate with Noah right in his seat of power. He texted Jeremy next.

Are you at the store?

He showered. Dried. Used Tanner's deodorant again. Tucked it away behind the feminine toiletries. He stepped out. Slid into his clean clothes. Tasha was already dressed. Wearing jeans and a T-shirt as usual. All business.

She put her hair into a ponytail. "Remember. Don't let anyone know we're sleeping together. No telling what Noah will do."

He made a zipping motion over his lips. "He won't hear it from me."

Carver knew exactly what Noah would do. Nothing. He wouldn't kill Tasha. She was valuable to him. But he might threaten to kill her. Just to see if it gave him more leverage over Carver.

Jeremy had responded to his text. *I'm here. Why?*

Meet me outside of Lee's.

Carver wrapped his arm around the small of Tasha's back. Pulled her in. Kissed her. She drew in a deep breath.

"You smell so good."

Because of Tanner's deodorant, he thought. It was almost funny. "I'm gonna head in. Better arrive a little bit after me just in case."

She nodded. "Good idea."

Carver went outside. Got in the Audi. Drove off. Tasha's unit was in the back of the building, so she probably hadn't seen what he was driving.

He parked outside Lee's shop. Jeremy was already there. Standing outside. Holding his backpack. Looking nervous. Carver rolled down the window. "Hop in."

Jeremy blinked. Came closer and peered inside. "Wow, where'd you get this?"

"Noah's carpool."

Jeremy walked around. Got in the other side.

Carver started driving. He looked over at Jeremy. "I'm going to ask you a question. I want an honest answer. It doesn't matter how you answer, you're going to be okay. Understand?"

Jeremy flinched. "What are you going to ask me? Do you want me to do something dangerous?"

"I want to know who your contact is with Enigma."

He looked confused. "I don't understand."

"You went to Enigma for help because of Noah. But the plan backfired and nearly got you killed when they came after me yesterday."

Jeremy stared at him openmouthed. "Uh, I wouldn't even know how to contact them. Only Noah and his top guys know that. And I would never betray you. You could snap me in half!"

Carver turned the corner. He was just driving up and down the streets. "So, you didn't have anything to do with those people chasing us yesterday?"

"No!" Jeremy looked Carver in the eye. Shook his head vehemently. "Absolutely not! I couldn't contact Enigma even if I wanted to. You've got to believe me!"

"I believe you."

"Please don't kill me. I promise—"

"I said I believe you." Carver did believe him. Jeremy was on the straight and narrow. Just a kid doing what he could to survive.

He pulled into a parallel parking spot on the side of the road.

Jeremy was shaking. "Do you really believe me, or are you going to kill me now?"

"I'm not going to hurt you." Carver thought over what he needed to do next. "Noah was looking for a briefcase."

Jeremy nodded. "Yeah. I heard he had his enforcers looking for it. Promised ten grand to anyone who found it."

"I found the briefcase."

"You did?" Jeremy's mouth formed a surprised O. "That thing must have something really valuable inside of it for Noah to offer a bounty."

"It does. It has a drug that blocks the opioid receptors in people's brains. Makes it so fentanyl and other opioids don't even affect them."

Jeremy frowned. "You're saying there's a drug that makes fentanyl useless?"

"Exactly. And it seems to permanently block those receptors. I think Noah wants to use it to destroy the drug trade and Enigma's black-market profits."

"Whoa." Jeremy nodded. "Yeah, that makes total sense."

"But there's nothing in the briefcase saying who made the drug or conducted the tests. It was done in a black lab."

"Like a secret lab?"

Carver nodded. "Off the books so they could do human trials."

"My God, that's so crazy." Jeremy frowned. "That drug would hurt big pharma too. A lot of major drug companies sell opioids."

"It would disrupt a market worth billions."

Jeremy's gaze went distant. "Enigma would probably have the resources to make a drug like that. But I don't think they would."

"There aren't that many big firms who could pull it off."

"Hang on, that reminds me of something I read yesterday." Jeremy opened his laptop. Opened a web browser. Opened the history. "Yeah, here it is." He clicked a link. It went to a website called *Underground Informer.*

"Is that a conspiracy website?"

"I never heard of it before. I only went there when I was looking for connections."

"Connections to what?"

"A lab was raided by the feds. They said it was conducting illegal human trials. The website said stories were suppressed by major news outlets because the lab was supposedly connected to Futuretopia."

Carver looked at the story on the website. Skimmed it.

Jeremy summarized. "Futuretopia is a smaller pharma company. It's a spinoff of Bayern Labs, a major company that is majority owned by an investing firm."

Carver reached the payoff before Jeremy did. "Marshall Investing."

"Yep." Jeremy grinned. "It's owned by Henry Marshall."

More pieces fell into place. "Marshall wants to disrupt the market. He's secretly working against Enigma."

"But not because he's a philanthropist or anything." Jeremy shook his head. "If the man had a secret lab running human trials, then he's as much a monster as the people running Enigma."

"Does Bayern not deal in opioids? Wouldn't that hurt their bottom line?"

Jeremy shrugged. "I have no idea. I could research it."

"Maybe Marshall is targeting specific markets. He doesn't want the drug released to the general public. He wants to use it where it will hurt Enigma the most."

"That sounds like a plan," Jeremy said. "So, why does Noah want it?"

"Noah wants to flood the streets with it. Get rid of fentanyl use in the city because he thinks it will hurt Enigma."

Jeremy nodded. "It would hurt them where it matters most. The organized retail crime and car break-ins are nothing compared to the money they make selling black-market fentanyl."

"Where is the fentanyl coming from?" Carver didn't know if that mattered. But maybe it did.

"Clandestine labs in Mexico. Noah has hundreds of mules crossing back and forth across the border every day. If they get caught, crossing into California, Enigma owns the judges, so they're released maybe a day or two later."

"Yeah, it's probably easier and cheaper to keep production south of the border." Carver considered his next move. Offering Noah the contents of the briefcase should be plenty. Deshawn's connection to Marshall was the ace up his sleeve.

But he had to be prepared in case Noah decided to double-cross him. Noah might agree. Take the goods. Decide that he was done with Carver and end him. He needed proof that his phone was still in one piece. That Noah would give it to him.

And that would be the hard part.

CHAPTER 39

It was do or die time.

Carver drove back to Lee's shop. "Put your backpack inside the store. Leave it, your phone, everything in there."

Jeremy stared at him silently for a moment. Nodded. He climbed out. Returned without his backpack or phone.

Carver drove across town. Stopped at a coffee shop near Golden Gate Park. He gave Jeremy his old burner flip phone.

Jeremy looked around. "What are we doing here?"

"You're going to go have some coffee and relax. I'm going to have a chat with Noah."

Jeremy sighed. "I'm useless."

"Not useless. You're collateral. I need you out of the way."

Jeremy looked confused. "So, you'd be sad if Noah killed me?"

Carver wasn't sure how to answer. "I prefer it if you keep on breathing. You've made some mistakes. Dumb mistakes. No need to die for them."

Jeremy sighed. "You're not the most tactful guy I've ever met."

"Will you stay here? Stay out of the way?"

Jeremy kept staring at him. "My family is all dead. They died in a car wreck when I was young. I haven't had anyone look out for me in a long, long time."

"You're alone?"

He nodded. "I made mistakes because I was eager to be independent. To survive on my own. But I'm not that good at it, it seems."

"You made mistakes. You learned from them."

Jeremy nodded. "Thanks for looking out for me, Carver. It means..." His voice cracked. "It means a lot." He cleared his throat. Wiped his eyes. "More than you know."

Carver patted his shoulder. "All good, kid." He leaned over to open the passenger door.

Jeremy hugged him. "Thanks."

Carver patted the kid's back. "Yeah. No problem. Now get out."

Jeremy took the flip phone. Got out. He watched forlornly as Carver drove away.

It was time to get real. Carver didn't have many assets. He had a Glock 45. A survival knife. His wits. He'd done okay with less. But if things went sideways, it wasn't much to count on. He wished he could contact Leon. Get him as backup.

The only people he could count on were Tasha and Tanner. And he wasn't sure how much he could trust them. He could probably use them as cannon fodder. Maybe.

First things first. He needed ammunition. Buying a gun wasn't realistic. Not in this part of the country. There were probably some back channels to getting a weapon, but Noah probably controlled all of them.

But there might be a few more options he could explore.

Carver ran some errands. Got his ducks in a row. It took him the better part of two hours. He ignored everything until he felt ready. Until it was time.

Then he got in the Audi and headed to Noah's. Speaking of the devil, there was a text from him.

Where are you? I want a progress report.

Tasha had texted him too. *Where are you? Did you skip town?*

Carver texted them back a simple message. *I'm on my way there.*

He parked the Audi out front. There was a trash bag in the back seat. Inside it was the briefcase and bunched up newspapers to make it look like a bag of clothing. He walked inside. Went to the basement first to take care of something. Then he went straight to Noah's office.

Tasha was already there. She was serving drinks to Noah. Playing the servant just like the first time Carver had seen her. She gave him a hard look. A questioning look.

Carver set the trash bag on the floor.

Noah was sitting behind his desk. He raised an eyebrow. "Bringing your garbage to me, Carver?"

"Something like that." Carver leaned against the door frame. Titus was standing to the left of Noah's desk. Deshawn was sitting in a chair to the right.

Noah sipped a glass of scotch. "Where have you been all morning?"

"Here and there. Running errands."

"I've decided to shorten your deadline, Carver. I feel like you're taking liberties with my generosity." Noah steepled his fingers. "You have until tonight to present me with a plan for handling Enigma."

"Easy enough." Carver folded his arms over his chest. It put his hand within easy reach of the Glock. "What if I told you that I already have a plan so amazing that you'll give me anything for it?"

Noah didn't look impressed. "I find it hard to believe you've done anything. Killing Bushner didn't do anything."

"I didn't kill him."

"Well, your adventure into his house certainly didn't accomplish anything."

"It actually accomplished more than I thought." Carver touched the hilt of the pistol. "I know who wanted him killed."

Deshawn looked up from his phone. He was suddenly all ears.

"Oh, really?" Noah leaned forward. "Enigma?"

Carver shook his head. "Henry Marshall."

Noah's eyes flicked toward Deshawn. It was subtle, but Carver noticed. It meant Noah had some suspicions about his friend already. Maybe he knew about the house in Strawberry.

Noah pursed his lips. "Let's skip to the part where you tell me this plan of yours, Carver." He tapped on his phone. "Bring him in."

Carver heard movement behind him. He backed out of the doorway. A pair of enforcers pushed through a double door. They dragged a hooded figure down the hallway. The figure was wearing a black robe, covering his body.

It looked strange. Almost ritualistic.

Carver kept out of the way. They took the figure into the office. Handed it over to Titus. Then they left. Vanished back through the double doors. Carver stepped inside the doorframe. Watched Titus holding the person.

Tasha looked pale. She'd probably seen this kind of thing before.

"What's this about?" Carver said. "Some kind of cult thing?"

"These are the sacrificial robes," Noah said. "I like to put them on the sheep before I send them into the afterlife."

"All of this for me?" Carver shook his head. "I was going to tell you the plan." He wondered who was under the hood. Was it Tanner? Herbert? Someone else?

"I know you're going to tell me your plan, Carver. And it better be a very good one." He snapped his fingers. Titus jerked the hood off the person. "Otherwise, this sheep is going to die."

The face beneath the hood was a surprise to Carver. A big surprise. Mainly because he shouldn't be anywhere near here.

It was Jeremy.

"I thought I told you to stay put."

Jeremy was gagged. He couldn't talk.

"Ah, so you're the reason he was all the way across town." Noah shook his head. "I had someone following him after your little adventure yesterday. I thought it might be a good idea to track my assets."

"No one was following us." Carver shook his head. "I would know. You must have a tracker on the car."

Noah shook his head. "I don't track my cars, Carver. That could be evidence used against me if the feds ever decide to raid us."

It didn't matter how. It just mattered that Noah had somehow tracked Jeremy.

Titus laughed. He reached under Jeremy's robe. Pulled out a small white disc. "It's as easy as putting one of these on his clothing."

Carver recognized it. It was a small wireless tag. Available at retail. It connected to Wi-Fi networks and provided location tracking.

"Think you're smart, don't you, boy?" Titus bared his teeth in a victorious grin. "You ain't shit."

Noah looked annoyed. "Don't give away our secrets, Titus."

The big man looked down. "Sorry, boss."

Carver got to the matter at hand. "I don't know why you think you can use him against me." He wondered if Jeremy had told them anything. But it sounded like Noah hadn't even questioned him. Noah had sent his people to pick him up. He might not have had time to question him yet.

"You took him far away from me for safety." Noah grinned. "You don't want him to mean anything to you, Carver, but he does. It's human nature to care. Even for someone like you." Noah stood. Mussed Jeremy's hair. "Hell, I like the kid. He's a hard worker. Keeps his head down."

Jeremy's face was tight with fear. His eyes were pleading. Carver kept a stony face, but he was pissed. He should have frisked the kid. Made him change clothes. He'd thought leaving his electronics behind would be enough.

Carver picked up the garbage bag. "I'll skip to the point then. What I have in here proves that I have something very valuable to you. And I will trade that for all of my stuff and for you to forgive Jeremy of all his debts. Wipe the slate clean and release him." He glanced at Tasha. Decided he might as well include her. "Also, Tasha and her sister will be free from you forever."

Tasha flinched. Like she was confused. "Carver, what in the hell is in that bag?"

Carver dumped it out on the floor. The titanium clanged on the floor.

Noah shot up from his seat. Stared open-mouthed at the broken briefcase. Deshawn jumped up too. Titus frowned like he didn't know what it was. Tasha's mouth dropped open.

Noah stared at the case. "Where did you get this?"

"It doesn't matter. What does matter is that I have the contents hidden somewhere. I'm the only one who knows where. All you have to do is agree to my terms and the contents are yours." Carver brushed off his hands. "We go our separate ways. Simple as that."

Noah nodded at his bodyguard. "Titus, bring that to me."

Titus glared at Carver as he crossed the room. He pulled the briefcase out of the newspaper. His lips peeled back as he looked at the warped remains. He set it on the desk in front of Noah.

Noah touched it. Looked at the inside. Nodded. "This is it." He looked up at Carver. "You found where Bobby hid it?"

Carver was confused. Shouldn't Noah know about Sally and Herbert? Hadn't his enforcer killed Sally? He played along. "I don't know who Bobby is."

"That addict killed two of my men." He laughed. "Can you believe it? A damned f-head hiding in the forest killed my men." Noah shook it off. Looked at Carver. "You don't know who Bobby is? You didn't get this from a guy hiding in the forest?"

"No. I heard rumors that you were looking for a briefcase. A very secure briefcase."

Tasha glanced at him. Frowned. She probably wondered if he was going to mention her.

"So, I started asking around the homeless crowd. Found a lead in the Tenderloin District. Followed it to a guy who was happy to trade the case for some fentanyl."

Noah burst out laughing. "You've got some crazy luck, Carver. I had a ten grand bounty on that case."

"You know what's inside of it?"

Noah nodded. "Of course, I do. I found out about a secret lab in the old, abandoned tech building. It was set up like a homeless shelter. But there were rumors something else was going on in there." He chuckled. "I finally got a story from a crazy homeless guy that sounded like an insane conspiracy theory. He said they were interviewing people. Asking them medical questions. And some of them were disappearing."

Carver was surprised the lab was right in town. It seemed risky for Marshall to have set up right under Enigma's nose. But maybe that was why it worked for so long. It was the last place they'd look.

Noah kept talking. "One guy escaped. He said he was given a drug that made opioids useless to him. He couldn't use fentanyl anymore. I didn't believe him. I thought it was just another crazy guy."

"He came to you and told you this?" Carver said.

Noah nodded. "He thought I might pay him for the information. I told him I didn't believe him. He said he could prove it. So, I had two enforcers hold him down and I dumped an entire bottle into his mouth." He snorted. "It was enough to kill an elephant and that son of a bitch didn't even blink."

Titus nodded. "It was crazy, boss."

"I had my people go undercover there. The whole place was disconnected from the internet. It was surrounded by a Faraday cage. Their own employees weren't allowed to leave."

"Sounds about right," Carver said.

"We found out they were shipping samples and the formula by armored truck." Noah spread his hands. "So, I set up an ambush."

"You got the briefcase, and then what? A drug addict stole it from you?"

"We ambushed them. A firefight broke out. My guy got the briefcase and went down. By the time the smoke cleared, and the dust settled, the briefcase was nowhere to be found. And we had to get out of there before the cops came."

"Aren't the cops on your side?"

Noah shook his head. "Enigma owns them lock, stock, and barrel." He sighed. "Turns out my guy made it a block from the truck before he died of blood loss. Bobby took the briefcase. Went into hiding up in the forest. The rest is history."

"Good to know." Carver crossed his arms again. Got ready with the Glock. "So, why don't you let Jeremy go. Let Tasha go. Give me my stuff back. And I'll give you the prize. You can flood the streets with Antifen and destroy Enigma's drug trade."

Noah laughed. "You think I want to use Antifen?"

Carver stared at him. "Isn't that why you wanted the briefcase?"

"No, Carver, no." Noah tutted. "Why would I want to cure thousands of opioid addicts when I can just kill them?"

The puzzle Carver thought he'd solved broke apart. Then he realized what Noah meant. "You want to flood the streets with Fentanyl X."

Noah clapped slowly. "Good boy, Carver. You figured it out." He looked at his empty glass. Snapped his fingers at Tasha. "Be a good girl and get me another drink."

Tasha looked stunned. Like she didn't know what to do.

Noah stood. Slapped her hard enough to leave a red handprint on her face. "I said, get me a drink, girl."

Tasha gasped. She took his glass. Filled it halfway.

Noah took it. Walked around the desk and sat on the edge. "It's simple, really. I'll be handing out free pills. The addicts will rush to get them. But the pill will be Fex. It will be ten times the dose in the same sized pill."

"And they'll drop dead in minutes," Carver said. "People will stop taking it."

Noah shook his head. "No. People will ignore the overdoses like they always do. And when they finally realize what's happening, it will be too late."

Carver saw the plan now. "If all the addicts are dead from a fentanyl overdose, it will trigger panic in the city. It'll cause a nationwide crisis. Fentanyl production will be shut down. Pharma companies' stocks will crash. Enigma will be financially devastated. Provided the sale of fentanyl is actually one of their major sources of income."

"Exactly!" Noah held up his drink in a toast. "Carver, you're not as dumb as you look."

Titus barked a laugh. "He looks real dumb, boss."

Deshawn was quiet. Dead quiet. He had the look of a man trying to think on his feet and failing to come up with a solution.

Tasha had a similar look on her face. Carver couldn't tell if she was thinking. She looked worried. As if she didn't know what Noah would do next.

Carver couldn't tell either. Noah was basking in the moment. Showing he was unpredictable. Proving his superior intellect. Letting Carver feel dumb.

It was okay for him to have a moment. To feel good that he was about to achieve his goals. If anything, it meant he'd be amenable to Carver's demands.

Carver let the moment play out. Then he repeated his offer. "So, let's seal the deal. Wipe the slate clean for Tasha, her sister, and Jeremy, get me my stuff, and then we'll go get your prize."

"That's not how it works, Carver." Noah sipped his drink. "I'll give you the ten grand bounty for finding the case just like I promised. I am a man of my word. Then you will help me implement this plan. Once it's complete, I'll give you your things. Then you can go do whatever it is you want. Jeremy, however, has his own obligations to meet. He's a grown man. He doesn't need an enabler rescuing him from his mess."

Carver stared at him. Remained silent.

"Tasha is also an adult. She will remain in my service until she pays her debts." Noah smirked at her. "She's slowly but surely getting there."

"So, no deal?" Carver said.

"Oh, we have a deal, just not the one you're trying to make." Noah set his drink on the desk. "I told you the terms. Ten grand for finding the case. But you're not getting your phone back until you help me drive Enigma out of my city."

"Like I said." Carver began to slide the Glock out of its holster. "No deal."

Noah walked around the desk. "Go get me the contents of the briefcase, or I'll kill Jeremy."

"I don't think so."

"I know he means something to you, Carver. Somewhere in that cold dead heart of yours, you want Jeremy to live." Noah spread his arms wide. "We can all walk out of here happy and alive."

Jeremy's eyes were wide. He was straining against the gag. Squirming in Titus's grasp.

"Don't be stupid, Noah." Carver was losing his patience with the man. "This is a win-win for all of us."

"I'm being very reasonable, Carver." Noah pursed his lips. "I have all the power here. I am the king."

"Enigma is the king. I'm offering you the keys to the kingdom."

Noah scowled. "Take me to get the contents of the case or Jeremy dies."

"And then what?" Carver said.

Titus frowned. Noah frowned. Deshawn was tapping away on his phone, seemingly unaware of the building tension. Tasha was looking back and forth between Noah and Carver.

Noah spoke. "I don't understand."

"You kill Jeremy and then what?" Carver stared him down.

"I guess we'll find out." Noah snapped his fingers.

Titus bared his teeth in a grin. Gripped the sides of Jeremy's head.

Jeremy gave Carver one last look. The fear was gone. All that was left was acceptance.

"Wait!" Carver shouted.

Titus twisted Jeremy's head violently.

— • —

CHAPTER 40

Jeremy's spine cracked like thunder.

Titus released him. Jeremy's head hung grotesquely to the side. His body toppled to the ground like a sack of rice. Carver stared at it for a moment. Rage boiled deep inside him.

He didn't know why it was there. He should be perfectly calm. This was nothing he hadn't seen before. But he felt it burning all the way up to his face.

Carver fixed his gaze on Titus. "You're a dead man walking."

Noah laughed. "And then what, Carver?" He nodded at his bodyguard. "Titus, why don't you show Carver what an ultimate fighter champ can do? But don't kill him. I need him to take us to the prize.

Titus smacked a fist into his palm. He grinned. "Gladly, boss."

Carver released the Glock. He wasn't in the mood for a quick kill. He was pissed.

Titus stalked toward him. Arms up. Spread out like a grappler. He was a constrictor, not a brawler. That didn't mean he didn't punch. It just meant he preferred to get up close and squeeze the life out of you.

Carver let him come. Titus lunged. Carver knocked his hands away. Sidestepped. Titus went past him. Carver rammed an elbow into the other man's back. Titus stumbled forward. Hit the wall.

He growled. Spun around. Came at Carver slowly. Methodically. He feigned a punch. Threw a kick. Carver blocked the kick with his arms. The force would have knocked him over if his feet hadn't been planted properly.

Titus's leg bounced off Carver's arms. Titus was off balance for an instant. Carver took the opening. Raised his right leg. Smashed his foot against the side of Titus's knee. There was a loud crack. Titus screamed. His other leg wasn't back on the ground. Gravity did the rest of the work and dragged him down.

Carver threw an elbow into Titus's throat on his way down. Titus choked. The big man landed on his backside. He struggled to his knees.

Carver was already behind him. He wrapped his arms around the other man's head. Bared his teeth at Noah. Twisted savagely. Titus fought back. His neck muscles tensed. He grabbed Carver's forearms. Tried to hit him in the face.

It was like fighting a bull. But this bull was wounded. Titus' airpipe was constricted from the elbowing. He was gasping for air. Carver kept up the tension. He twisted as hard as he could.

Titus was strong. Real strong. Carver's arms tensed. His muscles strained hard. He feigned a twist to the left. Titus tensed to stop him. Carver twisted the opposite way. Titus wasn't ready for it. Bones snapped.

Titus screamed. Went limp. He was still breathing. But his neck was broken. He was paralyzed. Carver dropped him. Let him smack face first into the floor.

Noah pulled a gun from the desk. Carver couldn't reach the Glock in time. He backed toward the door, but it was too far. Noah wouldn't kill him. Not if he wanted the contents of the briefcase. That gave Carver some wiggle room.

"You son of a bitch." Noah sighed. "Guess I'll have to take you myself." He turned to Deshawn. "Go get a car. Meet me out front."

Carver smirked. "I wouldn't trust your buddy too much, Noah. After all, he's working for Henry Marshall."

Noah laughed mirthlessly. "I know who he's married to. I know about his kid."

Deshawn bolted up from his seat. He reeled like he'd been hit. "You what?"

"Yes, I know, Deshawn." Noah sighed. "It wasn't until Carver told me everything that I began to realize maybe you're not just screwing Marshall's daughter. Maybe you're working for him too."

"Deshawn killed Bushner for Marshall." Carver began to think the ace up his sleeve was actually a joker. Because Noah didn't seem all that mad about it.

"Marshall is against Enigma, Noah." Deshawn held up his hands defensively. "He came to me. He thought he could help us. I promise I didn't betray you, man."

"And I appreciate that." Noah grinned at Carver. "You thought you'd make me do something crazy, Carver? Maybe piss me off enough that I'd kill my best friend?"

Carver shrugged. "I thought I'd get more of a reaction."

"I'm five steps ahead of you, Carver." Noah tapped a finger on his temple. "Always thinking ahead."

Tasha interrupted. "Carver, don't take Noah to the stuff from the briefcase."

Carver wasn't sure why she cared. Talking like this was going to get her sister killed.

"Tasha, be a good girl and shut up." Noah scowled at her. "Or I'll send someone to kill your sister right now."

Tasha pressed her lips together.

Noah waved the gun at the door. "Deshawn, go get us a car. I'll meet you out front."

There was a loud boom. Deshawn flopped over sideways. Blood spewed from his head. Noah's eyes flared. His mouth dropped open. Tasha held a Beretta. She aimed at his head. "Drop the gun."

Noah set the gun on the desk. "What do you think you're doing? You know if something happens to me your sister will die."

"I guess we'll just move her into hiding." Tasha stepped closer. "Now, be a good boy, Noah." She shot him in the leg. He screamed in pain. Fell back into the chair. She shot his other leg.

Noah cried out again. "Stop! Stop! I'll give you what you want!"

Tasha shook her head. "There's only one thing I want, Noah." She put the gun to his head. "I want you to be a good boy."

"I'll be a good boy," he hissed through clenched teeth. "Just stop, please."

"Aw, you'll be the bestest boy, Noah?"

"Yes." He was shuddering in pain. "Just stop. Stop. Please."

Tasha patted his head. "Okay. Now, be a good boy and die." She pulled the trigger. His head bounced back against the headrest. Blood and brain matter shot through the back of the chair.

Carver drew his Glock. He put a bullet in Titus's head. The man might be paralyzed, but he was still alive. He might still be able to talk. Much as Carver wanted him to be a paraplegic for life, this was better.

Tasha sighed. She lowered the gun to her side. "God, that felt good."

Carver went to Jeremy's body. He checked for a pulse. There was none. He sighed. Blew out a breath. "Sorry, kid."

"I can't believe Noah didn't take your offer." Tasha shook her head. "God, what a narcissist."

Carver's thoughts were turning to the near future. "You'd better get your sister on the move fast. No telling how long she has."

"I will right now." Tasha pulled out her phone. Tapped on the screen.

"How does Noah's vault open?"

"His thumbprint."

Carver took out his knife. "Which thumb?"

"The right one."

Carver put Noah's right hand on the desk. Took out his knife. It wasn't ideal, but it would do. He put the knife over the thumb. Pressed down hard on both sides. Rocked it back and forth. It slowly worked through the bone until the thumb came free.

Tasha grinned. "You've cut off a few thumbs before, haven't you?"

"More than I can count. Biometrics on everything these days." Carver took the thumb. Walked across the hallway to the vault. He put the thumb on the reader. The heavy metal door clicked open.

The vault was about twice the size of Noah's office. There was a mirror on the back wall. Glass shelves. Glass cases. Some were empty. Others displayed Noah's prizes. A gold-plated Desert Eagle. An antique Colt revolver.

Gold bricks. Stacks of cash. A shelf of old books. Probably first editions or collectibles. He even had toy action figures new in boxes, and a trove of comic books. A little bit of everything. Most of it probably stolen.

A pair of H&K MP5s with suppressors were set up on stands. They were facing each other, barrels crossed. A Colt M4 was leaning against the wall. Four ammo cans were on the floor next to it.

They were all Carver's. But he didn't care about them. His duffel bag was on the floor next to the M4. He dropped to his knees. Unzipped it. Rifled through it. His fingers closed around a phone.

He pulled it out. Saw the faint crack on the screen. Breathed a sigh of relief. It was his burner phone. He turned it on. The battery was dead. He checked the time on his other phone. The encrypted message would expire in thirty minutes. He needed to charge the phone.

Tasha stood next to him. "Found what you were looking for?"

He found the charging cable in the bag. Stood. "Yeah."

"Was that really the briefcase Noah was looking for?"

Carver nodded. "A case like that costs big bucks. You can't just go to a luggage store and find one."

"I don't know why he didn't agree to your deal." She sighed. "He was brilliant but that ego of his was huge."

"Yeah." Carver looked for a power outlet. Found one. He plugged in the phone.

"So, now what?" Tasha leaned against the wall. "Are you going to sell the contents of the case?"

Carver shook his head. Watched the battery charging process. It needed a little charge before it would start. "I don't care about any of that."

"You don't?" She looked genuinely puzzled. "That stuff has to be worth millions."

"Probably billions in the right hands." Carver shrugged. "But it would just put a bullseye on my back."

"Where did you hide it?"

Carver's other phone vibrated. He checked it. Saw a thumbs up emoji in a text. He didn't answer Tasha's question.

Tasha went to the vault door. Looked around. "We need to get out of here. Noah's enforcers are going to come down here any moment." She glanced back at him. "I'm going to check the rear exit."

"Okay." Carver stared at the charging phone. It was up to one percent. He almost regretted insisting on an encrypted messaging app. Otherwise, he could have directly texted Paola from another phone. Skipped out on this little adventure altogether.

He picked up the Colt M4. Checked the chamber. Rocked out the magazine. The chamber was clear. The magazine was full. There were more loaded magazines in the bag. It was always good to keep a few handy just in case.

He put the rifle in the bag. He rocked out the magazines in the MP5s. Removed the suppressors. Put everything in the bag. He didn't have anything to carry the ammo cans.

The bag was already heavy with the rifles. The ammo cans would add a lot more weight to it. There were hand trucks in the warehouse. He could grab one of those. Or he could make a few trips outside.

He picked up Noah's Desert Eagle. It was a heavy pistol. Probably weighed an extra pound with the gold plating. It was a ridiculous weapon. Something a gangster would carry just for looks. A stupid gangster, anyway.

Noah wasn't like that. He was smart. Played his cards right. For the most part, at least. Then he bit off more than he could chew. And he kept biting off bigger and bigger mouthfuls until it reached this point.

Carver looked for his Glock. Didn't see it. It was an old beater of a gun. One he'd taken from a thug back in Minnesota. But it worked just fine. Better than a gold-plated Desert Eagle.

He wiped the gun down. Pulled a pair of gloves from his duffel bag. Put them on. He hadn't touched the cases or the shelves. But he'd touched a couple of other things. He wiped them down. Checked the phone charging process.

Two percent. It still wouldn't turn on.

He went to Noah's office. Looked through his desk. Took his phone. Took Deshawn's and Titus' phones. He used Noah's thumb to unlock his phone.

Carver found what he was looking for. A kill switch app. It would erase all the security footage. Wipe all the servers on the premises. It was something a smart guy like Noah would have. Just in case of the feds.

Noah's thumbprint unlocked the kill switch app. Carver pressed the button. The app activated. A progress meter appeared on the screen. Below it was a message. *Wiping all data.*

Carver unlocked Deshawn's and Titus's phones with their prints. He checked the galleries. Found images of him on Deshawn's phone. Nothing on Titus's. He tried to factory reset the phone but it required a password.

He settled for erasing the images. Emptying the deleted items folder. He did the same for Noah's phone. Hopefully, it would be enough. Hopefully, there weren't more images of him around.

Carver tapped out a message on his phone. Received a thumbs up again. He returned to the vault. Checked the phone's charge level. Waiting for it to charge was like watching a pot of water. Waiting for it to boil.

Tasha returned. "I've got a clear path for us out back. Get your things. We need to go now."

"Not yet." Carver watched the phone. Three percent.

"We can charge the phone in the car." She sighed. "Are you sure you don't want to get the stuff from the briefcase?"

"It's better to let it stay hidden. You don't want that kind of attention, believe me."

"I'm willing to take the risk." Tanner walked inside. "It would mean a lot for our family. We'd have enough money to last a lifetime."

Carver wasn't surprised to see him. "Probably be a real short lifetime considering who's looking for it."

"What does it matter to you?"

Tasha looked annoyed. "Damn it, Tanner, I told you to wait outside."

"I'm here to speed things up before Noah's enforcers flood this place." Tanner motioned at the door. "Get your stuff, Carver. Let's go."

"You two can go. I'll meet you later."

"What?" Tasha shook her head like she hadn't heard him right. "We need to go, Carver!"

"Like I said, you can go."

"He just wants to get the drugs and the formula for himself," Tanner said. "He's going to get it after he leaves, and we'll never hear from him again."

"Wrong." Carver shook his head. "Nobody gets it, okay?"

"Think of the people it could help, Carver." Tasha walked toward him, eyes pleading. "No more fentanyl addictions."

Tasha and Tanner were holding their cards close to their chests. They were hiding something, but Carver had gotten a peek at their hands. He knew they weren't related. They were up to something. Were they con men? Or something else?

This was high stakes poker. No cash prize. Just his life in the balance. He'd have to play a wildcard and see what kind of reaction he got. He took a shot in the dark. "You don't want the drugs to save lives."

She tried to look hurt. Failed. "It's not just for money. I promise."

Carver kept his poker face on. Took another guess. "I know it's not for money." Carver checked the phone charge. Four percent. It still wouldn't turn on.

She looked confused. "What's that supposed to mean?"

Tanner pulled a Beretta from under his jacket. Aimed it at Carver. "Tell me the location."

Carver repressed a grin. If this was poker, Tanner just lost.

Tasha's eyes widened. "What are you doing, you idiot?"

"Don't tell me you actually caught feelings for this idiot, Tasha." Tanner shook his head. "He knows something. That's why he's not telling us."

"I know you're not doing it for money. You're not doing it to help people either." Carver kept turning over imaginary cards. Watching their faces.

Tasha looked confused. She backed away. Out of Tanner's line of fire. "What's going on?"

"Can't you tell? He knows something." Tanner kept the gun trained on Carver. "Give us the location and we'll say our goodbyes. Now, set the damned phone down and keep your hands where I can see them."

"It's not that simple, though, is it?" Carver set the phone on a shelf. Kept his hands up in front of his chest. "You can't let me go, can you?"

"Damn." Tasha ran a hand down her face. "Look, Carver, for what it's worth, I really want to let you go."

Carver laid another card on the table. "Your handler wouldn't like that too much, though, would they?"

"Okay, I have to know how you found out." Tanner shook his head. "There's no way you figured it out on your own. I swept my tent and Tasha's place for bugs, so you didn't find out that way either."

Carver's hand was almost fully revealed. He saw most of Tasha's and Tanner's cards too, but he didn't have confirmation. Not yet. Did he take a direct guess, or find a way to make them reveal it?

He considered the angles. Tried the indirect approach again. "It's obvious that you're not brother and sister. You're not even related. It's also obvious that you have something going on. Something physical, not emotional."

Tanner blinked. "How in the hell—"

Carver kept going. "There's not even a sister in danger. Probably just a person pretending to be the sister to keep the charade going. To make Noah think he owned Tasha."

Looks of realization formed on their faces. They knew the jig was up. But Carver needed the final card. Confirmation about who they really were. His gut told him he was right. They weren't con men.

They were soldiers. They'd infiltrated Noah's organization. Not because of this brief-case business. That was a recent development. Tasha had been working for Noah for much longer. She was a mole. Meant to keep an eye on him.

There was too much pointing in one direction for the answer to be anywhere else. So, Carver took the guess. It would either be a royal flush, or a royal bust.

"You can't let me go because your people want me dead. But first, they really want to get their hands on the drugs and the formula. They're desperate to get it because they don't want Henry Marshall using it."

Because the truth was, Tanner and Tasha worked for Enigma.

CHAPTER 41

"Bravo, Carver." Tanner clapped a hand against his wrist, all while keeping the Beretta trained on the target. "You're right."

"Setting up your tent in that park was no coincidence either." Now that Carver knew who they were working for, he knew how other things had played out too.

"That Dodge of yours was picked up on cameras entering the city. They kept an eye on you. After you parked, I set up my tent in the homeless encampment. Paid Tommy to say whatever I wanted him to say." Tanner shrugged. "Like clockwork, the meter maid marked your car for Noah's people and all your stuff was stolen."

Carver blinked. "The meter maids work for Noah?"

Tasha laughed. "You figured us out and not that?"

Tanner sighed. "Yes, Carver. Noah owns a lot of public servants. Technically, our employers own them. But Noah has been a thorn in their side. He was never quite obedient. He had enough power to cause a major headache if he wanted to, so they never acted against him."

Carver decided to ask direct questions. "Is Enigma the real name for the organization?"

Tanner shrugged. "It's one of the code names, yes. I don't think the organization has a real name. Everything is compartmentalized. We only know other direct team members and our direct commander."

"Sounds a lot like the people I used to work for in the government." It seemed as though the command structure from Scion was being mimicked by Enigma.

"I'm sure it is," Tanner said. "But let's get back to the point. Unlike Noah, I'm willing to cut a deal where everyone wins. We can go somewhere public. Somewhere safe. You tell us where the drugs and formula are, and then we go our separate ways."

"I want a guarantee that Enigma will leave me alone from here on out. I have zero interest in them."

"I don't think the people you blew up on the Farm would feel that way."

Carver shrugged. "They killed a former squad mate. I didn't know the first thing about them until then. I just exacted a little justice is all."

"You blew the place to kingdom come," Tasha said. "And your associate has been methodically hunting down our assets and killing them."

"My associate?"

Tasha rolled her eyes. "Leon Fry."

"I didn't know." Carver gave it some thought. "I think that no matter what I do, Enigma will keep coming for me."

"I'll be straight with you, Carver." Tanner nodded. "They probably will, and there's nothing I can do about it. But I can make this deal here and now. We can all walk away from this living and breathing."

"Please, Carver." Tasha looked genuine. "I actually kind of like you. I don't want to have to kill you."

"Noah is dead. You can blame it all on me if you want. This is a big win for you two." Carver was getting tired of holding his hands up. "Why don't you take the win, and we can all walk away happy?"

"I'm not giving you a choice, Carver." Tanner was practicing trigger discipline, but his finger was twitching. "Let me be clear. Killing you would be just as big of a win as getting the contents of the briefcase."

"Killing me and getting the briefcase would be the trifecta, wouldn't it?" Carver tilted his head slightly. "I think we both know that keeping Antifen off the streets would be even bigger than bringing back my head."

"Yeah, you're probably right." Tanner's trigger finger slipped into the trigger guard. "But that's okay by me. Last chance, Carver. I'm counting to three and pulling the trigger."

Now seemed like a good time to bring this to a stop. Carver said the magic words. "Aunt Lin wouldn't approve."

Tanner frowned. Blinked. "What?"

Tasha got the reference. "The Chinese woman?"

"My aunt." The hallway outside was suddenly full of men with guns. Zimo poked Tanner's back with a pistol. "Please lower your weapon."

Tanner lowered it. Held it out. Zimo took it.

"How?" Tasha stared at Carver.

Carver took Tasha's pistol. He cleared the chamber. Popped out the magazine. "I told Zimo I was confronting Noah today and needed backup. I wasn't quite expecting it to go like this. After you killed Noah and Deshawn, I told Zimo that we could take out the entire organization today."

"We ambushed his enforcers outside," Zimo said. "Took them prisoner without firing a shot."

"No wonder the enforcers didn't come running." Tasha shook her head. "This isn't over, Carver. Enigma will keep coming after you."

"Yeah, I know. Guess I'll have to deal with them at some point." He looked from her to Tanner. "What are your real names, anyway?"

"None of your business," Tanner said.

Carver checked his phone. It powered on at last. He used his thumbprint to get in. Opened the encrypted app. The message from Paola was there. He saw her new number. An instant later, the app deleted it.

He typed in the new number. Saved it. He'd get another phone soon. Install the encrypted message app on it. Use the encryption key saved on this phone to activate it. Then he'd find a better way of doing this.

Until he found one, this would have to do.

"My real name is Tasha," Tasha said.

"You're good," Carver said. "Real good. It's a shame we're not on the same side."

"Maybe we can be." She touched his hand. "They're always recruiting. Working for them would be better than being hunted like an animal."

"Nah. Not interested." Carver patted her hand. "I have a feeling the retirement benefits include paid funeral expenses."

She looked down. "Yeah. That's the catch."

"It usually is with employers like that." Carver stared at her a moment. "You don't know who's at the top?"

"Like Tanner said, everything is compartmentalized."

"Essentially terrorist cells." Carver nodded. "Got it."

"We're not terrorists!" Tanner shouted. "This country is broken and we're going to fix it."

"Flooding the streets with fentanyl and killing thousands sounds like a funny way to do it." Carver shrugged. "Guess it's not that much different than the government after all." He nodded at Zimo. "You can take them away. It's time for me to hit the road."

"You're really not going to tell anyone where the drug formula is?" Tanner struggled as one of Zimo's men put plastic cuffs on him.

Carver nodded. "It's better to let it stay hidden."

"Please, Carver." Tasha took his hand again. "What's it going to harm if you tell me? Enigma will destroy the research and be done with it. That's basically the same as keeping it hidden."

Carver thought it over. It really wouldn't make a difference one way or the other. But maybe someone high up in Enigma would reconsider. Decide that using Antifen was the right thing to do.

He leaned over. Whispered in her ear. "It's at Arty's."

Her eyes widened. "Are you kidding me?"

He shook his head.

She whispered back. "Meet me there later? I can give you a proper goodbye?"

"With a bullet in the head?" He laughed. "Not a chance."

"I promise I wouldn't."

"Just take the win, Tasha." Carver kissed her forehead. "Take care."

Carver walked into the hallway. Bowed at Zimo. "Thanks for the assist."

"The least I can do after what you did for my aunt." Zimo shrugged. "It's a shame that the police won't actually do anything to Noah's enforcers. But the money in the vault will go a long way to helping us fund security for our community. And without the head of the snake, perhaps life will improve."

"I have a good feeling about it." Carver sighed grimly. "A really good feeling."

"You don't seem happy."

Carver took him to Noah's office. Pointed to one of the bodies on the floor. "That's Jeremy. He doesn't have family. No one to bury him. And he was one of the good guys."

Zimo nodded. "We will treat him with honor, Carver. His soul will find peace."

"I'd like that, Zimo." Carver knelt next to Jeremy. Put a hand on his shoulder. "I'd like that a lot."

"We will also frame this incident as a fight between rival gangs, or something like that." Zimo shook his head. "What a mess."

"Yeah. A real bad one."

"What do you want us to do with the Enigma agents?"

Carver had already thought it through. "Hold onto them for two hours, then let them go."

"Consider it done."

Carver went back to the vault. Got his things. Zimo's men had already taken Tanner and Tasha elsewhere.

He took a little cash from Noah's big pile. He stuffed it in his bag. Then he went outside. Put his stuff in the Audi. Drove back to the Embarcadero. Back to his temporary encampment home.

There was another text on his recovered phone. One from Leon. Carver read it after he parked.

Carver, I'm in San Francisco. You're in danger. They have people who know you're here. They're after you.

Carver texted him back. *Thanks for the heads up.* He sent an address. *Meet me here in an hour.*

He went to his tent. Cleaned it out. Broke it down and packed it up. It took him the better part of fifteen minutes. That was a lot longer than it should have taken. Probably because his mind just wasn't on the task.

He kept thinking about Jeremy. About the sound of his neck cracking. It shouldn't have ended like that. Everyone should still be alive. Happy with the deal they got. Instead, there were four more corpses going into the ground.

It wasn't anything Carver hadn't seen countless times before. It was just one more person lost to a bad decision. It happened every day. Every passing hour. He couldn't put a finger on why it was bothering him this much.

He was losing his touch. Losing his professional detachment. That was no good. He slept like a baby most nights despite everything he'd seen and done. He didn't need something like this haunting his dreams.

Carver packed his stuff in the Audi. He paid final respects to the Ramcharger. Put a hand on the hood. "You were a good car. Thanks for everything."

"Do you realize how many tickets you've accumulated?" A familiar voice said.

Carver turned. Saw Reedus the meter maid in his little three-wheeled car.

"That boot isn't coming off until you pay up." Reedus got out. Marched over to Carver. "I might be willing to cut you a break for a small fee."

"That's nice of you." Carver resisted his first violent urge. "It's nice how you mark the cars for Noah's people to break into, too."

Reedus stumbled back. "What?"

Carver grabbed him by the shirt. Swung him around. Slammed him against the side of the Ramcharger. "Yeah, Reedus. They took something very valuable from me. I had to go to Noah and get it back."

"You what?" Reedus wriggled, but he wasn't getting free. "Noah will kill you, you stupid ape!"

"Noah won't be doing much of anything anymore, Reedus." Carver grinned. "In fact, his entire crime organization just got a big black eye. So don't expect any bounties from your work for a while. Not until someone else takes over."

Reedus shivered. "What happened? What did you do?"

"I didn't do anything, Reedus. I just knew the right way to start a small gang war. They did the rest."

"What?" Sweat poured down his forehead. "That's impossible!"

"I'm tempted to let them add one more casualty. To let them know where you live."

"No! Please no!"

"Yeah. That's what I'll do. Tell them you were one of Noah's inside guys." Carver released Reedus. Walked toward the Audi.

"Please don't! I'll do anything!"

Carver stopped. Turned. "Stop giving fake tickets. Stop marking people's cars. I'm going to be watching you." He pointed two fingers at his eyes. Pointed them at Reedus. "Behave, or else."

"I will! I promise! Just please don't tell them where I live."

"Remove the boot from my truck. Take all those tickets and throw them in the trash."

Reedus got to it. He unlocked the boot. Tossed it in his meter maid cart.

Carver watched him the entire time. "Now, get the hell out of here."

Reedus gunned his cart. Kept going without stopping until he was out of sight.

Carver got in the Audi. Took one last look at the Ramcharger. Saluted it and drove away. He got on the highway. Crossed the Oakland Bay Bridge. Drove to Arty's. Came in through the backyard again. It was daylight, so someone might see him.

He put on the hoodie. Put on a facemask. Went into the garage. He took the box of vials. He removed two vials. One Fentanyl X vial and one Antifen vial. He put them on top of the research paper. Then he tucked everything back in place.

He left the garage. Returned to the Audi. Drove back across the bridge. He parked near the encampment. Carver opened his bag. Took out the empty fentanyl bottle he'd taken from Bushner's house.

He cleaned it out with some bottled water. Opened an Antifen vial and poured the contents into the bottle. He got out of the car. Walked to Tommy's tent. Thumped on it.

Tommy crawled out. He looked haggard. Like he was recovering from a brutal bender. "What do you want?"

Carver took out the bottle. "I've got a present for you and your girl."

Tommy's eyes brightened. "Wow, that's the prescription stuff!"

"Yeah. It's good. Real good."

"Baby, come out here!" Tommy poked his head in the tent. "Get your ass up, you lazy idiot!"

"Shut up!" His girlfriend crawled out. Looked blearily at Carver. "What's the fuss about?"

"Open up." Carver showed them the bottle.

She gasped. Opened her mouth. Lifted her tongue. Carver dripped two drops. He turned to Tommy. He was ready. Carver dripped Antifen into his mouth too.

"Thanks so much!" Tommy giggled. "This stuff is the best."

"Yeah, it is." Carver gave him the bottle. "Spread it around. When I come back to camp I'm going to ask if you shared it. If you did, then I'll give you more."

"I promise!" Tommy took the bottle. "Everyone gets a taste!"

"Just two drops, though. It's potent."

Tommy nodded eagerly. "Two drops. That's it."

Carver left. No more opioids for Tommy and gang. Anyone who took it would have a long road to recovery. Provided they didn't have any brain defects that prevented the Antifen from bonding.

Maybe it was a cruel thing to do. Maybe he should have given them a choice. He wasn't even sure why he'd gone out of his way to give them the opioid cure.

Carver gave the encampment one last look. Then he put the Audi in gear. Pulled onto the road and left.

He drove south to a diner. Parked. Got out. An old van pulled in a moment later.

Leon hopped out. Hurried over. He looked dirty and tired. "I'm glad I reached you in time."

Carver looked at the van. "Nice ride."

Leon sighed. "You don't even want to know what I went through to get here. And that van is a whole other story."

"I'm looking forward to hearing it." Carver crossed his arms. "The people after me are with Enigma?"

Leon looked confused. "How do you know about that? And why weren't you answering your texts?"

"Let's get some lunch and talk." Carver went inside. Got a booth in the back corner.

Leon sat across from him. "I've obviously missed something."

"Just a little something." Carver ordered food. Spent the next hour catching Leon up on the events of the past few days.

Leon told him how he'd gotten the van. It was a good story. Better than Carver had expected.

"You're like a roaming crusader," Carver said. "It's cute."

"Yeah, real cute." Leon laughed. "I came here to warn you and you've already taken care of everything." He shook his head. "I put a body in the ground just getting a ride out of Arizona."

"That's the power of friendship."

Leon burst out laughing. "Hearing that come out of your mouth doesn't even sound real."

Carver took out his second burner phone. He sent Leon the pictures he'd taken of the research paper. "That's all the formulas, the white paper, everything."

Leon nodded. "I'll make sure it gets out. That the right people can replicate the results."

"Good."

Leon laughed. "The people at Enigma are going to be so happy when Tasha and Tanner bring them the formula. Then they're going to be pissed when they realize the formula got out anyway."

"If they'd agreed to leave me alone, they wouldn't have that problem."

"They're bad people, Carver." Leon shook his head. "They're trying to destroy the country from the inside out. They want to seize power."

"Maybe the country needs a little destroying." Carver sipped his coffee. Shrugged. "It's not my place to say."

"But—"

Carver held up a hand. "I'm not having that conversation again. If you want to be a crusader, then you go right ahead. I just want a beach. I want peace and quiet."

"Maybe you'll have that for a few years, but if Enigma gets its way, you'll be alive to see the fall of the country."

"Nah." Carver shook his head. "People are stupid. They'll screw it up somehow."

Leon laughed. "You're nothing if not a skeptical optimist."

"Is that what I am?" Carver nodded. "Sounds about right."

"You're plenty of other things too, but that's the only way I can frame it without calling you names."

"Fair enough." Carver nodded at the van outside. "It's off the radar?"

"It is." Leon finished his coffee. "Need a ride?"

"Yeah. I'll dump the Audi at the airport. Find a replacement somewhere."

"What about Paola?"

Carver raised an eyebrow. "What about her?"

"You went to hell and back to get that phone. Just so you could keep in touch." Leon shrugged. "She means something to you. Maybe more than you want to admit."

"She means a lot to me, and I don't know why." Carver stared down at his coffee. "But Jeremy reminded me that feelings are an Achille's heel. It damages my peace."

"I have to admit I'm a little relieved, though."

Carver raised his other eyebrow. "Relieved?"

Leon nodded. "It's nice to know there's human emotion buried somewhere in that dumb head of yours."

Carver laughed. "Whatever helps you sleep at night."

Leon took out his phone. Showed the map to Carver. "What say we continue your road trip? There's still plenty of forest south of town. Plenty of camping to be done."

That sounded nice to Carver. He'd had enough of the city. "Yeah, let's do it."

He looked at his phone. At the encrypted messaging app. He stared at Paola's number. Stared at it for a long minute. Then he turned off the phone. Tucked it away. She was better off without him. But he would always be there if she needed him.

And that was about the best he could do.

BOOKS BY JOHN CORWIN-

PSYCHOLOGICAL THRILLERS
The Family Business
AMOS CARVER THRILLERS
Dead Before Dawn
Dead List
Dead and Buried
Dead Man Walking
Dead by the Dozen
Dead Run
Dead Weather Days
Dead to Rights
Dead But Not Forgotten
CHRONICLES OF CAIN
To Kill a Unicorn
Enter Oblivion
Throne of Lies
At The Forest of Madness
The Dead Never Die
Shadow of Cthulhu
Cabal of Chaos
Monster Squad

Gates of Yog-Sothoth

Shadow Over Tokyo

Into the Multiverse

THE OVERWORLD CHRONICLES

Sweet Blood of Mine

Dark Light of Mine

Fallen Angel of Mine

Dread Nemesis of Mine

Twisted Sister of Mine

Dearest Mother of Mine

Infernal Father of Mine

Sinister Seraphim of Mine

Wicked War of Mine

Dire Destiny of Ours

Aetherial Annihilation

Baleful Betrayal

Ominous Odyssey

Insidious Insurrection

Utopia Undone

Overworld Apocalypse

Apocryphan Rising

Soul Storm

Devil's Due

Overworld Ascension

Assignment Zero (An Elyssa Short Story)

OVERWORLD UNDERGROUND

Soul Seer

Demonicus

Infernal Blade

OVERWORLD ARCANUM

Conrad Edison and the Living Curse

Conrad Edison and the Anchored World

Conrad Edison and the Broken Relic

Conrad Edison and the Infernal Design

Conrad Edison and the First Power

STAND ALONE NOVELS

Mars Rising

No Darker Fate
The Next Thing I Knew
Outsourced
Seventh

Printed in Dunstable, United Kingdom